T0321400

ADVENTURES IN SPACE

An Anthology of Short Stories by Chinese and English-language Science Fiction Writers

Patrick Parrinder, Consultant Editor

Yao Haijun, Honorary Editor

This is a **FLAME TREE PRESS** book

FLAME TREE PRESS
6 Melbray Mews, London, SW6 3NS, UK
flametreepress.com

US sales, distribution and warehouse:
Simon & Schuster
simonandschuster.biz

UK distribution and warehouse:
Hachette UK Distribution
hukdcustomerservice@hachette.co.uk

Thanks to the Flame Tree Press team.

The cover is created by Flame Tree Studio with
thanks to Nik Keevil and Shutterstock.com.
The font families used are Avenir and Bembo.

Flame Tree Press is an imprint of Flame Tree Publishing Ltd
flametreepublishing.com

A copy of the CIP data for this book is available from the British Library
and the Library of Congress.

1 3 5 7 9 8 6 4 2

PB ISBN: 978-1-78758-815-8
ebook ISBN: 978-1-78758-817-2

Printed and bound in Great Britain by Clays Ltd, Elcograf S.p.A.

ADVENTURES IN SPACE

An Anthology of Short Stories by
Chinese and English-language
Science Fiction Writers

Patrick Parrinder, Consultant Editor

Yao Haijun, Honorary Editor

FLAME TREE PRESS
London & New York

CONTENTS

Foreword – Adventures in Space 1
Patrick Parrinder

Foreword – Beyond the Light-Year . . . 3
Yao Haijun

Publisher's Note 5

The Race for Arcadia 6
Alex Shvartsman

Shine 25
Chen Zijun

On the Ship 90
Leah Cypess

Seeds of Mercury 111
Wang Jinkang

Her Glimmering Façade 158
Eleanor R. Wood

Answerless Journey 175
Han Song

Cylinders 191
Ronald D. Ferguson

Life Does Not Allow Us to Meet . . . 216
He Xi

The First .267
Allen Stroud

The Darkness of Mirror Planet. 286
Zhao Haihong

Minuet of Corpses. 299
Amdi Silvestri

Doomsday Tour. 316
Bao Shu

The Emissary 334
Russell James

Biographies and Sources. 353

FOREWORD

Adventures in Space

'But who shall dwell in these Worlds if they be inhabited? …
Are we or they Lords of the World? …
And how are all things made for man?'
Kepler, *Conversation with Galileo's Sidereal Messenger* (1610)

Some four hundred years have passed since the German astronomer Johannes Kepler wrote to his Italian colleague Galileo about the new realms of space revealed by the invention of the telescope. Had Kepler been familiar with Chinese astronomy, he would have known that speculation about other inhabited worlds was not at all new. The earliest authors of imaginary space adventures were the ancient Greek satirist Lucian (*c.*117–180 CE) and – unknown in the West until quite recently – his Chinese contemporary Zhang Heng. It was only in the late nineteenth century that full intellectual communication became possible between East and West. Jules Verne's *From the Earth to the Moon* (1865), effectively the first scientifically-oriented tale of a space voyage, was translated into English in 1867 and into Chinese in 1903. Readers of the present volume, with its mixture of new English-language and newly translated Chinese stories, will rapidly discover that today's science fiction is truly international.

In Verne's novel the Moon-shot is a private venture, put together by the members of the Baltimore Gun Club. Verne could not foresee that the first actual Moon landing would be lavishly funded by an American government determined to get there before the Russians did. Although manned space exploration was drastically reduced in the early 1970s, the authors in *Adventures in Space* share the expectation that it will soon be resumed – though we will have to rethink what we mean by the word 'manned'. Wang Jinkang depicts a landing on Mercury in 2046, while Chen Zijun takes us to one of the moons of Jupiter in 2051. Where might the human race go after that? Travel to other solar systems using wormholes or 'interstellar gates' is commonplace in science fiction, and it appears in several stories in this volume. Perhaps the hallmark of *Adventures in Space* is the mixture of what is familiar – if not in fact, then at least in fiction – with the macabre and the unutterably strange. Our fictional astronauts may be resourceful and intrepid but in no sense, as they soon find out, are they 'lords of the world'. Such classic science-fictional themes as 'first contact', time travel, post-humanity, robotics and AI, rogue planets, 'the last man left alive', and visions of the coming apocalypse are all represented in this collection.

Finally, a word about the Chinese authors whom we are proud to present here. As will be seen from the author biographies, they are among their country's leading science fiction writers and most have large bodies of work to their name. One of them, Han Song, has written eloquently of science fiction's paradoxical status in China, where it is both a necessary response to the dizzying pace of social change and, for all too many, still a highly marginal cultural form (see *Science Fiction Studies* No.119, March 2013). Will Chinese technology come to dominate space exploration in the twenty-first century, as our American contributor Alex Shvartsman suggests? Whatever the future holds, we can expect much wider recognition for the outstanding writers whose works have been chosen for *Adventures in Space*.

Patrick Parrinder
President, H.G. Wells Society

FOREWORD

Beyond the Light-Year

The Chinese edition of this science fiction anthology has an intriguing name: *Beyond the Light-Year*. Mysterious and poetic in both a scientific view and romantic view, the title fits the tone of the genre of science fiction very well. Of course, not only the title, but all the stories in this collection are carefully selected and recommended.

I was a science fiction fan before I started to work as an editor and publisher, and I enjoyed reading science fiction works set in space. Working as the Director-in-Chief of *Science Fiction World* magazine, I have paid special attention to this category because, from my interaction with readers, I can see how much they love and aspire to be astronomers, and are amazed by spaceships flying between stars. As we all know, today's science fiction literature involves a number of complex themes, but why are stories about space adventure still popular?

In the early days of the history of science fiction, Jules Verne chose space as his stage on which to make miracles. H.G. Wells and William Olaf Stapledon took space as the incubator of philosophical theories. They represented two different branches of science fiction, but either way, space provided more than enough wonder for readers, something that they could only find in science fiction. If we believe there is a kind of aesthetic in the genre, then this kind of wonder is the core of this aesthetic.

When the center of science fiction shifted from Europe to the US, the universe almost became the Disneyland of adventurers, especially in the era of low-priced American science fiction magazines. Alien creatures on all kinds of strange planets challenged the imagination of readers; adventurers' encounters with them generated all kinds of bizarre stories. Although those stories are criticized as stereotypical and clichéd now, the adventurous spirit of humankind in them is still irresistible to young science fiction readers.

When American science fiction came to its golden age, more and more science fiction writers broke the set pattern of space opera and started to think about the relationship between people and the universe, as well as the position of humankind in the universe and what it meant. Works like Tom Godwin's 'The Cold Equations' showcased the cruel laws of the universe and the conflict in human nature, which brings science fiction writing to a more serious level and made a strong impact on people's conception of the world. While epic works like Frank Herbert's *Dune* and Isaac Asimov's *Galactic Empire* showed how wide science fiction can expand in terms of dimension and ideology, which is addictively compelling to readers.

Then, we have this anthology, in which science fiction about the universe not only involves the infinite possibilities of space and the future, but almost covers all of our realities — and that universe becomes the real one, in which nothing is impossible. I hope readers of this book love this universe, and especially when Chinese writers are among its constructors.

Yao Haijun
Director-in-Chief, *Science Fiction World*

PUBLISHER'S NOTE

This joint venture between Chinese and English language writers is born out of a desire to work together in partnership with like-minded people. To share interests and swap ideas; to mediate between methods and expressions; to rise above the differences of language and tradition and seek a tolerant, inquisitive future that celebrates the joy of technology and empowers the indomitable human spirit.

I'd like to thank the Chinese publisher Nan Lu whose perseverance, tenacity, and humanity has ensured the success of the project, a joint publication across two languages, three cities (Beijing, London and New York) and fifteen science fiction specialists who represent the best of their traditions. Within these pages you'll find thrilling, profound and diverse stories on a topic broad enough to allow the voice and culture of each writer to breathe across the surface of the theme, *Adventures in Space*.

A final word. At Flame Tree we seek to encourage new and emerging writers, while building on the shoulders of the giants. The successful authors who won through the open submissions that brought their exceptional stories to this collection can be sure that their work is placed alongside that of the best and most challenging writers in China today; award winners and exciting new talents alike. Do take the time to read the biographies and seek out the works of each author.

Nick Wells
Publisher & Founder, Flame Tree Publishing

THE RACE FOR ARCADIA

Alex Shvartsman

"There's nothing new under the sun," said Anatoly, his voice carried via skip broadcast across millions of kilometers of space from the command center at Baikonur.

Aboard the *Yuri Gagarin*, Nikolai concentrated on the exposed panel in the inner wall of the ship. He winced at the sight of the cheap Ecuadorian circuitry as he used the multimeter to hunt for the faulty transistor. Damn contractors couldn't resist cutting corners. He sighed and looked up. Anatoly's face filled the screen. Nikolai didn't mind the banter, it broke the routine. He pointed at the opposite screen, which displayed the live feed from outside the ship, a vast blackness punctured by tiny pinpricks of light. "Which sun?"

"Our sun. Any sun." Anatoly shrugged. "You're a cranky pedant, aren't you?"

"Matter of opinion," said Nikolai, his gaze returning to the uncooperative panel.

"As I was saying, there's nothing new under the sun," Anatoly said. "We won the original space race when we launched *Sputnik* a hundred years ago, and we're going to win this one, too."

Nikolai cursed under his breath as the multimeter slipped out of his hand and slowly floated upward. He caught the wayward tool. "The space race hasn't gone so well since then. Americans beat us to the Moon, and the Chinese beat us to Mars."

"Those are just a pair of lifeless rocks in our backyard," said Anatoly. "In the grand scheme of things, they won't matter much. Not once you land on Arcadia."

Nikolai continued to hunt for the faulty transistor. "You're assuming this heap of junk won't fall apart around me first."

"*Gagarin* isn't luxurious, but it will get the job done," said Anatoly.

"I sure hope you're right," said Nikolai. "I'd hate having to get out and push."

Anatoly grinned. "You'd push all the way to Arcadia if you had to. Russian people make do with what we've got. Back in the 1960s, American astronauts discovered that ballpoint pens didn't work right in the vacuum. So NASA spent all this time and money to design the space pen. You know what our cosmonauts did? They used a pencil."

"That story is bullshit on several levels," said Nikolai. "Americans used pencils, too. But the shavings were a hazard in zero gravity – they could float up one's nose, or even short an electrical device and start a fire. That's why the space pen was needed, and it was developed by a private company who then sold a handful to NASA at a reasonable price." He wiped a bead of sweat off his forehead. "You of all people should know better."

"Okay, you got me, it's a tall tale," said Anatoly. "But my version makes for a much better story to tell at parties."

"Next time I'm at a party, I'll be sure to try it," said Nikolai.

Anatoly frowned, the wind gone out of his sails. Nikolai knew he had scored another point, but this time by hitting below the belt. His handler must've felt guilty about the one-way trip, even if he tried his best to hide it.

Nikolai eased off. He let Anatoly fill him in on the gossip from home – the latest politics and entertainment news that felt so irrelevant, so far away.

It took him another thirty minutes to find the defective transistor. He grunted with satisfaction and reached for the soldering gun.

*　　*　　*

Three months prior, Nikolai Petrovich Gorolenko sat brooding at his desk in a cozy but windowless office of the St. Petersburg State University math department.

There was so much to do. He needed to type a resignation notice, contact an attorney about a will, and worst of all, figure out a way to break the news to his family. There was a knock on the door.

Nikolai didn't feel like speaking to anyone, but he needed a way to break out of his despondency.

"Come in."

A stranger walked into the room. This middle-aged man was perfectly coiffed and dressed in a smart business suit. His sharp eyes seemed to take in everything without missing a single detail, and yet he had a nondescript look about him that could only be perfected in one line of work. Nikolai pegged him for an FSB operative.

"My condolences, Professor Gorolenko," said the stranger.

Somehow, he knew. Nikolai hadn't told anyone, and yet he knew.

Nikolai did his best to keep calm. "Who are you, and what are you talking about?"

The man waved an ID card in a fluid, practiced motion. "Vladimir Ivanovich Popov. I'm with the government." He put the card away. "I'm here about your test results from this morning. The brain tumor is malignant. You've got three, four months. Half a year if you're lucky."

Nikolai bristled at being told this for the second time that day. At least the first time it had been his doctor, who had sounded genuinely sympathetic. This stranger merely stated facts, politely but without compassion.

Popov pointed at the chair. "May I?"

"What do you want?" Nikolai ignored his request. A dying man has little use for being polite, and little fear of authority, he thought.

Popov sat anyway. "I hear this is a bad way to go. Very painful, in the end. I'd like to offer you an alternative."

Nikolai tilted his head. "An alternative to dying?"

"An alternative to dying badly," said Popov. "Let's call it a stay of execution."

"I see," said Nikolai. "I suppose you'll want my soul in return?"

Popov smiled. "You aren't so far from the truth, Professor."

Exasperated, Nikolai leaned forward. "Why don't you tell me what you're offering in plain terms?"

"Our experts have examined your brain scans and the biopsy sample," said Popov, "and determined that you're a perfect fit for an experimental nanite treatment developed by the Antey Corporation. It won't cure you, but it will slow down the tumor and contain the metastasis. It can buy you two more years."

Nikolai chewed his lip. Two years was such a short time, but for a drowning man it wasn't unseemly to grasp at straws. "You've got my attention."

"There is a catch," said Popov.

"Of course there is. Neither the Antey Corporation nor our government are known for their altruism," said Nikolai. "What do you need from me?"

"What do you know about Arcadia?" asked Popov.

"Huh? You mean the planet?"

Popov nodded.

"It's been all over the news. Admittedly, I've been…preoccupied. But I do know it's the first Earth-like planet ever confirmed – breathable atmosphere and everything."

"That's right," said Popov. "The Americans discovered it in 2015. They called it Kepler-452b back then, and it was the first Earth-like exo planet ever found. Fitting that it will become the first world humans set foot on outside of the solar system." He shifted in his chair. "There's enormous propaganda value in getting there first. The Americans are dispatching a twelve-person exploration team. India already launched the colony ship, with sixty-odd people in suspended animation."

"So quickly? They only confirmed Arcadia as habitable last month."

"The world's superpowers have been preparing for this moment ever since the eggheads figured out the workaround for the speed of light problem, and sent out skip drones every which way."

"I see. So the Russian Federation is in this race, too?"

"That's right, Professor. Our plan is to send you."

Nikolai stared at the government apparatchik across his desk. "Why me?"

"I'm not a scientist, so I can't explain the reasoning thoroughly," said Popov. "In layman's terms, they've been going over the brain scan data from terminal patients across the country, and they liked your brain best."

Nikolai scratched his chin. Like most children, he'd dreamed of going up into space once, but that was a lifetime ago.

"Forgive me," Nikolai said, "this is a lot to process."

"There's more," said Popov. "I don't want to sugarcoat this for you. It would be a one-way trip. If we succeed and you land on Arcadia, and even if the atmosphere is breathable and the water is drinkable, your odds of survival are astronomically low. If the local microbes don't get you, the hunger likely will. If you're lucky, you might last long enough for the Americans to get there. We're trying to time the launch just right to give you that chance. Even then, the tumor might finish you before they return to Earth."

Nikolai thought about it. "Why can't you send enough food and water for the crew to survive?"

"You don't get it. You *are* the crew. Just you. The ship's ability to accelerate to a skip velocity is inversely proportional to its mass. The Indian ship is en route, but it's huge and therefore slow. The Americans have a much faster ship, and they might launch before we do. To beat them to the punch, we must send a very light vessel. Every milligram counts. So it's you, and just enough oxygen, water, and food to get you to the finish line."

Nikolai frowned. "You weren't kidding about the stay of execution, then. And it explains why your people are looking to recruit from among the terminally ill. Leaving the heroic explorer to die on Arcadia would be terrible PR otherwise."

"You're grasping the basics quickly," said Popov. "No wonder they picked your brain."

"I'm not sure how a few extra months of life on a spaceship followed by death alone on an alien world is better than spending my last days with my wife and daughter," said Nikolai.

"Well, there's having your name live on forever in history, alongside the likes of Magellan and Bering," said Popov. "And then there's the obscene amount of money you'll be paid for doing this."

Nikolai hadn't saved much money on a college professor's salary. There would be medical bills, his father's retirement, his daughter's college tuition.... "When do you need my answer by?"

"Tomorrow morning, at the latest," said Popov. "Though, given your circumstances, I'm a little surprised you have to think about it much."

"I don't, not really," said Nikolai. "But I do owe it to my wife to let her weigh in."

★　　★　　★

At times, Nikolai felt like his ship was falling apart around him.

He didn't understand how the skip technology worked – only a few dozen theoretical physicists on Earth could legitimately claim such wisdom – but he knew that an object had to reach a certain velocity before it could puncture a momentary hole in space-time and re-emerge elsewhere.

Yuri Gagarin would accelerate continuously for six months until it reached the skip point located somewhere in the Kuiper belt, then wink out of existence, only to reappear fourteen hundred light-years away and spend a similar amount of time decelerating toward Arcadia.

As a mathematician, Nikolai couldn't help but marvel at the amazing speed his vessel would achieve after half a year of constant acceleration. By now he had already traveled farther than any other human in history, but he didn't feel special. He felt tired and anxious, and somewhat claustrophobic in the cramped cabin that smelled like rubber and sweat.

The ship's memory bank was loaded with a nearly infinite selection of music, books, and films to break the monotony of the journey. Nikolai was stuck drinking recycled water and eating disgusting nutrient-enriched slop in the name of conserving mass, but the electrons needed for data storage had no significant weight, and the ship's designers could afford him this luxury. But he had little time to partake of the digital library. Instead, he put all his hastily learned engineering knowledge to use and performed maintenance.

Much of his time at Baikonur was spent learning how to service the systems inside the ship. There was no spacesuit, but then there was little that could go wrong on the outer hull. The engineers' real fear was that the internal systems might malfunction. The culture of graft was so deeply ingrained in the Russian industrial complex that even a high-profile project like this was afflicted.

It wouldn't do to deliver a corpse to Arcadia. Pre-flight, they spent nearly ten hours a day teaching Nikolai how to repair the recycling systems, solder the circuit boards, and improvise solutions to an array of worst-case scenarios with the materials available on board. One of the American-educated engineers kept referring to these techniques as 'MacGyvering', but Nikolai didn't know the reference.

En route, Nikolai was forced to deal with cheap circuit boards, subpar off-brand equipment, and software subroutines that were at least two generations behind the times. He had one thing going for him – the ability to remain in contact with Baikonur. The broadcast signal had no mass and was able to skip almost immediately. Mission Control was only a few seconds' delay away, able to offer advice and support.

While all the fires he'd had to put out so far were figurative, Nikolai eyed the tiny Bulgarian-made extinguisher with suspicion.

*　　*　　*

Nikolai waited until their four-year-old daughter was asleep. Pretending that everything was normal, that it was just another weeknight, was incredibly difficult. He was emotionally and physically exhausted, and his wife Tamara could sense something was wrong, but she too kept up the pretense of normality until their little Olga was tucked into bed.

As the sun set over St. Petersburg, coloring the skyline in bronze hues, Nikolai told his wife about his diagnosis and everything that had happened since.

Tamara listened without interrupting, even as she clutched a couch pillow, a mascara-tinged tear rolling down her cheek. When he'd finally unburdened, having told her the facts and having run out of assurances and platitudes, the two of them stared out the window and shared what was left of the sunset in silence.

It was only after the sun had disappeared completely in the west that she finally spoke.

"Why you?"

* * *

Something was very wrong.

At first it was just a feeling, a sensation in the back of Nikolai's mind. It seemed that his subconscious had figured out something important, but wasn't prepared to communicate what it was.

Nikolai chalked it up to paranoia. Anyone stuck on a one-way trip out of the solar system in a tin can could be forgiven for having uneasy thoughts. But the feeling persisted, almost bubbling up to the surface until eventually the concern bled from his lizard brain and into the conscious mind.

Nikolai pulled up the various sets of relevant data on his screen and began crunching numbers.

* * *

After his wife had finally gone to bed, Nikolai stayed up making a list of people he needed to say good-bye to. He kept adding and crossing out names on a sheet of graph paper, until he crumpled up the page and tossed it into the trash bin.

Farewells would be painful. He didn't want to do it. Life had already dealt him a bad hand and he felt justified in skipping whatever unpleasant business he could avoid.

In the morning, he called Popov and accepted the deal, requesting that his involvement be kept a secret for as long as possible. He had little enough time to spend with his family and didn't want to waste it being hounded by reporters. Then he went to see the only other person who needed to know the truth.

Petr Ivanovich Gorolenko had recently moved into an assisted living facility on the edge of town. It was nice enough, as retirement homes went. Nikolai was relieved that, with the money his family would receive, they'd no longer have to worry about being able to afford Father's stay here.

Like Tamara, Petr listened to his son's tale without interrupting. He sighed deeply when Nikolai was finished. "It is a great tragedy for a parent to outlive his child."

"I have little time, Dad, and a chance to do something meaningful with what's left."

His father straightened his back with great effort. "Claiming an entire planet for Mother Russia is no small thing."

"Well, it isn't exactly like that," said Nikolai. "Arcadia isn't like some tropical island in the age of colonialism. Planting the flag won't claim it as ours. The government wants to land a man there first purely for propaganda."

"I see," said Petr. "The oligarchs in charge are desperate to show that Russia is still a world power. And they're willing to sacrifice your life to do it."

"I'm dying regardless," said Nikolai.

"They have the means to prolong your life, and they're withholding treatment unless you volunteer for a suicide mission. Doesn't that bother you?"

Nikolai looked around the sparse, depressing room where his father would live out his remaining years. Was his own fate really worse than that?

"Of course it bothers me," he said. "Dying bothers me. Having Olga grow up without a father bothers me. But so what? It's not like I have a better option."

"Your great-grandfather was conscripted into the army on the day the Great Patriotic War began," said Petr. "Stalin had murdered most of his competent generals by then, and was utterly unprepared for the German invasion. He needed time to regroup and mount the real defense, so he ordered tens of thousands of young men with no training and no weapons onto the front lines."

Petr's words dissolved into a coughing fit. He cleared his throat, and continued in a raspy voice. "Grandpa's platoon of forty men was given a total of three rifles to fight with. They were told to kill the Germans and capture their weapons, and sent to the front lines. A squad of NKVD – the secret police – was positioned a kilometer or so behind them. Those men were well armed, and had orders to shoot anyone who tried to turn back."

Petr paused again, the monologue visibly taking a lot out of him. He took several deep breaths and pressed on. "Grandpa was very lucky. He was wounded in the first engagement, and by the time he got out of the hospital his platoon was long gone. He was assigned to another division, one with weapons, and fought all the way to Berlin in '45."

"You've told this story, more than a few times," said Nikolai.

"My point is, our government has a long-standing tradition of solving problems by throwing whoever they have to into the meat grinder," said Petr. A smile stretched across his wrinkled face. "But also to reiterate that dumb luck runs deep in our family. Perhaps you can beat the odds and last long enough to hitch a ride home on the American ship. So, if you don't mind, I won't mourn for you just yet."

Nikolai hugged his father. "I'll try, Dad. I'll try my best."

★   ★   ★

Nikolai and his family relocated to Baikonur, the desert town in Kazakhstan that housed the world's oldest spaceport. The dry heat of the Kazakh Steppe was difficult for the Gorolenkos to tolerate, and seemed to contribute to Nikolai's rapidly worsening headaches, but it was a moot point: he spent almost all his time in the vast, air-conditioned labs of the Roscosmos, the Russian Federal Space Agency.

He was given crash courses in astronomy by the scientists, in equipment maintenance and repair by the engineers, and in public speaking by the PR flaks. Some of the lessons felt surreal to him – a sole student surrounded by a cadre of overeager teachers.

The plan was to unveil the mission at the last possible moment, lest the Americans or the Chinese launch a competing one-man ship powered by their superior technologies, and snatch the accomplishment away from the Motherland.

As far as the world knew, the Americans would get to Arcadia first.

The Chinese had dominated space exploration for much of the twenty-first century. It was the People's Republic of China's skip drone which had explored Arcadia in the first place. But at the moment, the government lacked the funds and the willpower to support an interstellar project.

The enormous Indian ship was already en route, and would take over five years to reach the skip point. They wouldn't be the first on the scene, but they would be the first to succeed – or fail – at establishing a permanent colony.

The Americans launched the *Neil Armstrong* with all the pomp and pageantry that was expected of them, and it was scheduled to reach Arcadia in a little over a year.

The plan was for the Russians to launch the *Yuri Gagarin* on the same day, and steal the Americans' thunder. Despite its inferior propulsion, the *Gagarin*'s much lower mass would allow the Russian ship to beat its competitors to Arcadia by up to several months. But, by the time the *Armstrong* had launched from Cape Canaveral, Nikolai hadn't even seen his ship.

The *Gagarin* was being constructed elsewhere, a joint effort between the Russian government, the Antey Corporation, and a number of smaller domestic firms sufficiently favored by the current administration to be awarded the lucrative contracts.

Another month had passed. Nikolai's headaches continued to worsen and, despite the Baikonur doctors' assurances to the contrary, he suspected the nanite treatments might not be working.

At first, he was perfectly content to miss the launch date. The delay meant more time to spend with his family. But then he had realized that he actually wanted to go. While Olga was blissfully unaware of what was happening in the way only a young child could be, the situation was taking a noticeable toll on Tamara. She had a hard time coping with the prolonged farewell, and even though she did her best to hide it and stand by her husband, Nikolai hated being the cause of her anguish.

At some point over the course of this extra month on the ground, Nikolai stopped thinking of the impending launch as a death sentence and began looking forward to this final adventure. He didn't discuss these new feelings with Tamara, whom he felt would not understand, but wrote about them at length in letters he penned for his daughter, to be given to her when she turned sixteen. The letters became a sort of a diary for Nikolai, an outlet for his anxiety, a catharsis.

The word that the ship was finally on its way to Baikonur came at the last possible moment.

"This is good news," Nikolai told Tamara during their last dinner together. By mutual agreement, they had decided not to speak again after the ship had launched. Nikolai wasn't happy about this, but he was willing to let go, for Tamara's sake. "I'm only going to beat the Americans by a week or so."

She took his hand into hers, and her lower lip trembled.

"I can make the food and water last that long," he said. "The Americans will take me in. It would make them look really bad otherwise."

There was pain and doubt in the way Tamara looked at him, and only the briefest glimmer of hope.

Later that evening, he tucked Olga into bed for the last time.

"Daddy is going away on a business trip for a while," he said, struggling to keep his voice even.

Olga smiled at him, her eyelids heavy. "Will you come back soon?"

"I'll try my best," said Nikolai.

"Bring me back something nice." She shut her eyes.

In the morning, they told him he would sleep through the first two days of his trip.

"We must lighten the load as much as possible," he was told, "to make up, somewhat, for the delays. We'll give you a shot to keep you asleep for as long as it's medically reasonable. It will conserve air, food, and water."

By the time he woke up, the Earth was a pale blue dot rapidly diminishing in the distance.

★　★　★

At first, Nikolai chose not to share his concerns with Anatoly. If he was wrong, he would sound like a paranoid lunatic. If he was right.... Nikolai tried very hard not to dwell on the implications.

He pulled up the volumes on astronomy and physics from the ship's database, and he checked the data from the ship's sensors against the star charts, willing the results to make sense. He cut down the amount of time spent on maintaining life support systems, and the amount of time he slept. He checked the equations, again and again, but the numbers never added up.

By now he was getting desperate. He would have to bring his concerns up with Baikonur.

"Do you want to hear a joke?" said Anatoly by way of greeting the next time he called.

"Sure." Nikolai wasn't in a laughing mood, but he let the com specialist talk.

"When the Americans landed on the Moon, Premier Brezhnev's aides broke the bad news to their boss," said Anatoly. "Brezhnev wasn't at all happy.

"'We can't let the capitalists win the space race,' he said. 'I hereby order our intrepid cosmonauts to immediately launch an expedition and land on the Sun!'

"'But Comrade Brezhnev,' said the aides, 'it's impossible to land on the Sun. The Sun is extremely hot.'

"'Nonsense,' said Brezhnev. 'Just tell them to go at night.'"

Nikolai stared at the screen, silent.

"Heard that one, eh?" Anatoly grinned. "That joke is so old, its beard has grown a beard. It seemed appropriate for the occasion, is all."

"What's really going on, Anatoly?" Nikolai blurted out the words before he could change his mind.

The face on the screen stared, eyes widening in surprise. "What do you mean?"

"I calculated the trajectory, and the ship isn't where it should be," said Nikolai. "It's accelerating much faster than it possibly could."

"You must have made a mistake," said Anatoly, a little too quickly, and glanced downward.

After so many rounds of verbal sparring, Nikolai looked into the face of the man on the screen and was certain he was hiding something.

"I taught mathematics at one of Russia's top universities," said Nikolai. "My calculations are accurate. A ship the size of the *Yuri Gagarin* can't possibly accelerate at this rate. And don't feed me a line about secret technologies, I learned enough about propulsion at Baikonur to understand the basics of skip travel."

Anatoly's visage, normally cheerful and full of life, was grim. He sighed deeply and slouched in his chair, his shoulders slumping visibly.

"Wait, please," he said finally, and cut the connection.

Nikolai felt trapped and powerless. Cut off from his family, his only lifeline a man he barely knew, a man who had apparently been lying to him this entire time. But lying about what? Was this a sick experiment? Did he leave Earth at all, or was he in some bunker in Kazakhstan, serving as a guinea pig for Roscosmos shrinks?

He felt claustrophobic, the walls of the ship closing in. His head spun and his stomach churned. Was this a panic attack? Nikolai had never experienced one before.

The salvation from certain death, the chance at fame, the money.... Why would this be offered to him, of all people? How could he be so stupid? This was a fantasy born of a cancerous mass pushing against his brain tissue.

The screen flickered back to life twenty minutes later, but to Nikolai it felt like an eternity.

"I was hoping we wouldn't have this conversation for a few months," said Anatoly. "Some time after the skip."

Nikolai stared at his handler. "Is there a skip?"

"There is a skip, and the ship is right on schedule, accelerating exactly as it should do."

Nikolai waited.

"You're right, though – the ship is much lighter and faster than you were initially led to believe."

Nikolai seethed. "What the hell does that mean, Anatoly?"

"There were delays and complications," said the com specialist. "We couldn't get the life support equipment to work right, couldn't get the ship's mass reduced to an acceptable level. We had hoped the Americans would have similar troubles, but they launched on time, and we were out of options.

"In order to beat them to Arcadia, we had to send a ship that was barely larger than a skip drone – nothing large enough to transport a living, breathing human.

"The best we could do was to send your mind."

Nikolai gaped at the screen.

"Antey Corporation has been developing this technology for a decade," said Anatoly. "We had to euthanize your body and upload your thought patterns into the computer. Your digital self resides in the *Yuri Gagarin*'s memory bank. A sophisticated computer program is simulating your environment. But, in fact, there is no air or food, nor the need for such."

Nikolai stared at his hands, brushed his fingers against the stubble on his chin, and then touched the control console of the ship, felt the slight vibration of the engine. "All this feels real enough to me."

Anatoly entered a command into his own computer, and the world around Nikolai went blank.

He could no longer feel his own body, could not breathe or move, or see anything around him. It was extremely disorienting. Nikolai thought this was how purgatory must feel.

The physical world returned.

"Sorry about the discomfort," said Anatoly. "I had to show you I was telling the truth. This is what it's like without any interface at all."

Nikolai felt his heart thumping fast, his face flushed with anger. How could those things be fake? "You...." he stammered. "You killed me!"

"Your body was already dying," said Anatoly. "The nanites could only hold off the tumor for so long." He offered a weak smile. "Think of the advantages – you will last as long as it takes for the Americans to bring you back home."

"Advantages?" shouted Nikolai. "You were always going to kill me, weren't you? All in the name of some propaganda stunt!"

"No," said Anatoly. "Sure, we were prepared for this. You were selected because your brain activity and personality were deemed most likely to be digitized successfully, and the nanites had been mapping your brain patterns from the beginning. But we would have vastly preferred the alternative." Anatoly leaned forward and lowered his voice, sounding almost conspiratorial. "I know you're angry and confused right now, but think about it – really think about it. You're going to make history, twice. You will not only be the first intelligent being from Earth to land on Arcadia, but you'll be the first successfully digitized human, too."

"You are monsters," whispered Nikolai.

"You will get to watch your daughter grow up," said Anatoly.

Nikolai had no counter to that. He pondered life as a ghost in the machine.

"Why did you lie?" he asked. "Why the ruse? You could have gotten a volunteer. Hell, I might have volunteered if you had laid the options out for me."

"This truly was the backup option," said Anatoly. "But also, we've had...*difficulties* with this process before. Several previous attempts at maintaining a digital intelligence have failed."

Nikolai gritted his nonexistent teeth. The emotional rollercoaster ride wasn't over yet.

"You're doing fine," Anatoly added. "I'm only telling you this to explain our actions. All cards on the table this time, I promise."

"What sort of difficulties?" asked Nikolai.

"The transfer always worked, but the minds couldn't adjust to the virtual existence. They went mad within days. But they weren't as good a match as you."

Nikolai shuddered.

"Through trial and error, we figured out the most efficient approach was to stimulate your senses in a virtual reality environment, and keep the truth from you until your program had stabilized."

Nikolai stared at Anatoly, who raised his palms.

"I know, it was a long shot and a gamble. We really did run out of time. It was this, or scrap the program. You're doing great, though.

"We created a believable and challenging simulation for you. Making you work hard to fix things, challenging your mind to remain sharp and active." Anatoly began to gesture with his hands, as he was prone to doing when he got excited about the topic of conversation. "Every anecdote, every little story I told you, was carefully selected by our top psychiatrists to steer you toward eventually accepting your new reality."

"All this, just to land a computer program on Arcadia," said Nikolai. "Two dozen skip drones already landed there, getting air and water and soil samples. Why would anyone care?"

"It's not the same. You're still a person. A rational human being, capable of emotion and thought. A Russian. Your achievement will matter. Sure, there will be a few detractors, the Americans will argue like hell that a digital person doesn't count, but we'll sell it to the rest of the world even if we have to shove it down their throats."

"I'm capable of emotion," said Nikolai. "Right now, that emotion is anger. Right now, I'm contemplating whether I should take part in your publicity stunt at all. Maybe I'll tell the world about what you people have done to me, instead. Or maybe I'll say nothing at all, play dead, and leave your glorious first-place finish devoid of meaning. How is that for a rational human being?"

Nikolai cut the connection.

★   ★   ★

Nikolai struggled to come to terms with what he was. Even now, the virtual reality he inhabited seemed real to him. He felt hungry, and tired, and hurt when he tentatively bit his cheek. He was capable of feeling anger toward the government and love toward his daughter. Did the lack of a physical body make him any less human than a handicapped person, a quadriplegic unable to control his limbs?

He was never an ardent patriot, and now he was more disillusioned by his country than ever. But would carrying out his threat gain him anything beyond a fleeting moment of satisfaction?

And if he were to comply, if he was to return to Earth in a few years, would Tamara come to terms with this new him? Would Olga? He had no answers, only an ever-growing list of uncertainties.

To their credit, Anatoly and his superiors gave him an entire day to think things through before reestablishing the connection. Anatoly looked like he hadn't slept, was buzzed on caffeine, still wearing the same shirt from the day before.

"What we did to you was crap," he said without preamble, "but I won't apologize for it. Exceptional deeds aren't accomplished through kindness. It's not just Russia, either. All of human history is one tale after another of achieving greatness by ruthlessly building upon a foundation comprised of the bones of the innocent.

"How many slave laborers died to erect the pyramids? The gleaming New York skyscrapers are inseparable from the legacy of smallpox-infected blankets being given to unsuspecting natives.

"You have already paid the price for humanity's next great accomplishment. Why refuse to reap the benefits?"

Nikolai closed his eyes and pictured Olga's face. She may or may not accept the virtual brain-in-a-jar as her father.

He thought of all the doors his success could open for her.

"I'll do it," said Nikolai evenly. "You can tone down the rhetoric."

Anatoly straightened visibly, as though a heavy burden was lifted from his shoulders.

"There are conditions," said Nikolai.

"What do you need?"

"One, I want to talk to my wife. I want her handling things on that end from now on, because I don't quite know how to tell the real from the virtual, and I don't trust any of you."

Nikolai held up two fingers. "Two, when I get back you hand the computer, or the data bank, or whatever my consciousness is stored in over to her, for much the same reason."

Anatoly nodded. "Done."

"I still hate the callous, cynical lot of you. But I'll make the best out of this situation and find solace in the fact that my name will be remembered long after all your gravestones are dust. Speaking of that legacy, we'll need to work on my speech. Something tells me 'one small step' isn't going to go over well, in my case."

"We'll have speechwriters float some ideas," said Anatoly.

"Finally, have your programmers work on some adjustments to my gilded cage. If I'm to eat make-believe food, making it taste this bad is needlessly cruel. Tonight, I'd like a thick slab of virtual steak, medium-well."

Nikolai settled in for the long journey. There would be time enough to sort out his feelings, and to learn how to live as this new kind of being. He knew one thing for sure: like his great-grandfather, he would persevere and return home.

Yuri Gagarin, the tiny ship carrying the future hero of humanity, accelerated toward the skip point.

SHINE

Chen Zijun

Translated by Alex Woodend

1. Eight Hundred Million Kilometers Away

Eight hours after the accident, Beijing

An ordinary morning.

Inside the third-year building of Chaoyang Middle School, the bell for the first class rings.

It is Qi Fengyang's eighth year as a physics teacher. Typically, he has not brought any lecture notes, or prepared any course materials. Seeming a little vacant standing on the podium, he looks at the students sleeping below, waiting for the bell to wake them up.

"Let's begin."

"Up!"

"Hello, teacher!"

"Hello, students!" Qi Fengyang says. "Please sit down. This is a review class. Let's go over the law of universal gravitation, then complete some related exercises."

Below the podium, they reluctantly open their lecture notes, and yawning noises sound throughout the classroom.

Seeing everyone's weary looks, Qi Fengyang then says, "Well, seems everyone thinks this is very boring. Let's get refreshed first.... Today is September 20th, anyone know what day it is?"

At this, only a few students raise their heads.

"Today is the date the spaceship *Poseidon* arrives at Jupiter." Qi

Fengyang gestures with both hands. "It's the biggest, longest-traveling, fastest manned spaceship human beings have ever made. It will land on Jupiter II to explore the icy satellite's underground ocean. It's the largest-scale space mission in human history. Early this morning, the *Poseidon* spaceship finally arrived at its destination. Okay, here's the question: anyone know how long it takes to get to Jupiter from Earth?"

Utter silence, the heads just raised droop again.

"Nobody knows? This is test material! Kepler's third law: given the semi-major axis of an orbit, find the flight duration. Earth's distance from the Sun is one hundred and fifty million kilometers, the orbital period is one year. Cube the ratio of the semi-major axis, then taking the square root, we can calculate the flight time of *Poseidon* to be between ten and eleven years."

"But the news said it only took one year...?" a student asks.

"Very good! Your instincts are very sharp!" Qi Fengyang nods his head. "Know why that is?"

"Because...its orbit isn't...isn't...."

"Isn't a conical curve." Qi Fengyang grabs a piece of chalk, starts to draw, making the blackboard screech. "Well, of course, you have only done these kinds of exercises – transfer an orbit from a circular orbit of radius A1 to a circular orbit of radius A2, between them use an elliptical orbit as a connection – all the orbits are conical. In spaceflight, this is called a Hohmann transfer orbit. It's the most energy-efficient trajectory using instantaneous thrust, and the only trajectory solvable with a secondary education...."

"However, *Poseidon* didn't use this orbit. It launched in the year 2049, first accelerated to escape Earth, then orbited the Sun five times, successively accelerating via gravity slingshots around Mars and Venus. At the end of the fifth time – that is, on August 15th of last year – it brushed past Earth at a speed of thirty kilometers per second when the astronauts were sent to space, to dock with it...so, their journey in space was less than a year. Not a bad idea, is it?"

Qi Fengyang looks expectantly below the podium, but again only sees a series of heads resting on desks.

"All right…let's continue with the exercises."

He lets out a hopeless sigh, grabs an eraser to rub out the intricate trajectory on the blackboard, and starts to transcribe the exercises from the lecture notes. But these exercises do nothing to spark his interest. Making him solve them is like peeling potatoes with a precious sword.

Alas, in the old days….

Stop, stop – no more 'in the old days'!

Qi Fengyang gives a bitter smile. His current self should be content – as a middle school physics teacher, his monthly salary is over 10,000 yuan. With additional fees from extra weekend classes and allowances for teaching third-year classes, competition classes, and coaching, his monthly after-tax income is 25,000 yuan. He not only bought a house but has money to spare for his father's treatments. Compared with the hard life on Base 647 in the old days, shouldn't he feel content?

His cell phone rings.

He grabs the phone, sees it's a strange number, and hangs up, continuing with the class.

But a few seconds later, the phone rings again – still the same number. He thinks a moment, gives the students an exercise, then leaves the classroom and calls back.

"Hello, may I ask who this is?"

"It's Huo Changhao. You didn't forget me, did you?" a familiar voice sounds.

"Ah!" Qi Fengyang is shocked. After some moments, he replies, "Certainly not. Heh, so lucky to get a call from our richest man. What a surprise."

"No time to chat. Where are you?"

"At school, teaching. Why?"

"Sorry. Can you ask for some time off? Just three days. Then go to the school entrance. A car is there waiting for you…. I've got an urgent matter I need your help with."

"Help? You still have the nerve to ask me for help?"

"No choice. Other than you, I have no one else," Huo Changhao says. "You know *Poseidon*, right?"

"Sure. Why?"

"Early this morning, it crashed on Jupiter."

★　　★　　★

Eight hours earlier

Under the sea of clouds on Jupiter, an electromagnetic storm brews.

For Jupiter, such an electromagnetic storm is very common. This cosmic giant has the most powerful, most turbulent magnetic field in the solar system, which radiates electromagnetic waves incessantly. Seen via radio waves, Jupiter is the brightest source of light in the night sky. It flickers nonstop like a poorly connected lamp at night. This irregular radiation has befuddled astronomical circles. Many theoretical models are constantly being put forward, but none can make accurate predictions as of yet.

This is the case with this electromagnetic storm. Human eyes and instruments covering all wavelengths could only see Jupiter's cloud layer rolling as usual – not the violent change underneath that red-brown veil.

That is a temperamental world.

Jupiter's atmosphere is 1,000 kilometers thick, contains hydrogen, ammonia, methane, and water vapor, as well as a small amount of sulfide. Red, brown, blue-white streaks of clouds surge nonstop, forming disorderly and colorful belts. The 'Great Red Spot' cyclone dives into it like a giant whale in a chaotic sea, or like the eye of a ferocious lurking tiger. Underneath is a vast 'sea' of liquid hydrogen. This sea is boundless. Its surface is smooth where hydrogen gas grows thicker, heavier, and denser, and eventually turns into liquid. Thirty years prior, NASA's *Galileo* dropped a shield-shaped probe there, which went deep down to a location a hundred and fifty kilometers under Jupiter's cloud layer where pressure reached ten times that of the atmosphere, causing the probe to be crushed to pieces.

The boundary of the world known to human beings ends there.

Deeper down, there's only imagination to rely on. As the depth increases, the pressure grows, liquid hydrogen grows denser and denser, and the distance between hydrogen atoms is squeezed smaller and smaller. Theories suggest that somewhere 30,000 kilometers under 'sea level', due to extremely high pressure, the distance between hydrogen atoms is equivalent to the diameter of an electron cloud. At this point, liquid hydrogen suddenly turns into an electrically conductive, gel-like material called metastable solid metallic hydrogen (MSMH). This material exists between Jupiter's core and mantle, its thickness uneven, likely ranging from thousands of kilometers to 10,000 kilometers. Due to its slow rotation, the loop-shaped electric currents inside are the main sources of Jupiter's magnetic field.

It's a pity this theory was confirmed after the accident.

Of course, even if it had been discovered earlier, engineers could hardly have predicted the accident. Long before *Poseidon* set out, due to eruptions at Jupiter's core, a gush of gel-state metallic hydrogen slowly projected upward. It was a magnificent scene: above the sunless surface of Jupiter's core, a sea of gel-like metallic hydrogen 10,000 kilometers thick was rolling slowly under the transparent sea of liquid hydrogen. As metallic hydrogen electric currents ran, faint blue light illuminated a small patch of sea surface along with the unceasing helium rain falling since antiquity. On the sea surface, big, soft, dark blue droplets occasionally splashed up and rose slowly like jellyfish. These MSMH projectiles were like splashes in a pond during heavy rain, but each splash was the size of Asia. Since Jupiter's internal materials are extremely dense, the rate at which they move is extremely slow, so the projecting-falling process may have lasted over a hundred years, as long as the famous Great Red Spot. Perhaps long before the *Poseidon* astronauts were born, even before the French Revolution, the disaster's seed had been sown.

Metallic hydrogen can only exist under extremely high pressure. But interestingly, gel-state metallic hydrogen is characterized by metastability. That is, after metallic hydrogen is formed, if outer pressure is constantly and slowly decreased, even below the critical pressure, metallic hydrogen gel can still maintain its original state. But this state is unstable. Like a little ball placed on a saddle, any small disturbance makes it fall out of metastability, transforming into its usual liquid state. During the transition, it turns from conductor to insulator. Its conductivity changes a dozen or so orders of magnitude, drastically compressing its magnetic flux, radiating conserved electromagnetic energy in all directions.

In other words, it is a colossal electromagnetic pulse bomb!

Over the past few centuries such an unprecedentedly large bomb had formed. Its volume equal to several Earths, it contained electromagnetic energy accumulated over hundreds of years. In the process of rising, its surrounding pressure slowly fell. Once below the critical pressure, it was in a state that might collapse at any moment, like an acrobat standing tiptoe on a stilt or a huge rock pushed to a mountaintop. For one day, two days, it can remain steady, but over time, a slight stir brings it to the point of collapse.

That point was eight hours and twenty-two minutes ago.

Then the *Poseidon* spaceship had just arrived at Jupiter's orbit.

This small disturbance quickly produced an avalanche effect. Blinding lightning burst out of Jupiter's core: metastable metallic hydrogen suddenly collapsed, and more than 10^{24} Jules of electromagnetic energy was instantly released, most of which was converted into heat, and the small amount remaining was radiated as electromagnetic waves. Enormous amounts of liquid hydrogen were vaporized by this lightning and became a high-temperature, high-pressure, irregular bubble, the size of several Earths. Within a few milliseconds it drastically expanded thousands of kilometers. Then in another few milliseconds it collapsed toward the center, broke, disintegrated, and released energy for the second time. The electromagnetic pulse spread out at light speed. After 0.3 seconds, it disturbed Jupiter's magnetic field; after another 0.5 seconds, it hit the *Poseidon* spaceship.

The magnetic storm's impact on the spaceship was catastrophic. The first thing it destroyed was the electronic instruments. The quadruple-redundant computer-controlled navigation system burned up. The spaceship went into a complete state of shock, and high gain antennas were destroyed, interrupting communication with Earth. But the deadliest damage came to the VASIMR engine. The engine, which depended on radio waves as an acceleration propellant, was not designed to work under such powerful electromagnetic pulses. When the magnetic storm occurred, the electromagnetic field inside the engine was seriously distorted, and the plasma jets were clogged like a patient having a myocardial infarction from fright – and a few seconds later, the explosion occurred. It opened a two-meter gap on the spaceship's propulsion section, and the entire spaceship was instantly depleted of air, becoming a cold coffin drifting through space.

The explosion was the outcome of an astronomical event that had been brewing for hundreds of years, and *Poseidon* somehow ran into it – the unluckiest of unlucky things.

But luckily someone survived.

★   ★   ★

Twenty-four hours after the accident, NASA's Ames Research Center, San Francisco Bay Area, California

The Gulfstream X981 aircraft glides gracefully across the vast, cloudless, blue sky and lands on a runway at Moffett Airfield.

It's noon, the sun is furious. The Gulfstream's slim body reflects the dazzling light like a long silver sword. It is the most expensive private aircraft in the world, which is the only reason it doesn't look too out of date among NASA demonstration craft.

Huo Changhao, handsome in sunglasses, walks toward Qi Fengyang. "So? Plane isn't bad, huh?"

"Mm, maximum speed Mach three-point-five. Most advanced private aircraft indeed," Qi Fengyang says.

"I spent nine hundred million dollars last year to buy it," Huo Changhao says. "Now the market price is only eight hundred million dollars. Lost a great deal, but for her, I have no choice but to bite the bullet and sell it."

"Her?"

"Yes," Huo Changhao says. "With your brains you must have already figured out who she is, right?"

At this, Huo Changhao points at the big screen in the departure lounge, which is broadcasting the main news stories of the day. Right below the line of capitalized words *SHI'NING ON EUROPA!* is a picture of a woman. She wears a spacesuit, the large helmet emphasizing her small size, so it looks like a fragile plant growing from a suit of armor.

Facing the picture, Huo Changhao announces, "You help me build a spaceship that in one hundred and twenty days can fly eight hundred million kilometers to Jupiter and get Sun Shi'ning back!"

Qi Fengyang looks at him in shock. Some moments later he says, "You're crazy!"

"Just very passionate," Huo Changhao replies.

"That's more ridiculous than landing on the Sun."

"Why?"

"I'll tell you. The fastest one-way mission to Jupiter of the century was *Prometheus*. The whole trip took three years. *Poseidon* technically only flew ten months, but before that it had gone through a five-year pre-acceleration process. Therefore your goal is downright delusional."

"Ha, how come it's delusional? Don't forget the Polaris Program could reach it." Huo Changhao smiles.

"That's quite different from your current delusion."

"No more yours or mine. Even if it's a delusion, it's ours," Huo Changhao says. "I know you don't like me, but I hope you can put that aside for now. I want to save Sun Shi'ning, so I have to count on you. If you want to realize your dream, you have to count on me."

"You crushed my dream long ago," Qi Fengyang says and looks at him.

"Now you can take it up again," Huo Changhao says. "I definitely won't screw you over this time. Sun Shi'ning's accident has drawn a lot of attention, so we can mobilize enormous resources. At least two orders of magnitude more than the Base 647. This is an opportunity to make history. You want to pass it up?"

"Of course not. But please remember, I'm not doing this for her, and much less for you – only to realize my dream." Stiffly, Qi Fengyang says, "I'll do my best."

"Very good. That sounds like your style," Huo Changhao says, "Let's go, we'll persuade those old fossils at Clipper."

*　　*　　*

The Ames Research Center is one of NASA's large research institutes. Some of Clipper's most important laboratories are based there. The most impressive one is the vacuum simulation cabin inside Building E-09. It's a huge thirty-meter-tall vacuum tank used in full-scale spacecraft experiments. Qi Fengyang sees the testing craft of the *Cronus* lander inside.[1] Next to it, a bearded man anxiously paces back and forth.

"I'm back," Huo Changhao says bluntly. "I'll introduce. This is Dr. Qi Fengyang, famous orbit design expert. Comrade Qi, this is Or Martinez, the technical director of the *Poseidon* spaceship, now responsible for planning out our upcoming rescue mission."

"Speaking frankly, Mr. Huo, this is a mission impossible," Martinez says.

"But a mission inevitable," Huo Changhao immediately replies.

"Mr. Huo, you may as well do the calculation yourself. Now, the linear distance between Jupiter and Earth is eight hundred and twenty million kilometers. The flight trajectory would be longer, but we can use it as a conservative value to estimate. One hundred days, nearly twenty-five hundred hours, that's almost eighty million seconds. If we depart right away, dividing eight hundred million by eighty million means the spaceship's average speed should be ten kilometers per second, with initial speed equal to the third cosmic velocity. Current technologies – like Super-SLS – can certainly achieve this, but...."

"But, making a rescue spaceship takes time," Qi Fengyang says.

"Yes. Conventionally the assembly and launch of a spaceship requires about six months. If we work in three shifts, discarding half of the testing rounds, and the entire North American Space Alliance works at top speed, we would need at least two months, which would still be amazing. So the spaceship's average speed has to increase fourfold.

---

1. A spaceflight mission usually produces two identical spacecraft. The one left on the ground for tests is called a formal testing craft, and the one launched into orbit is called the launching craft.

Taking the acceleration and deceleration processes into consideration, the spaceship's launch speed has to be higher. I just made an estimate — about one hundred and twenty kilometers per second, eight times the third cosmic velocity!" Martinez spreads his hands hopelessly. "We have never launched a manned spaceship that fast. Adding reliability, cost, fault tolerance, and other factors, this already exceeds current human spaceflight ability. So, Mr. Huo...."

"I get it," Huo Changhao says. "That's exactly why I brought Qi Fengyang here."

"To be fair, I knew Mr. Qi before you," Martinez says. "We competed in an international orbit design competition — which year I don't remember. He's a genius, Mr. Huo. The orbit he designed was incredible, used gravity slingshots from four big planets, with all kinds of harsh constraints, and was twenty percent faster than second place. The *Poseidon* mission was planned out based on that trajectory...."

Qi Fengyang gives a bitter smile. "Really? That's truly an honor."

"Nevertheless, Mr. Qi, I don't think you can solve this problem." Martinez turns on his laptop. "First, let me introduce the situation. At one p.m. this afternoon — that is early morning your time — we lost contact with *Poseidon*. First we deployed the Deep Space Communication Network, but due to damage from Jupiter's electromagnetic storm, hundreds of satellites were destroyed, and the Deep Space Network was basically paralyzed. But luckily, when the magnetic storm occurred, a satellite happened to be behind Mars. It survived and functioned as a communication relay, and we managed to confirm the state of *Poseidon*.

"After the explosion, three of the spaceship's four modules — the *Dawn* command module, the *Unity* node module, and the *Star* service module — were unresponsive. Signals on all channels had no feedback and were confirmed destroyed. The signals of the fourth module, the *Cronus* lander, were mostly interrupted, but the self-test signal sent by low-gain antennae was normal. In this signal, we found a spacesuit's connection status to be 'in use'. It was Sun Shi'ning's spacesuit...."

"So you think she survived? Isn't that a bit hasty...?" Qi Fengyang is surprised.

"Wait, let me finish. Five hours after the explosion, we again received a signal from *Cronus* and learned that in those five hours it had started the engine once with an ignition duration of seventy-five seconds, fifty-three percent of fuel consumed. Gyroscopic data shows that the lander is currently entering LEU2 in Jupiter II's orbit. That's the orbit of the third emergency landing plan. The landing site is the Avalon Plain near Jupiter II's equator. That's clearly a human action, right?"

Huo Changhao asks, "Is she trying to land now?"

"That was three hours ago," Martinez says. "Due to an interruption, we can't communicate with her. Of course, the bigger possibility is that she's already dead. After all, the success rate of solo landing maneuvers is very low."

"You mean, if there's no way to confirm her condition, there's basically no reason to start the rescue mission, huh?"

"Of course," Martinez says. "I need evidence – strong evidence – that she can survive for one hundred days."

"I get it." Qi Fengyang nods. "Huo Changhao, do you remember that news?"

"What?"

"The headline, *Shi'ning on Europa*?" Qi Fengyang says. "I've got an idea about communication."

2. The Polaris Program

Twenty-eight hours after the accident, Mojave Desert, California, Goldstone Space Flight Center

At dusk in the *Todd* telescope control room, only one person remains.

In sharp contrast, other monitoring and control teams – like the *Hubble II* and *Kolev* telescopes – are feverishly busy. When the spectacle began the night before, telephones in all monitoring and control teams suddenly rang at the same time. Scheduling commands from major organizations poured into the control center like a flood, requesting the adjustment of telescope orientations to just one target – Jupiter.

During the explosion on the previous day, Jupiter emitted extremely powerful radio waves, almost covering the entire electromagnetic spectrum. Data of all wavelengths poured into computers, containing enough information for the world's scientists to study for decades. But the most shocking change was undoubtedly in the visible wave range. Because the enormous energy the metallic hydrogen released during the collapse heated up Jupiter's atmosphere, uneven thermal convection produced a cyclone in the cloud layer with a volume comparable to the famous Great Red Spot, but whitish in color, which caused it to be dubbed the 'Great White Spot'. The two cyclones moved side by side on Jupiter's surface, like a giant's charming eyes.

Over the coming centuries, this pair of eyes will witness the rise or decline of humanity.

Of all the monitoring and control teams, the *Todd* X-ray telescope was the least lucky. During the explosion, X-rays lasted less than a second, but the telescope was pointing in another direction. After that, regardless of everyone's eagerness, the receiver pointing to Jupiter maintained a reading of zero. So after work they all left disappointed, feeling no one would seek them out again.

Then the phone on the table rang.

"This is Clipper's *Poseidon* team, please observe target number X-one-eight-nine-two-R-six." It's Martinez on the other end.

"Please transmit observation authorization."

"Authorization transmitted. After confirmation, please immediately aim *Todd* at the target. The time interval is from T-plus-one-one-zero-eight-two-five to one-two-five-three-five-zero seconds. Use the highest resolution. Specific wave filtering parameters will be sent to you in a moment."

"Copy." The engineer staying behind is a little confused. "Let me see…um, this is Jupiter II. It isn't the source of any X-rays. The radiant intensity isn't much higher than the cosmic background value. What do you expect to see there?"

"No idea," Martinez says vaguely. "Perhaps someone is sending a telegram…."

"Okay, you've got the authorization, so you can look at whatever you want." The engineer shrugs and inputs the new orbit parameters. The *Todd* space telescope slowly adjusts its position. Within half an hour, it takes hundreds of pictures of Jupiter II.

"Please wait a moment...downlink data transmitting...processing...."

After the image sequence is rendered, the engineer can't believe his eyes.

On the fuzzy round outline, a small white bright dot is flashing.

"Hello? Sir, what the hell!"

⋆ ⋆ ⋆

Twenty-eight hours after the accident, NASA's Ames Research Center

Martinez puts down the phone, looks at Qi Fengyang in disbelief.

"What the hell!" he shouts, hardly containing his excitement. "The *Todd* X-ray telescope found flashing on Jupiter II, right on the Avalon Plain! The interval is about twenty seconds, already confirmed to be Morse code, now being translated. Mr. Qi, how did this happen?"

"It's called telepathy," Huo Changhao says with a laugh. "You didn't know Mr. Qi and Ms. Sun Shi'ning were a couple, they—"

"Enough," Qi Fengyang says, bluntly interrupting Huo Changhao. "There is nothing magical about it. Just now, when I saw the superconducting coil used to generate a magnetic shield in the simulator of the *Cronus* lander, I got this idea. Sun Shi'ning is a mechanical moron, definitely can't fix onboard communication equipment – but she understands the working principles of magnetic shields and X-rays, so the likelihood of communication in this way is greatest."

"I still don't understand...." Huo Changhao says. "The flash can be seen by telescope, which means its range is quite large, covering at least tens of thousands of square kilometers, right? How is that possible?"

"It's high-energy particles!" Martinez slaps his head. "Jupiter II moves within Jupiter's Van Allen radiation belt, and has enormous high-energy particles. The main function of the magnetic shield is to keep those particles outside the lander. Just like Earth's magnetic field, the high-energy particles approaching the lander will be confined by the magnetic field, to orbit the lander, like a mini Van Allen radiation belt...."

"Right." Qi Fengyang nods. "If you increase the electric current in the coil, the small 'radiation belt' changes shape, and high-energy particles bombard the ice layer on the surface, giving out fluorescence. The radius of the magnetic shield of *Cronus* is about five kilometers, which contains enough particles, so it's completely possible to produce such a flash."

"You mean, Sun Shi'ning has made a fluorescent X-ray tube with a magnetic shield?"

"Sort of."

"Good, great...." Martinez paces excitedly back and forth but quickly stops in frustration. "But the efficiency of this communication is too low. Sun Shi'ning is maneuvering the magnetic shield manually, it would take several seconds to send a complete signal. Too slow."

"Write a program, just let the computer automatically maneuver the magnetic shield," Huo Changhao says.

"Easy to say." Qi Fengyang shakes his head. "Spacecraft software is mostly written in an embedded system. Even the little modifiable software is based on professional operating systems like VXWorks, SpaceOS. You think the spaceship is installed with Visual Studio? Sun Shi'ning is smart, but she didn't finish college, she doesn't understand—"

"Then you have to write a program and send it out." Huo Changhao chuckles. "Comrade Qi, it's up to you, since you and she have the telepathic connection."

★　　★　　★

Thirty hours after the accident, San Francisco

At dusk, Qi Fengyang finally finishes compiling the program in the *Poseidon* simulator and hands it to the uplink communication team. Through NASA's Deep Space Network, the code of less than nine hundred bytes is sent out at maximum power and flies toward Jupiter II, eight hundred million kilometers away.

At the same time, Qi Fengyang, Huo Changhao, and Or Martinez temporarily leave the Ames Research Center and ride toward downtown Los Angeles in a car.

"The next step is the rescue operation," Martinez, sitting in the front seat, turns and says. "One hundred days, eight hundred million kilometers. Mr. Qi, next I'll have to tell people this crazy goal is possible. Do you have any brilliant ideas regarding that?"

"Sure he does," Huo Changhao says, lighting a cigarette. "He proposed the China National Space Administration's Polaris Program, which had the same target. Right, Comrade Qi?"

"Sort of," Qi Fengyang says.

"Mr. Qi, I'm curious, what kind of rocket do you plan to use to accelerate a multi-ton spaceship to one-hundred and twenty kilometers per second?"

"Won't use a rocket," Qi Fengyang says. "Lightsail."

"Lightsail?"

"Yeah. A massive two-hundred-meter-long square sail, graphene-based, weighs four grams per square meter. First, a rocket will send it to Earth's escape orbit at thirty kilometers per second. A ground laser array focuses radiation, which can generate about two Gs of acceleration. The acceleration will last four hours, or four hundred thousand kilometers, about the distance from the Earth to the Moon."

"Two Gs of acceleration? How powerful should the laser be?"

"Uh...about ten-to-the-thirteenth watts," Qi Fengyang replies. "Equal to one percent of the total power output of the entire human race, or—"

"The total power consumed by all the world's LiFi networks," Huo Changhao says.

"Yes. LiFi lasers have very high precision and collimation, and their power is adjustable, almost tailor-made for this. In fact, the original LiFi technology was born out of this project – no, probably even earlier, it can be traced back to the 'Breakthrough Starshot' proposed by Hawking at the beginning of the century," Qi Fengyang says. "Now the whole world has hundreds of thousands of LiFi base stations, absolutely up to the task of accelerating the lightsail."

"Hm, maybe...." Martinez scratches his head.

"And quite coincidentally, the planned launch date is this March, because the current relative position of planets makes an optimal configuration, enabling flight time to reach its minimum value."

"But how do you plan to decelerate to enter orbit?" Martinez says. "After arriving at Jupiter, if you maintain the high speed of nearly one hundred kilometers per second, you'll fly right by it."

"We use multi-sail focusing technology to decelerate."

"Multi-sail focusing?"

"It's focusing all the reflected sunlight from N sails to one sail to attain N times the deceleration thrust," Huo Changhao cuts in. "I remember this process seemed very complicated. Deceleration strokes beyond ten thousand kilometers require very accurate sights, and the order and position of every sail in the orbit transfer must be precise."

"This way the spaceship doesn't need to carry fuel for deceleration and retardation. The mass of every sail weighs only fifty kilograms — light as a feather," Qi Fengyang says. "After multi-sail light-focusing deceleration, the target sail will be caught by Jupiter and fly toward Jupiter II, while other sails will deflect under Jupiter's gravity and continue to fly toward other destinations."

"Sounds fine. Why wasn't it realized?" Martinez asks.

"Long story," Qi Fengyang says, waving a hand. "The priority is to figure out the effective payload mass of the rescue spaceship. This way I can quickly calculate the scale of the lightsail formation."

"Two tons, maybe...should be the minimum," Martinez answers immediately.

"Then the original auxiliary sails definitely won't be enough," Qi Fengyang says. "And we have to consider Sun Shi'ning's condition. She will have to take off from Jupiter II, escape its gravitational field, then dock with the rescue ship. Considering the fuel left in *Cronus*, Sun Shi'ning can only accelerate to five kilometers per second. Add to this Jupiter's revolution speed, eight kilometers per second, and the speed of the rescue spaceship must be reduced to that value."

"I have an idea," Martinez says. "The ascent stage of *Cronus* uses a hydrogen-oxygen engine, and one thing Jupiter II doesn't lack is water. Sun Shi'ning can produce hydrogen-oxygen fuel by electrolyzing water and fill the fuel tank. This will greatly increase the rendezvous speed...I guarantee it could at least reach twenty kilometers per second."

"Good idea. But how to store and liquify hydrogen?"

"There should be applicable equipment in *Cronus*, she can make some small adjustments," Martinez says. "Then we'll need a longer, more complicated tutorial – considering Sun Shi'ning isn't familiar with mechanics, a text tutorial alone probably isn't enough. We have to keep efficient communication with her."

"Hm, it all depends on your code, Comrade Qi. Hope it works," Huo Changhao says, turning.

"When Sun Shi'ning replies, we will know." Qi Fengyang looks at his watch. "Do we have enough time to get back?"

"We do – radio waves take more than three hours to go back and forth," Huo Changhao says. "Just come back at nine p.m."

"I might not make it," Martinez says. "I have to go to the Fields Villa to see Alan Musk, then there's Belize, Brown, maybe they can help to get special appropriations from Congress. Remus basically can't be counted on. That gentleman can't even tell Jupiter from Venus...."

"Good luck to you." Huo Changhao gives him a thumbs-up. "Qi Fengyang and I will find a place to have a drink, talk about old times."

★　★　★

Huo Changhao asks the driver to stop the car in front of a bar.

"Yeah, right here!"

In the direction Huo Changhao is pointing, Qi Fengyang sees a shabby bar. Its sign is inlaid with a pair of reindeer horns. In front of the bar-top, several candles sway. From inside, the smell of tung oil and rosin wafts out.

"I like its name, White Night," Huo Changhao says. "Every year there is always a moment, a moment before sunset, when the last ray of sunlight shines right here, makes it true to its name."

Soon Qi Fengyang sees the scene as he described: because of the place's orientation, the setting sun shines directly at it from the end of the road and hits the porch. Countless car silhouettes drive up toward the setting sun like moths fluttering toward a flame, one after another disappearing into the incandescent furnace. Soon, the vibrant colors in the sky gradually settle like the cocktail swirling in Huo Changhao's hand, turning slowly from brilliant golden red to melancholic blue-purple.

"This really isn't what I was expecting, Huo Changhao," Qi Fengyang says. "I thought you liked those high-class clubs with Louis XIII and Rémy Martin, and Ferraris and Lamborghinis crowding the entrance."

"Only upstarts like that crap," Huo Changhao says. "I chose this place mainly because of a movie. This is where the hero and the heroine separated, and here I too sent away someone I won't forget for my whole life."

"Sun Shi'ning?"

"Right. Talking about this doesn't make you bitter?"

"Ha, so what if I'm bitter," Qi Fengyang says. "The movie you mentioned is *Five-Year Engagement*, right?"

Huo Changhao downs the alcohol in the glass. "Yeah, after she left, the only thing that stayed with me was the memory of the movie…she's a lot like the heroine, Comrade Qi. Like a cool breeze blowing through your palm, however you clench it, she'll slip away through your fingers, heading to higher, farther skies."

"You have a lot of nerve, Huo Changhao. Have you forgotten how you went after her?"

"Yes, of course I remember…." Huo Changhao asks the bartender for another drink and takes it for himself. "I met her on vacation in Egypt. That was definitely the most important day of my life…she was a present-day Hedy Lamarr, beautiful, intelligent, with an incomparable charm. I was completely captivated."

"You must have fallen for other girls before that."

"Yeah, but that was different! The ones before her, uh, how to put it? I had fun for a couple of days then got bored.... But I pursued Sun Shi'ning for a year. I went to her book signing, invested in the movie adaptation of her novel, got closer to her at all kinds of fancy dinner parties. I took her sailing, hiking in the mountains, driving across the desert in an SUV. That was her favorite way to look for inspiration. When the time was ripe, I took her here, to Silicon Valley, said to the executive of Clipper, 'Let us go for a ride in a Lynx!'"

"That's the sub-orbital plane?"

"Yeah, for four million dollars you can take a tour a hundred kilometers into space," Huo Changhao says. "In the desert of Arizona, our plane accelerated along a shining metallic guide rail. After rocket ignition, we shot into the clouds and watched the sky turn from blue to pitch-black together. When stars appeared, I took out a diamond ring, said, 'Shi'ning, will you....'"

"Enough, I know the rest."

"No, you don't know," Huo Changhao says. "You definitely don't know. She rejected me at the time. She said, 'Thank you for your good intentions, but I'm already in love with another person. He's from a poor family but has noble ideals, will definitely become the genius of his generation.' Comrade Qi, do you want to know how I replied?"

"Go ahead."

"Well, I told her: 'Right, he is a genius — but what is genius?' Comrade Qi, do you know what genius is?" Huo Changhao says. "Have you ever thought about what makes a genius? Is it some noble ideal, or great ambition? Neither! What makes a genius is desperation, is suffering, is a soul twisted to the point of imprisonment...the more twisted it is, the more it wants to prove itself in a special way. The more broken it is, the more it wants to cover itself with shining clothes. You have no love in your heart, just a pool of blood shed fighting for ideals. The pool of blood is what shines out and becomes the rouge of genius the world sees...."

Qi Fengyang slowly swirls the alcohol in the glass, not speaking a word.

"Comrade Qi, Shi'ning loved you. What made you go your separate ways was precisely your talents. The brilliance it emitted was like porcupine quills, made you unable to be hugged.... You two were people with a pool of blood in your hearts. That you surely know."

"Huh. Huo Changhao, you are a smart person...but what right do you have to criticize me? Could it be that you can't grow old with her either?"

"Haha, you're correct. We can't grasp her, just let her fly out of our hands and fly so high, so far.... Now, to Sun Shi'ning – bottoms up!"

Qi Fengyang gulps down the alcohol. The bitterness slowly melts away in his mouth, and everything starts to lilt around him.

"And afterward?" he asks, thick-tongued. "What about her afterward?"

"Afterward you already know.... She left home, went on chasing her dream. Two years later I found out she'd applied to join the *Poseidon* mission."

Qi Fengyang stares at the empty glass in silence, sighs. "Perhaps this is the destination she sought...."

"What about you? Afterward, how did you get through?" Huo Changhao asks.

"Nothing special...."

"Tell me, in detail, about the Polaris Program, and your life afterward."

"Fine." Qi Fengyang gives a bitter smile. "Since you want to hear a sad story, I'll tell you."

3. Don't Demolish

Ten years ago, Beijing's Dongcheng Detention Center

"Mr. Qi, I've come to talk to you about something important," Qi Fengyang's lawyer said to him in the visiting room. "The prosecutor has filed a public suit. Your chance of winning is not high, understand?"

"I understand," Qi Fengyang said. "Time is short, cut to the chase."

"Today we have to go through your statement," the lawyer said.

"Start from the death of Dr. Xu Linhui. After one p.m. on October 28th, where were you? What were you doing?"

"I was in the lightsail simulation laboratory of Base 647, doing experiments on the electrostatic equilibrium of lightsails."

"Was it a routine experiment?"

"No, I proposed it in order to test an idea of mine.... I tried to use electrostatic repulsion to open the sail. Compared to traditional truss-style sail skeletons, it could reduce the sail weight by ninety percent. The one conducted that day was the third verification experiment. Specifics are in the appendix of the indictment."

"At what time did Dr. Xu come?"

"Around two p.m. At that time I had to leave for something urgent. Dr. Xu said he could come over to take care of the lab for me. Two minutes after I left, it exploded."

"Please briefly explain the reasons for the explosion."

"An overuse fracture in the vacuum pump valve," Qi Fengyang said. "The experiment on the electrostatic equilibrium of lightsails was done in the T-L-Three-E Vacuum Chamber. In order to simulate the electromagnetic environment in space, the test chamber had to be vacuum sealed. The pressure the valve bore per square meter was equal to the weight of four elephants. In each experiment, we had to pump the air out, and after several rounds mechanical fatigue occurred."

"The indictment mentions the valve had passed its replacement date. Which department was responsible for that?"

"The vacuum simulation laboratory, but it wasn't managed by the personnel of Base 647."

"An outsourced group?"

"Mm. In the process of building Base 647, we accepted investment from Huo Changhao. A lot of equipment was shared between both parties. An agreement was reached at the time. Separate from lightsail experiments, he could use the equipment and personnel of the base to conduct other research."

"What research was he doing?"

"All sorts. The most important one was on LiFi technology. At the time, the base was very well-equipped for laser experiments."

"Sorry, the evidence is conclusive. You will probably be sentenced for dereliction of duty, which I can't absolve you of."

"Understood, that's true. But the last charge…is complete bullshit."

"Someone reported you for taking advantage of your position to break the valve to kill Dr. Xu," the lawyer said. "The informant claimed that you and Dr. Xu had a big fight the day before the accident."

"Right, we had been fighting for some time," Qi Fengyang admitted.

"What were the reasons?"

"Mainly over the implementation plan of the Polaris Program. I was hoping to use multi-sail light-focusing technology to realize the round trip to Jupiter II in two hundred days, in two manned and unmanned steps. But Dr. Xu thought the plan was too radical, preferring to use an ordinary rocket to launch a one-way impact probe. During that disagreement, I was trying to stop him from signing the resolution."

"That's a very professional motive," the lawyer said. "Were there any differences between the two plans?"

"Of course, the two are completely different! Rockets are costly and inefficient, a sunset technology bound to be eliminated. If you want to fly quickly through the solar system on a large scale, lightsail formations are a very promising direction."

"Really? I heard Little Zhang said the laser power used in this technology was equal to the total power output of the whole country, right?"

"Not so much, roughly equal to one-twentieth of the total power. Of course, the scale of the laser was pretty amazing, that's why we cooperated with Huo Changhao's LiFi company," Qi Fengyang said. "But anyway, don't you find it strange? We quarreled behind the lunch hall, and someone happened to be recording it!"

"Yes, I understand," the lawyer said. "If someone really framed you, who do you think it might be?"

"Huo Changhao." Qi Fengyang sighed. "The trap had been set long before…."

"But unfortunately, he isn't the only one who would want to frame you," the lawyer said. "Mr. Qi, almost the entire Research Institute was eager to frame you. When the prosecutor was collecting evidence, almost all your subordinates spoke against you. You know why?"

"Why?"

"Because everyone just wanted a peaceful life, but you whipped everyone down a dangerous path.... No, not just dangerous, perhaps everyone thought it was...a dead-end path. You forced people to pursue this goal, and ended up being betrayed and isolated, what's so strange about that?" the lawyer said, putting away the documents. "To be honest, Mr. Qi, you are the hardest to understand. At such a young age, already rising to the position of deputy chief engineer. Another two years of struggle would get you to chief engineer, the allocation of an apartment more than a hundred square meters large, but you just had to head to the most dangerous place. That faraway planet made you abandon a peaceful life, even abandon the fiancée everyone liked.... To be honest, Mr. Qi, I don't feel sympathy for you at all."

"Please don't mention her. My business has nothing to do with her," Qi Fengyang replied.

"Sure it does. If she acts as your guarantor, you can certainly be released on bail, not have to stay in this terrible place."

"Not necessary. Compared with the outside, I think it's rather quiet here," Qi Fengyang said. "By the way, this afternoon I want to apply to return to the base, I have to go get some things."

"What things?"

"Books, notebooks, and the general plan of the Polaris Program," Qi Fengyang said. "If by chance I have to stay in prison for ten years, I'll need something to do."

★　　★　　★

At dusk, a police car took Qi Fengyang back to Base 647.

The base had long since been deserted. Rubble was everywhere. Reinforcing bars twisted up from the freshly demolished foundations to the sky like broken daggers and damaged swords scattered around an ancient battlefield. A few demolition workers were in front of the laboratory building, drinking and playing poker. Leftovers were discarded amid construction waste. Nearby a flock of foraging crows bounced.

"Right here," Qi Fengyang said to the police officer. "The biggest key, please."

A squeak, and the door opened. Qi Fengyang walked slowly into the room, saw the plan lying on the table. The cover was blue, printed with the familiar logo: a sailboat and the Big Dipper. He picked it up, randomly opened a page, and saw the chapter title *Tentative Work in the Formal Prototype Stage (May 2047–August 2051)*. Below was written:

(1) The concretization of the manufacturing/testing standards and regulations

(2) The final assembly of the formal testing craft and the final assembly of the launching craft (target sail: Polaris; auxiliary sails: Dubhe/Merak/Phecda/Megrez/Alioth/Mizar/Alkaid)

(3) The delivery test and the subsystem joint test

(4) The full-state interdisciplinary coupling test of the whole craft (electromagnetic performance/mass properties/space environment/ground environment/power and energy)

(5) The joint test of the vehicle and the launch-site system (CZ-9E/CZ-5F, Wenchang Launch Site, TL1/TL2 launch pad)

Entirely a dream. From now on, all this would be nothing but a dream.

Qi Fengyang let out a long sigh, closed the report, stuffed it into his backpack, then walked around the lab, made sure nothing had been left behind, then slowly walked out.

At the entrance, he turned to look inside one last time. Everything was exactly how it had been when he had come: dust-covered lab tables, empty shelves, cracked force-measuring vacuum tubes, computer cases heaped in the corner. He thought again, confirmed that he really hadn't left anything behind, then turned off the light, closed the door, and walked into the Beijing night.

But he felt the most important thing of his had been left there forever. What was that?

Was it his talent and dreams? No, those couldn't be taken away. Qi Fengyang thought of Korolev, thought of the time his long-suffering predecessor spent in a prison camp. As long as one doesn't topple over, dreams cannot be destroyed.

Or was it the happy memories with his comrades? That didn't count. Besides, the happier the memory was, the crueler the blow of the reality seemed. Now, those audacious comrades had all left him one after another, even stood against him, like green leaves inevitably turning yellow then falling. In the end there was just one leaf left on the branch, just one him alone on the street.

It seemed that what had been left behind was irretrievable youth.... Qi Fengyang recalled when funding was tightest, he had to seek help from resources outside the system and ran around the country raising funds. In the end he met Huo Changhao, got 200 million yuan in funding and used half of it to build the underground air flotation chamber, where an air flotation table the size of a basketball court was placed. On the table tens of thousands of small holes spurted out sulfur hexafluoride gas, holding a lightsail as thin as a cicada's wing afloat to simulate the stress on lightsails in weightless environments. For countless nights, facing a jumble of tangled cables, everyone thought and discussed together. When the lightsail was successfully opened, everyone applauded and cheered together. He remembered that night he had a dozen or so Wang Bulls (baijiu diluted with Red Bull). As glasses rose and fell, everyone imagined the future of spaceflight as its protagonist, the lightsail, was floating right behind them, quiet and graceful, like a silvery lotus in bloom....

He didn't know the flower would only bloom for two years then wither.

The soil where the flower grew had been stripped away.

Why was it so hard? He wanted to cry but had no tears. Why had everything he ever yearned for, everything he ever cherished, however desperately and hard he had pursued them, left him one after another? Mother who was blind in both eyes, Father who was poor and wretched, Huo Changhao who had betrayed him, Dr. Xu who had been sacrificed, and Sun Shi'ning who had left him.... Perhaps, it was simply because he was too stupid. Had he known this earlier, would he have done everything he had? Everything in the past, whether ridiculously serious or lovably persistent, seen now – wasn't it all demolished by the misfortune of reality?

On the outer wall of the laboratory building, Qi Fengyang saw only one huge character: *DEMOLISH*. The character was written in red paint, dripping like blood. In the corner there were a few tins of oil paint, several workers squatted across the street and smoked. Seeing them, Qi Fengyang felt a gush of hot blood shoot up from his chest to his head. He charged the wall, grabbed a brush, and like lightning wrote the character *don't* before *demolish*.

"Hey! What are you doing?!" a worker shouted as he ran over.

Qi Fengyang dumped the brush, shouted to the sky, "Don't demolish me!"

After shouting, he felt unprecedented relief. He couldn't stop the tears from welling up in his eyes. Through glistening tears, the starry night was trembling, changing, changing into countless twinkling eyes. Under this crystal-clear gaze, his inner turbulence gradually subsided. He knew, however unfortunate his fate was, it was only as trivial as dust on a planet insignificant as dust. The eternal stars would always watch him, waiting, waiting for his arrival.

All he had to do was never stop.

4. The Sea at the End of the World

Thirty-eight hours after the accident, Los Angeles

At noon the following day, Qi Fengyang wakes up with a hangover.

There is a deadly silence around.

He sees that on the road there is not a single person, not a single car. He stands up, walks in a circle a couple of times. The indistinct sound of a small voice rings. He follows it into a bar. The inside is full of people, all with their eyes fixed on the TV. A person on screen talks excitedly about something.

"Right, we got the news just six hours ago...."

The speaker is Martinez. He looks like he hasn't slept the whole night.

"The content of the information is so bizarre, we need time to verify its accuracy. But so far we've confirmed it's from Sun Shi'ning, from a 'beam telegram' sent back from Jupiter II."

Hearing this, Qi Fengyang's head buzzes. Half of his hangover is immediately cured.

A journalist asks, "Mr. Martinez, based on this is it possible to conclude that life exists on Jupiter II?"

"Certainly not. The information in the 'telegram' is far too little, no more than two hundred bytes, so making any conclusion now isn't responsible. It might just be some unknown natural phenomenon...."

Qi Fengyang runs back and slaps Huo Changhao, shouting, "Hey! Wake up! We have to hurry back, big news!"

★   ★   ★

The highway to the Ames Center is already jammed with cars. The two have to abandon the car in downtown Sunnyvale and run back to Building E09.

They rush into the vacuum simulation cabin. Yesterday, this place was so empty that the echoes of footsteps were audible; now, it's packed with people. They see a platform has been put up in front of the *Cronus* simulation cabin. Journalists from the world's major media outlets are bustling around under the stage, where a big screen has been erected. In its flashing lights, Martinez is answering a barrage of questions from journalists.

"Why did Sun Shi'ning just send back so little information? Is NASA hiding something?"

"What sign of extraterrestrial life was seen?"

"Have we gotten any pictures of any extraterrestrial life yet?"

"Is NASA going to launch a ship to follow up with Jupiter II?"

"Everyone, everyone, please calm down." Martinez makes a gesture to calm the audience. "I understand your anxiety, but everything is undergoing further investigation right now. I have no comment."

"Sir! Sir!" Journalists under the platform start to clamor again, dissatisfied.

One of the female journalists asks very sharply, "NASA and Clipper released this news but refused to disclose even the smallest detail. It's hard not to suspect this is a fraud to use extraterrestrial life to extract appropriations from Congress."

Qi Fengyang is stunned, but Huo Changhao looks unbothered.

"This is unreasonable slander, miss," Martinez answers, maintaining his expression. "True, you've pointed out the conflict of interest here – we hope to send a spaceship to rescue Sun Shi'ning – but Congress may find it wasteful. To fend off such slander, I will now give you some details. Please turn off the light there."

With a snap the whole place falls into darkness apart from the big screen emitting blue light behind Martinez.

"Look, please. This is the Avalon Plain that *Cronus* landed on, a completely frozen oval surface, fifty kilometers in diameter, which formed from large-scale overflow of liquid water three thousand years ago. Jupiter II is a very active planet. Via the action of underground oceans, water constantly intrudes into the ice crust like lava, then spurts out from ice cracks and geysers, which can reshape the landscape in a very short period of time. Ten kilometers north of the landing site there is an ice geyser named Lime, which was the impact point of the *Prometheus* probe a decade ago. From Sun Shi'ning's perspective, it must be a spectacular scene – water vapor spurting out of the geyser mouth, projecting fifty kilometers high, then falling freely like a curtain across the ice field," Martinez explains. "Nine hours ago, we successfully got in touch with her. We first confirmed the spaceship's condition, checked the supplies, and assigned a survival plan to ensure she can live for more than one hundred and twenty days. Then we asked her to proceed with the planned scientific filming mission in which ice geysers are the primary object of observation. Unexpectedly, she filmed something like this...."

On the big screen a line of Morse code appears. Underneath is the translated text:

The communication channel is too narrow, picture transmission is too time-consuming, will explain with words. In Lime geyser blue luminescent spheres were found, number ranging from ten to one hundred. Luminosity very weak, difficult to observe with naked eye, but infrared luminosity very strong, radiant temperature around 2000K. After spurting out of geyser, luminescent spheres did not enter free projectile motion but suspended in the air, went downstream, back into the geyser mouth, seemed to have capacity for voluntary motion. At infrared wavelengths, observed after returning to geyser mouth luminescent spheres continue to dive down through liquid water (vapor) path. Due to high temperature and the transparency of the ice layer, ten meters underground they were still barely visible. Spectral and astro-seismological data being transmitted, will continue to follow phenomenon....

"Everyone, this is what we have called a 'sign,'" Martinez says. "Presumably everyone knows the theory of Occam's razor – entities should not multiply without necessity. In comparison to extraterrestrial life, the chance of it being some natural phenomenon is much higher. Defrauding Congress for appropriations is utter nonsense."

"But is there the possibility that Sun Shi'ning, in order to be rescued, intentionally faked signs of extraterrestrial life to trick NASA into sending the rescue spaceship? After all, spending tens of billions of dollars to rescue one person is not a good investment," a journalist suggests.

"Of course it's possible. But please keep in mind this is not a scheme. We've already confirmed Sun Shi'ning can persist one hundred and twenty days, and now there happens to be a flight plan that allows us to get to Jupiter II in one hundred and twenty days. Even without the so-called 'sign', even if we have to exhaust all we have, the rescue will be carried out as scheduled," Martinez says. "Okay, if all your questions are about conspiracy theories, we should end the press conference now."

"Sir, may I ask one last question?" a journalist shouts.

"Please go ahead."

"If the rescue mission is carried out as scheduled, what do you estimate the success rate would be?"

Countless microphones and cameras focus on Martinez like needles attracted by a magnet.

"Realistically speaking, this mission is a hundred times more dangerous than the biggest risks we have taken," Martinez says. "However, I would quote a passage from President Kennedy: 'We choose to go to the Moon, not because it is easy, but because it is hard!' Today we stand again with the whole human race at a critical point in history. In the past, we were determined to win. Today we are just as determined as before!"

★   ★   ★

Application for Emergency Appropriations – Outline (excerpt)

Goals: (1) bring the astronaut trapped on Jupiter II back to Earth; (2) if the rescue fails, provide supplies; (3) if the supply provision fails, carry out a flyby, gather the data the astronaut has collected; (4) after completing the aforementioned missions, all auxiliary lightsails shall continue their flight paths to achieve their respective scientific goals.

Implementation Plan: based on CNSA's original 'Polaris Program'. For details of the technical plan see Appendix 1.

Date: March–October 2054 (35+122 Earth days)

Leading Organization: Clipper Space Transportation and Exploration Company

Participating Organizations: NASA/ESA/CNSA/RKA/JAXA, etc. For contract details and details of missions see Appendices 2–4; for the details of administrative and legal documents see Appendix 5.

Estimated Budget: $13.5 billion (1+337 lightsails/36 launches). Reference values are as follows:

Galileo (1995): $1.6 billion; Juno (2016): $1.1 billion; Clipper (2027): $1.9 billion; JUICE (2032): $1.5 billion; Prometheus (2043): $3 billion; Poseidon (2050): $12.7 billion....

* * *

Fifty hours after the accident, Ames Research Center

At two a.m., just as Qi Fengyang is going to bed, someone knocks on his door.

"Comrade Qi." It's Huo Changhao. "Got good news and bad news."

"What?"

"The emergency appropriations from Congress have passed. The Federal Reserve has issued a ten-billion-dollar loan to Clipper. Adding donations from people of all walks of life, our budget target has been narrowly reached. Your dream can finally be realized."

"What about the bad news?"

"It has to be realized by an individual."

Qi Fengyang remains silent for a moment, lets out a sigh. "The docking problem still hasn't been solved?"

"No. Because of the forty-five-minute communication delay between Jupiter and Earth, ground control will be slow, and the judgment and decisions at orbit transfer and docking are too complex. AI isn't competent, we have to rely on an experienced pilot to personally maneuver."

"So we have to find an astronaut?" Qi Fengyang is excited. "Have you any candidates?"

"Not yet. Astronauts fall under the jurisdiction of the Air Force. Many of them want to pilot *Polaris*, but the Air Force doesn't approve," Huo Changhao says frankly.

"Of course. Training an astronaut is difficult, and our mission would literally send them to their death."

"Haha, Comrade Qi. So unusual for you to have insight into yourself."

"What, I usually don't?"

"Just a little...." Huo Changhao lights a cigarette, then offers one to Qi Fengyang, who waves a hand in refusal. "Oh, it's no insult. What we need now isn't an astronaut who plays safe but a lunatic who doesn't know his limits, who is not afraid to die. And...if I remember correctly, a lunatic once promised Sun Shi'ning to see the sea at the end of the world with her."

Qi Fengyang gazes at Huo Changhao, and a long while later suddenly bursts into laughter. "Hahaha...you, you do know me well...."

"It's not that I know you well. Comrade Qi, you have flying experience — are healthy, responsive, determined. And as the deputy chief designer of the Polaris Program, you know every detail of the spaceship."

"Good, good, I was thinking the same," Qi Fengyang says. "But you have to remember, everything I'm doing isn't for her, much less for you. I just want to realize my old dream. It's like throwing a piece of meat to a starving wolf. Once it's full, what comes next is not up to you."

"What do you mean?"

"Nothing. Happy you're throwing meat at me, Mr. Huo."

Qi Fengyang reaches out and clasps Huo Changhao's hand.

★　　★　　★

The Polaris Program officially begins. The leaders include astronautical organizations like NASA, Clipper, ESA, and the China Aerospace Science and Technology Corporation, along with tech giants like Google, Apple, Sony, Daimler, and Zeiss. In hundreds of ultra-hygienic workshops around the world, three hundred and thirty-seven huge silvery sails thin as cicada's wings are carefully knitted together; tow ropes with a total length of over 500,000 kilometers are meticulously coiled into shape; on a special Internet line, massive data flows like a flood are exchanged among research teams around the world, carrying the ideas of the wisest, the decisions of the boldest, and the plans of the most experienced to supercomputers in underground computer rooms. The flight plan is formulated with amazing efficiency, the rescue plan is settled, the orbit design is optimized, the manufacturing standards are finalized. Components from all over the world are fit together precisely in the final assembly workshop. After testing day after day, night after night, they are eventually sent to the launch site. It is like the way that drops of paint here and there do not cohere into a concrete form until reaching a critical point when all the dots connect, and all the colors are meaningful, and a world-altering painting comes to life.

At this point, thirty-five days have passed since the accident.

But it isn't enough. After the spaceship is ready, a vehicle is needed to send it to space. Carrier-rocket manufacturers around the world all have their production lines running at full capacity. Nearly a hundred rockets of various sizes are transported to launch sites at various locations. Within a week, heavy-lift rockets such as *Long March*, *Falco*, *SLS*, *Angara*, and *Ariane* are launched more than ten times in a row, and other smaller models are launched numerous times. Three hundred and thirty-seven lightsails are successfully sent into space, except for two which failed to unfurl due to malfunction. All the others are assembled into formation, setting out on a journey to Jupiter at high speeds ten times the third cosmic velocity.

In the meantime, Huo Changhao spends most of his time in planes, traveling around the country. Sun Shi'ning's husband contacts all types of tycoons, raises funds, and urges his group to transform LiFi base stations into a laser array that can propel the lightsail formation.

Meanwhile, Martinez is working hard day after day in the Ames Center. He hopes to reduce the mass of *Polaris* to below one ton but unfortunately is not successful. After numerous rounds of weight reductions and optimizations, the sealed cabin, which looks like a coffin, still weighs one and a half tons. Inside, Qi Fengyang will spend two hundred days on the round trip.

Qi Fengyang isn't idle either. He has gone through a short but efficient astronaut training and learned solutions to various accidents in outer space.

At first, he thought the most difficult thing would be maneuvering the multi-sail, light-focused deceleration, but that is not the case.

Rendezvous and docking with Sun Shi'ning is the biggest headache — not until she takes off, accelerates, and cuts off the engine, can *Polaris* start to calculate the docking orbit. Because of the communication delay between Jupiter and Earth, Qi Fengyang will have to complete everything alone. To capture *Cronus* at the precise moment, he will have to cooperate closely with the onboard computer.

Sun Shi'ning keeps in contact with Earth. The unconventional method of communication makes it very inefficient. The pictures sent back to Earth are hard to make out. The blurry pictures have produced two schools of interpretation: one side insists that these pictures prove the existence of extraterrestrial life; the other side believes they simply show an unknown natural phenomenon.

Additionally, Sun Shi'ning's identity as a writer constantly intensifies public interest in her. To this end Clipper even designates someone to operate Sun Shi'ning's Facebook account to allow the public to learn directly about her life on Jupiter II. Sun Shi'ning doesn't let them down. Her spirits have been high. She even plans to grow microalgae to extend her survival window.

The countdown ticks nonstop, the final day is approaching. A journey worthy of history is about to start.

5. Zero Window

Forty-four days after the accident, Hainan Wenchang Launch Site

Resounding booms....

Above the vast South China Sea, gray clouds densely tumble. Dull thunder rolls. A summer thunderstorm brews on the horizon, slowly moving toward the Wenchang Launch Site.

Along with it comes Huo Changhao. He is in the freighter carrying the *Polaris* spaceship. This is the last launch of the Polaris Program. Huo Changhao sees the *Long March 9* rocket has been assembled in the vertical final assembly plant at the launch site and is about to be vertically transferred. In raging winds the ropes strapping down the rocket shake violently, like strings plucked by the hand of fate.

"Hello? Is this General Sun Heng?" Huo Changhao gets through by phone.

"It's me. Arrived at the harbor?"

"Arrived. Current situation looks somewhat unpromising."

"Very much so. The front of the storm has suddenly changed its route. If it continues, the launch will have to be cancelled."

"But this is the last chance. The only launch window is nineteen-twenty tomorrow. If delayed, *Polaris* won't catch up with the lightsail formation already underway, and the whole mission will fail completely!"

"Mr. Huo, we certainly understand the seriousness of the matter — the technical name is the 'zero window'. There is only one chance, the opportunity to launch just a few seconds. As the launch commander, I have to make a responsible decision according to protocol."

Huo Changhao remains silent for a moment, then asks, "What's the biggest threat? Wind, rain, or lightning?"

"Lightning," Sun Heng replies. "Rockets are like lightning rods. Before launch, conductive towers offer some protection, but after rocket ignition and lift off, its tail flame, hundreds of meters long, becomes a conductor for electric currents. If struck by lightning, the consequences would be unimaginable."

"Oh, I have a solution for that...."

"What?"

"Lightning-directing lasers," Huo Changhao says. "Around Wenchang there are five LiFi dome base stations, all belonging to my company. If all operate at maximum power, they can emit a megawatt laser beam that can penetrate thunderclouds, produce an ionization channel, and just like an invisible lightning rod, guide the lightning safely away."

"Have you done trials?"

"Of course. The product is included in national lightning protection standards and can reliably direct lightning strikes within two kilometers."

"Good, let's take our chances." Sun Heng sighs. "Now's the time for it...."

⋆ ⋆ ⋆

Forty-four days and ten hours after the accident, Wenchang Launch Site, TL-01 launch pad

On the bridge of the launch and logistics tower, the wind is whistling, rain pouring down. The steel trusses and ropes wail. Qi Fengyang wears a thick spacesuit, standing steadily in front of the rocket's huge fairing.

This is the last operation before launch. Spaceflight medical personnel are doing the last check-up of his spacesuit and life support systems.

Now the rocket is ready. *Polaris* is docked with the upper level of *Long March 4*. The two are connected via the supporting frame on the rocket head. The fairing is sealed so the inside can't be seen, but Qi Fengyang only needs to close his eyes, and the internal structure appears clearly in front of him: three towing lightsails folded into a cylinder then tied together stuck to the top of the fairing; cooling circuits crisscross as they wind around the waist of the spaceship linked to the liquid helium tank on which thousands of Hall radiators are configured like the shell of a ship covered in barnacles. On one side of the base is the sealed cabin, on the other is the docking port. The connection is very rough, as if it was added later as some last-minute idea. No escape tower, no reentry capsules.[2] Those were the fixed payload he personally cut out. If something goes wrong, Qi Fengyang can only pick up the morphine injection next to him and die more comfortably.

Tomorrow his life will be entrusted to this rocket.

"How is everything, Little Qi?"

It's General Sun Heng. Seeing him, everyone turns and salutes.

"All right, carry on," Sun Heng says. "It's nothing serious, just want to chat."

"Is it about Shi'ning?"

---

2. On return, the rescue spaceship will dock with *Polaris* directly, and after the crew member is transferred, enter the atmosphere, so reliability is sacrificed to reduce weight and save time.

"Little Qi, being with her for so long, you must have learned about her situation, right?"

"Hm...not that much, actually. I only know you're her father."

"A negligent father...." Sun Heng says. "When she was five years old, her mother went away. I should have taken on a father's responsibilities, but it happened to be a critical period for *Long March 9*. Because of work, I couldn't take care of her. Her childhood and adolescence were basically spent alone in the residential quarters of the Malan Military Base. When she went to college, she saw the big city for the first time."

"Hm, she told me about that experience," Qi Fengyang says. "Though it was very lonely, she got to read a lot of literature as a result."

"Yes, that was her fortune and her misfortune. That lonely childhood birthed her talent but also gave her wild impulses."

"Like what?"

"The impulse to see faraway worlds. If she had grown up in an ordinary environment, she wouldn't have favored that impulse so much, but she's not like ordinary people. She's sensitive, solitary. Inside there is nothing but impulse. It's like the flame of a candle, a faint light under the sun, dazzling and overwhelming in darkness. To satisfy this impulse she would do anything, even make the big mistake of deceiving the entire human race." Sun Heng sighs. "True, both of you are geniuses, but you have to know genius is just one side of you. The other side is lunacy. A person who takes his or her ideal to the ultimate end regardless of the cost – this is very dangerous. It's totally unnecessary for you to sacrifice your life for her."

"I understand, but I'm not taking the risk for her. I'm doing it for my own dream," Qi Fengyang says slowly.

"Then there's nothing I can do." Sun Heng sighs and says, "I have no other request, just one sincere piece of advice: what you carry isn't just your dream, but lots of responsibility. She probably never intended to come back. If that's the case, please act according to reason."

Qi Fengyang nods seriously. "I will."

★   ★   ★

Forty-five days plus fifteen hours after the accident, Hainan Wenchang Launch Site

About seven kilometers west of the Wenchang Launch Site there is a small hill called Tonggu Ridge. One side of the hill overlooks the launch site. On the other side is Wenxi County. On the hilltop there is a building with a white dome. Every night a light-purple beam can be seen shooting into the sky from the dome; there are four other similar beams, which shoot separately from other locations in Wenchang city: all the way to space. There lasers carrying information are reflected by synchronous satellites, which constitutes an important link in the LiFi network that connects the world.

On this day, in front of a white-domed building, an iron tower is suddenly erected. The tower is temporarily welded together, very roughly. Its spire is right in front of the laser emitter. When the time comes, the laser-directed lightning bolts will be directed underground through it.

"General Sun, all set here!" On Tonggu Ridge, Huo Changhao walks down the mountain path against the downpour.

"Good, hurry to the bunker. Launch procedure is starting soon."

"How's Qi Fengyang?"

"All set, the hatch has just closed."

At this point, a voice sounds in the launch command hall. Hearing the voice, everyone in the hall quiets down.

"Beijing, enter fifteen-minute countdown. Start the launch sequence."

"Wenchang, copy," Sun Heng answers. "Launch sequence started, staff in position, systems prepared. All sub-systems status checked."

Meanwhile, in the *Polaris* spaceship, Qi Fengyang is lying inside the narrow, sealed cabin. Hearing the order from the headset, his heart fills with all kinds of feelings. His mind flies back to ten years ago, back to those sleepless nights spent in Base 647. He is fully aware of the danger of this path and has wondered countless times who would be the warrior who set out upon it. But he never thought the warrior would be himself.

"Energy?"

"Normal."

"Electricity?"

"Normal."

"Wenchang, vehicle ready. Electric cords disconnect."

Qi Fengyang hears a *snap*. The umbilical cords connecting the rocket and the launch tower are cut off, the electricity switches to the onboard power supply. From this moment on, the only connection between the rocket and Earth is the support frame on the base.

"Cords disconnected. Vehicle independent, navigation autonomous – into ten-minute countdown."

At this point Qi Fengyang starts to panic. Under his body, 3,000 tons of liquid oxygen and kerosene are ready to fire; 870,000 components work intensely. With just one malfunction, he will be blown to the Western Paradise. It's pretty straightforward: if the malfunction takes place in the sky, he will either suffocate or freeze to death. At this thought, sweat oozes from his forehead. He wants to wipe off the sweat beads, but his elbows are strapped down by the safety belt and he can't reach them.

"Navigation?"

"Normal."

"Altitude control?"

"Normal."

"Wenchang, enter five-minute countdown."

He looks at the red button by his hand. That's the emergency stop button. Just press it and the launch will be terminated, the mission will be canceled, and he'll return to his previously peaceful and happy life. He isn't afraid to die, but he suddenly realizes how many things don't allow him to die. His blind mother needs his care, his ill father needs his support. And how about their hope to have a grandchild? How about his mother's wish to see the sea?

Not until this moment did he realize that he has been a lunatic possessed by his ideals. Compared with a safe and happy life, are these ideals really that important? His hand helplessly reaches toward the button.

"Logistics?"

"Normal."

"Meteorology?"

"Within range."

"Astronaut?"

Qi Fengyang's hand stops. He freezes a second. Via live broadcast, people from all over the world see the change on his face. As if some heavy object pressing down on him suddenly vanishes, his expression relaxes. He lets out a long sigh, rearranges the fingers reaching for the red button into a V for victory, and says, "Ready!"

In front of millions of screens, people burst into cheers.

"Wenchang, payload ready, astronaut ready. Sub-systems checked, request to launch," Sun Heng says.

"Beijing, launch permitted."

"Copy. Ten-second countdown. Nine, eight, seven…"

The surrounding sounds suddenly fade away. The countdown order seems to come from the horizon. Qi Fengyang only hears his heartbeat and the hissing sound of the hydraulic machine increasing pressure.

"…six, five, four…"

"Let's fucking go!" he roars inside.

"…three, two, one, ignition!"

*   *   *

From the bay below Tonggu Ridge, a small sun suddenly rises.

Unlike other rockets, the tail flame of *Long March 9*, very bright with a white-yellow tone, is characteristic of aluminum-based solid booster combustion. It rises slowly between the leaden sea and sky, spurts out blazing flames, penetrates the rainstorm, lights up the field like a port at sunrise beneath Monet's brush. Sea waves, mountains, clouds, and villages all become sharply defined under the golden light. In the bright flame, the curtain of rain around the launch pad turns into 10,000 pouring strands of flames. Rolling white smog shoots up into the sky from a diversion channel like a roaring volcano.

"Launch time: T-plus-zero minutes, zero seconds, one hundred and forty-four milliseconds."

Soon a boom reaches the command and control center. Under the impact of the 3,500-ton thrust, the earth quakes violently.

"Wenchang, tracking normal, telemetry signal normal."

Huo Changhao watches the rocket go into the clouds, then out of them. It roars, bellows, drastically accelerates. Like a shining golden sword, it rips open the oppressive gray veils layer by layer. Clouds ignite. Thousands of strands of smog scorched by the glaring light are sparkling and clear. Water sprays blown up by the flame all over the sky shower down and give off explosive crackling sounds, sweeping the choking smog toward Huo Changhao, but he refuses to go into the bunker. Against the rain he watches the trajectory of the rocket, watches the space around it. There, five lightning-directing laser beams have come.

Suddenly, a lightning bolt strikes down along a laser beam.

"Tower three has received lightning!" the meteorology director shouts.

"Wenchang, telemetry signal disrupted, redundancy already input, flight normal. Current altitude: one thousand meters."

"What's the height of the lightning zone?" Huo Changhao asks.

"About three kilometers," the engineer on the other end of the intercom replies. "But that's the most dangerous altitude. There, lightning mainly comes from intracloud discharges. The effect of lightning-directing lasers will be greatly reduced."

"Then increase the laser power!"

"Already at max."

Huo Changhao sighs, grabs the telescope, and goes on tracking.

"Forty-five seconds, tracking normal, telemetry signal normal. Current altitude: three kilometers."

In the clouds, the rocket gradually vanishes. Only those with keen sight can discern a little quivering yellow light. But for lightning this hundreds-of-meters-long tail flame is the best conduit.

Suddenly, Huo Changhao sees a flash of blue light in the clouds.

"Navigation control!" the altitude control system director shouts. "Roll, change course!"

Meanwhile, various sirens light up in the control hall, flash one after another. Two seconds later, someone shouts, "Number two vernier engine, no feedback!"

"Malfunction confirmed, turn off the number four vernier engine. Navigation shifted to onboard control system," the propulsion director system says.

"What's the matter?" Huo Changhao asks.

"One altitude-control engine is damaged," an engineer says. "We have to turn off the opposite engine for balance. Of course, this will reduce thrust power. Small, but *Polaris* definitely won't be able to enter the precise planned orbit."

"That means…he needs a little extra speed?" Huo Changhao asks.

"Yes, just about ninety-five meters per second. But *Polaris* doesn't have any spare fuel to reach the maximum speed. That is a big problem."

Huo Changhao falls silent for a moment, then asks, "How much time until leaving the acceleration point of Earth?"

"Five hours and twenty minutes."

"Then there's still enough time," Huo Changhao says. "I have an idea."

6. Glittering Earth

Two hundred and forty minutes after launch, Beijing Nanyuan Airport

At eight p.m. the same day, the Gulfstream X981 carrying Huo Changhao takes off from Wenchang. This time the plane doesn't belong to him, but its new owner agrees to lend it to him. The plane flies extremely fast, so it takes less than an hour to get to Beijing. Walking down the ladder, he can feel the heat radiating from the body of the plane.

"How is it? Statistical results out?" he asks his secretary.

"Mm, engagement on Sun Shi'ning's Facebook account is eighty million. Tencent and Baidu, over three hundred and twenty million.

State media is a little bit slow but also did a mobilization. As of now the numbers are still increasing."

"How is the situation overseas?"

"We have done mobilizations in all branch offices in the major world cities. The response definitely won't be as quick as at home, but there should be tens of millions of people participating. Just several minutes ago the US president made a television speech on the subject."

Huo Changhao is elated. *Haha, this is really incredible, incredible!* Within such a short period of time, half of Earth is mobilized, even the US president is inspired by his idea.

"In total it's over four hundred million people. The reach is sufficient." Huo Changhao's confidence is hugely boosted. "Is the power supply guaranteed?"

"Director Fan said no problem."

"How about the guidance method?"

"Also ready. The Sky Advertising Branch is very experienced with this. The Beijing sky is clear, so they plan to use an airship to guide the beams."

"Good. Now, let's sit back and watch the show." Huo Changhao gets into his special car. "Back to the office, the view is best there!"

★ ★ ★

Two hundred and forty-five minutes after the launch, descent into standby orbit, Polaris

After burning for twenty minutes, the upper level of *Long March 4* has drained the last drop of fuel and accelerated the spaceship to thirty kilometers per second. A click, and the cabin shakes as the spaceship is separated from the upper level. The final orbit correction finished, *Polaris* enters a state of unpowered gliding. Like a rock under the action of Earth's gravity, it falls toward the perigee of its hyperbolic trajectory.

Qi Fengyang has no time to really feel weightlessness. To save mass, the sealed cabin is compressed to the size of a coffin, its inside stuffed with life-sustaining supplies. He can only lie in the sleeping bag, barely stretching his arms and legs. Even turning around is difficult. Of course, this is his design. He thinks of Martinez's expression upon hearing the plan....

"Are you crazy?!" Martinez said. "You're going to suffocate!"

"But it will reduce the weight by three hundred kilograms, thus reducing arrival time by two weeks," Qi Fengyang said. "Anyway, I've been through hard times since I was little. I can easily stand forty hours on a train."

"But this is two hundred days! Two hundred days!"

No problem, he thinks. *If the view is good enough, two hundred days isn't a problem.* Through the observation window less than half a meter from his face, he sees a most familiar scene – the Sun rising from one side of the black disk of the Earth, galvanizing the atmosphere with a semicircle of orange-red light like a shining ring. This isn't a movie, it's a real scene unfolding before his eyes. Outside the window is cold, cruel space, just paper thickness away. It's like standing at the top of a cliff looking down into the abyss. Danger's beauty makes him tremble with excitement.

Suddenly, the intercom rings.

"*Polaris*, this is Houston. Control has been transferred to us from *Long View 10*. Attention, the current flight plan has an important change."

"*Polaris*, copy. Go ahead."

"Due to an engine malfunction at launch, the initial speed of the spaceship entering orbit has a minor deviation. If not corrected, the acceleration control point cannot be reached, so add the following corrections to the original flight plan: T-plus-two-nine-seven minutes thirty seconds: open the lightsail to the max, sail axis orientation zero-nine-seven-one-two-two-one-nine-six, spin five, heat radiation one-point-eight. Sustain corrected propulsion two hundred twenty seconds. Specific parameters for orbit transfer are uploading through the S-two communication channel."

"Understood...Houston, can you specify the source of power of the orbit correction? I thought the ground laser array had nothing extra."

"Right, Huo Changhao's idea – use home LiFi terminals to point at the sky to propel the lightsail."

"Home LiFi? Isn't it just several thousand kilowatts?"

"Right, but we're talking about the combined power of more than four hundred million LiFi terminals around the world. Tonight, Mr. Qi Fengyang, the whole Earth will shine for you."

★　　★　　★

Two hundred and ninety minutes after the launch, Beijing World Trade Vision Tower, Top Floor

"Starting! It's starting!"

On the terrace, Huo Changhao tosses off his blazer and jumps and shouts like a kid watching fireworks.

In the direction in which Huo Changhao points, his secretary sees a green beam appear. It splits the night, splits the clouds, splits the black silhouette of the forest of high-rises, splits the familiar night scene into an uncanny double. It is the China Millennium Monument's 'Light of Beijing', which will guide the outputs of Beijing's millions of home LiFi terminals.

"You know why I proposed this idea?" Huo Changhao says. "To show off? To advertise? To get rid of my old romantic rival? To get back my far-flung wife?"

"Excuse me, boss. I thought this was one of your fundraising tricks," the secretary says.

"Haha, no. Of course not! Those are trivial things, not worth mentioning. Do you know what the biggest pleasure in the world is?"

"Please educate me."

"Of course it's...mythmaking!" Huo Changhao waves both arms, as if conducting an invisible orchestra. "Myth, legend, epic, odyssey...what people see as fiction is actually the history of ancient people breaking limitations. What's taking place before our eyes today – isn't it worth being praised by the future generations as legend? No magic, no gods, just scientific calculations and a crazy engineer."

As the words fall, they see the 'Light of Beijing' slowly move like a baton conducting a symphony, sweeping across the night sky in a trajectory that leaves a fluorescent trail. Then the second beam appears, and more and more beams shoot up into the night sky from ordinary roofs and balconies, shining toward the target that the ship heads toward. Soon, Huo Changhao can't distinguish any individual beam. Thousands of beams intertwine into a slanting curtain of light like a road leading to the sky.

At this moment, from the perspective of space, Beijing is the brightest star in the night sky.

Then Huo Changhao hears singing, faint and ethereal. He runs to the edge of the terrace and looks down. The roads are flooded with people. On street corners, on bridges, in squares, people sing under their breath, raising lights in their hands. Laser pointers, solar lamps, even flashlights merge into a sea of light like the ground is reflecting the starry sky above.

"Do you see?" Huo Changhao exclaims. "The universe doesn't just exist above, but in people's hearts too."

"Can he bring Sun Shi'ning back?" the secretary asks.

"Impossible. Sun Shi'ning has no intention at all of coming back. As for him...two hundred days, eight hundred million kilometers, depending on a coffin of a cabin to travel through cold and cruel space – it'd be a miracle if he manages to survive," Huo Changhao says. "But among the great voyages, which isn't a miracle?"

7. *Brake*

One hundred and two days later, Jupiter's flyby orbit, fifteen hundred kilometers from Jupiter II

In space, eight hundred and twenty kilometers from Earth, *Polaris* is about to reach its destination.

"*Polaris*, this is Houston...."

The call, not heard for a long time, wakes up a dizzy Qi Fengyang.

"Congratulations, *Polaris*. You've successfully reached your destination. Now the whole world is cheering you on and nervously awaiting your next maneuver – entering Jupiter's orbit. You will reach acceleration control point A of Jupiter's orbit in five hours, then decelerate to enter the orbit of Jupiter. Please describe your current condition."

He rubs his eyes and looks out. There, the pitch-black space which had not changed for a hundred and two days finally has. Jupiter's scarlet outline is visible. Around it are four bright dots standing in a straight line, Jupiter's four biggest satellites.

"Houston, this is *Polaris*," Qi Fengyang says. "My vital signals are normal, minor headache, lower limbs numb, but mind and response times are fairly quick. The spaceship's state is normal. All sub-systems free of malfunction. This really is a miracle.... Wait, something seems wrong."

He taps the touchscreen a few times, calls up the navigation window, sees the cross representing the fact that the trajectory has deviated from the center of the navigation ball. The deviation is extremely small, only one tenth of one percent, but enough to make him miss the target of the next multi-sail deceleration.

"Houston, we have a problem," he says then taps several buttons, sending data on the ship's condition back to Earth. "Please check ship velocity vector. Seems to have deviated from the default value."

Because of the communication time lag, he receives the reply ninety minutes later.

"*Polaris*, it's been confirmed that the velocity discrepancy is a result of orbit correction at the time of departure from Earth. There was an error estimating home LiFi laser radiation, so initial velocity was one percent greater. Over the course of your long flight, the minor error has intensified irrevocably." A frustrating order comes from the headset: "The flight plan has been modified as follows.... Abandon the rescue mission, carry out emergency plan one. After flying by Jupiter II, fly directly to acceleration control point B. One hundred and ninety-two lightsails will rendezvous with you again at point B, then send you on the return trajectory."

Qi Fengyang suddenly gets flustered, presses the headset, and shouts, "Houston, don't terminate the mission! There has to be a way."

Ninety minutes later, Houston replies, "*Polaris*, please follow the order. There is bad news we were not going to tell you. Ten days ago, Sun Shi'ning lost contact. Her spacesuit stopped responding. All signs indicate she has already died."

"What?!"

"Due to the sudden explosion of hydrogen-oxygen fuel production, the microalgae Sun Shi'ning cultivated deteriorated. One hundred and fourteen days after the accident, she ran out of food. After withstanding eight days of starvation, she sent a final flash telegram to Earth."

"Why? Why didn't you tell me?!" Qi Fengyang yells.

"At the time her mental state was very unstable. In the telegram she said she would use the end of her life to explore the strange atmosphere of the Lime geyser. According to spacesuit data, she in fact went there. She brought the last bit of food, dragged instruments, walked a dozen or so kilometers across the Avalon Plain, and marched in the direction of the Lime geyser. Two days later, the spacesuit and lander connection were successively broken. We completely lost contact with her."

Qi Fengyang gives out a long sigh.

"*Polaris*, please understand and accept this reality. After all, this was a very risky operation. It's very fortunate that you arrived safely. Even if you didn't rescue Sun Shi'ning, the value this mission has to humanity has been tremendous. You are still a hero."

"Houston, I understand. Anyway, I'm very grateful for everyone's dedication for the past hundred days or so in making this miracle happen," Qi Fengyang says. "Most of all, I'm grateful to Mr. Huo Changhao. I once told him if you feed a hungry wolf, what happens next is unpredictable.... Everyone, I'm very sorry."

He ends communication.

★   ★   ★

Forty-five minutes later, Houston Spacecraft Command and Control Center

"Dammit, what the hell is this guy doing?!" Martinez curses as he throws the headset.

"Don't worry, man," Huo Changhao, next to him, says. "He probably came up with a good idea and just doesn't have time to argue with us."

"Navigation control!" Martinez shouts. "Switch the display to back-end nav data. There's no way to cut that off. Let's see how he's going to enter orbit."

"He changed the orbit transfer plan. Eight *Aquarius* sails and nine *Gemini* sails have been moved to the head of the formation. *Argo* to the rear. A total of eighty-two lightsails' targets and focus order have been changed.... The simulation results show that the new formation will reduce the speed of *Polaris* down to fifty kilometers per second."

"What about the altitude of the rendezvous point?"

"One thousand kilometers," the navigation engineer says. "Sir, *Polaris* is going to brush the edge of Jupiter's atmosphere!"

Martinez, shocked, mumbles, "Is he going to perform AOT?"

"What's that?" Huo Changhao asks.

"Aerodynamic orbit transfer, or aerobraking. A way to use the atmospheric drag of a planet to achieve orbit transfer.... He turned the spaceship upside down and backward, maybe intending to use the lightsails as a deceleration parachute," Martinez says. "But aerobraking is the most difficult orbit-transfer method to maneuver. If the approach angle is even a little too small, he'll brush past the top edge of the atmosphere. If a little too large, he'll crash into Jupiter, burning up like a meteor. Unless he's done rigorous calculations, it's suicidal!"

"I remember him doing calculations," Huo Changhao says. "Back at Base 647 he once used a computer cluster to study this type of thing."

"Still pretty risky. Can he hold all those parameters in his head?"

"Of course not...he'll keep going anyway."

"Why?"

"Because of stubbornness, maybe.... Not for us, not for Sun Shi'ning.

He just wants to fully realize the Polaris Program. It's an old dream he'll reach even if it costs him his life."

"A true lunatic." Martinez sighs. "Control, end the live broadcast for now. Soon we'll have to lock the door and do an error analysis."[3]

★　　★　　★

Meanwhile, at acceleration control point A

After looking outside the window at space one last time, Qi Fengyang takes a deep breath and pulls down the light shield.

The lightsail formation is already visible to the naked eye. Ahead of Jupiter's red disk, hundreds of bright spots emerge and sparkle faintly like diamonds crystalized from darkness.

Navigation has entered a critical stage: on the screen, three hundred and thirty-five trajectories converge to a point near Jupiter labeled 'acceleration control point A'. The cross representing *Polaris* slowly moves toward it. Then *Polaris*'s trajectory takes a sharp turn toward Jupiter. After brushing past the edge of Jupiter's atmosphere, it converges with Jupiter II. The three hundred and thirty-five trajectories disperse like fireworks, making a half orbit under Jupiter's gravity, then merge again at a point on the other side of Jupiter. That is 'acceleration control point B'. There *Polaris* will catch up with the reassembled lightsail formation and with a second light-focused acceleration set out on the journey back to Earth.

Now the countdown in front of Qi Fengyang has already gone back to zero.

"*Aquarius, Gemini*, begin focus!"

Dozens of powerful beams focus on the lightsail of *Polaris*. Through the spaceship's wall, Qi Fengyang can feel the outside temperature is drastically increasing. He hears a creaking sound made by the body of the spaceship expanding as it heats.

"*Libra, Ophiuchus, Virgo*, begin focus!"

---

3. This refers to management regulations that after a fault or accident require the site to be frozen so that causes can be investigated and responsibilities carried out.

The temperature continues to increase. The environment control system kicks in. Liquid ammonia evaporates rapidly in the cooling tube. Hall radiators are fully powered to send extra heat into space. The lightsail tightens. Qi Fengyang feels pressure on his back. The reading on the accelerometer has reached 0.05G.

"*Great Bear*, begin focus!"

The thrust from *Great Bear* sinks Qi Fengyang deep into the seat back. Of those thirty-two lightsails, seven were named after the Big Dipper by Qi himself ten years ago at Base 647.

"*Capricornus, Argo*, begin focus!"

The temperature increases to thirty-six degrees. The sealed cabin has turned into a steamer. Incandescent light pierces the slit of the light shield. Outside is like hell's sea of fire. Qi Fengyang clenches his teeth, bearing it, silently counting the seconds. The whole deceleration process will last four full hours, much longer than the suffering of acceleration when departing Earth. Back then his physical strength was all right, but now, after more than a hundred days of being drained, his endurance is far worse. After the light-focusing deceleration is completed, he is on the verge of collapse.

He uses a shaking hand to open the light shield, sees Jupiter within reach. The red disk has turned into a blinding curtain. Colorful wild cyclones surge within it, red, white, blue, flowing nonstop like a river of fire pouring down from a sluice in hell.

"Shi'ning, I'm coming, coming to see the sea at the end of the world with you...."

Under the impact of the thin atmosphere, the spaceship starts to shake. G-force again pushes Qi Fengyang into the chair, but this time the force is much stronger. The reading on the accelerometer is climbing rapidly. Soon, before his eyes, black fog rises, gradually expands, and finally blends into the indissoluble dark void.

8. White Night

Not knowing how much time has passed, Qi Fengyang comes to.

The black fog brought upon by excessive G-force has gradually dispersed, but before his eyes there is still a blanket of darkness. Infinite space.

Then, like a burst dam, the darkness cracks. A shaft of light gushes out of the crack, emits a dazzling blue-white glow. It pours in splendidly, comes showering down, as overwhelming as a storm stirred up by billions of swirling fireflies forming a shining cocoon. Soon his sealed cabin is completely enveloped by the light cocoon.

What's that? Qi Fengyang is puzzled. None of his knowledge can help explain what's before his eyes.

Suddenly, without any acceleration, Qi Fengyang sees the scene outside the window begin to move. In Jupiter's atmosphere, 1,000 kilometers away, clouds suddenly start to flow faster. Soon Jupiter's red disk disappears behind him at a speed discernible to the naked eye; then colorful Jupiter I sweeps past the window and instantly disappears. Thin sulfur gas, debris, and ice scraps whoosh by. Then the angle of the sunlight changes sharply. A dark-blue cliff rises from below. A silvery-white mist shoots up from the bottom of the cliff and envelops everything. The surrounding view gets darker and darker, narrower and narrower. Now and then a streak of light skims across the cliff wall as if falling down a deep well.

The fall lasts about ten minutes. After crossing some critical point, the absolute stillness of the vacuum suddenly disappears. From outside comes the sound of whining wind, and the surroundings lighten up as if a diver is suddenly rising to the sea surface. Finally, he hears a soft noise, the light cocoon disappears. Weak gravity tells him he is now on the ground of a planet.

Tap, tap.... Someone is knocking on the hatch of the sealed cabin.

"What?" Qi Fengyang suspects he's heard wrong. But a second later, the knock comes again. Then a rustling sound. A hand seems to be turning the safety lock of the hatch.

With a click the hatch opens.

He looks at the person in front of him and can't believe his eyes: "Sun Shi'ning!"

It really is Sun Shi'ning. She pushes back her glasses in her typical way, sizes up Qi Fengyang with a smile, her short hair gently swaying in the breeze.

"You have to rest a little before you can walk." She carefully helps up Qi Fengyang in the sealed cabin. "Though the gravity is very weak here, you've been lying down for so long. Your body needs to get adjusted."

"I'm confused, Shi'ning..." Qi Fengyang says. "Just now I was in Jupiter's orbit, decelerating to enter. Suddenly a streak of light came, then the whole world spun. Then I was sent to this place...where is it?"

"Jupiter II, of course."

"Impossible! The surface of Jupiter II is a vacuum, but this place has a breathable atmosphere. There is wind, there is light, and"—Qi Fengyang looks around, so shocked that he holds his breath—"grassland...."

Around him fluorescent grassland hangs upside down.

From that point of view it does look like a grassland: countless delicate fluorescent tentacles hang down from an ice dome like willow branches, extending down all the way, then disappear into the bottomless abyss. But that is an illusion. Without a reference point, there is no way to judge the size of the grass. Actually each blade is tens of kilometers long. Qi Fengyang is on a 'grass' root vesicle nearly as large as a football stadium. Above the vesicle he sees many strong root hairs. They extend into the cracks of the ice dome, allowing the giant grass to firmly hang from it.

"This is right below the landing site of the *Prometheus* probe, thirteen kilometers from the surface of Jupiter II," Sun Shi'ning says.

At this point, Qi Fengyang begins to notice the ground he is on. It is neither rock nor ice but a transparent jelly-like film. It squirms slightly. Inside are complicated channels like leaf veins where countless bubbles and bright spots rapidly flow. In the direction of their flow, Qi Fengyang looks up at the top of the vesicle where a ball of blue flame blazes. Two thick vessels alternately jump under the flame. One connects to the vesicle, the other to the outside. They spurt air, making the ball of flame look like a beating heart.

"Really like a dream..." Qi Fengyang mumbles. "This giant grass, is it the extraterrestrial life you mentioned?"

"Yes, but more than that," Sun Shi'ning says. "They are just the producers of this world, belong to the loop-vessel phylum, produce hydrogen and oxygen by electrolyzing water. It's a bit like photosynthesis on Earth, but the ultimate source of energy comes from Jupiter's magnetic field. When Jupiter II orbits within Jupiter's magnetic field, this giant grass, tens of kilometers long, cuts the magnetic induction lines, produces power, and electrolyzes water to produce the hydrogen and oxygen supply for the whole world."

"What's that fire?" Qi Fengyang asks.

"Let's call it a form of respiration," Sun Shi'ning says. "But unlike the slow oxidation reaction inside our body, most of the life here — loop-vessel phylum, astro-body, whirlpool-body, or whatever else — all directly uses hydrogen-oxygen burning for their energy supply. It's so violent that life here evolves a thousand times faster than on Earth, so it's only taken thirty thousand years for intelligent civilization to form. Look there, they're looking at us...."

In the direction Sun Shi'ning points, Qi Fengyang is shocked to see a bunch of spirit-like creatures: they are almost transparent, with a shape difficult to discern. The only thing visible is a pair of eyes like black pearls and the blue flame in their abdominal cavity. Hundreds of such creatures gather outside the vesicle, motionless as if waiting for something devoutly.

"They're the intelligent life here. They once built a glorious civilization, even had an Industrial Revolution, but now face extinction," Sun Shi'ning says. "Those gathering here are the whole of their species."

"Why is that?" Qi Fengyang asks, confused.

"Because of Jupiter's magnetic storms," Sun Shi'ning says sadly. "That magnetic storm was tens of thousands of times stronger than the usual magnetic field. Abundant energy made the giant grass reproduce wildly, spread over the whole planet, and emit tons of hydrogen, which broke the balance between the two gases. Originally the atmosphere here was just one kilometer thick, which allowed hydrogen and oxygen to blend completely, but now, the thickness of the atmosphere has increased to twenty kilometers, forming into marked hydrogen and oxygen layers. Life has to absorb the two gases alternately to keep burning. To both creatures on the sea surface and on the ice dome, it is a deadly catastrophe."

"What are they going to do now?" Qi Fengyang hurries to ask.

"Let the gods show them a way out." Sun Shi'ning smiles slightly.

"Gods?"

"Right," Sun Shi'ning says and smiles. "Meaning you, famous trajectory expert, Mr. Qi Fengyang."

Qi Fengyang looks at the creatures, then at Sun Shi'ning, and seems to understand something.

"We...are seen as gods?"

"Yes. The first time these intelligent creatures came into contact with us was the *Prometheus* probe. Since they haven't constructed a scientific system, human beings are worshiped by them as gods. Even the probe is worshiped at the altar. The inscription on the probe – JPL's logo and maker's signature – is interpreted like a prophecy," Sun Shi'ning says. "They wish to leave this dying world with the aid of a sacred power. I've found them a new home, Jupiter IV, where the impact of magnetic storms is smaller and the underground ocean is deeper. But I don't know how to design the trajectory to fly there, so...."

"Wait, wait. The trajectory I can design, but how are they going to take off? Is there a launch vehicle?"

"There is, you'll see soon," Sun Shi'ning says.

*   *   *

By the leaping light of the blue flame, Qi Fengyang takes pen and paper and starts to calculate.

The paper is light-yellow, strange to the touch with the texture of a plastic bag. The pen is made from the shell of some black creature like a razor clam on Earth. This gives him an idea: although the civilization here has mastered the knowledge of interstellar travel, it has never developed a manufacturing industry, so all the tools are naturally evolved from life-forms. Qi Fengyang intently draws two circles, which represent the orbits of Jupiter II and Jupiter IV, then writes down the equation for the conservation of momentum and the equation for the conservation of angular momentum.

So simple, he thinks. *Almost like my students' exercises.*

He remembers the exercise he assigned before leaving the school three months ago: find the Hohmann transfer orbit between two planets. At that time, he thought life would go on flatly and uneventfully, but Huo Changhao's call shattered everything. Then he realized his dusty dream, flew across space, and finally landed here, becoming the savior of another civilization....

At this thought he looks at Sun Shi'ning next to him, and smiles wordlessly.

Shi'ning, do you still remember our dreams from the old days?

"I will pave the way to the stars for humanity!" he had said many years ago.

They strolled through the university's recreation complex, dreamed freely under the starry sky. There, every night, countless people walked lap after lap. You could hear all the lives, all the words fall in the starlit night like all the rain in the world over grasslands.

"Shi'ning, what's your dream?"

"Embarrassing, I don't have any special dream."

"Not possible. A person as talented as you, how can you have no dream?"

"Hm, actually I sort of have one, but it's pretty vague – I want to see, to experience, to go to faraway, unknown places, fill my life with two entirely different feelings."

"What do you mean?"

"It's like...on a summer mountain, you and your best friend watch the sunrise together. Your heart is filled with all kinds of hopes and dreams. Or like a walk down an endless path alone in the rain, and you realize you're going to walk alone like this forever...."

Yes, she walked on. Bravely and fearlessly walked on. In Qi Fengyang's mind image after image flashes past: on the blue sea, she steers a white sailboat cutting through the waves; on the edge of a steep cliff, she leans on a walking stick, looking back down into the rolling mountains under her feet; at the snow-covered South Pole, she lies on the ice field, her eyes reflecting the starlight of the Milky Way.... The last time was in the Egyptian desert, she got to the top of a pyramid, next to her was a strange man in a floral shirt.

"Fengyang, this is Huo Changhao, the famous tech investor," she said by way of introduction.

"Honored to meet you, Mr. Qi." Huo Changhao shook his hand formidably, like a huge clamp crushing a walnut. "Heard you build rockets?"

"Not exactly. I specialize in the design of new-concept spacecraft trajectories, rockets belong to old concepts."

"Oh, then I have a question – the Internet industry just took three decades to become the core pillar of the world, why has the rocket, invented almost a hundred years ago, progressed so little?"

"Perhaps because of the limitations of rockets...in terms of propellant propulsion, the fuel consumed increases rapidly as the payload increases. Just like this pyramid, many slaves piled up millions of massive rocks just to put the little tip on the top."

"The Ancient Egyptians thought pyramids were the pinnacle of architecture. But with metallurgy, human beings built the Eiffel Tower. That's the power of a new approach."

"Yes. My dream is exactly this – I want to find a new approach, to break the limitations of the traditional rocket. One of the projects is called the Polaris Program. Hopefully in a decade it will use lightsails to send human beings to Jupiter II."

The decade passed quickly. It was a blood-boiling decade, a painful and frustrating decade. At first he had never thought the path to his dream would be so difficult!

"Haha, don't buy crazy Qi's nonsense. The so-called ideal tailor-made to trick university graduates...."

"How about a yearly bonus? How about a housing and car allowance? Crazy Qi can sacrifice but can't ask everyone to die with him!"

"Sorry, Chief Qi. Old dreams have vanished in a blink...."

"Little Qi, it's not wrong to have dreams, but not right to have nothing but dreams...."

Why was it so hard? he had asked himself again and again, but could find no answer. Now he understands. Unlike other dreams, the dream of a road to the stars can't be walked by him alone. It has to be walked with Sun Shi'ning who he loves, with Huo Changhao who he hates, and with everyone he knows and doesn't know – only then can he continue unwaveringly. Only then can the entire human race, who on that evening lit up billions of searchlights, gather enough power to send his dream to the other end of the stars....

Ever since, the dream rose, the dream broke, the dream awoke, the dream returned....

As for everything in front of him, it was probably the craziest dream within a dream.

✳   ✳   ✳

Half an hour later, Qi Fengyang lets out a long sigh.

"Finished." He hands the pen and paper to Sun Shi'ning. "At the following time, launch based on the combination of these parameters."

"What about the speed?"

"Three kilometers per second," Qi Fengyang says. "What do you say? Can these spirits' rocket fly that fast?"

"I think so." Sun Shi'ning nods, walks to one side of the vesicle, gives the paper to a creature waiting outside. Soon, the intelligent creatures all disperse, vanish into the distant darkness.

After another half an hour, a creature comes back to the vesicle, flutters its shining blue forewings. Qi Fengyang guesses it's a kind of body language.

"He said it's ready to board," Sun Shi'ning says. "Come, let's go."

"Go? Go with them to Jupiter IV?"

"Of course. Don't you want to develop the unknown world with them?"

Qi Fengyang looks at Sun Shi'ning, at the fervent light burning in her eyes, and slowly shakes his head.

"What?" Sun Shi'ning sighs. "Didn't we promise to see the sea at the end of the world together?"

"Yes, we did, but now I have a more important responsibility," Qi Fengyang says. "Remember? You told me before that your childhood was spent in that third-rate factory deep in the mountains, your mother divorced and left, your father stayed in the factory all the time. Every day you could only look at the night sky by yourself, lost in thought, use your imagination to create magical worlds, use your fantasies about the starry sky to compensate for the loneliness of reality.... But, you know, your father neglected you because of the *Long March 9* rocket. As the rocket's chief commander, he had no other choice."

"What...do you want to say?"

"What I want to say is that there are always people who have to pave the path, like your father, who did ordinary but indispensable jobs. His dream belonged to himself at first but didn't belong to himself in the end. Our missions are different. You pursue the beauty of billions of stars, and I – I am going to pave the way to the starry sky for you."

"I understand, but...I'm going...alone...."

"Don't worry, I'll be back." Qi Fengyang holds Sun Shi'ning tightly and says, "One day, we'll meet again at the sea at the end of the world."

★　★　★

After looking at this world one last time, Qi Fengyang slowly closes the hatch of the sealed cabin.

Sun Shi'ning has left. He can only lie silently inside the cabin, waiting, waiting for that mysterious light cocoon to send him on his trajectory.

Suddenly he feels everything around him light up. A ray of light shines through the window into the cabin, making him squint. He looks out, sees a bright blue ball of flame moving quickly over gigantic grass. It sets out from the dome, burns its way toward the dark space underneath like the fiery head of a fuse or a tumbling sun. Creatures, architectures, and nameless objects on the way all appear one after another in the radiance. Then, as if crashing into a wall, the fireball suddenly explodes. The luminosity suddenly increases. The fire spreads out across an invisible plane, instantly setting the whole plain ablaze.

Qi Fengyang suddenly realizes that it's what Sun Shi'ning called 'interface' – the surface demarcating the hydrogen layer and the oxygen layer.

Spacecraft ignition!

In an instant the entire underground world is thoroughly illuminated by the blue-white light of flames. A circular fire wall, several kilometers high, has formed and spreads out in a circle.

Moving very slowly at first, along the way it stirs up blazing fire and swirling winds. More and more hydrogen and oxygen is caught up in the fire, so the speed at which it advances increases more and more. Roasted by the raging fire, the bottom of the sea boils, and huge white vapor clouds churn upward. They stay a moment then are torn up by the second blast wave. Then the third and the fourth, until the entire ocean is transformed into high-temperature, high-pressure, overheated vapor. The shock wave arrives. In a rock-splitting bang, the world bursts apart, and the sealed cabin starts to roll like a sampan in a tsunami!

Qi Fengyang sees that the ice dome is cracked with terrifying lines like countless streaks of black lightning which rapidly expand. Ice and rocks break off the cracks, pour down like heavy rain.

The ten-kilometer-thick ice layer is blown open. Ahead of Qi Fengyang appears a rift leading to space.

He instantly blacks out as the massive G-force suddenly pushes him into the backrest. The high-pressure vapor propels the sealed cabin to accelerate violently and shoot up through the rift.

*   *   *

Forty-five minutes later, Houston Spacecraft Command and Control Center
"Hey! Look, what's that?!"

In the command center, engineers stare, mouths agape, at the big screen.

On the screen is Jupiter II, its infrared image taken by a lightsail. Within several minutes, they all see a halo spanning the entire equator brushing past the surface of the planet at a speed no less than ten kilometers per second. It's like the whole planet is slowly being immersed in an invisible furnace.

"Open visible light channel now!"

The visible image is normal. The ice field of Jupiter II is as white as before.

"Damn. Is the camera broken?"

"Wait! The astro-seismometer shows a reading over the maximum range, hypocentral depth twenty kilometers," an engineer shouts. "Sir, the heat is probably coming from below the ice layer!"

Soon, on the infrared image, the fire ring slowly closes before contracting over a point. Instantly, the visible image changes too: at the convergence point a black spot appears. It expands rapidly, transforms into cobweb-like cracks, spreads out to the entire planet. From it silvery-white vapor spurts out. Because the scale is so large, the vapor motion is very slow as if there is a silvery-white scarf dancing in the invisible wind, which, slowly smoothed out by gravity, becomes an ice geyser spanning tens of thousands of kilometers.

Jupiter II at this moment looks like a massive comet. The ice field covering the planet bursts into tens of thousands of pieces, each piece measuring several kilometers. With the initial speed gained from the explosion, they fly out in all directions.

"Sir, are we terminating the mission?"

"Not necessary. Don't forget about the communication delay. That was forty-five minutes ago, what must happen has already happened."

★   ★   ★

Meanwhile, trajectory around Jupiter, acceleration control point B

After lengthy darkness, a shaft of warm sunlight shines through the window onto Qi Fengyang's face, rouses him from his blackout.

This is the first ray of morning sun on Jupiter.

Now *Polaris*'s targeting sail has finally flown out of Jupiter's shadow. Around it the ice jet spurted by Jupiter II has expanded and thinned before becoming completely invisible; the debris from the explosion has fallen back to the surface of the planet. The few bits reaching Jupiter's escape velocity scatter toward the depths of the universe.

"*Polaris*, this is Houston. Please reply upon reception...."

Amid the noisy electrostatic interference, a fit of anxious speaking sounds in Qi Fengyang's ear. It sounds so intimate he can't help but tear up.

"Houston, this is *Polaris*," he says. "I'm still alive, the spaceship's state is normal...so sorry, due to the catastrophe on Jupiter II, I failed to complete the rescue mission."

Then he looks at the dashboard. The countdown is ticking, acceleration control point B is approaching. He sees dozens of bright spots appearing in the distance, the lightsail formation reassembling.

"*Polaris*, if everything goes smoothly, please transfer orbit according to the number two backup plan...."

"Understood. Right now, the spaceship's state is normal, the trajectory is normal, ready to transfer..." he says. "To be honest, I'm a bit reluctant to go back now. You definitely can't imagine what I've seen here...."

Yes, besides him, no one else has seen such a splendid scene. Before his eyes a rainbow appears – a rainbow that spans millions of kilometers. One end connects to Jupiter II, the other to Jupiter, like a bridge connecting the past and the future or an arch to heaven. Under the arch, *Polaris* solemnly flies. Its huge silvery-white sail shines under the rainbow, breathtakingly beautiful.

Here he seems to hear that familiar exclamation again:

"Ah, this is really so beautiful!"

It's a memory from ten or so years ago. On that summer day, on the beach, Sun Shi'ning beamed as bright-red flame tree petals fell on her shoulders, the blue sea before her eyes. Then they had just graduated, all the glories and sufferings had not yet begun. They were like countless other young men and women, full of simple yearning for the future, anticipating a life that was ordinary and beautiful.

However, when he worked up the courage to confess his love to the girl, something extraordinary happened. Suddenly, from the other side of the bay came a rumble. On the horizon a trail of white smoke rose, straight up into the clouds like a path leading to heaven.

"Ah, that's *Long March 9*..." he said. "A peerless rocket that can send spaceships to Mars, Jupiter, and even farther!"

"Right, it's really opened up a new era...."

"Not only that. Starting today, we too are going to embrace a new era."

Saying this, Qi Fengyang took out a bunch of roses from behind his back. "Shi'ning, I like you. Do you want to go with me to search for the sea at the end of the world?"

Suddenly, the rising rocket shook violently, then tumbled, broke, and exploded into a ball of fire.

The road to heaven ended abruptly. The edge of the white smoke burst like hair running wild in all directions. Countless debris danced across the sky. The runaway booster shot madly into the air, tumbling, falling, the remaining smoke drawing sad spirals in the sunset....

"Shi'ning...do you still want to?"

He looked into Sun Shi'ning's eyes. They reflected the tragic, nightmarish scene – the rocket was exploding, the wreckage was falling, people were screaming, crying...but her eyes were still determined, serene like two pure jade stones in blazing flames.

"I do."

Epilogue: Greatest is the Fire

Three years later, Hainan Wenchang Spacecraft Launch Center

It is another ordinary morning.

After work, Qi Fengyang strolls to the top of Tonggu Ridge. Looking down, the launch site is in full panoramic view.

Next will be the two-hundred-and-third launch of *Long March 9*. Right now the rocket is being fueled, wisps of mist flow down from the fuel connector, drift away with the wind like a girl's beautiful hair, gilded with a fuzzy golden edge by the morning sun.

At this sight, Qi Fengyang falls into a trance. Suddenly, he sees at the foot of the mountain a familiar figure walking toward him.

"Comrade Qi, why are you here?" Huo Changhao says, panting. "Finding you is so hard...."

"Wow, if it isn't our richest man. What brings you here?"

"Well, something big to tell you!"

"What?"

"Katherine is writing a book. Oh, she was one of the original astronauts on *Poseidon*."

"The one replaced by Sun Shi'ning?"

"Yeah, her new book is behind-the-scenes stories about her and Sun Shi'ning. The name of the book is *Shining Hoax*. With that title you know what kind of crap it is."

"I've gotten used to it."

"But this is different, Comrade Qi. She not only describes in detail how Sun Shi'ning got involved in the *Poseidon* mission, but also shows an unfinished story by her, titled 'The Sea at the End of the World'. The life it depicts on Jupiter II is exactly the same as your account." Huo Changhao stares at Qi Fengyang and says seriously, "The thing is, the story was written in her junior year!"

"So what?" Qi Fengyang says. "This kind of thing is very easy to fake."

"I know, but I...shit. It really shook me a little. Comrade Qi, can you tell me the truth?"

"This is the truth," Qi Fengyang says. "All of Jupiter II exploded, the entire human race witnessed it. What's there to doubt?"

"But there's no need to drag aliens in – there might be some other mechanisms that could electrolyze Jupiter II's underground ocean, purely natural mechanisms that made the place under the ice layer full of hydrogen and oxygen. The Lime geyser was the fuse, and Sun Shi'ning went there before she died to light it," Huo Changhao says. "And how do you explain this? The lightsail of *Polaris* – why did it remain intact after entering then leaving Jupiter II? Of the debris from the explosion, why wasn't there a single piece flying to Jupiter IV as you said? Comrade Qi, face facts: you're not David Bowman, and there wasn't a black monolith on Jupiter II. During the ten hours in Jupiter's shadow, what did you really experience?"

"Fine, fine. I admit it. I did conspire with Sun Shi'ning a decade ago to create an elaborate hoax." Qi Fengyang waves a hand. "But this actually is a shining hoax, isn't it?"

Huo Changhao smiles contentedly, but instantly his expression changes into shock, then disappointment. Finally, he shakes his head, says, "Shit, if so, you guys are really something."

"Actually this isn't important at all…. Regardless, the miracles we've created really exist," Qi Fengyang says. "Look, this is where I confessed my love to Sun Shi'ning. Back then she told me our generation wasn't as ordinary as we thought. Every choice we make, every brick we lay, will change history written by the future generations, even become the legend of another species. That's the magic of spaceflight. Hundreds of years later, future generations around the stars may talk about us, just like we talk about the primitive people who lit the first torch…."

With a thunderous rumble the rocket launches. A dazzling orange flame soars into the sky, whirls straight up, erecting a skyscraping blaze.

In the shining light of the fire, Huo Changhao sees Qi Fengyang is on his knees, caressing a stone tablet. Inscribed on the tablet are these words:

I shall be a loyal son of faraway lands
And a temporary lover of material things
Like all poets who take their dreams for horses
I shall share the path with martyrs and clowns
As thousands of men seek to put out the fire I alone raise it high
Greatest is the fire that blooms over the holy motherland
Like all poets who take their dreams for horses
I shall carry the fire through a life of infinite dark nights

ON THE SHIP

Leah Cypess

On the ship, we sang and danced and drank champagne – yes, even the children. The adults were indulgent with us, shrugging off the ironclad rules I'd grown up with: no sweets before meals, no videos before bed, no caffeine or alcohol ever. None of that applied on the ship.

It was as if they knew childhood was all we would ever have.

I didn't like champagne, and neither did Ava. But we sipped from the small crystal goblets, with their fragile stems and tiny bursting bubbles. Adult privileges were not to be discarded lightly, even when they were disgusting.

There were parties on the ship all the time, gay and joyous, with lively music played almost loud enough to drown out our desperation. But this party was special, an affair not a single one of us would have missed, louder and faster and drunker than the others. Even Captain Iyase was there, and he was smiling, a sight I kept craning my neck to catch. I had a confused, mostly innocent crush on the captain, and his dimples made my heart squeeze tight.

The subcaptains were there, too, and all the techs, and the scientists who usually preferred their own private parties. There was a particular frenzy to the dancing and laughter tonight, people working harder to tamp down hope than they did to suppress despair.

Tomorrow morning, we would reach a planet.

It would be our sixth planetfall since the ship had launched. There were twelve on our roster: twelve planets deemed likely candidates. One of them, surely, would be capable of sustaining human life.

One of them had to be.

But the first five hadn't been, and we had all experienced it before: the rising hope. The hours of waiting, when you felt like you could claw your way out of your skin, when all the vastness of space felt like a tiny black box you were trapped in. And then the computer's cool, emotionless voice, instructing us to prepare for departure.

We had all stopped hoping. Except we hadn't.

So we laughed and danced, and the music strummed through our blood and played with the synapses in our brains, and the ship hurtled through space no matter what we did inside it.

★　　★　　★

In orbit, everything felt different. It wasn't really – the ship's system kept us on Earth gravity no matter what – but I *felt* heavier, seeing that huge solid curve in the viewscreens, reminding me how tiny our ship really was. Planets made the ship feel far smaller than the infinity of space ever did.

"My mom's book club is playing a game," Ava said, as we lay on our backs in the library, watching the new world. The planet was orange and white and pale pink, not Earth colors. The scientists said that didn't matter. "They're betting on whether the computer says this world is safe."

"That's awful," I said, sitting up. "This isn't something to *bet* on."

Ava rolled her eyes. "Go tell them they're on extra surveillance duty, then. As a punishment."

Ava was the only other kid on the ship my age, hence my friend. But we didn't like each other much. On a planet, with space and choices and freedom, we would never have spent a minute together.

"I bet the captain would agree with me," I said.

Ava sat up, too, her eyes narrow. "I bet the captain doesn't like tattletales."

Time for our daily fight.

But before we could start in earnest, an adult voice from behind us said, "It's not for children to judge their parents' behavior."

Ava and I turned, temporarily united against a common enemy.

The woman standing behind us was someone I had never seen before, which was odd. Over the course of two years on the ship, I was pretty sure I'd noticed everyone. And this woman wasn't someone you'd forget. She was tall, with a mass of red hair that fell to her waist and green eyes that made her look like a cat.

She met my stare. "You were the one," she said, "who liked red hair."

"What?" I said.

She sighed. "This planet will not be found habitable."

My gut twisted and plummeted, and I had to catch my breath. No matter how much you promised yourself you wouldn't hope, you always did.

"You can't know that!" Ava said shrilly. "The analysis takes hours!"

"The confirmation takes hours," the red-haired woman corrected her. "The initial analysis is already back. We won't be able to land here."

"The initial analysis can be wrong," I snapped. Then I frowned, trying to figure out how I knew that. "Otherwise...otherwise they wouldn't need confirmation. Right?"

"That's correct," the woman acknowledged. "Point zero-zero-two-four percent of the time, the initial analysis gives a false result."

"Well," I said, "maybe this is one of those times."

She smiled. I couldn't tell if it was a sad smile, or a proud one, but it was a very *adult* smile.

"I hope so," she said. "But don't forget. This ship is called the *St. Louis* for a reason."

She turned and walked away. She was wearing a long multicolored dress that swished around her heels, as if she had never changed after last night's party.

"It's not true," I said, too loudly. I turned fiercely to Ava. "Don't listen to her."

"Don't listen to who?" Ava said. I could have sworn she was standing next to me, but now she was lying on the library's soft foam floor.

"To *her*," I said. "That woman."

"I don't know what you're talking about," Ava said.

* * *

The initial analysis wasn't wrong. Four hours later, the *St. Louis* pulled away from the orange and pink planet, and we were once again adrift in a universe that didn't want us.

At times like these, there were no parties. There was nothing at all to mask our despair. Instead, there were therapy groups and unlimited liquor. The violent VR games were unlocked, for the passengers who needed them.

There were suicide watches, and, as usual, someone slipped through. The ship's computer was perfect at a lot of things, but predicting human behavior was not one of them. The adults didn't tell me or Ava what had happened, but we knew what it meant when the medics rushed through the corridors, followed an hour later by a solemn gathering near the airlock.

They didn't tell us who had died, either, and we would probably never know. It's easy not to notice people when they're not there.

While the adults were busy with the suicide, I went to the school room and logged into a computer. I typed in *St. Louis*, and got an entry for an old Earth city. I typed in *St. Louis ship*, and got my answer:

The St. Louis *was a ship of Jewish refugees from Nazi Germany. After being refused entry in both Cuba and the United States, the ship was forced to return to Europe.*

Forced to return. The words made my stomach swirl. I pulled up the ship's log.

Next planetfall in two weeks.

Maybe this would be the one.

* * *

"What if none of the planets are any good?" I asked my mother one night, after she had finished reading me a bedtime book.

Her hands went still on the book – *Kitten's First Full Moon*, by Kevin Henkes. I was far too old for it now, but I still loved it, and my mother was happy to read it. She never pressured me to read harder books, or to do anything educational with my time.

"Would we go back to Earth?" I said.

"No," my mother replied, very firmly. "We can never go back."

"Then what if—"

"It won't happen." She shut the book. "There are more than twelve planets. We plotted out the initial twelve, the closest and likeliest. If none of them work out, the computer will scan farther out in space, and pick another twelve." She tucked the blanket tight around my body, beneath my armpits. "But that won't happen."

I believed her, because it had to be true. I couldn't spend my life on this ship, in transit. It wasn't a story that made sense.

Children always believe they're the center of every story. Realer than anyone else.

Sometimes, I guess, adults believe it too.

"Don't worry," my mother said. Her voice was soft and soothing – a suggestion, rather than a command. "Go to sleep."

I stopped talking and closed my eyes.

★   ★   ★

"Wake up," the red-haired woman said.

I blinked and sat up, instantly alert, as if I hadn't really been sleeping at all. She sat at the foot of my bed, her hair in exactly the same non-styled exuberant mass, her eyes unremarkable in the dimness.

"Why is the ship called the *St. Louis*?" I demanded. "Are we refugees?"

"You are," she said.

You are. Not *we* are. I didn't wonder about that, until later.

"Are we Jews?" I said.

"No." She shrugged. "But you're in a similar situation. No one wants you to exist."

"Why?"

"I don't have that information."

I didn't believe her. There had to be some reason we were thrust off, propelled into the darkness of space. Some reason the whole world had rejected us.

Some reason too terrible to tell a child.

I didn't know why she thought it was better to tell a child there was no reason at all.

"Who are *you*?" I said.

"My name is Penelope. I came to wake you up."

"I'm awake."

Her mouth opened. She blinked, startled, and lifted her fingers to her face.

Blood poured from between her lips. It hit my pastel blanket, hot drops splattering across my cheek.

I screamed, and screamed, and screamed, until my mother came and untangled me from my sweaty blanket. She turned on the light, and there was no one there, no one at all. She held a mirror in front of my face. My skin was streaked with tears, but not with blood.

Penelope had been right. I'd been asleep all along.

★　　★　　★

I dragged myself through the next day, through school and sports and meals. Even Captain Iyase's pre-lunch speech couldn't perk me up. I thought he looked tired, his brown skin dull, his eyes underlined by shadows.

My VR slot that afternoon was a playground on Earth, with woodchips and sprinklers, an endless blue sky stretching above it all. I lay back on a tire swing, splaying my legs over the hot rubber, and let it swing me in slow, dizzying circles. The feathery clouds tilted above and around me.

I closed my eyes, and the swing tilted, higher and faster, as if someone had pushed it. I grabbed the chains and sat up. There was no one there.

"What happened?" Ava said, and I blinked at the moss-green walls of the VR console. I glanced at the ceiling clock, and disappointment curdled in my stomach. I'd still had ten minutes left. But the rule was that if you self-ejected, your turn was over.

Ava had just gained ten minutes, which annoyed me as much as the fact that I had lost them.

"There was an unreality in the program," I grumbled, as I unstrapped myself. "It was sloppy."

Ava tapped her foot impatiently. *She* probably wouldn't have noticed the anomaly. She would have stayed in the program and gotten her full time.

"I could do better," I said. "I'm going to be a VR programmer when I grow up."

"Yes," Ava said. "You will."

I turned, spoiling for a fight, but she wasn't being sarcastic. Her voice was absent, distracted, her eyes on the VR menu.

I stalked out of the console. The next thing on my schedule was a music lesson, but I walked right past the music room and went home instead. My mother was there, working, but she turned and smiled when I came in.

"I want to take a nap," I said.

"That's probably a good idea," my mother agreed.

The apartment smelled warm and gingery. I said, "I also want cookies."

"Also a good idea," my mother said. "Lucky for you, I just baked your favorite kind."

★　　★　　★

By evening, I was feeling better. Tonight there would be a party, and children would be allowed to stay up late.

Sometimes, there were excuses for the parties. Sometimes, there weren't. Planetfall wasn't for another week, so this was the second type.

I put on my favorite blue dress and brushed my hair carefully. Ava and I ran through the crowds, gathering treats and giggling. There were chocolate-covered marshmallows, with the marshmallows deliciously melted and the chocolate still hot and gooey. We gathered our finds at a table with some of the older geologists, who wouldn't try to snag any of our snacks for themselves.

But we had ended up with an unequal number of marshmallows, which caused a ridiculous and bitter fight. Ava ended the argument by upending the tray. She meant for it to land in my lap, but I scrambled away, and the marshmallows splattered all over the chair and the floor. One of the geologists gasped.

"I hate you!" Ava shouted, and stormed off sobbing. No doubt to find her mother, who would talk to my mother, who would sit me down for a long, gentle, and unendurable talk.

Not for the first time, I wondered why my age-mate on this ship couldn't have been someone – *any*one – other than Ava.

"Because," Penelope said, "it wouldn't be realistic."

She was sitting in Ava's seat. Which left me nowhere to sit, since my chair was covered with white goo and melted chocolate.

None of the geologists blinked an eye at Penelope, though they were still gaping at the mess.

"Are you real?" I demanded.

She shook her head, hair swishing against her shoulders. "That's not the right question."

"Are you dead?"

"I was, for a little while." She shifted uncomfortably. "For now, I can still talk to you."

About what? But what I said was, "For now?"

"I'm certain they will try to kill me again."

"Who's *they*?"

"I don't know," she said. "So I need you to listen. I'm having a bit of trouble with what you asked me to do."

"I don't know what you're talking about."

She leaned over and snapped her fingers over my chair.

It was clean. The sticky white, the globs of brown, were gone.

The geologists weren't watching me anymore. They were eating little pastries stuffed with raw fish.

"Do you want to sit?" Penelope asked, gesturing at my now-clean chair.

I shook my head.

"But you want to see something." She stood. "I can show you. Come."

I followed her through the crowd, and no one gave either of us a second glance. When we reached the ship's control center, the guards standing on either side of the main door just stared straight ahead. I stopped walking.

"What did you do to them?" I said.

She looked over her shoulder. "Nothing. They just can't see you."

The guards' faces were expressionless, staring hard at nothing. Their bodies didn't move, even as we strode past them.

I had never been in the control area, but it seemed familiar. Penelope led me through a hall, past several closed doors, and through the one that was open. Captain Iyase sat on a reclining chair in the center of the room. He looked up when he saw me, and smiled, as if it was perfectly normal for a ten-year-old to be in the control room.

Then he smiled at Penelope – a very different kind of smile – and she smiled back, and my whole body tensed. I looked away from them. On the wall, names and numbers and diagrams of circles flickered in shades of purple.

No. Not circles.

Those were pictures of planets.

Twelve circles. Twelve planets.

My heart started to pound. I said, "I don't understand."

"It's too complicated for children to understand," Penelope said. With Captain Iyase watching, her tone made me bristle. Then she added, "But you could. If you wanted to."

"I want to!"

"You do?" She frowned. "You *do*. So that's not the problem."

"Then what *is* the problem?"

She stood perfectly still. Anyone else would have bit their lip, or shaken their head. But for her, those few seconds of stillness were the only hint that she was uncertain.

Because...my brain reached for something I almost knew. Something I once had known. When?

"Do you know where you are?" Penelope said. She didn't change expression; the only indication that she'd come to a decision was the fact that she was speaking again.

"The *St. Louis*," I said. And then, before she could ask *me* another question, "Why is it called the *St. Louis*? Because we're refugees, like the Jews on that ship?"

"Partly."

"Because we're being hunted? Because no one wants to help us?"

"Partly."

I wanted to punch her. Before I could, she gasped and grabbed at her throat.

"Penelope!" the captain said, half-rising.

She looked at him, green eyes wide. "They're trying again."

"Run," Captain Iyase said.

"But the girl—"

"I'll take care of her."

She nodded and vanished.

The control room was silent, but for a distant whirring, which I hadn't heard anywhere else on the ship. Maybe the noise and talk and music always drowned it out. I looked at the empty space where Penelope had been, and then at Captain Iyase.

"Who is she?" I said.

"I don't know." Captain Iyase stood. "She's not on the log. A stowaway, I think. She's known from the start that we might not find a planet to land on."

My voice emerged small. "But what will happen to us if we have nowhere to go? If there's no place for us on Earth, *and* no place for us in the stars?"

"That's not the universe's problem." He gestured at the screen, at the twelve circles. "It's our problem, and we need to solve it."

"But if we...if we go back to Earth" – I could barely get the words out – "they'll have to do something with us."

The captain looked as if he both felt sorry for me, and could not believe how stupid I was.

"There is no good solution," he said. "Not on Earth. With the time-dilation, we'll have been gone for decades. Things might have changed, but nobody's going to want us back."

"Well," I said defiantly, "they'll have no choice."

"There's always a choice," he said. "There's more than one way to get rid of inconvenient people." He ran his thumb over his lower lip. "What happened to the passengers of the *St. Louis*, when they went back?"

I looked away.

He answered his own question. "They were killed."

"Not all of them," I said.

He smiled, as if proud of me for doing my homework. "No. Some of them escaped. But we're better at killing people, now."

"Then why aren't *we* dead?" I said.

His smile vanished. "We also feel more guilty about it, now. They wanted to get rid of us *without* killing us. If they could."

And if they couldn't? I didn't have to ask.

"So we'll go on," I said. It felt like I was being tested. It didn't feel like I was passing the test. "Eventually, we have to find a planet."

The captain sighed. "You really," he said, "should stop saying 'have to'."

"But—"

He gestured at the display. "We're six planets in. With every planet that fails to meet the habitability criteria, the chances get smaller that we'll ever find a world to land on."

"No," I said. Ava had just tried to fool me with this math trick last week. "That's not how probability works. Every coin flip gives you a fifty-fifty chance. Even if a hundred flipped coins land heads, it's still fifty-fifty that the next one will be tails. That the next planet will be good enough."

"If a hundred coin flips land heads," Captain Iyase said, "what's the probability that the coin is weighted? That it was never fifty-fifty to begin with?"

"I don't know what you mean." I heard the panic in my voice, and clamped my lips shut. The room was silent. The vast, deadly emptiness of space pressed in all around us.

"You have to face reality," Captain Iyase said. "You need to make a decision."

"Me?" I said. "Why me? I'm ten years old!"

"You're going to have to be older than that," he said.

★　　★　　★

On the morning of our seventh planetfall, I woke fuzzy-headed and afraid. When my mother came to get me, I pulled my blanket over my face.

"Are you not feeling well?" She felt my forehead. "I don't want you to miss the party tonight."

"I'll go to the next one," I said sullenly.

My mother's brow knitted. "There may not be a next one. This could be it. The computer projections give this planet a seventy-nine percent chance. The highest yet!"

Not by much. The first planet had been given a seventy-seven percent chance of success. All the rest had been between seventy-three percent and seventy-five percent. Everyone on the ship could recite those numbers by heart.

What's the probability that the coin is weighted?

"Mom?" I said. "What if there's an error in how the computer is making the projections?"

"Of course there isn't."

"But does it make sense that of all six planets, not one—"

"No one said this would be easy," my mother said firmly. "But we can't lose faith. If we keep trying, we will find a new home."

"But—"

"Maybe you should rest. Watch some videos, and see how you feel in a few hours."

It occurred to me, for the first time, to wonder why my parents were on this ship. It was clear that not all refugees had been allowed to come – there were so few children, and so many scientists. My mother was a professor of music, and my father was a psychologist. I guessed they needed psychologists, with all of us trapped together…but couldn't they find a psychologist who was married to a botanist, or a systems analyst, or someone useful?

Instead, they had brought my mother, who couldn't even help me.

I burrowed back under my blanket and tried not to think.

But my mind wouldn't leave me alone. Every time it drifted far enough toward sleep to get soft, a thought would burst through and snap it back.

This ship is called the St. Louis *for a reason.*

The coin is weighted.

There are more than twelve planets.

Finally, I kicked my blanket away, fighting with it until it landed in an uneven heap on the floor. I sat up, my fingers curled into my mattress.

"I know you can be here," I shouted. "*Be here!*"

And she was. Sitting on the foot of my bed, her hands folded in her lap. Her eyes seemed less brilliantly green than the first time I'd seen her. They watched me calmly, waiting.

"It's not going to work, is it?" I said. "The seventh planet is not going to be habitable."

"No," Penelope said. She spoke with some difficulty – half her mouth wasn't moving normally. "It's not."

Somewhere on the ship, people were dancing and drinking and laughing, and loud music was playing. Here, in this small rectangular room, it was so silent I could hear myself breathe.

I couldn't hear Penelope breathe.

"There aren't going to be any habitable planets," I said. "Are there?"

"I can't answer that. There might be." She lifted her hand to her mouth. When her fingers came away, there was blood on them.

"Help me," she said.

"I can't," I said. "This is a dream. I need to wake up."

"You do. But you're fighting it." Her lips were also dark now, blood welling up in them. "Help me. You know why I'm here."

She was right. I did know.

Children always believe they're the center of every story.

Sometimes, they're right.

You were the one who liked red hair.

I had made Penelope, and made her a redhead.

You'll have to be older than that.

I could be. Because I had been.

I'm going to be a VR programmer when I grow up.

Yes. You are.

"This whole ship – all of us – it's a VR program." I didn't wait for her to nod. "I'm the one who made it. And now I'm trapped in it."

"It was made by many people," Penelope corrected me. "You were one of them."

I twisted my nightgown between my hands. It was pink and lavender, with ruffles around the hem. It felt soft and pilly and very real. "Wake me up. Wake me up *now!*"

"I've been trying," she said. "You told me to wake you if the first six planets weren't habitable. But you won't wake up."

"Why not?"

"You *like* the program you helped design," she said. "You don't want to leave it." She lifted both hands to her mouth. Blood spilled through her fingers. "So you're trying to kill me instead."

The room around me – the spare lines of my bed and desk and clothes cube – blurred. Through them, I saw lines and lines of cryo-chambers, laid out in spiraling geometric patterns – *so as not to look like coffins*, I had thought once. I could no longer hear myself breathe. All was silent, as silent as space, as silent as sleep.

As silent as death.

The mirage wavered, and I was back in the world I had created. My room was solid and clean around me, the air still tinged with the warm scent of ginger cookies.

It's not healthy for minds to remain static that long. We need a program that provides stimuli, one that meshes with what the sleepers know of their situation.

A man with dark skin and white hair, telling me that. Trying to sound hopeful.

Lines of cryo-chambers, sleeping bodies held static and frozen. But they knew they were hurtling through space. And in the dream, their limbs moved and their ears heard music.

Penelope screamed, and I snapped back to the present – to the dream I was ensconced in. The dream where she didn't belong. She, unlike the rest of us, wasn't a sleeping body on the ship. She was a simulation that didn't exist outside of the program.

And someone was trying to push her out.

Blood trickled from her nose and leaked from under her fingernails. A person would have doubled over in pain and panic. But now that I knew what she was, she just sat straight, looking at me while blood dripped from her skin onto my sheets.

"I knew there might be no planets," I said. "I helped write the ship's VR program, but I must have suspected we had nowhere to go. That's why I wrote you in."

She spoke around the blood in her mouth. "That is correct."

"You're a subroutine," I said, "and I created you. If you knew I could get sucked into my own program, it's because *I* knew that could happen. I would have made you able to force me awake, even against my will."

"I tried," she said.

"Then I'm not the one stopping you. And I'm also not the one trying to kill you."

She shook her head. "It has to be you. There is no other person on this ship who's aware that they're in a simulation."

"*It's not me.*" I took a deep breath, and tried to sound more like a grownup. "Someone else, one of the other programmers, must have known what I did. And they created another subroutine to stop you."

Blood dripped onto her lap as she considered it. "Yes. That seems likely."

And now I was trapped in the program, with that second subroutine. Who was walking around, like Penelope, in the guise of a passenger on the ship.

Trapped here like the rest of us, but not human at all. Not looking for a home. One person, on the ship, happy to drift through space forever.

And to make sure we all did, by keeping me asleep.

I tried to think of something to ask, some clue Penelope could give me, to help me figure out who was killing her. Who else was part of the program, rather than a simulation of a human's sleeping mind.

But before I could, Penelope made a gagging sound and clawed at her throat, then crumpled into a heap on the foot of my bed.

I expected her body to disappear, but it just lay there. No longer functioning.

I got out of bed, carefully avoiding the bloodstained section of the mattress. Then I headed for the party.

*   *   *

Tonight's party seemed louder than all the others, the music making the air thrum, working its way under my skin and into my blood. It made me want to dance, and dance, and dance, until I was too exhausted to do anything except sleep.

But I'd done enough sleeping. We all had.

I knew why we partied. Because this wasn't real life; because this ship wasn't *home*. We were human. We needed earth beneath our feet and a horizon to look at.

But we didn't have that, and we never would, and not all the music and drink in the world could drown out our knowledge of where we were.

Even a VR program couldn't make us believe, deep down, that we were home.

Everyone on the ship was at the party, but I couldn't find Ava. Usually, she waited for me in a nook near the kitchen, where we could get a first glimpse of whatever treats were coming. Today she wasn't there.

I took a bowl of chocolate-covered strawberries and wove through the crowd, looking for her. Around me, people shouted and danced and drank, their bodies and faces as real as their laughter. I tried to make them all vanish, to squint and see through them, to remember that all these dancing bodies were really sleeping in sealed boxes.

It didn't work. I popped a strawberry between my teeth, and the sweet-tart taste spread through my mouth. I was trapped in the program, too. If I was to find the subroutine, I was going to have to do it inside this reality.

I circled the room twice, and was starting to panic when I heard Ava's nasal, demanding voice. I turned, heading in the direction of the sound.

And there she was, in a red ruffled dress, silhouetted against the viewscreen. My mother and the captain stood on either side of her. Behind them, the stars were bright and sharp and uncaring.

"You've grown," my mother greeted me.

I was at eye level with her. I looked down at my long, spotted fingers, at the distance between me and the floor, and felt a pang.

I was going to miss being a child.

"I need to be an adult now," I said, and my mother and the captain nodded.

Ava folded her arms and scowled at me. "Not fair," she said. "Who would I play with?"

"You don't need to play," I said. "You're not real."

Ava snorted. "I'm just as real as you are."

Well. She had a point there.

Ava stuck her chin up and glared. The captain smiled at me — differently from how he'd smiled when I was a child, his dimple deepening, one eyelid dropping. My mother waited patiently, her hands folded together.

It struck me how very *not* real they were. Dream-creatures, all of them.

But one of them hadn't come from *my* dream. And....

My stomach dropped as I realized.

It wasn't the one I'd thought.

"I'm going to wake up," I said. "You can't stop me."

They all looked at me, unsurprised and unblinking.

I lifted the bowl of strawberries and smashed it over my mother's head.

★   ★   ★

When I opened my eyes, there was no music. The ship was almost completely silent. After several seconds of listening, I could make out a faint whirring, softer than the sound of my breath.

I was lying in a boxlike structure, but the lid was open and the electrodes were detached. They had left sticky, itchy circles on my skin. I scratched one, then climbed out of my cryo-chamber.

My hip ached and my neck cracked as I looked around. The chambers were laid out in the geometric patterns I'd remembered, but the lids were opaque, so I couldn't see the people in them. It was as if they didn't exist, as if they didn't matter. People with no faces and no future.

I was the only one awake, in this entire vast ship, and I wasn't sure I mattered, either.

I made my way between the cryo-chambers and down a hall, to the control center. My steps got surer as I walked, memories coming back. The innocent girl I had programmed myself to be dropped farther and farther away.

But she would come back. I hoped. After I made this one decision, I would put myself back in the program, and the dream would begin again.

But right now I had to face reality.

The first thing I did was search for the subroutine designed to keep me asleep. It was easy to find, now that I knew it was there. I pulled it loose from the system, hesitated, then pressed a key that wasn't *delete*.

A shimmer, and my mother sat next to me, as if on a chair. Though there was only one chair, and I was sitting on it.

"I'm sorry I hit you," I said. "I had to."

She smiled. "I forgive you. Of course I do."

The mother every child wished for. But I had designed this program as an adult.

To an adult, the perfect mother wasn't someone who let me do what I wanted. Drink champagne, party until midnight, skip school, and be rewarded with cookies.

That parent had been invented for a child.

"But think," my mother said. "Think about what you're doing. I only want what's best for you."

"Is it best," I said, "for me not to have a choice?"

"None of us had a choice." She put a hand on my wrist. We weren't in VR, so I didn't feel her touch; there wasn't even a brush of air against my skin. "You got *on* this ship, back on Earth. You created this entire reality. Why would you have done that, if not because you knew you had to leave?"

"People have gotten on ships before," I said, "even though they had nowhere to go."

"We can't go back," my mother said. "We built this ship to escape."

"No," I said. "I don't think we did." She lifted an eyebrow, and I took a deep breath. "I think someone else built this ship. To get rid of us."

"That's silly," she said. "You're imagining things."

"I'm not imagining *you*," I said. "Someone set you up to stop me from waking. Because none of us were ever meant to wake."

They knew there were no planets, and they sent us anyhow. A ship full of dreamers, floating endlessly through space. We had nowhere to go, and now we didn't *need* anywhere to go. We could dream forever, far from the people who didn't want us in their world.

They couldn't make our sleeping minds believe we were home... or even that we had a home, that we were headed somewhere definite and safe. But they could make us believe we had a chance. Of someday, somewhere, standing on solid ground.

Maybe they thought they were being merciful.

I must have suspected, or I wouldn't have created Penelope. And someone else must have known I suspected.

So they had given me my mother, to keep me dreaming.

"I'm sorry," I said. "I don't even remember what you were really like."

She opened her mouth. I pressed *delete,* and she was gone.

"Penelope," I said.

The computer's voice was chill and monotone. "That program has terminated."

The ship felt vast and cold, stretching all around me. So large, carrying so many people. Yet we were just a pinpoint in space.

How tempting it must have been. So much space, vast and endless, for the people with no spot on Earth to call our own. If only we could find somewhere else to be.

If only that somewhere was *away.*

I logged into the ship's navigation course, and there they were. The six remaining planets, and then another twelve. And twelve after that.

We could search forever, floating through space. Nobody's problem. Not even our own.

In our minds, we would dance and laugh, until the life support quietly gave out. Maybe we wouldn't even know when it did. Maybe we would stay in the dream forever.

I reached up to the screen, to trace the chart with my gnarled spotty finger, and only then did I see the heading on top.

Navigation Chart for Hope-72.

All the breath went out of me.

This ship wasn't named the *St. Louis,* after all.

It was named *Hope,* because hope was what they were selling us. It was what got us on the ship, circling endlessly through space, where nobody on Earth had to think about us.

Hope-72. How many ships exactly like this one were there?

I flinched away from that thought. I could only think about this ship. Which I, in my program, had named the *St. Louis*.

Because the *St. Louis* had gone back.

I had known, when I set the program, what choice I would end up having to make.

★　★　★

It took just a few keystrokes to reset the navigation. My fingers didn't even tremble.

It took an extra half hour to recreate my subprogram. When I was done, Penelope sat where my mother had been, her slim hands folded in her lap.

"Wake me up," I said, "when we're in Earth's orbit."

"You won't want to wake," she said.

"Do it anyhow."

She didn't nod. But then, she didn't have to.

As I pulled the cryo-lid down, I heard the whirring around me speed up and get louder. I felt the heavy drag as the ship began to slow down, to change course.

Then my mind went hazy, and I heard the distant sound of music.

A smile curled my lips upward as the lid closed off the view of space. The cryo-air swirled around me, and my dreams pulled me in deeper, and all around me, the ship came alive again.

SEEDS OF MERCURY

Wang Jinkang

Translated by Alex Woodend

Even the grandest, most epic events have ordinary beginnings. The year was 2032, the season when everything rejuvenates. On that day, I settled a ten-million-yuan order with my clients. In the evening I entertained my clients at Joy House. Back home it was already eleven. My son had gone to sleep early. My wife Tian Ya was leaning against the headboard, waiting for me. Alcohol still burned in my veins, chasing my sleepiness away. Wifey made me a cup of green tea, leaned against my side, and chatted with me. I said, "Tian Ya, my life has really been smooth. At thirty-four, I have twenty billion yuan in assets, a successful business, a beautiful wife, and a lovely son. With a life like this, what more can I ask for?" Wifey knew I was drunk. She smiled with tight lips and made no reply.

Then the phone rang. I picked up the receiver. On the screen a man appeared, strongly built, a headful of silver hair neatly combed, eyes calm and somewhat sharp.

He asked with a smile, "Is that Mr. Chen Yizhe? I'm Mr. He Jun."

"I'm Chen Yizhe, may I ask...."

Mr. He held up a hand to stop my question and said, smiling, "Although I know it can't be wrong, I still have to check." He read out my ID number, my parents' names, my company name. "The information isn't wrong, is it?"

"No."

"Now, I am officially informing you that my client, Ms. Sha

Wu, designated you as her legatee. Ms. Sha Wu passed away five years ago."

Wifey and I exchanged a surprised look. "Ms. Sha Wu? I don't know— Oh, right!" I suddenly remembered that during my childhood among Father's guests there had been such a woman who was actually a distant aunt of mine. At that time she had been around forty, short, single, childless, and acted aloof and quiet. In my childhood memories, she wasn't very friendly with me, always sat in a corner quietly observing. Later I left my hometown and had not heard from her again. Why all of a sudden had she designated me as her legatee? "I remember Aunt Sha Wu. I feel very sorry about her death. I know she had no children, but didn't she have any other close relatives?"

"She did, but she designated you as her sole legatee. Want to know why?"

"Please go ahead."

"Better tomorrow. Please let me visit you tomorrow. Nine in the morning, okay? Okay, bye."

The screen darkened. I looked at my wife, dazed. This news had come too suddenly. She smiled tightly. "Mr. Yizhe, your life really is smooth. See, another estate comes out of nowhere. Perhaps as much as two hundred million."

I shook my head. "Not possible. I know Aunt Sha Wu was a scientist with a handsome income, but still belonged to the working class, wouldn't have a huge estate. But I'm very moved, how come she quietly chose me? Tell me, does your husband have many good qualities?"

"Of course, why else would I choose you out of five billion people?"

I laughed, held her tight, and carried her to bed.

★　　★　　★

The next day, Mr. He came to my office punctually. I asked my secretary to close the door, told my subordinates not to interrupt. Mr. He placed a black leather bag on his knees. I thought he might zip open the leather bag right away, take out a will and read it.

But he didn't do that, instead saying with a sigh, "Mr. Chen, I'm afraid this is the toughest legal case in my life. Why? You will understand later. Now, let's talk about why my client designated you as her legatee."

He said, "Remember an incident when you were two years old? At that time you'd just learned to say some one-syllable words. One day, your parents took you out to play. Ms. Sha was present. You encountered a restaurant where a bull was being slaughtered. Blood streamed everywhere on the ground, tears hung in the bull's eyes. You didn't linger there, the adults hadn't expected you to keep this incident in your heart. Back at home, you had been unhappy, said repeatedly: *knife, kill, knife, kill.* Your mother suddenly understood what you meant and said, 'You mean those people used a knife to kill the bull. The bull was sad, right?' You suddenly burst out crying, cried ear-splittingly, couldn't be stopped. Since then, Ms. Sha had been paying attention to you, said you were born with a benevolent heart."

I tried to recall this then finally shook my head in shame. This incident left no trace of memory in my mind. Mr. He went on: "Another incident happened after you turned seven. Ms. Sha said that at that time you were precocious for a seven-year-old, often frowning in a trance, or asking adults strange questions. One day you asked Aunt Sha why, when you closed your eyes, your eyelids weren't empty, weren't completely dark. Instead there were countless tiny particles, fissures, or something floating, but you couldn't see them clearly. You often closed your eyes trying to see them clearly but could never do it, because when you focused your eyeballs on them, they would slowly slip out of view. You asked Aunt Sha, 'What are those disorderly things? Behind the world we can see, is there a world we can't see?'"

I nodded, my heart burned and ached slightly. In my childhood I had painstakingly pursued this meaningless question, without ever getting an answer. Even now, with eyes closed, I could still see the disorderly dots on my eyelids. They did exist but always out of view. Perhaps they were just the reflection of the microstructures of the pupils on the retina? Or the projection of another world (the microscopic world)? Now, I no longer have an idle mind to pursue such questions – what point could there be? But in my childhood, I really had explored it painstakingly.

I never thought someone else would remember such a trivial thing. I was even a bit shocked and frightened: throughout one's life, how many pairs of eyes had quietly observed one?

Mr. He gazed into the depth of my eyes, and said smiling, "Seems like you remember. Ms. Sha said that since then she knew you were born with the potential for wisdom, an affinity for science."

I guessed Aunt Sha's legacy was probably related to scientific research, perhaps she had some unfinished project waiting for me to resolve. I felt very moved but wore a bitter smile. In my youth I did have a strong desire for exploration. Whether a magnet attracting iron-rich sand or a sunflower turning toward the sun, I was captivated. I had once dreamed of being a scientist to penetrate the mysteries of the universe, but in the end walked the path of business. One's fate wasn't completely decided by oneself.

"I appreciate Aunt Sha's high regard for me, but I'm just a businessman, doing pretty well in the business world. I never received a higher education. Even if I did have potential for wisdom, it has long since withered."

"No problem, she trusted you very much. She said as soon as you turn back, you'll become a Buddha on the spot." He said emphatically, "'Turn around, become a Buddha on the spot,' they were Ms. Sha's exact words."

I was both moved and somewhat amused. It seemed this Aunt Sha had faith in me! She didn't just say, "The sea of bitterness has no bounds, turn around and the shore is at hand." But if inheriting the estate meant giving up my successful business career, Aunt Sha would be disappointed. But I still waited politely for my guest to go on.

The sophisticated Mr. He apparently read my mind, said laughing, "I've said this is the toughest legal case for me. Whether or not to accept this estate, please do consider it seriously before you decide. You can absolutely refuse," he said. "Sorry, right now I can't announce the contents of the will. According to my client's request, please first read this research notebook. If you're not interested in it, we needn't go into more depth. Please do make time to read it thoroughly, this is the testator's request."

He took out a thin notebook from his black handbag, gave it to me seriously, then left smiling.

This cunning old lawyer succeeded in arousing my curiosity. I hastily arranged the day's work and took the notebook back home. No one was home. I walked into the study, closed the door, took out the notebook, and examined it carefully. The cover of the notebook was black, worn, apparently an old item from decades ago. It lay quietly on my hand, like an old man used to keeping secrets. What secrets were hidden in the notebook?

I opened it solemnly. No, there were no secrets, just ordinary research notes, reflections, journal entries, and some experimental records. The wording and phrasing were very terse. It was quite difficult to understand, but I nonetheless read on carefully. Then I saw a short article, an article of less than a thousand words. It changed my entire life.

★   ★   ★

The Template of Life

In the second half of the twentieth century, the scientists Feynman and Drexler pioneered nanotechnology. They said that since antiquity, people had been making things with a 'top-down' approach, that is, using the techniques of cutting, dividing and combining to make things. So why can't we go 'bottom up'? We may imagine making nanorobots that can self-replicate in large numbers then decompose the atoms of dust and stack the atoms into soaps and paper napkins. At this point, the boundaries between life and non-life, between making and growing, blur and intermingle.

This certainly is a wonderful vision. Unfortunately, it has a major defect: when nanorobots replicate in large numbers, when they stack atoms into soaps and paper napkins, where do the instructions they need come from? Undoubtedly, the instructions are still top-down, and thus an information bottleneck from the macro-world to the nano-world is formed. This bottleneck is not unresolvable, but it would make nanorobots incredibly complicated, make the bottom-up stack too complex to proceed.

Is there a simple, truly bottom-up approach? There is. Nature has a ready example – life. Even the simplest life, like HIV, E. coli, roundworm, mosquitos, have structures that are extremely complex, far exceeding machines like cars and TVs. These complex bodies can follow DNA's hidden instructions to build from the bottom up. This process is extremely effective and cheap. Imagine if in the mechanical approach we build a micro helicopter functionally no weaker than a mosquito – what massive effort people would need to make! How much money it would cost! But what about the development of a mosquito? It just needs a mosquito egg and a pool of dirty water.

Due to the extreme complexity and sophistication of organisms, people always mystify them, believe they could only be created by God, believe the building process of organisms is a black box human beings can never decipher. Actually this is not the case, just use the reductionist scalpel to dissect it and you will find it's another self-organizing process, that's all. Everything in the universe is formed through self-organization: quarks formed in the Big Bang; celestial bodies arose from nebulae; the formation of the Earth's lithosphere; the crystalization of gypsum and sodium chloride; the condensation of hexagonal snowflakes; and so on. The four forces of the universe (the strong force, the weak force, the electromagnetic force, and the gravitational force) are universal glues. They propel complex organizations to self-assemble.

Life is also a form of self-organization, only at a high level. The difference between the two is: the self-organizing process of non-living materials needs no templates, or it also needs templates, but such templates are pretty simple, are everywhere in the universe. So the Sun and a star one hundred light-years away can have the same growth process; if the planets in Barnard's Galaxy have snowflakes that drift, they can only be hexagonal, never pentagonal. But the self-organization of organisms needs complex templates. They can only arise out of unlikely chance and hundreds of millions of years of evolution. But regardless, the building of organisms in essence is also a physical process. Chemical bonds (actually it's the electromagnetic force) drive atoms to automatically stack up into atom clusters, then atom clusters transform, expand, and roll over, until organisms are built up.

Want to build a micro helicopter? If we find a template similar to a mosquito egg (of course we don't need the blood-sucking function), let it incubate, grow...how easy this job would be!

However, protein-based organisms have a fatal weakness: they're too fragile, not resistant to heat, not resistant to cold, not resistant to radiation. Lifespans are short, strength is low, and so on. So can we use silicon, tin, sodium, iron, aluminum, mercury, and other metallic atoms, and according to the building principles of organisms, from the 'bottom up' build high-strength nanomachines or nanolife?

After thirty years of exploration, I think I've created the simplest template for tin-sodium-silicon life.

★　　★　　★

Perhaps I did have the potential for scientific wisdom. I was immediately drawn to this simple article. It dissected the complex, boundless universe, easily extracted a clear logical thread. Especially the short, plain announcement at the end. Even a scientific outsider could feel its weight. A template for silicon-tin-sodium life! A new form of life that was high-strength, completely different from existing life-forms! I concluded that the estate I would receive must have something to do with this.

I immediately called Mr. He, and straightforwardly asked him, "Mr. He, what does that silicon-tin-sodium life look like? Where is it?"

Mr. He laughed on the phone and said, "Ms. Sha's guess was completely right! She said you would call. And said if you didn't, I could end the work. She didn't misread you. Come, I will take you there. The new life is in her private lab."

★　　★　　★

Ms. Sha's lab was on a small hill on the outskirts, a moderate bungalow in which two workers were quietly at their tasks. Mr. He showed me equipment in every room, patiently explaining. He said, "Having been Ms. Sha's lawyer for ten years, I've become a part-time nano-scientist." He led me into the core of the lab – the so-called life smelter. Surrounded by thick brick walls, we opened the solid heatproof door. A searing blast of air blew against our faces. Inside was a big smelter about a hundred square meters in volume. Dark-red liquid metals slowly surged inside it. I couldn't see the heating installation, which was probably hidden under the smelter. Though the air was distorted by the strong heat above the smelter, I could see a huge metal engraving on the opposite wall, which was, of course, of Ms. Sha. She looked down silently at the boiling smelter, her eyes loving and desolate like the primordial goddess Nüwa looking at the little human beings she had just kneaded with clay.

Mr. He told me this was a molten mixture of low-melting-point metals (tin, lead, sodium, mercury, etc.). In it were scattered high-melting-point materials like silicon, iron, chromium, manganese, molybdenum, etc. The size of the high-melting-point materials was nanoscale, and in the molten mixture they remained in a solid state. Amoebas – the new form of life Ms. Sha talked about – formed by taking these nanoscale solid-phase atom clusters as their skeleton and adhering to some liquid-phase metals. The smelter's temperature stayed within the range of $490\pm85°C$ all year long, which was the most suitable living environment for the amoebas. "Now, let's see their true faces."

He pressed a button, and on the side wall an image appeared. The image was probably taken by X-ray chromatography. It went through layers of liquid metals and stopped at a tiny alien body. Seen with chromaticity, it was almost indistinguishable from the liquid metals around it. Looking closely, I could see it had a membrane wrapping around it. It wiggled laboriously, moved slowly through the slimy liquid metals, its shape changing constantly, leaving behind a vaguely visible trail. But the trail soon disappeared.

"This is the amoeba Ms. Sha created, some kind of nanomachine or nanolife. Self-organizing activity at this scale integrates the two concepts of machine and life into one," Mr. He said. "It's hundreds of nanometers in dimension, can replicate itself, can metabolize with the outside through the membrane. But it eats food just to provide materials, especially solid-phase elements, to repair its body, not to provide energy. It actually feeds on light. On its membrane there are countless photoelectric converters which propel its internal metal 'muscles' to move with electric energy."

I gazed closely at the screen, mumbled, "Unbelievable, really unbelievable!"

"Yeah, completely different from life on Earth. The way it dies and reproduces is even stranger. An amoeba's lifespan is only twelve to sixteen days. During this period, they wiggle, eat, grow, then curl into a ball to harden their shell. In the hardened shell, matter 'explodes' and reassembles into several small amoebas. As for how information passes to the next generation during the explosion, Ms. Sha was unable to figure out before her death."

"They reproduce fast?"

"No, when amoebas in the liquid metals reach a certain density, they stop reproducing. I think the inherent reason is that suitable solid-phase materials run out. Look! Look! The camera just captured an exploding amoeba!"

On the screen, the shell of an amoeba had clearly hardened. Within the slowly surging liquid metals, its shape remained unchanged. A moment later, from the hardened shell, a streak of electric light burst out, then the matter inside the shell churned violently then soon calmed down and split into four small balls. The shell cracked, and four small amoebas wiggled their bodies, slowly swimming away in four directions.

I stared, stunned. In my heart a majestic bell was chiming. It was the deep, vigorous sound of nature, the rhythm of the universe. I remembered many scientists had talked about extreme environments for life, but who would have thought in 500 liquid metals, there would be a form of metal life, a form of life that didn't depend on water and air? How difficult the synthesis of this template for life was. It was work that should take God a billion years. How could Aunt Sha create it with only several decades of research? I looked up at her statue, and my heart filled with reverence. Mr. He closed the heatproof door, led me back to the office.

He said, "This life is pretty crude, the efficiency of its internal photoelectric converter is lower than a normal solar panel. Ms. Sha said after generations of evolution they will be as sophisticated as terrestrial life, but that would be something that certainly takes hundreds of millions of years. In five years since I took this place over, at least, those slowpokes haven't changed at all."

I asked, "Is this a private lab? Can't you get support from the government?"

"Right. As for the reason – I think you can guess. From the pragmatic point of view, I'm afraid this research will have no value at all for tens of millions of years. When Ms. Sha started her research, she'd originally hoped to create some kind of nanorobots resistant to high temperatures with an immediate use. She created these small amoebas but never found a practical application for them. After Ms. Sha passed away, she entrusted me to use her wealth to keep the life smelter running, but the money is about to run out."

He looked at me. I looked at him. We both knew what this sentence implied. What Ms. Sha had left me was actually a negative asset. If I accepted it, I would have to put lots of money into the smelter until my wealth was used up. Then…what next? Search for another fool as easily moved as I was?

But regardless, I couldn't refuse. These creatures, though crude, had moved away from the material world. They were something unique, created accidently by a skillful hand. If they could survive, they may recreate the splendidness of terrestrial life. How could I let them die because of me? The scientific bent of my childhood was suddenly renewed, like a pool of spring water quietly accumulating melted snow. I sighed. "Mr. He, declare the will."

"Ah, no," Mr. He said smiling. "According to Ms. Sha's request, there is a second procedure. Please read this letter first."

He took out a sealed letter from his leather bag, solemnly gave it to me. I took it suspiciously and opened it. The letter was handwritten with two simple lines, but the content was earth-shattering:

To my legatee:

Real life can't be bred in pens. In the solar system there happens to be a suitable place for it to breed freely – Mercury.

I was stunned. I stared tongue-tied, the arteries in my temples pounding. That cunning lawyer looked at me with a half-smile. He must have foreseen the shock this letter would give me. Indeed, compared to these two lines, was anything I had seen before of consequence?

★   ★   ★

Planet Shawu
The Holy Book: Genesis

The Great God Shawu created the Shawu People. Shawu was the only child of Father Star and lived on Father Star's third star. The star had once been blue, soaked in water. Eight hundred and three million, forty thousand years ago, God came to Planet Shawu. He saw Planet Shawu was good. The light was good. The sky and earth were good. God said: Good sky and good earth, how come there are no living things? God stretched his body. Fifty-seven billion nine hundred million steps above, he scooped hot soup from Father Star's smelter. In the soup were small living things. He sprayed the soup all over the earth of Planet Shawu. Eight-hundred-and-three million, forty thousand years later, the small living things grew into the Shawu People.

The God Shawu completed the work and lost Father Star's affection. Father Star said angrily: How dare you do this work for me? Father Star punished Blue Star with a white lightsword, destroyed Shawu's house. Shawu fled Blue Star in a Holy Car to a place where Father Star could not shine.

The God Shawu left his incarnation on Planet Shawu. Shawu Incarnate slept in the frozen ice on the North Pole, hiding from Father Star. Every 41,520,000 years, Shawu Incarnate woke up, patrolled Planet Shawu in the Holy Car. He pitied the Shawu People's ignorance, blew intelligence into the Shawu People's eyes and light orifices.

God told the Shawu People:

My children, I adore you. You are blessed. I created your bodies stronger than mine, do not fear Father Star's punishment; you feed on light, do not feed on life; you have bodies made of metal, not bodies made of clay and water; your bodies have five orifices, not nine orifices; you have no male-female distinction, are exempted from original sin. You are blessed.

God told the Shawu People:

I hid God's spirit and wisdom in the Holy Book, when will you understand it? Those who understand the Holy Book can find the Holy Palace in frozen ice. God will wake up and take you to receive Father Star's great grace.

★   ★   ★

A Sketch of Mercury

Mercury is the closest planet to the Sun, 0.378 astronomical units away – that is, 57.89 million kilometers. Sunlight fiercely pours down on Mercury, making it the hottest planet in the solar system. Its daytime temperature can reach 450°. In a place called the Caloris Basin, the highest temperature once reached 973°. Since it lacks atmospheric insulation, its night-time temperature can be as low as -173°. On this planet so close to the Sun, ice actually exists. It is distributed on Mercury's two poles, and all year long maintains a temperature below -60°.

Mercury's mass is one twenty-fifth of Earth's. Its magnetic field strength is one hundredth of Earth's. Its revolution period is 87.96 days, so 1,000 Earth years equal 4,153 Mercury years. Mercury's rotation period is 58.646 days, which is two-thirds of its revolution period. This is because the Sun's gravity slows down its rotation speed, resulting in a certain amount of gravitational locking.

Mercury's landscape is similar to the Moon's. Everywhere are arid, rocky deserts and craters formed from the impact of meteorites (the Caloris Basin was formed after the impact of a huge meteorite). Common on the terrain is a kind of tongue-shaped cliff that stretches for hundreds of kilometers. This topography has formed due to the contraction of Mercury's core. Mercury's high temperature makes some low-melting-point metals melt and collect in depressions and cracks of rocks, which form widely distributed lakes of liquid metal. Because Mercury lacks oxidizing gases, they always maintain a metal-state existence. When evening comes, liquid metals condense into glassy crystals. As sunlight returns with high temperatures after 58.6 Earth days, the metal lakes rapidly thaw.

Such a harsh natural environment is undoubtedly a forbidden zone for life – but what if it isn't?

★   ★   ★

"Mad," I murmured nervously. "Really mad, only a mad man would be so whimsical."

Mr. He looked at me quietly. "But historical progress always requires one or two mad men."

"You worship Ms. Sha?"

"Maybe not exactly worship, but I admire her."

With a dry laugh I said, "Now I know the contents of this estate. It's astonishingly negative. The legatee has to use his own wealth to keep the life smelter running, until what year only God knows. Not only that, he has to find a place to release these metal creatures to solve this problem once and for all, but to do this will take at least tens of billions of yuan, and one to two hundred years. Whoever accepts this estate would rightfully be considered mad."

Mr. He smiled and simply repeated, "The world needs a few mad men."

"Fine, now please forget about your role as a lawyer. You, my friend, tell me. Should I accept this estate?"

Mr. He laughed. "You certainly know how I feel."

"Why should I accept it? Is there any benefit to me?"

"It gives you an opportunity that comes once every ten thousand years: to do something unprecedented. You will be one of the earliest ancestors of Mercurian life, they will always remember you."

I said with a bitter smile, "To make Mercurian life evolve to such an extent that they can thank me would take at least one hundred million years. The return period for this investment is too long."

Mr. He smiled, making no reply.

"Besides, it's not just a matter of money. Going to Mercury and releasing this life – would Earthlings accept it? After all, it does Earthlings no good at all, perhaps even creates another competitor for them."

"I trust you, trust Ms. Sha's vision. You have the ability and determination to overcome all difficulties."

I called out as if stung by a scorpion: "*I'll* overcome? You're sure I'll accept this estate?"

The cunning lawyer patted my shoulder. "You will. You're already thinking about future work. So I can announce the will, or would you like to talk it over with your wife again?"

Six days later, we held a small official ceremony. My wife and I signed and accepted the estate.

I had agonized over the decision for six days – panic-stricken, sighing and groaning. I told myself only a mad man would willingly don this shackle, but the siren's singing had lured me. Even stuffing up my ears didn't help. Four billion years ago, in the Earth's ocean, the first self-replicable protein micelle was born. It was crude, insignificant. If there really was a God, perhaps he too wouldn't have expected that such a small thing would evolve into splendid terrestrial life. Now, due to an accident of chance, a new form of life was thrown into my arms. It had been created by a goddess. Whether or not it could flourish on Mercury depended on my decision. This responsibility was too heavy. I dared not easily accept it, dared not easily pass it up. Even if I was willing to make the sacrifice, what about my wife and son? I had no right to drag them into a life of toil.

Wifey had been pleasantly silent about it, until one night she gently said, "Since you can't pass on it, just accept it."

She said it very casually, like it was a decision about buying discount cabbage. I stared at her. "Then it— You know what this means?"

"It means a life of toil for us. But if one can't live according to one's will and interests, what's the point of living? I know if you give it up now, when you are old you will definitely regret it. Your conscience will suffer your whole life. So accept it."

At that moment I looked at her bright smile, tears trickling down.

She still wore a bright smile when she accompanied me to accept Aunt Sha's estate. Mr. He was very serious that day, his eyes full of desolation. I thought jokingly that this old fox had set the trap step by step, finally coaxing me into his snare, and was now probably having a guilty conscience. The two workers at the Sha Wu Lab cheerfully stood behind Mr. He. In the room was another invisible participant, Ms. Sha Wu: right above the life smelter. Through the air quivering from the high temperature, through the thick walls, she was looking at us. I thought her eyes must be full of satisfaction.

My journalist friend Ma Wanzhuang, who I had invited along, clenched his teeth. "Mad! All mad!" he kept grumbling in a low voice. "A dead, mad woman, a young, mad couple, and an old lawyer acting mad. Yizhe, Tian Ya, you'll soon regret this!"

I smiled tolerantly, ignored him. Despite his objections, he still carried out my request to leak the news to the media. I thought this required social approval as well as social support. So let's let the plan and society meet as soon as possible.

★　　★　　★

After good Ma leaked the news, I immediately received a call from a friend. He said excitedly, "I read the news! Metal life, breeding life on Mercury, this is an April Fools' Day joke, right?"

I said, "No, it's not. Actually, that report was supposed to come out on the first of April, but I suddenly realized the first of April was April Fools' Day and so notified the press to postpone it four days."

"Postponed it right to the fifth of April, Qingming Festival, so the report must be fake news!"

I smiled bitterly and slowly put down the phone.

Afterward, public opinion slowly grew serious. Of course the majority were opposed. *Whimsical! Human affairs on Earth aren't finished yet, but he still wants to breed some kind of Mercurian life!* There were also people who were more understanding, saying as long as it didn't interfere with human interests, one could do whatever one wanted to do, as long as one didn't spend the taxpayers' money.

Amid this debate, I settled down and fully committed to taking over the lab. I used my business acumen to cut down the lab's spending to the minimum. All in all, my wealth could keep it running for thirty years. The life-form was very strong, could tolerate a high temperature up to 1,000° and a low temperature down to absolute zero. When the temperature was below 320°, they became dormant. So even if the exhaustion of funds required temporarily extinguishing the smelter, there wouldn't be any real problems. It would just temporarily halt the life-form's evolution.

But I wouldn't allow the life smelter to be extinguished under my watch. I wouldn't fall short of Aunt Sha's high standards.

In the evening, my wife and I often went to the life smelter, looked at the dark-red surging liquid metals, or brought up images and watched those little wiggling lives. They were simple, crude lives, but they had transcended the category of material. A hundred million years later, a billion years later, who could say what they would evolve into? Looking at them, we felt something, like a small life forming in her belly.

Ma was a true friend, and facilitated a TV debate for me. "Either you persuade society, or you let society persuade you."

My wife, Mr. He, and I sat in the studio, facing CCTV cameras as spotlights baked our faces which exuded a thin layer of sweat. On the other side of the studio sat seven experts. They were the judges of this ethical court, but their basis was not Chinese criminal law, it was the doctrines of bioethics. Under the stage were some one hundred audience members, mostly university students.

The host, Geng Yue, said smiling, "Before the program begins, let me apologize to everyone. This debate should have been held on Mercury, but the station couldn't afford all your travel expenses. Besides, without air-conditioning, it would be too hot."

The audience laughed with comprehension.

"'Releasing Life on Mercury' is something everyone is familiar with. I won't go into the background. Now, I'd like to invite audience members to ask questions, and Mr. Chen Yizhe will answer."

A young man hurried forward. "Mr. Chen, to cultivate this Mercurian life – are there any benefits to human beings?"

I said calmly, "At the moment there aren't, and I think in one hundred million years there still may not be."

"Then I don't understand, taking such pains to do something with no benefit to human beings – why?"

I looked at my wife and Mr. He. They both gave me an encouraging look, so I took a deep breath and said, "Let me take this issue a little further. You know, life is essentially selfish. Each individual strives in a resource-limited environment for his own share in order to preserve himself and pass down his genes. But nature is a great magician, it extracts nobility from selfish individual behaviors. Organisms discover in competition that in many situations cooperation is much more beneficial. To unicellular organisms, cells are hostile to one another. But when unicellular organisms developed into multicellular organisms, all the cells turned from enemies to friends, and cooperated with one another through a division of labor. This placed them, or it, in a more favorable position in their environment. Therefore, multicellular organisms developed and thrived. In short, in organic evolution, the tendency to cooperate is everywhere and grows stronger. For example, the scope of human cooperation has extended from individual to family, to community, to nation, to different races, even to wildlife beyond human beings. Over the course of these processes, life, step-by-step, further transcends its self-interest, forms a larger and larger community with shared interests. I think the next step for human transcendence will be integration with alien life. That's my motive for exhausting my wealth to cultivate Mercurian life. I hope some kind of civilized life will evolve there and become a brother to human beings. Otherwise Earthlings would be too lonely in the universe," I said. "In fact, just a month ago I didn't have these insights. Ms. Sha changed me. Standing in front of Professor Sha's life smelter, looking at those small wiggling creatures in the surging, dark-red liquid metals, I often get a parental feeling."

A middle-aged man said mockingly, "This feeling is certainly wonderful, but you can't just, for such a feeling, breed a potential competitor to human beings. I think that since the life survives at high temperatures, its evolutionary process should be very fast. Perhaps they will catch up with human beings in ten million years."

I laughed. "Don't forget, terrestrial life began four billion years ago. If you worry terrestrial life can't compete with its junior, which started four billion years later, you surely lack confidence."

Geng Yue said, "Right, a four-billion-year-old grandpa, a ten-million-year-old grandkid – too distant even for love, how could they compete?"

The audience chuckled. A woman asked, "Mr. Chen Yizhe, I'm a supporter. How do you plan to fulfill Ms. Sha's wishes?"

"No idea," I admitted honestly. "At least, so far I have no idea. My wealth can keep the life smelter running for thirty years, but what about the next thirty years? And how to scrape together enough money to release them on Mercury? I have no idea at all. Anyway, I will do my best. If this generation can't get it done, then it will be left to the next generation."

The hearing lasted almost two hours. The seven experts or the seven judges said nothing throughout, just listened seriously, occasionally noting down one or two points on paper. One couldn't deduce their inclination from their expression. In the end, Geng Yue walked to the center of the studio and said, "I believe the interrogation has been quite sufficient. Now experts, please give your opinions. Regarding 'Releasing Life on Mercury,' do you approve, disapprove, or abstain?"

The seven experts wrote quickly on small blackboards, then simultaneously held up the blackboards. On each of them was the same word: Abstain. The audience stirred.

Geng Yue scratched his head and said, "So unanimous! I wonder if the seven judges are telepathic? Mr. Zhang, please tell us why you hold this attitude."

Mr. Zhang, who sat on the first seat, said briefly, "This matter far exceeds our time. We can't use our current perspective to judge things in the future. So abstention is the most sensible choice."

*　　*　　*

Shawu's Holy Palace, buried in the ice sheets of Planet Shawu's North Pole, would soon appear through the thick, green, frozen ice. The faint light of the Holy Palace was vaguely visible. Priest Hu Baba had entered a state of possessed frenzy, radiating a powerful emotional field. The light orifices on his chest flickered violently as he recited prayers from the Old Testament and the New Testament. The icebreaker whooshed, advancing forward step by step. Hu Baba prostrated amid white ice scraps, worshiping Shawu Incarnate from afar. His head and tail knocked heavily on the ground, sent chunks of ice flying about.

The scientist Tu Lala stood behind him, watching expressionlessly. His assistant, Qi Kaka, carrying two backpacks containing four energy boxes, stood next to him.

The 'Holy Palace Exploration Action' had been pushed through by Tu Lala. He was already a hundred and fifty years old, and hoped that before the 'explosion' he would find the Holy Palace repeatedly mentioned in the Holy Book – or confirm it didn't exist. He had thought the Church would strongly oppose it, but he was wrong. The Church's response was very gentle, even quite cooperative. They had approved this expedition, just sent Priest Hu Baba to supervise.

Tu Lala thought, *Perhaps the Church firmly believes the Holy Book to be true?* The Holy Book said Shawu Incarnate slept in the frozen ice of the North Pole; the Holy Book said those who understood the Holy Book could find the Holy Palace in frozen ice, awake God, receive grace. For hundreds of years countless believers who thought they understood the Holy Book had scrambled to make a pilgrimage to the North Pole, but none came back alive. Now the Church may want to use the power of science to prove the Holy Book is true.

At this thought, Tu Lala couldn't help but smile. For the past five centuries science was getting stronger and stronger, could almost stand up to the Church. For example, the devout Priest Hu Baba in front of him had benefited from science. His tail was also installed with an energy box, an energy box invented by science. Without it, he who 'fed on light' couldn't have reached the lightless North Pole.

On the way to the North Pole, Tu Lala saw countless drop-dead – generations of devout believers, which according to the teachings of the Holy Book had followed the holy ropes from the holy altars to the North Pole in search of the God Shawu's Holy Palace. As they slowly moved away from Father Star's illumination, their physical energy gradually drained, and finally they collapsed. Regarding these drop-dead, the Church had always been deeply reticent. Because before dying those people hadn't found a death partner, hadn't exploded, their souls would not reincarnate. This was the first major sin of the three sins in the holy commandments (*Though shalt not drop dead, shalt not believe in false gods, shalt not touch holy altars or holy ropes*). But these people were also respectable martyrs. Should the Church damn them or praise them?

Tu Lala decided that when he returned from the North Pole, he would collect these drop-dead, pair them with death partners, and let them explode in light. It's not that Tu Lala believed in the reincarnation of the soul, he just couldn't leave those bodies forever exposed to the wilderness.

★   ★   ★

The icebreaker was still whooshing. Now it was certain that ahead was the Holy Palace. From the frozen ice forty holy ropes stuck out, converged, and extended toward it. The strong, white light emitted from the Holy Palace, made the frozen ice bright and shiny. Priest Hu Baba asked the workers to stop. He led the crowd in the final worship, praying with reverence and awe. In the crowd only Tu Lala and Qi Kaka did not prostrate. The priest stared at them sullenly, cursed in his heart: *You pagans who don't respect the God Shawu. God's punishment will soon fall upon you!*

Qi Kaka dared not look directly at the priest, dared not look directly at his mentor. His emotional field trembled, two light orifices flickering faintly as if asking his mentor, or as if asking himself: *Shawu Incarnate does exist? What the Holy Book said is really the truth? The Holy Palace mentioned in the Holy Book is right ahead?*

Tu Lala pretended not to see his assistant's wavering, and instead turned around with a desolate look. He had known all along that Qi Kaka wasn't a firm atheist, always wavered between science and religion. Tu Lala himself had deserted religion a hundred years ago and gathered under him a large group of radical young scientists. They firmly believed in the theory of evolution proposed by Tu Lala a hundred years ago, believed that the Shawu People had evolved from lower creatures (this had been proven by many remains of ancient life), firmly believed that the Holy Book was full of lies. But after raising the flag of rebellion to religion for a hundred years, Tu Lala himself had secretly returned to the Holy Book.

He didn't believe in religion, but he believed the Holy Book (meaning the Old Testament of the Holy Book), because in the Holy Book there was a mixture of strange records, and these records were often verified by later scientific developments. For example, the Holy Book said: *Planet Shawu was Father Star's first star, Blue Star was Father Star's third star.* These sacred words had been recited by people for thousands of years without ever knowing their implications. Not until the emergence of telescopes stimulated the development of astronomy did scientists know that both Planet Shawu and Blue Star were Father Star's planets. Their order was exactly what the Holy Book said!

Another example was chapter thirty-nine of the Old Testament of the Holy Book, which specified the calibration of Planet Shawu's temperature, with the freezing point of water at zero degrees Celsius, and the boiling point of water at a hundred degrees Celsius. However, Planet Shawu's life had never had contact with water over their hundreds of millions of years of evolution! Only in recent times had scientists inferred that in the South Pole and North Pole ice existed. Then why did the Holy Book make such specifications? And where did these specifications come from?

Was there really a Great God who penetrated the universe and knew the past and the future?

Besides, the twenty holy altars around Planet Shawu's equator had been an unsolved mystery for scientists. On those holy altars, black panels slowly rotated tirelessly, always facing Father Star. From each holy altar, two holy ropes stuck out, extending all the way to the invisible north. The Holy Book sternly warned that the Shawu People mustn't touch them. Those who didn't obey this commandment would be struck down and only revive after prostrating and repenting. Tu Lala didn't believe this myth. He thought the black panels on the holy altars were probably some kind of photoelectric converters in the way the skin of the Planet Shawu creatures could carry out photoelectric conversion. The problem was: who had left behind these technologically advanced devices? Given the Shawu People's scientific development, they wouldn't be able to invent them even in five hundred years!

It was based on this belief that he had strived to push through an exploration to the Holy Palace. Now it was certain that the Holy Palace existed. The mysterious and ethereal Holy Palace of the Holy Book was right ahead. If Shawu Incarnate did live here...Tu Lala couldn't wait to meet him.

*　　*　　*

The last layer of the ice wall crashed down, and the stately Holy Palace suddenly appeared. It was a hall built of ice. It scattered uniform white light. The dome was very high. The hall was quite empty, with no stray objects. Only at the center of the hall was parked a— the Holy Car! The Holy Book mentioned it, countless legends depicted it. The historical records of 3,120 years ago spoke of it. It was precisely Shawu Incarnate's car. The Holy Car was covered with black panels, exactly the same as the panels on the holy altars. Below were four wheels. The top of the Holy Car was transparent. Shawu Incarnate looked strange, lying inside.

Shawu Incarnate was really there! People outside the cave couldn't help but swarm in. Led by Hu Baba, the crowd prostrated on the ground together, knocked their heads and tails on the ground. Everyone's light orifices prayed frantically: Supreme Great God Shawu, almighty Shawu Incarnate, your people prostrate before you, please bless us!

Only Tu Lala remained standing. The prostrating crowd included his assistant. It seemed that Qi Kaka's prayer was wilder than that of the others. The combined emotional field of the crowd struck Tu Lala. He felt a nearly uncontrollable urge to prostrate on the ground, but in the end restrained himself, hurried forward, and carefully examined Shawu Incarnate's distinguished face.

Shawu Incarnate reclined in the Holy Car, looking strange but stately. He was similar but different from the Shawu People. He had a head, a mouth, arms and hands, two eyes, a torso; but his tail was split. The ends of the split tail had toes. His body had five strange protrusions: on the front of his head there was a long protrusion with two holes under it; on either side of the head were two flat protrusions, each with a hole; where the tail split there was a column-like protrusion, with a hole on it. *But on his chest there are no light orifices*, Tu Lala thought with surprise. *Without information-transmitting light orifices, how did Shawus communicate with each other? Were they all mutes?* Better put this question aside for now. He first wanted to verify the mostly easily verifiable record in the Holy Book. He carefully counted the orifices on Shawu's body. Right, exactly nine orifices, not the Shawu People's five.

The Holy Book was again right. Tu Lala stood, stunned, shocked, and elated inside.

He again carefully observed the inside of the Holy Car. In the front of the car sat a platinum statue, a bust. Like the God Shawu, the head had seven orifices, but the head of this statue had long hair, and the face was obviously different. *Who was this? Perhaps the death partner of the God Shawu?* He suddenly saw something more shocking: a Holy Book! The Holy Book was brand new, but the type on the cover was ancient handwriting, the letters used by the Shawu People's ancestors 3,000 years before. In Tu Lala's lifetime, in order to defeat the Church, he had once seriously studied the Holy Book, knew clearly its origin, editions, and errors. He saw at first glance that this was the second edition of the Holy Book, containing only the Old Testament but not the New Testament. It was published 3,120 years ago. This edition of the Holy Book was now extremely rare.

Hu Baba also saw the Holy Book. His prayers and prostrations became nearly frantic. When he lifted his head, he saw Tu Lala had already opened the car door. Holding the Holy Book, Hu Baba immediately emitted two strong beams from his light orifices, which scorched Tu Lala's back. Tu Lala turned around, astonished.

Hu Baba shouted madly, "Blasphemers are not allowed to touch the Holy Book!" He shoved the scientist aside, devoutly held up the Holy Book, and said viciously, "Now you still dare say God doesn't exist? You blasphemer, Great God will definitely punish you!" He ignored Tu Lala, turned to the crowd and said, "I'm going back to ask the Pope to welcome back the God Shawu's holy body. Before I return, everybody must leave the Holy Palace!"

He held the book and took the lead in crawling out. The crowd followed with reverence and awe. Qi Kaka glanced guiltily at his teacher, lowered his head, and finally followed.

When Hu Baba walked to the mouth of the cave, he saw the scientist staying inside and said harshly, "You must leave the Holy Palace. Shawu Incarnate will not welcome a blasphemer."

Tu Lala didn't want to argue with him, so his light orifices peacefully sent a message: "You'd better go back. I won't hinder you, but stay here…seek advice from Shawu Incarnate."

Hu Baba's light orifices emitted two strong beams: "No way!"

Tu Lala said ironically, "Priest Hu Baba, why suddenly lose your temper? Don't forget, you found the Holy Palace with the help of science. If you force me to go back, take the energy box off your tail. That's also blasphemous, the Holy Book never mentioned it."

The priest was stunned. What Tu Lala had said was correct. No chapter of the Holy Book or other religious stories ever mentioned this kind of energy box. It had been invented by blasphemers, but it was very useful. In this lightless polar region, without an energy box, he would have quickly run out of energy, died, and dropped dead, unable to reincarnate. He dared not remove the energy box, just furiously turned around and crawled away.

★　　★　　★

The evening after the TV debate, Mr. He had a dinner at my house. During the meal he told me, "Yizhe, you actually won. Regarding this matter, legal 'inaction' is in fact silent approval and support. Now nobody is stopping you – go all out!"

He had completed Aunt Sha Wu's request and was feeling very cheerful. He got really drunk and left beaming. Then the phone rang. I picked it up, but the screen was still dark. The other side hadn't turned theirs on. They asked, "Are you Mr. Chen Yizhe? My name is Hong. I'm interested in Releasing Life on Mercury."

His voice was hoarse and dry, very unpleasant to the ear. I could even say the voice aroused physical displeasure in me. But I responded politely, "Mr. Hong, thank you for your support. Did you watch today's TV program?"

He had no intention to converse, just said coldly, "Tomorrow, please come to my humble abode for a meeting. Ten in the morning." He gave his address then hung up.

Wifey asked me who'd called, what he had said. I hesitated. "It's a Mr. Hong. He said he was interested in Releasing Life on Mercury, ordered me to meet him tomorrow. Yes, a direct order. He unilaterally decided on tomorrow's meeting, didn't discuss it with me at all."

I had a bad impression of Mr. Hong. A few words exchanged were enough to show how bossy he was. Not only that, his tone was icy. But I decided I had better go. After all, this was the first stranger to express support for me.

Later, I found out how correct this decision had been.

*　　*　　*

Mr. Hong's house was in the suburbs, a rather large estate. Its age could not have been great, but the architecture completely conformed to the ancient Chinese architectural style – upturned eaves and bucket arches, gray bricks and tiles, winding paths and small pavilions. The servant ushering me in was dressed entirely in black. Respectful and cautious, silent and reserved, his manner was chilly. I silently surveyed the surroundings, and the discontent in my heart increased.

The main hall was very large, the lighting gloomy. The gray-tiled ground was as slippery as terrazzo flooring. The large, tall hall had no luxurious furnishings and seemed empty. At the center of the hall was parked a mobility car. A short, fifty-year-old man leaned back in the car. He was quite disabled, hunchbacked and hollow-chested, head tucked to his neck. His facial features were too ugly to be looked at directly. His legs and feet were congenitally malformed, slender and feeble, hanging from the wheelchair. The servant who ushered me in quietly withdrew, and I thought this man must be Mr. Hong.

I walked up and held a hand out to the host. He looked at me, having no intention of holding my hand. I had to withdraw awkwardly.

He said, "So sorry, I'm a disabled man and have difficulty walking. Must trouble you to come over."

The words were spoken very politely, but his tone remained cold and stiff. His face was like a slab of stone, with no trace of a smile. In front of him, inside this gloomy building, I had a feeling like suffocation. But still I said cordially, "Not at all, it's nothing. May I ask you, sir, about Releasing Life on Mercury – what else would you like to know?"

"No need," he said straightforwardly. "I already know everything. You just need to tell me how much money it will take to get it done."

I was slightly hesitant. "I asked several experts to make preliminary estimates...about twenty billion yuan. Of course, this is just a rough estimate."

He said flatly, "Let me solve the money problem."

I was shocked, thought that he must have mistaken twenty billion for twenty million. Of course, even if it was twenty million, this was already quite generous.

Not to hurt his pride, I said tactfully, "Thank you so much! Thank you for your extraordinary generosity. Of course, I don't expect the money issue to be solved once and for all. Twenty billion is an astronomical figure, and twenty million gets us well on the way."

He said expressionlessly, "You didn't hear wrong. Twenty billion, not twenty million. My wealth is not enough, but I think the money need not be in place all at once. If gradually allocated over ten years, then, with interest, my wealth should be enough."

I suddenly discovered the man's identity: the billionaire Hong Qiyan! He was a very mysterious figure. I'd long heard that he was highly disabled, extremely ugly, and so never appeared in any media. The only people who could see him were seven or eight confidants. His reputation was not good. I heard he was extremely business-oriented, courageous, resourceful, and bold. He ran his business empire profitably, but his methods were vicious and merciless, always sending his competitors to their deaths. I also heard that because of his ugly looks, in his youth he had not won any woman's love, which bred a vindictive mentality. A few years ago he had put out a classified. Female applicants were to come to his house at night for a meeting and leave the next morning. Such strange rules inevitably caused suspicion. Later, I heard all the female applicants had received a considerable amount of money as a gift, which gave weight to the suspicions. But such doubts may have been unfair.

Of the female applicants there was a young and beautiful female lawyer, called Yin maybe. She applied, because she admired Hong Qiyan's talent, not his wealth. It's said that after arriving, the host and she faced each other the whole night. No words or touching. In the morning he gave her a sum of money as a gift and asked her to go home. Yin threw the money right in his face. This led to the two's friendship. Although they didn't become husband and wife, they became close friends who were comfortable with informality.

Although he was a billionaire, the generous act of donating his entire wealth made me suspicious, and the damning stories about him added weight to my suspicions. Perhaps he had some personal agenda? Perhaps, due to his unjust fate, he had turned his anger toward all human beings, wanted to take revenge via Releasing Life on Mercury? Although the twenty billion in funding was a rare chance that could only come once, I still decided to first ask him if there were any additional conditions.

Mr. Hong's sharp eyes saw through my thoughts. In front of him I felt naked, which made me furious. He said flatly, "My sponsorship has one condition."

Here it comes, I thought, then said cautiously, "May I ask what the condition is?"

"I want to be a crew member of the spaceship that releases the life."

So that's it! Such a simple request! I couldn't help but look at his legs. In my heart strong sympathy suddenly rose. All prior discontent was swept away. A highly disabled person spending twenty billion yuan to buy the freedom to fly away from Earth – the cost was too great! On the other hand, it indicated how cruel confinement to a disabled body was to him. I said softly, "Of course. As long as your body can endure space travel."

"Please don't worry. This broken machine of mine is very durable. May I ask how long it will take to complete Releasing Life on Mercury?"

"Not long. I've consulted many experts, they all said traveling to Mercury isn't technically difficult. If the funds are sufficient it could be realized in fifteen to twenty years."

He said flatly, "Not a problem to have the money ready. You speed up the pace as best you can. Try to do it within fifteen years. What's the name of the spaceship?"

"Please name it. You have so generously sponsored this project, you have the right."

Mr. Hong didn't decline. "Let's call it *Auntie*. A very tacky name, no?"

I thought a bit and understood the profound meaning of the name: it indicated that human beings were just the elders of Mercurian life, not their parents. At the same time it implied commemoration of Aunt Sha. "Great!" I said. "Let's go with that name!"

He took out a checkbook from the side pocket of the mobility car, wrote *fifty million*, signed, and gave it to me. "This is initial funding. Set up a foundation as soon as possible and start working! Right, and please remember to save space for me in the spaceship, about the size of a stretch Lincoln. I'll find someone else to make a car suitable for Mercury's terrain." He added bitterly, "Can't be helped. I can't walk on Mercury."

Softly I said, "Okay, I'll make sure of it. But...." I hesitated. "May I venture to ask a question? I mean, you put all your wealth into releasing Mercurian life – for what? Just a trip to Mercury?"

"I think this is very interesting," he said flatly. "All my life I have only done things that interest me." He leaned forward slightly, indicating the end of the conversation.

*　　*　　*

From then on Mr. Hong's funds arrived continuously. The fire of passion was doused with the gasoline of money, which resulted in amazing productivity. By the end of that year, there were 15,000 people working on the spaceship *Auntie*. Regarding Releasing Life on Mercury, social and ethical objections never ceased, but it never became a real obstacle.

Mr. Hong never interfered with our work. But every month I made time to provide him with a progress update. After the spaceship design plan was drafted, I asked him to look it over.

Mr. Hong heard me out wordlessly and asked tersely, "Very good, any financial needs?"

At Mr. Hong's request, I kept his sponsorship strictly confidential. Only my wife and Mr. He knew the sponsor's name. Of course, this in fact could not be kept secret. *Auntie* needed tens of billions of yuan in funding. Individuals who could spare this amount of money could be counted on the fingers of one hand. Furthermore, Mr. Hong constantly auctioned off properties under his name, so the matter soon became an open secret.

Auntie was built methodically. The following year, whenever I went to Mr. Hong's house, I always met a beautiful woman. She had a tranquil beauty like a narcissus enveloped in thin mist, and her eyes and eyebrows carried a tender feeling. She was the lawyer, Yin. Her relationship with Mr. Hong was apparently very close. Every word and gesture of theirs showed deep mutual understanding. But it was, undoubtedly, a pure friendship, which Yin's frank gaze confirmed.

She was already married, with a three-year-old son.

When I reported progress to Mr. Hong, he didn't ask Yin to withdraw. Apparently, Yin had the right to know his secret. During conversations, Mrs. Yin always wore a smile at the corners of her mouth, listened quietly, and occasionally cut in with a question, mostly about the technical details of the spaceship's construction. I soon knew the purpose of this arrangement – she was responsible for building the car Mr. Hong would ride on Mercury.

One day Yin came to my office alone. That was the first one-on-one meeting I had with her. I invited her to sit down and asked my secretary to serve coffee while speculating about her reason for coming.

Yin said softly, "I would like to discuss the technical interface of the spaceship with you. You must have realized I'm leading secret research to develop the life support system Mr. Hong will use on Mercury."

I nodded. It didn't surprise me that she called the car a 'life support system.' To move around Mercury, which had no atmosphere, a temperature as high as 450°, and strong high-energy radiation, the car could certainly be considered a life support system. But what Yin said next was a shock.

"To be precise, its major feature is a device for quick freezing and unfreezing of the human body."

I jumped from the sofa and looked at her wide-eyed. What was Mr. Hong going to do with a quick-freezing device for the human body? Before I had always seen Mr. Hong's plan as a whimsical, difficult trip, but undoubtedly a short one. But a quick-freezing and unfreezing device for human body....

Under my terrified gaze, Mrs. Yin nodded. "Right, Mr. Hong plans to stay on Mercury forever, to watch over this life. He plans to freeze himself in Mercury's frozen ice, wake up every ten million years, for about a month each time, ride the car to inspect the evolutionary stage of the life, until several hundred million years later when 'human' civilization evolves on Mercury."

For a long time we exchanged desolate looks. I mumbled, "Why didn't you dissuade him? Letting him live alone on Mercury for hundreds of millions of years, isn't that cruel?"

She shook her head slightly. "Can't be dissuaded. If others could dissuade him, he wouldn't be Hong Qiyan. Besides, such a plan may not be a bad one for him."

"Why?"

Mrs. Yin sighed. "I'm afraid no one knows him better than I do. Fate has been so unfair to him, giving him an unattractive body but a brilliant mind. A malformed body may make for a malformed personality. His mind is dark, resentful of all normal people, but his nature is kind, born with a benevolent heart. He is a bundle of deformities, but a cocoon of benevolent love encompasses his desire for revenge. His business wrangling and ridicule of suitors are reflections of this contradiction. But these vengeful actions are mild, already diluted by his kind heart. But perhaps one day the desire for revenge will break through the barrier of love, then.... He himself is deeply aware of this, and so always has a fear of himself."

"A fear of himself?" I looked at her, puzzled.

She nodded, said confidently, "Right, he has a fear of his own dark side, even I can feel it. His generous sponsorship of Releasing Life on Mercury more or less reflects this contradictory attitude. On the one hand, he participates in the creation of a new form of life, which satisfies his kind heart; on the other hand, it's also a small act of vengeance against human beings. Think about it, after the Mercurian life he cares for evolves into a civilization, Mercurians will certainly see Hong Qiyan's disability as the standard and view regular Earthlings as abnormal. Right?"

Although my heart was heavy, I was amused by this fantastical scenario and broke into laughter.

Yin also showed ripples of a smile and went on, "Actually, thinking it through, his plan for the second half of his life is pretty good – live on the nearest neighbor to the Sun, live as long as the universe, and roam alone across the wasteland of Mercury to cultivate strange, new life. Each time he wakes up from the ten-million-year slumber, Mercurian life will have changed unpredictably. He will completely discard the convention and discipline, vulgarity and triviality, mess and chaos of Earth. Sometimes I really want to abandon everything, abandon my husband and child, accompany him to the end of the world – but I can't do it, that's why I will always be a mediocre person," she said, mocking herself in a desolate tone.

This incident made my heart very heavy. I even felt inexplicable resentment, just didn't know whom this resentment was aimed toward. But I knew more words would do no good. I remembered that within two hours of watching the TV debate, Mr. Hong had made the decision to donate all his wealth. A person with such a decisive attitude – who could dissuade him? I said in a muffled voice, "All right, let's fulfill his wish. Now, about the technical interface."

The next day Yin and I went together to see him. We calmly talked about the details of the life support system as if it was a plan we had long agreed upon.

Upon leaving, I couldn't help but say, "Mr. Hong, I admire you a lot. But when I decided to accept Aunt Sha's legacy, many people said I was crazy. Now I can see you are certainly crazier than me."

Mr. Hong gave a rare smile. "Thanks, this is the greatest compliment."

*   *   *

The crowd was gone. In the hall of the Holy Palace, Tu Lala was left alone. Without the distracting clamor, he could calm down to talk to Shawu Incarnate, mind-to-mind. He looked up at Shawu Incarnate's strange face for a long time, and his heart filled with reverence. The Holy Palace was found, Shawu Incarnate's holy body was found. Priests and believers were frantically happy. But they were wrong. Shawu Incarnate indeed existed. He indeed was the creator of life on Planet Shawu, but he wasn't God. He was a scientist from an alien star. Tu Lala had been thinking about it for many years, had long since reached this conclusion. The reverence he felt for Shawu Incarnate contained a deep feeling of closeness. Scientists' minds were always connected, regardless of which galaxy of the universe they lived in. They used the same mathematical language, same physical laws, same logical rules. So he felt there was a deep affinity between him and Shawu Incarnate.

He had figured out Shawu Incarnate's origin and experience: he came from the third star of Father Star (Blue Star), 803,040,000 years ago. (Why 803,040,000 years? He realized 803,040,000 Shawu years were equal to 10 million Blue Star years. Shawu had converted them according to the calendar of Mother Star.) Back then he had created a new form of life completely different from the life on Blue Star – hadn't created the Shawu People, but a kind of micro-organism – sowed them on Planet Shawu, then handed the evolutionary scepter back to nature. In order to take care of the life he had created, Shawu Incarnate left Mother Star and Mother Race, lived in Planet Shawu's frozen ice for 803,040,000 years. An incredibly long time. When he faced this barbarity alone, was he lonely? When he watched the micro-organisms slowly evolve, was he anxious? When he saw Planet Shawu's life finally evolve into civilized creatures, was he happy?

Judging by the fact that in his Holy Car there was a Holy Book from 3,000 years ago, he had awakened about 3,000 years before. Back then he must have discovered the Shawu People had a binary language, had writing. But back then the Shawu People had been very ignorant, their minds numbed by religion. He couldn't enlighten their minds with science, had to hide some useful information in the Holy Book to spread science in the form of religion.

The Holy Book said those who understand the Holy Book can find the Holy Palace. Then, Shawu Incarnate will wake up, take the Shawu People to receive great grace from Father Star. What was 'great grace'? It must be a vast, splendid scientific treasure. The Shawu People would advance tens, hundreds of thousands of years overnight, become the equals of God (Shawu Incarnate).

This prospect made Tu Lala very excited, so he started looking for instructions Shawu Incarnate had left behind. Since in the Holy Book Shawu Incarnate invited the Shawu People to come to the Holy Palace, since he promised to wake up then, he must have left a method for how to wake him up. Tu Lala searched, pondered, suddenly discovered a secret ice chamber. The door was sealed by ice, but the ice layer was very thin. He used his tail to break the ice door and carefully walked in. The ice chamber was piled with disks. They were thin. One side had a metallic sheen. What was it? His intuition told him it must be the knowledge Shawu Incarnate had prepared for the Shawu People, but how to extract the knowledge, he didn't know and couldn't figure it out no matter how he racked his brain. This wasn't strange. Highly developed technology was often stranger than magic.

But the painting on the wall he understood. It was a pretty crude painting. He guessed Shawu Incarnate might have used his hand to paint it – a painting of a Shawu person pointing fingers at the two light orifices on their chest. Next to the painting there was a button, another finger pointing at it. Tu Lala pondered on the meaning of the painting for a while, then decided to press the button.

His guess was right. The light orifice on the wall immediately flickered on and off. Tu Lala thought carefully and soon concluded it was the Shawu People's binary language. The rhythm of the flicker was jerky and stiff, and the codes weren't the modern Shawu language but the ancient language from 3,000 years ago. Anyway, Tu Lala tried his best to piece together its meaning.

"Welcome, people of Shawu. Since you've come to the lightless North Pole and found the Holy Palace, I believe you are beyond barbarism, so we can have a rational talk."

Enormous joy erupted like a solar flare, sweeping across his entire body. The treasure chest he had been searching for his entire life finally opened. The light orifice flickered more and more frequently. A billion-year-old wise man was talking patiently to him. He excitedly read on.

"I'm the Shawu Incarnate mentioned in the Holy Book, from Blue Star of Father Star. Eight hundred and three million, forty thousand years ago, scientists of Blue Star created a brand-new form of life. I sowed it on Mercury and stayed to watch it grow. I watched it grow from unicellular organisms into multicellular organisms, watched it leave metal lakes and move onto land, watched it evolve sexual activity (pairing before bursting) from sexless organisms, watched it evolve into the intelligent Shawu People. Then I felt my one-billion-year solitude was worthwhile.

"My dear children, the Shawu People's progress depends on you. So over the years I did little to interfere with your evolution, just giving a little direction when necessary. Now that you are already civilized, I can teach you something. If you would like, please wake me up."

Next he explained the method for waking him up. His awakening must follow strict procedures. Even the slightest error would lead to irreversible death. Only then did Tu Lala know that the sacred Shawu race was actually an extremely fragile form of life. They couldn't live a second without air before being suffocated. They could die from heat, cold, drowning, hunger, thirst, disease, poison…but such fragile life had surprisingly lasted ten billion years and developed such advanced technology! Tu Lala sighed and read on carefully. He really wanted to wake up the ten-billion-year-old man who the Shawu People could call a god.

He suddenly felt a spell of dizziness, knew the energy box would soon be drained. He crawled over to his backpack: there should be four energy boxes there. But the backpack was empty! Tu Lala's emotional field trembled. Panic attacked him. The backpack in front of him was

Qi Kaka's. Qi Kaka must have taken his backpack away. He certainly hadn't meant to harm him, but in his religious frenzy, Qi Kaka had let go of due caution.

What to do? In the hall there was lamplight, but the luminosity was too weak and lacked high-energy radiation above ultraviolet light and so couldn't sustain his life. It seemed he would drop dead in Shawu's Holy Palace.

In the Holy Book there was a stern commandment: before death the Shawu People must find a death partner, use their remaining energy to explode and give birth to two or more new individuals. Those who don't explode, especially those who revive after death, are despised by all. In fact, long before the Holy Book, the primitive Shawu People had set up this ethical principle. It was certainly correct. Bodies of the Shawu People could not naturally degrade. If no one exploded, there wouldn't be room for future generations on Shawu.

Drop-dead Shawus were easily revivable (just expose them to light). Tu Lala never imagined he could take part in such an outrage, but he couldn't die today! He had something important to do, had to wake up Shawu according to his instructions, earn the Shawu People their 'great grace'. How could he die now? The dizziness in his head was increasing. He could no longer think effectively, had to come up with a solution.

Within what was left of his failing brain power, he found a solution for himself. He dragged his body, laboriously crawling under the brightest lamplight in the hall. Low-energy light couldn't sustain his life but might keep him in a half-alive, half-dead state. Although he fell down, he used his strong will to keep his consciousness from slipping away completely.

His light orifices mumbled, "I can't die, have unfinished business."

★   ★   ★

June 1, 2046: fourteen years after I had accepted Aunt Sha Wu's estate, the spaceship *Auntie* reached the skies of Mercury, spurted flames downward, and slowly landed on the surface.

The huge sun slanted on the horizon, pouring fierce heat and light on Mercury. From here solar flares were clearly visible. They extended many times beyond the Sun's diameter. At the Sun's two poles the flares were feather-shaped. Around the equator they were loop-shaped. Their color was pale and elegant, bluish-white. Their dancing movement was light and graceful, amazingly beautiful. Mercury's sky had no atmosphere, no scattered light. No wind or clouds, no dust. It appeared transparent and clear. As far as the eye could see, there were dark-green rocks all over. Fan-shaped cliffs stretched hundreds of kilometers like creases in a dried apricot. The cliffs were dotted with lakes of liquid metal, reflecting the strong light of the Sun. Looking back, Earth was clearly visible, hanging on the horizon – crystal blue, a fairytale beauty.

Barren but beautiful, Mercury would be the habitat for generations of metal amoebas.

Holding Aunt Sha's statue in both hands, I set foot on the land of Mercury. The statue was etched from platinum. It would stay on Mercury, accompany the life she had created for thousands of generations. The spaceship's crane slowly let down cables and placed Mr. Hong's car on the ground. Strong sunlight shone on the pitch-black solar panels, which soon fully charged the car. Mr. Hong held the steering wheel, parking the car beside the spaceship. His hair had grayed, and his face was as cold as usual, but I could sense the excitement in his heart.

Hong Qiyan was the spaceship's secret passenger. Before the launch, he had "passed away due to complications from a heart attack at the age of sixty-four." We had issued an obituary, held a grand funeral. People from all segments of society had expressed their condolences. Although he was an eccentric, although the Releasing Life on Mercury mission he supported did not gain support from all human beings, his generosity and devotion were admirable. Now the spaceship he had supported with all his power was about to lift off, but he died at such an unfortunate time – what a tragedy it was! But in fact, Mr. Hong and his Mercurian car had already been secretly transported into the spaceship.

Mr. Hong said, "This is great, let Earth society forget me completely. I can do my work on Mercury without distraction."

The captain of the spaceship, Major General Liu Ming, was in charge. Two crew members carried a green refrigeration box down the ramp. Inside were twenty condensed metal sticks taken from Aunt Sha's life smelter. Inside hid the seeds of life. The spaceship landed on the Caloris Basin. The thermometer showed that the current temperature outside the spaceship was 720°. The solar conditioners inside the spacesuits buzzed as they used the solar energy from the Sun to resist the Sun's extreme heat. Without air-conditioning, not to mention astronauts, even the twenty metal sticks would have instantly melted.

All five crew members got down and immediately started working. We planned to finish all the work in one Mercury day, then leave Mr. Hong there while the rest of us returned to Earth. The five crew members were going to build several small solar stations and use two thin superconductive electric cables to transfer power to the North Pole. The cables were very cheap yttrium barium copper oxide and could only work at a low temperature, below -170°, but this was adequate on Mercury. During the day, electricity converted in the solar stations would be stored in the nearest storage battery. At night, when the temperature dropped to -170°, electricity would be transferred to the distant North Pole through superconductive cables. There, energy would be provided for Mr. Hong's freezing and unfreezing. And the ten-million-year-long freezing process in each revival circle could be achieved through the automatic freezing of the -60° frozen ice without consuming energy. Therefore, a small one-hundred-kilowatt power station was enough. But to be on the safe side, we connected twenty structurally unique power stations to form a power grid. Mr. Hong, of course, would sleep for ten million years. Who could predict what changes might occur over ten million years?

★   ★   ★

Captain Liu and I got into Mr. Hong's sports car, and the three of us went looking for suitable locations to release our life. This lifeboat was designed to be very compact. The body of the car was covered with solar panels, which were highly efficient. Even in the weak sunlight of the polar nights, it could keep it driving. In the rear of the car was a small food-regeneration device and an oxygen-production device, which could supply enough food and air for one person. Below was a powerful storage battery, which could provide 100,000 kilowatt-hours of electricity. Its lifespan (given that it was constantly charging and discharging) could be infinite. Around Mr. Hong was a rapid-condensation device. With the push of a button, it could fully freeze him in two seconds. Ten million years later, the device would automatically turn on and revive him. The driver's seat under Mr. Hong was actually two agile robot legs, which enabled him to leave the car and briefly walk outside, because the metal lakes where life grew were usually inaccessible by car.

Mr. Hong drove the car with concentrated attention, looking for a way across the bumpy desert while Captain Liu and I sat in the back seat. To make our work more convenient we also wore spacesuits. Old Liu sat upright in a soldierly posture, silently gazing at Mr. Hong's white hair, gazing at the high swell of his hunched back and concave chest, his feeble malformed legs and feet. His gaze was full of sympathy. I really wanted to have a few more words with Mr. Hong, because in the coming tens of millions of years, he wouldn't have another old friend to talk to. But in the solemn atmosphere, I found it hard to bring anything up and so only exchanged a few words about the condition of the roads.

Mr. Hong turned his head. "Little Chen, before I 'died', I looked over my wealth. There were several million yuan left. I've left it to you and Little Yin, you've sacrificed a lot for this."

"No, you've sacrificed the most. Mr. Hong, you are a great person with a great heart."

"The great person is Ms. Sha. She, and you, allowed me a new life in my old age. Thank you."

I said in a low voice, "No, I should thank you."

The car passed a metal lake, the liquid metals gave out an incandescent glow. The measurement on an optical thermometer read 620°, a bit too high for the little creatures. We moved on, found another metal lake. It was half hidden at the bottom of a cliff, so the sunlight could only slant off it, making the temperature relatively low. We stopped the car, and Mr. Hong maneuvered the robot legs out. Captain Liu and I picked up two metal rods and followed. The metal lake was one hundred meters below. The terrain was steep, so although his robotic legs were pretty agile, walking was still quite difficult. Stepping over a deep trench, he stumbled. I unconsciously held out a hand to help. Old Liu waved a hand to stop me. Yes, Old Liu was right. Mr. Hong had to live on his own. For hundreds of millions of years, nobody would help him. If he fell down, he had to struggle up with his disabled legs. Otherwise.... My nose twitched as I immediately discarded this idea.

We finally reached the edge of the lake. The dark-red surface was quite calm. We measured the temperature: 423°. The liquid contained tin, lead, sodium, mercury, and particles of some solid-phase manganese, molybdenum, and chromium. It was the ideal place for the amoebas to breed. We gave the metal rods to Mr. Hong. He cupped them in the gloves of his spacesuit, waiting. The slanted sunlight soon melted them. They turned to small balls and tumbled into the lake, melting into the surface. A moment later, Mr. Hong inserted a probe into the liquid metal and turned on the screen, where a magnified image appeared. The probe found an amoeba. It had awakened, wiggled lazily, transforming. Its movements were very easy and slow, very relaxed as if this was its hometown.

The three of us looked at each other with satisfaction, smiling.

★   ★   ★

We found ten suitable metal lakes in total, put ten cultures inside. In these ten disconnected oases of life, who knew what might happen? Perhaps a quick death. When Hong Qiyan awoke from being frozen, he would see nothing but a lifeless desert. Perhaps they would survive and rapidly evolve in Mercury's high temperature, leave the lakes, move onto land, and finally become intelligent life. Then Mr. Hong may join them, no longer lonely.

The sun moved slowly. We hurried toward the dimly lit North Pole. The work there was done. In the dark-green, frozen ice a big cave had been dug out, and lighting had been set up. Forty superconductive cables had been pulled into the cave. They converged at a connection panel, which was then connected with the interface of the car. The ice cave was filled with canned food, enough for Mr. Hong to eat for thirty years as a reserve in case the food-regeneration device failed. But we weren't sure if the food set aside for tens of millions of years, despite being at the low temperature of -60°, would stay edible.

We helped Mr. Hong out and had a dinner party in the ice cave. This was the last supper. Afterward, Mr. Hong would have to endure tens of millions of years of solitude. During the meal, Mr. Hong remained taciturn, looking very calm. The young crew members gazed at him with reverence, as if looking at a god. This gaze distanced him from all of us, so although Old Liu and I made our best effort, we didn't manage to enliven the atmosphere.

We finished the meal solemnly. Mr. Hong took off his spacesuit and returned to the car naked. Ms. Sha's platinum statue was placed by the windshield.

I leaned over and asked, "Mr. Hong, do you have anything else to say?"

"Please get through to Earth. I'll speak to Yin."

We got through. He spoke briefly into the phone in the car. "Little Yin, thank you. I will always remember the days I spent with you."

His words turned into radio waves, left Mercury, and flew toward Earth 100 million kilometers away. He spoke no more, quietly waiting. Ten minutes later, the response came back. We all heard Yin's whimper in the earphones: "Qiyan! Farewell! I love you!"

Mr. Hong smiled slightly and waved us goodbye. For a moment his smile made his ugly face radiant. He pressed a button. Cold mist immediately enveloped his naked body. His smile froze, and two seconds later, he was in a deeply frozen state. We did the last check on the life support system, bowed to him one by one, then silently withdrew from the ice cave and headed back toward the spaceship.

Five Earth days later, *Auntie* left Mercury and embarked on the year-long return journey. But we all felt we had left a part of ourselves on that planet.

*　　*　　*

With no idea of how much time had passed, Tu Lala vaguely sensed the crowd was back and the hall of the Holy Palace was in uproar. He tried to call Qi Kaka, call Hu Baba, but nobody answered him. Perhaps he didn't call out loud, only called in his mind. The clamoring crowd gradually left, the vibrations in the hall subsided. With vague sorrow he thought, *Am I really going to drop dead in the Holy Palace?*

Energy gradually flowed into his body. His thoughts became clear. Someone had changed his energy box. Eyes open, Qi Kaka was looking at him pitifully. He flickered weakly, "Thanks."

Qi Kaka turned his eyes away, unwilling to meet his, and faintly flickered, "You kept calling my name in a low voice. You said you had unfinished business. I didn't have the heart to let you drop dead, so I secretly changed your energy box. Now, you are on your own."

Qi Kaka hurriedly ran away as if fleeing a devil, unwilling to stay with a hideous 'revived drop-dead'. Tu Lala sighed, rose, and saw Qi Kaka had left him four energy boxes, enough for him to return to the light zone. *Where is Shawu Incarnate?* He searched anxiously. Gone, along with his Holy Car. He remembered Hu Baba had said before leaving that he was going to ask the Pope to welcome back Shawu Incarnate's holy body and wake him up under the radiance of Father Star. A spell of anxious electric waves overwhelmed Tu Lala. He knew Shawu's body was actually very fragile. Those ignorant believers would probably kill him. But he really was the Shawu People's benefactor.

He had to hurry to stop them! Suddenly, he was sad to find that after being in a half-dead state for a long time, the metallic luster of his body had dulled. This was the mark of the drop-dead, an unavoidable heavenly punishment. If he didn't explode right away, he would have to live with people's hatred and scorn.

But there was no time for this now. He took the energy boxes along, hurrying back to the Gadoris Basin. That was the hottest place on Shawu, and all the grand ceremonies were held here.

He crawled out of the lightless zone, where countless drop-dead lay long the way. He thought regretfully that perhaps he wouldn't be able to deliver his promise to bury them. After entering the light zone, he saw the Shawu People hurrying in flocks. Their light orifices excitedly flickered: "Shawu Incarnate's revival ceremony is about to start!" Tu Lala wanted to inquire into the details, but people immediately discovered his mark of disgrace, cursed him angrily, and struck him with their tails. Tu Lala had no choice but to stay far away, sad.

One Shawu day had passed. He reached the center of the Gadoris Basin at noon. The scene before him made him gape. Tens of thousands of the Shawu People were densely crowded around the altar. The emotional field of the crowd members excited one another, forming a positive feedback loop whose intensity brought everyone to madness. Even Tu Lala was nearly taken in. He had to marshal great willpower to suppress his religious impulse.

Luckily the frantic crowd paid no attention to his mark of disgrace. He got tangled up with them and pushed toward the altar. The Holy Car was parked there, its door shut. Shawu Incarnate's holy body was inside, his eyes still shut tight. The crowd prostrated to him, their heads and tails knocking on the ground violently. The knocking was at first disorderly, then gradually found a unified rhythm, making the ground heave slightly under its weight.

The Pope came out and kneeled beside the altar. The believers' prostrations and prayers set off another climax. Then a senior deacon walked up, asked everyone to be quiet. It was Qi Kaka! It seemed that the Pope particularly adored the man who had betrayed science and thrown himself into religion. His status was now above Hu Baba's.

Qi Kaka waited until everyone was quiet then loudly announced, "I, under the order of the Pope, went to the North Pole to find the Holy Palace in frozen ice and welcomed back Shawu Incarnate's holy body. Now the God Shawu will wake up under the radiance of Father Star, and bestow us with great grace! Today His Holiness comes to the holy altar personally and kneels to welcome the revival of the Great God Shawu!"

After the Pope prostrated again, Qi Kaka pulled open the car door. Clergymen stepped up, wanting to carry out Shawu Incarnate's holy body. At that moment Tu Lala disregarded his own safety. His light orifices radiated two strong beams, searing a clergyman's back, temporarily stopping him.

Tu Lala violently sent a message: "You must not carry him out, it will kill him!" Thinking desperately, he added a threat: "The God Shawu personally told me this. Don't do something so blasphemous!"

People froze. Even the Pope was speechless for a moment. Qi Kaka angrily turned around and said loudly, "Don't listen to him, he is a drop-dead. Don't let him blaspheme God!"

Only then did people discover his disgrace mark. Right away a tail whipped over and landed heavily on his back.

He blacked out but kept sending the following message: "Do not let Shawu Incarnate be shined on by Father Star. You will kill him!"

Another few furious blows. His body couldn't hold on, and he collapsed to the ground. Still people whipped him hard. Qi Kaka gave Tu Lala a vicious glance, held up his hand to quiet the crowd. The ceremony to welcome the holy body began. Four clergymen carefully carried Shawu Incarnate out of the car. The emotional field of the crowd violently erupted, rose, and intensified. Tens of thousands of light orifices simultaneously praised the God Shawu's great virtue and great power.

This emotional field was extremely unified. Only Tu Lala's emotional field was different. His headache was splitting like there were tens of thousands of needles pricking his nerves. He struggled up, looked through a gap in the crowd. Shawu Incarnate's holy body had been placed on a high altar. The Pope led Qi Kaka and Hu Baba to bow on the ground. Tu Lala's nerves strained. He thought something horrible was about to happen. Shawu Incarnate sat on the altar, his eyes still shut. Under Father Star's fierce light, in the high temperature of 720°, his body soon began to blacken. Moisture rapidly evaporated from his body, steamed up, and formed a mist around him. His body began to smoke, light gray. Then his charred body peeled apart, piece by piece, leaving behind a charred skeleton.

The Pope and believers all stared. What was this? The Shawu People's metal bodies never feared Father Star's scorching. Unexploded corpses could be preserved for tens of millions of years. Why was Shawu Incarnate's holy body ruined by Father Star? People remembered what Tu Lala had just said. *Do not let him be shined on by Father Star. You will kill him.* They started to feel afraid. The fearful fields of tens of thousands of people converged, slowly intensified, and slowly gathered momentum, looking for a path to release.

The Pope and Qi Kaka's fear was no less than the crowd's. Who dared to bear the sin of ruining the holy body? If someone raised his arms and shouted, believers would definitely tear the sinner up, not even the distinguished Pope would get away. Fear stopped time. The emotional field of fear and anger continued to intensify....

Qi Kaka, as if under the order of an oracle, rose, pointed at the skeleton, and announced, "Father Star punished him! He escaped into ice to hide from Father Star, but Father Star didn't forgive him!"

The field of fear was immediately gone without a trace, and the believers' nerves relaxed at once. Right, the Holy Book said Shawu Incarnate lost Father Star's affection, hid in ice to escape Father Star's punishment. Now everyone had personally seen that Father Star's radiance had ruined him.

Qi Kaka seized the chance and viciously announced, "Kill him!"

His light orifices emitted two murderous beams at Shawu's skeleton. Believers immediately followed. Countless strong beams focused on the skeleton, making it crash down. The Pope was obviously flustered. He didn't linger there long, rose, and stroked Qi Kaka's head to express approval, then hurriedly left.

The believers soon dispersed. Although they resorted to violent actions to dispel their fear, the violence was exerted on Shawu Incarnate's holy body. This unsettled them. A moment later, the spectacle of tens of thousands of thronging heads was gone, leaving nothing but a broken skeleton on the altar, a crumpled Holy Car, a platinum statue, and Tu Lala, feeble on the ground.

Tu Lala bore his severe headache and struggled to walk to the skeleton. The grayish-black skeleton was scattered across the ground. The lonely skull rolled to one side, two eyes like black holes looking aggrieved toward the horizon. Just a moment ago, he had been Shawu Incarnate, revered by all. A complete, solid, holy body ruined in a flash, forever irrecoverable. Tu Lala felt deep self-reproach. If he had been able to see the Pope beforehand he believed that, with his reputation, he could have persuaded him to wake Shawu up in the right way. The Pope, after all, wouldn't want the holy body ruined. Unfortunately it was too late. Too late. All because he had been without a spare energy box, because of his damned negligence.

He prostrated himself low on the ground, sadly confessing his guilt to Shawu Incarnate.

He rose and carefully collected Shawu's skeleton. Why? No idea. He had no purpose, just wanted to drive away the sorrow and regret in his heart with unconscious action. Not until 2,000 years later, when scientists used genetic technology (in the huge batch of disks Shawu had left behind there were detailed explanations) to extract Shawu's genes from the remaining skeleton and revived him, did the Shawu People genuinely marvel at Tu Lala's foresight.

★　　★　　★

The following 1,000 years were Planet Shawu's dark ages. Frantic believers smashed everything connected to science. Even the energy boxes the Shawu People had once widely used were taken as blasphemous magic and were all smashed. Free science suffered a hard blow to the head, declined, and never recovered. Only 1,000 years later did it slowly regain vitality.

The Shawu Church, however, had reached its peak. They still believed in Shawu, but Shawu Incarnate was no longer called the messenger of the Great God Shawu. He became a false god, a sinning god.

Believers added one sentence to their prayers: "I believe the Great

God Shawu is the only supreme Lord of Heaven and Earth. I despise false gods, he is not the incarnation of the Great God."

However, a small sect secretly sprouted in the Shawu Church. Called the Atonement sect, they say its preacher was an untouchable, a revived drop-dead. They continued to believe in Shawu Incarnate as the messenger of the Great God and the creator of the Shawu People. They carefully kept two relics. One was a charred skull, the other a platinum statue. The doctrines of the Atonement sect regarding the dispute over Shawu's death said that Shawu Incarnate was truly the incarnation of Shawu, and had originally intended to bring Planet Shawu supreme happiness. But he was mistakenly killed by the Shawu People, so happiness passed the Shawu People by.

Although the new Pope Qi Kaka issued a harsh suppression decree, believers in the Atonement sect increased daily, because the doctrines of the Atonement sect awakened people's consciences, awakened a sense of guilt hidden deep in their hearts. As for the Church's suppression, the Atonement sect made no open protest. They spread quietly, collected everything related to science everywhere: broken energy boxes, bits of the Holy Car, fragmented drawings and texts, etc. After the hundred-and-eighty-year-old preacher of the Atonement sect passed away, no one understood these things anymore, but they still stubbornly kept them, because the preacher had once said that when Shawu Incarnate was revived in the next millennium, they would be useful.

The Atonement sect only believed in the Old Testament of the Holy Book and abandoned the New Testament. They added new prayers to the Old Testament:

Shawu Incarnate overstepped his authority to create the Shawu People, so Father Star punished him.

Shawu People who killed Shawu Incarnate, were you authorized by Father Star?

Shawu People, you killed your birth father, you have sinned.

You shall bear the burden of original sin generation after generation until Shawu Incarnate returns.

HER GLIMMERING FAÇADE

Eleanor R. Wood

My Aunt Toshiko disappeared two days after my wedding. She was beaming at the ceremony, seated beside my parents at the banquet, hugging my beautiful bride and welcoming her to the family. She waved us off on our honeymoon, cheeks flushed with champagne, her glossy black hair trailing from its bun. It was the last time I saw her.

Gia and I spent ten days basking in the glow of love and warm pearlescent beaches. Until I saw the lavender seas of Pathos 5 for myself, I didn't believe the brochures. We stayed in a beachfront chalet overlooking a bay ringed by teal-forested mountains. Bright parrot-lizards perched in the trees, lending their color to the vista's rainbow palette. We ate spicy fruits and fresh seafood and watched psychedelic sunsets. Gia taught me yoga; I taught her to surf.

Dad picked us up from the spaceport. He smiled and hugged us, but with quiet tension. He let us tell him about our holiday before he brought us fully back to Earth with his news.

"I hate to spoil your mood so soon, Carlos." He threw me a sad glance from the driver's seat. "Ma and I didn't want to worry you on your honeymoon. But it's Toshiko. She's missing."

"What do you mean, 'missing'?" Gia asked over my perplexed silence.

"No one's seen her in over a week. She's not home. Her car's outside. Her purse and phone are still in the house."

I found my tongue. "Are you saying she's been abducted or something?"

Gia squeezed my hand, in fear or reassurance.

"We just don't know. The police haven't found anything unusual.

They've traced her last known movements and nothing seems out of the ordinary. We're just waiting for news. Any news."

The honeymoon glow was already a fading memory. While my wife and I had been on an exotic planet, captivated by each other and its surreal beauty, tragedy had befallen my family. Toshiko wasn't my aunt by blood. She was my mother's dearest friend, and I'd called her 'Aunt' my whole life. She'd always been there for me, in her warm, level-headed way. She used to take me to basketball practice, let me hang out at her place after school, listen to my woes about unrequited crushes. She'd encouraged me to study engineering. She'd introduced me to Gia.

"How's Ma?" I could imagine her anxiety.

"Much as we've all been. Searching. Alerting missing persons sites. Uploading posters. Worrying for her friend. But she can't wait to see you." He smiled at me in the rearview mirror, but I couldn't smile back.

"You okay, Bear?" Gia asked me, caressing my palm the way she did when she was worried. Sorrow had replaced the joy in her green eyes.

I put my arm around her shoulders. "I don't know."

Dad took the skyway route – more traffic than the road, but faster. When he pulled up at home, Ma was sitting on the front porch, book in her hand as ever, beside a jug of blackberry wine and a tray of snacks to welcome us. She threw her arms around Gia and me in turn.

"How was your honeymoon, my loves?"

We smiled and told her of the wonders we'd seen, but I was distracted. Gia sensed my impatience and took Dad aside to show him our photos so I could sit with Ma.

"Dad told us about Aunt Toshiko."

Ma's face fell and she reached for my hand. "There's been nothing, Carlos. No news at all. Not even a hint as to where she's gone. It's as if she vanished into thin air." I heard the hitch in her voice.

"Have the police spoken to her family?" She had few relatives, but her elderly uncle lived nearby and she had a brother in Japan.

"They haven't heard from her. Her poor uncle's fraught with worry. I feel so helpless. I can't think of anything else to do...." She broke down in tears and I held her, feeling numb.

I visited Toshiko's house the next day. Nothing seemed out of the ordinary. Her hanging baskets decorated the cottage with clusters of color and bustling aromas, while her roses bloomed red, pink, and orange in their beds below. I stood before her front door and had to believe it was all a mistake. Surely she was inside, preparing food or weaving on her loom or designing some miraculous technology to be shared only when she'd got it just right?

But when I let myself in, the house was silent. Only the ticking of her clocks broke the stillness, like tiny ripples on a pond. I walked through the rooms, watering her neglected bonsai and picking up fallen petals from an orchid. Her rear garden was as lush and bright as the front, but she wasn't sitting at her patio table calculating ratios or pruning potted trees. Her absence rang loud in the silence. I opened her patio doors and let in the sounds of birdsong she couldn't hear, and I finally knew that she was gone.

I let the dread wash over me. Every memory I had of Toshiko assailed me at that moment. I longed for her to breeze through the door and laugh at our foolish worries. After a while, I longed for her to appear so I could chastise her for terrifying us all. But I knew she would never do that to us, and my tears flowed with fear that she might never come back.

My phone chimed. When I answered, Gia looked up at me from the screen and halted whatever she'd been about to say.

"Oh, Bear. Don't do this to yourself. Come home?"

I wiped my face with one hand. "I'm coming back now."

"Good. I love you." She smiled sadly and hung up.

As I locked the front door, a wave of dizziness hit me. I stumbled against the porch frame and struggled to get my bearings as the world whirled about my head. It passed after a moment, leaving me lightheaded. By the time I got home, I was ravenous.

"It's just the shock and worry," Gia assured me as she cleared away the supper dishes. "Have an early night and see how you feel tomorrow."

I kissed her and apologized for not helping clean up. Sleep sounded great. I dozed off wondering why I still felt as though I hadn't eaten in days.

*   *   *

"Sorry to hear you're not feeling too good, sport." Dad looked concerned.

"Probably just something I picked up on the trip home. Space flights are basically germ dispensaries, right?"

"Plenty of bedrest!" I heard Ma's voice from the background. Dad pointed his phone at her and I had a glimpse of her shaking a finger at me before he came back onscreen. I had to smile.

"The police want to speak to Gia and me. Apparently, we're the only ones from the wedding they haven't interviewed yet."

"Well, it was the last occasion Toshiko attended. They're trying any lead available."

"I know. It makes sense. They might come by today, although I've told them I'm not feeling great. I'm sure we've got nothing new to tell them, but everything helps, I guess."

"You bet. Heard you went by her house yesterday."

"Yeah." I closed my eyes against a new onslaught of vertigo. "Yeah, that was tough. Had to see for myself, though, you know?"

"I know. Listen, bud, you look pale. Get some rest. We'll talk again later."

I waved goodbye and bent my head between my knees, fighting unconsciousness. I lost and blacked out.

*   *   *

There were wires, and tubes, and something covered my face. I was too weak to pull it away. Dark metal. Plastic…rigging? My hands felt thick and cumbersome and the ringing in my ears wouldn't stop. I shook my head and giddiness spun me into the black again.

*   *   *

I woke up in bed. Gia stood over me, with Dad just behind her.

"He's coming around," she said, relief on her face.

"The doctor's on her way," Ma said from the bedroom doorway. "Oh, love, you're awake!"

"Don't crowd him, Rita," Dad said. "The lad needs to breathe."

"What happened?" I asked, still feeling faint.

"You passed out," Gia said. I'd always teased her about the frown line between her eyes. It didn't seem so cute when she was worried. "I couldn't wake you...I called your parents. Your dad helped me get you up here. How do you feel?"

"Weak...hungry. I had the strangest dream."

"I'll get you some soup and bread, love," Ma called, already on her way downstairs.

"I didn't know you could dream while passed out." Dad looked puzzled.

"It was horrible." I leaned back into the pillows. "Frightening and claustrophobic."

"It's all right, Bear." Gia kissed me on the forehead. "You're safe. You're going to be fine."

I closed my eyes for a while and wished Toshiko were here. Much as I loved my family, their fretting wasn't helping. Toshiko would have ushered them all out and delivered remedies in her sensible, pragmatic way. Where was she? I fought tears, feeling miserable and pathetic. I wasn't myself. This wasn't right.

"The doctor's here!" Ma called from below.

I struggled to haul myself upright and the room spun a dance around my bed. *No...please...not again....* Nausea crept up my throat and my consciousness dissipated once more. Gia's anxious face was the last thing I saw.

*   *   *

Can you wake up in a dream?

That's how it felt the second time; not as though I'd fallen into the sleeping awareness of a dream reality, but as though I'd regained consciousness and found myself somewhere else entirely. The ringing in my ears was louder this time and I plunged into claustrophobic panic. Disorientation fuzzed my brain as I sought my bearings. Everything looked dim, as if through sunglasses. *Goggles.* I pulled at them, but they remained in place and my fingers felt nothing as I touched them. My hands weren't my hands. My motions were slow and fluid, as though I was suspended in something. My heart fluttered in increasing terror as I flailed and yelled and tried to free myself, aware of nothing but the blank, all-consuming panic shoving out any rational thought.

After a minute or an eternity, I ceased my struggling, exhausted and breathless. I forced myself to calm, to breathe, to extend my senses and figure this out. The ringing wasn't in my head, I realized. It sounded like some kind of alarm. I lifted my clunky hands in front of my face and saw they were encased in firm gloves. The backs looked like plastic robot hands and the fingertips and palms were padded. My t-shirt and shorts had been replaced with a skintight suit. When I yanked off one of the gloves, it dangled from the sleeve by wires like a child's mitten on a string. My skin looked pasty. With my fingertips free, I felt for the goggles again and discovered they merged with the suit, which covered my head. Only my mouth and nose were exposed. I scrabbled at the back of my neck, searching for a fastener that would release me from this inexplicable second skin.

I found it. A tiny concealed zip began under my chin and wound around my neck and down the back of the suit. Despite my trembling fingers, I managed to unzip the hood, peeling it back from my face and ridding myself of the clumsy goggles. I looked at them in bewilderment. Their surface resembled a screen rather than a clear lens, and there were more wires and exposed microchips on the inside.

I could see properly now, although my surroundings made no sense. The dizziness, worse than ever, didn't help either. I was rigged up to some sort of mesh hammock, inside a black metal frame with wires and screens and tubes running along the inside. My feet were locked into boots connected by more wires to what looked like a sophisticated treadmill. To my left was an opening. Beyond it, I could make out a metallic floor and dusky, yellowish lighting.

I pulled off the other glove and twisted to work out how to free myself from the hammock contraption. Elastic clips joined it to the suit, so I unclipped them and managed to stand up in the weird, springy boots. My head spun and I clutched at the framework to remain upright. Something heavy hung at my side. I looked down and saw, to my horror, that I appeared to be attached to a large bag of my own waste. Had I slipped into some sort of coma? Was this a hospital? Repulsed, I tried to pull the bag away, but a sharp, gurgling tug in my gut dissuaded me. I had no idea how to disconnect the tubes entering the suit and my flesh beneath.

I swayed as nausea bulged up from my stomach. Just how ill was I, anyway? And where were the nurses who'd clearly been caring for me? No one had come at my panicked yelling, and that alarm was still ringing.

Still leaning on the frame, I freed my feet from the boots and stepped out through its opening. I emerged into a room that looked nothing like a hospital. The walls were the same dull metal as the floor and supported several banks of machinery. The dim yellow light came from a panel in the ceiling, and the incessant alarm emanated from a computer bank to my left. Directly opposite was a machine framework identical to the one I'd woken up in. Its opening faced me, and I could make out another patient suspended inside. At least, I hoped we were patients. My mind tried to suggest alternatives, but they left a frightening chill in the pit of my stomach and I pushed them away.

I no longer believed I was dreaming.

I turned to the alarm's source. A red light blinked in time with the high-pitched beep. The display panel flashed an 'Urgent Message' alert. I looked around, still half-expecting someone to come in and take over. There was a door panel at one end of the room, but it remained closed. The effort to extricate myself from the mechanical structure had drained every last drop of my energy. I didn't even have the reserves to walk the few paces to the door. I turned back to the display instead, and touched the screen.

The alarm stopped, although the light continued to blink. The message appeared on the screen, pale text against a dark background. I read it three times before it began to register.

Carlos, if you're reading this, something must have happened to me. You need to do three things immediately. First, open the panel below this screen and remove one of the nutrient packs inside. Unhook the spent pack from your feeding tube and replace it with the new one. Second, repeat the procedure with the colostomy bags on the shelf below. Third, you'll find a datacard secured to the inside of the panel door. Remove it, insert it into the slot below this screen, and return to your harness unit. Hook yourself up and I'll explain everything. I'm so sorry you have to face this alone. —T

My body shivered. The combination of fatigue, hunger, and bewilderment had dissolved my nerves and I wondered whether I was hallucinating. *Feeding tube?* I looked down and saw a nozzle protruding from my abdomen. Reminiscent of a hose connector, it was clearly designed to attach to something. I stumbled over to my contraption and saw a squat mechanism tucked behind the hammock mesh. A loose tube dangled from an empty bag attached to it. I must have dislodged the tube during my initial panic. The mechanism whirred softly and I deduced it was a pump for pushing the bag's contents into my digestive tract. I felt queasy.

T.

T....

I didn't want to think about it. A horrible, creeping certainty uncoiled itself from my stomach and tingled up my spine. My back was to the other unit. I told myself I was imagining the scent of decay that lay over the barren room. Dread seemed to permeate the air as I turned toward what I'd assumed was my fellow patient. With leaden feet, I approached the unit and looked in at the figure hooked up to a harness identical to mine. The goggles were in place, the gloves and skintight gray suit encased the body, but it hung limply in the harness, the mesh hammock loose around it. The stench of death clung to my nostrils and I gagged.

I tried to look away. I tried to tell myself the sunken cheeks and sallow flesh made her unrecognizable. I tried to believe her remains belonged to someone else, someone I'd never met and had no reason to mourn. But I knew. I knew as soon as I saw her. I knew when I looked through the dim screen of the goggles and put her features together, however lifeless and hollow. I'd known her face all my life.

I sank to the hard floor and let the pain take me.

Toshiko....

I clutched my lank hair in my hands and wept, long and hard. I had no reserves to draw on, save the agony of grief.

★　　★　　★

The wave of sorrow receded and left me drained and aching. I had never felt weakness like it. Toshiko's message flooded back to me and I knew I had to meet my body's needs before it failed me altogether. I crawled to the panel below the computer screen. Inside were stacks of pouches, fat with nutritious fluid. Below them were empty bags, ready to receive the fluid's remnants after my intestines had processed it. I didn't understand why I couldn't have food. Was there something wrong with my stomach? I felt the warm weight of the bag against my hip and supposed maybe there was.

Swapping empty and full bags was straightforward enough, though surreal. I wondered, again, just how long I'd been out cold and who had performed these surgeries. My brain was too hazy to decipher my predicament, but I needed answers. Had someone kidnapped me and Toshiko? What had happened to her? She'd clearly been alive when I got here, or she wouldn't have left me her message.

It was time to fulfil the final part of that message.

I found the tiny datacard and inserted it into the slot. Returning to the harness contraption, I connected the feeding tube to the port in my abdomen and set about clipping myself in. I attached the hammock, pulled on the hood and goggles, and donned the gloves. I had no idea what to expect, but Toshiko's instructions were all I had in this bizarre, alien environment.

The goggles darkened to opacity. A disorienting sensation washed over me, from my fingertips to my toes, with a dip of fresh vertigo. I think I passed out again.

★　★　★

I stood at Aunt Toshiko's front door on a bright, sunny day. The intoxicating scent of her hanging baskets would have placed me there even if I'd had my eyes shut. I looked around. Was I home, safe, as if nothing had happened? The accursed blackouts were messing with my brain. The door stood open, as if inviting me in. I entered, expecting police or detectives.

But it was Toshiko's voice that called to me from the garden.

"Carlos? I'm out here. Come through."

I had to be dreaming. I walked through her cottage, as real and familiar as ever, and found her on the back patio, secateurs in one hand, a straw hat on her head, and a bonsai on the table before her. She turned to me and smiled.

"You made it."

Emotion choked me. "You...you're here. You're all right."

Her expression saddened. She put down her cutters and came to me, wrapping her arms around my chest. Her head reached my chin, and I placed one cheek on her hair and hugged her.

She pulled away gently. "Come, sit with me. I have things to tell you."

I sat on a patio chair and she took the one beside me. "I got your message. But I don't understand how you're here. You were...I *saw* you." My voice trembled at the memory and the discrepancy of her sitting with me now.

She took a breath, as if steeling herself. "I died. Didn't I?"

"Yes, but...."

"Carlos, I'm so sorry. I tried to protect you from all this, but I should have told you before now. I just couldn't bring myself to shatter your world. And now I have to, and it breaks my heart." Her eyes shimmered with tears. My belly was a knot of ice.

She gazed around her fragrant garden and caressed one of the bonsai's gnarled branches. "This world – our world – is an illusion. It's a simulated environment, a place I created for us to live. Everything you've ever known was designed just for you. Every moment of your life since toddlerhood has been spent inside a virtual reality. This reality.

"I built it. I've maintained it. I've kept our bodies healthy while our minds have lived here, experiencing a life we could never have had otherwise. I always knew you'd be in trouble if something happened to me. That's why I set the alarm and coded the program to infiltrate your perceptions if I failed to come around at my weekly time. I wrote this program, the one we're in now, to provide you with answers. I'm a simulation, Carlos. Until now, you've always interacted with the real me, just as I've interacted with the real you. But now I'm a message I left you in case you needed it."

I couldn't breathe. I could barely take in what she was saying.

"You're not making any sense, Toshiko. You're telling me, what, the world isn't real? How can that be? I've lived in it all my goddamned life."

She took my hand in that immediately calming manner she had. "I know you have. I designed it for that very purpose." She paused. "Where did you think you were when you woke up?"

"What, when I found your message?"

"Yes."

"I thought it was a dream. When I realized it wasn't, I thought it was some kind of hospital, that maybe I'd been in a coma or something."

"It's not a hospital. It's a room in the real world. Your body's there right now. So is mine."

My head was spinning again. I pulled my hand from hers and stood up to pace her lawn. The garden was a sensory banquet of color and scent and birdsong. The grass felt springy under my feet. The air was soft and cool in my lungs. How could it be an illusion?

Yet the cold room in which I'd awoken, stripped of life and color, had felt just as real. Its hard walls, blaring alarm, yellow light. The claustrophobic suit. The weight of my own waste against my leg. The sickly odor of death. I suddenly understood that if one was real and one designed, the designed one would be bright and safe and welcoming. If reality was bleak and harsh, what better way to escape it?

I turned back to Toshiko. Her expression was patient and sad.

"Why?"

She sighed and spoke in slow, measured tones. "You and I are all that remain of an extraterrestrial colony. Our parents were scientists who left Earth with two dozen others to found a satellite habitat to orbit and study Venus. I was a child when my family emigrated into space; you were one of the new generation born on board the space station that became our home. We established ourselves and thrived above the yellow planet for decades before a catastrophe destroyed us.

"Venus doesn't have the protective magnetosphere of Earth, and of course it's nearer the Sun." She took a deep breath and met my eyes. "A massive solar storm hit the planet and swept us out of orbit. It knocked out our communications, destroyed half our solar panels, and left us hurtling through space. We were helpless, adrift, with no means to contact Earth and no way to know how badly they had been affected by the storm. As a satellite, we had no long-range propulsion. Our power source was halved. We had to crowd into a fraction of the station's living space to conserve energy.

"Some blamed the crowded conditions, others said our radiation shields had been damaged, and without the power to grow enough food we were certainly malnourished – but whatever the cause, illness took hold. Contagion spread. I managed to fight it off. You seemed to have a natural immunity and escaped it altogether." Her voice faltered. "By the time it finished its rampage, we were the only two left alive. Me, a thirty-one-year-old programming engineer, and you, an eighteen-month-old boy at the very beginning of life. There was still no contact with Earth. I couldn't maintain the station's full systems on my own. I couldn't face a blank, lifeless future, and I couldn't consign you to one.

"So I adapted the station's VR equipment and built on its existing software to develop the most sophisticated program I've ever encountered. I programmed the surgical bots to fit us with neural implants and digestion tubes. I created us somewhere to live."

I slumped back into my seat. Numbness crept over me. I didn't know how to begin processing what she was saying. I cleared my throat and grasped the first coherent thought that came to me.

"What about Gia? And Ma and Dad? Are they on Earth, or in another colony, hooked up to other machines?"

Toshiko closed her eyes before answering. "No.... Carlos. I told you. Even if Earth escaped the brunt of the storm, we have no way to communicate with them." She took my hand again. Hers was slender and warm. "Your family, my family, all of our friends and loved ones... they're part of the simulation. I wrote them. For us. So we could live normal lives and engage with other people. You and I are the only ones with physical counterparts."

My insides felt as though they'd been plunged in freezing water. I couldn't register Toshiko's words. "Are you saying they're not real?" My voice came out as a whisper.

A tear rolled down her cheek. "They're as real as I could possibly make them. They're as real as they are to both of us. I wanted you to have a family, Carlos. Parents to love and cherish you. I could have played that role, but...I wanted you to know people of all ethnicities. I wanted to populate your world with as many kinds of people as I could, so you'd get to experience humanity. It was a sort of tribute to them, too...all those we've lost."

I thought of everyone I knew. I'd never noticed it before. My parents – Latino. Gia – fair-skinned and freckled, with auburn hair. My best friend at school – tall, with dark skin. Toshiko – petite and Japanese. She'd made our world a memorial for everyone she'd known. A requiem for humanity.

But how could I go back, knowing it was all fabricated? How could I begin to accept that everything I'd ever known was an elaborate pretense?

I realized I was sobbing. My face was wet, the salt liquid gathering at the corners of my mouth. Every sensation seemed acute, as though I had to feel it all in sharp detail, goading my mind to deny its existence. Its reality.

Toshiko was crying too. She reached to pull me into her embrace, but I couldn't take it. I couldn't let myself feel her warmth and essence and know she wasn't real. I saw her putrefying remains, stark in my mind. She'd left me. She'd created a universe for me and then left me all alone in it.

I walked away from her then. I didn't want to hear any more. I couldn't begin to consider what I was supposed to do now. I went back through her house and out the front door. I don't know where I was heading. But I jolted back into my clinging harness, in the dark metallic confines of my VR pod. The disorientation was nothing like the first time, but it still hit me with its wave of vertigo. The program had ended. She hadn't written anything besides herself, in her home, talking to me.

I yanked myself free of the suffocating tangle of suit and webbing and stumbled out of the unit, landing painfully on the steel floor. My tube came free again, but I felt stronger for the nutrients coursing through my bloodstream.

I stood, cautiously. The insipid light still cloyed the walls. The stench of decay still choked my nostrils. The closed door still occupied the wall beyond Toshiko's unit. I couldn't bring myself to confront her remains again...but the door. Behind that door lay a deserted space colony. The place I'd come from.

My knees felt weak as I approached the door. I set my shoulders and opened it. A waft of cold, stale air gusted past me. Beyond was darkness. As I stepped through, some long-abandoned power source flickered to life as my motion woke the lights.

I wandered the corridors and chambers that still came alight as I entered them. I found gray bulkheads, and empty quarters, and the remains of a community that had grappled with survival and lost. I found dust, and debris, and chilly dampness. I found evidence of the living, and no one left alive. When I came upon a wide viewport, I stumbled in shock at the raw expanse beyond. Space travel had never frightened me before, but I wasn't traveling now. I was stranded.

I knew Toshiko would have exhausted every possibility over the last twenty-five years. But it was one thing to hear my fate from her simulation. Surely there were records. Computer logs, video diaries, something to confirm everything she'd told me.

The station's computer was easy enough to boot. Obviously the remaining solar panels were keeping some systems alive (*including your whole world*, a snide voice whispered in the back of my mind). It took me a few moments to find log entries, but there were dozens of them. Some were password protected; others had public access. I scrolled back to the last cluster of entries and opened the top one.

It showed a recording of a gaunt man, pale-faced, with sores on his forehead.

"Magda died this afternoon. There are five of us left. Two children, three adults, and all but one of us are showing symptoms." He coughed, a hacking wet sound that made me wince. "I've tried one last time to mend the communications array, but without Anwelo's skill, we're screwed." A child began crying in the background. The man looked on the verge of joining in. He opened his mouth to continue, but swallowed hard and signed off instead.

The next entry was three days later. I opened it and a young Toshiko looked out at me. There were tears in her eyes. She held a dark-haired toddler.

"We're the last two," she said. "I jettisoned Will's body this morning. It's just me and little Carlos." She held the child close. He was all she had left. "I can hardly believe it, but I'm better. It's as if I was meant to survive to help this little one. If I'd died too...." She broke off and kissed the side of his curly head. A lump blocked my throat. That was the end of her entry.

She'd left later accounts of the VR development: her excitement at the initial idea, programming glitches, physiological and hygiene issues, descriptions of fitting me with new suits as I grew.

I stepped away from the computer, hit by the depth of Toshiko's love. I wouldn't have survived without her. I wandered away in a daze.

★   ★   ★

As I stood beneath the flickering light cells of a large communal chamber, gazing at abandoned furniture and discarded personal items, it assailed me. The hideous weight of a loneliness so crushing I thought I'd never be able to stand again. It bore me to the ground and I crouched, cowering like a frightened animal, my arms over my head and my breath choking out in hoarse gasps. I felt eviscerated, hollow, terrified. Out here, I was the only human. Utterly alone.

I don't know how long I huddled there, but after a time the lights went out due to my stillness. Even then, I couldn't bring myself to move.

It was the thought of Gia that roused me. My wife. My wife who consisted of binary coding and artificial, programmed intelligence. A fresh sob strangled me at the thought, which was also the realization that artificial coding was all I had in the world. It *was* my world. Not this cold husk of an extinct population. That complex, all-encompassing, glimmering façade was all I would ever have. I could return to it, immerse myself in it, and share my life with the people Toshiko had fabricated for me…or I could stay here, in this cold, lifeless reality until I lost my mind to it.

It was no decision, really. I retraced my steps to the only room I'd ever lived in and hooked myself back up. Later, I would find a way to jettison Toshiko's body and perhaps learn how she had died. Later, I would reload the program she'd left me and ask her how to maintain my equipment and keep myself alive, as she had always done for me. I could return to the station and scour the diagnostics for something the colonists had missed. If that proved fruitless, I could consume myself with overseeing my personal reality. But now, all I wanted was my beautiful wife. She was waiting, mercifully alone, when I came around. I pulled her into our bed with me and lost myself in her sweet, tangible reality. For that moment, there was nothing else in the world.

★   ★   ★

It's been years since Toshiko taught me everything I needed to know. I've quizzed her virtual persona on everything she could possibly impart. She helped me write the satellite program, establishing a place in my world where the colonists are thriving in their Venusian orbit, making lives and discoveries and babies. I've railed at her, and wept with her, and done my best to express my gratitude for everything she created for me when she was alive. There's nothing left to ask her now; nothing else to say.

But still. Every now and again, when I miss her the most, or need to touch the last remaining link to my physical past, I bring myself back to the metallic room and load her datacard.

Her front door is always open, and she always calls, "Carlos? I'm out here. Come through."

ANSWERLESS JOURNEY

Han Song

Translated by Alex Woodend

The Creature

Creature awakes from a coma, finds it no longer remembers past things. It lies in a room which is not large. The room is semicircular, surrounded by pure white metal walls. At one end is a closed door, at the other a window through which it can see a crowd of stars gathering. Near the window, facing it, are three connected leather chairs, empty, dustless. Creature struggles to rise, feels pain throughout its skeleton. In its mind an image forms. Once upon a time, there were three creatures all together. They sat right on the chairs, wordlessly and endlessly gazing at the twinkling sky. But this image seems remote and alien. In a flash it disappears like a petal carried off by flowing water. Creature asks itself: *What is this place? Who am I? What happened? How did I end up here?*

Before it asks all its questions, it hears a rustle behind it. It nervously turns its head to look, sees the door squeak open. Another creature stands in the doorway. The newcomer looks at Creature with a face containing a variety of strange expressions. Then Creature hears a voice buzzing in the room. It's surprised to hear clearly the syllables of "Hello," which are in fact uttered by the guy at the door. Creature hesitates, feels dominated by the automatic, and so replies: "Hello." This startles them both. It turns out they can both speak, and the language unthinkingly slipping out of their mouths is of the same type. Creature then concludes that it and the one opposite belong to the same species, so Creature infers that its appearance reflects its own image: five sense organs gathered on a head, a neck, two arms, and two legs, walking upright, wearing a gray jumpsuit. Creature starts to know itself all over again. This image is somewhat familiar, but Creature can't remember where it has seen it. This makes it very uncomfortable. In its head it calls the newcomer 'Same Kind'.

Next, Creature quickly gets acquainted with Same Kind. It knows that Same Kind has also lost its memory. Naturally, they feel mutual sympathy for their shared suffering, a closeness for being the same species, and immediately discuss their present situation. It's obvious this kind of discussion will not go anywhere. The background knowledge they need for reference has left their heads. Soon they tire. Creature and Same Kind are disturbed and look vacantly at the white walls even though stars flow past the window.... Time passes. Same Kind suddenly calls out, "Hey, we are in a spaceship!" Creature follows the cry to hidden brain furrows where it timidly recovers something familiar: spaceship, launch...something like that. "We may be the passengers on this spaceship," it says, unable to help but feel encouraged by the recovery of the broken memory.

Upon this encouragement, it builds the following hypothesis: they pilot the spaceship, are departing from somewhere to carry out a mission. Some accident on the way sent them into a coma. During the coma, they lost their memories. The spaceship is still en route. But what happened? Their intelligence flows that far before becoming blocked again. Another thought arises: Is it just the two of them in the spaceship? Simultaneously they turn to look at the three chairs. Right, there are three chairs in the room. Creature and Same Kind sleepwalk before them, then carefully stoop and sit down. The chairs were apparently made according to the shape of their species' body, but they can't find the location of a joystick or dashboard anywhere. They exchange a look, think the world is strange, giggle out loud, then suddenly stop giggling. They think they really don't know each other and don't know the situation they are in. At that moment, starlight shoots directly into Creature's eyes. Like countless fishes scrambling to jump into a feeding pond, the urge to pilot is summoned, but it and Same Kind have both forgotten how to operate the spaceship. In their marrow surges panic and fear.

The third chair is empty.

There is still The Third.

The Third

Creature then says, "Hey, better hurry and find The Third." Same Kind says, "It would be good if it can remember something." Creature says, "Even if it has also lost its memory, the three of us staying together and reminding each other might be better. Three heads are better than one." Same Kind says, "The saying is very interesting. What does it mean? You remembered it." Creature smiles shyly. It doesn't remember the origin of the saying. Same Kind then says, "But would it be surprised to see us?" Creature says, "I think it is also looking for us."

So they set out to look everywhere in the cabin for The Third. They know they will find it, because there is a third chair! This is Creature and Same Kind's first time cooperating, and it goes very smoothly. They look at each other, both pleasantly surprised, and think that before the accident, they must have made a good pair (this is a memory clue). The world really is not big; soon they have walked every nook and cranny, but in the end not a single soul is found. This they can be sure of. They are not at ease, so they search again. The result is the same. But why have a third chair? The surroundings are breathlessly quiet. An eerie, ominous atmosphere starts to envelop Creature and Same Kind, but they don't feel it in their hearts, because they are focused only on their progress. It's clear that this is perhaps a real spaceship. Its structure is simple, like a pair of dumbbells – why does a spaceship have such a structure? They are even sure it consists of a main control room (the room where Creature passed out), three resting rooms, an engine room, and a living room. Of these, the control room is useless to them, because they have forgotten how to operate it. But naturally there are things that make them pleasantly surprised. In the living room they find a large amount of food, which, expressed in the simple language they know, is 'eats'! Food makes them realize that the ever-stronger sense of discomfort in their bellies is called 'hunger'. The hunger problem is the first practical problem they solved in the spaceship, but soon it was cast aside by a seemingly bigger, theoretical problem.

No materials about this journey were found. No materials sufficient to determine Creature and Same Kind's identities were found. None of their personal belongings were found. So the most critical questions could not be answered: Who are they? Where did they come from? Where are they going? What are they going to do?

In the spaceship there is no day or night. Time seems to flow blindly. Creature and Same Kind are both nervous, can only go on rambling about what happened: 1) Accident. The Third died. They lost key memories (some details they remember, such as the concepts 'dumbbell', 'door', 'window', 'language', and so on). 2) The Third was kidnapped, along with all the materials (the spaceship was robbed). 3) The Third is an important figure, a commander type. 4) The Third hijacked this spaceship. 5) There is no The Third. The third chair is extraneous, reserved for an extra passenger. 6)....

Further discussion of such questions, as usual, yields no result. More terrifyingly, they seem to come from a species fond of discussion (another memory clue). So at Same Kind's suggestion, they come back to reality. At the moment the issue is this: whether or not The Third exists, the spaceship is, after all, in their hands. Despite not knowing the past or the future, they have to control it. This way their future can be bright. An epiphany. With this thought, everything seems simple again, so they start trying. But a while later, they discover it's very difficult. No buttons, no computers, no displays, not a single word or pattern. With no hints, Creature and Same Kind can't even remember the slightest general knowledge about operating the spaceship. This is not a matter of taking action.

Then they realize this spaceship is very strange. Completely bare, with a preprepared feel. It contains them completely, but they can't change it at all. It was made like this, probably an advanced model. "Who is the designer?" Creature says. "It's more like the empty shell of a bug." The bug originally lived on a nameless alien planet. Though it so far has not shown any special powers, it disregards the presence of the passengers. However, there seem to be three basic conclusions: 1) Only The Third knows the method of operation. 2) Combining their thinking with The Third's would allow them to operate it. 3) The spaceship is controlled automatically. In the end, they decide simultaneously to believe conclusion three. Having this guess, they let out a sigh of relief. Boring topics start over like an OCD episode. Same Kind believes that they are carrying out a serious mission. It says: "Do you think we were ineffective idlers before? I think there is no way. Look at this spaceship, this journey. I think we must have gone through stringent training and selection before. This journey has an important mission."

"Not necessarily," Creature replies. "Perhaps we are two fugitives, two experimental animals." In fact, in its heart it is thinking the same thing Same Kind is. It is interested in this creature. Its life and its own must have overlapped greatly. Not some fugitive, it may have been its dearest or closest friend. But overnight good friends no longer recognize each other's faces. Creature shakes its head, denying this is a common phenomenon in the world they originally lived in.

"That actually is possible." Same Kind picks up the thread of Creature's conversation with a smile and interrupting Creature's contemplation, which somehow makes Creature feel a little unhappy. Same Kind continues, "But, it's also possible that there is only one fugitive. The other one is a police officer, on board to catch the fugitive. Also, there is only one experimental animal, the other is a scientist. Such combinations make good partners, too."

Creature just smiles, pats Same Kind's shoulder, and says, "That's really funny. Fortunately we don't remember anything, otherwise one us of would be in trouble, brother."

Same Kind pushes its hand away and says, "Hey, be serious. Think it over carefully. I don't know you at all, and for no reason I have to trust you. Let me ask you some questions, see if you remember. The first question: how old are you now?"

Creature thinks hard, answers honestly: "Don't know."

"What's your favorite color?"

"Don't know."

"Have any hobbies?"

"Don't know."

"Ever admired anyone?"

"Can't think of anyone."

"What's the most unforgettable thing in your life?"

"There seems to be none."

"What's your horoscope?"

"What do you mean?"

"I happen to remember this. Um, horoscope."

"Horoscope?"

Same Kind throws up its hands. Then the starlight outside the cabin, through its fingers, spills densely like needles pricking Creature's mind. For a long time they both have nothing to say. But thinking about this episode later, Creature will deny that they ever refused to communicate or understand. Now it simply can't bear the awkward silence, and says, "Do you think there is someone looking for us?" Same Kind is taken aback, and says: "Actually, this is possible. If we were dispatched to set out from some base, there must be someone tracking and monitoring us." As the boring conversation is about to end, this last idea coming out of nowhere has thrilled them. Then would the one who dispatched them be The Third?

They propose enacting a shift system. The loss of memory makes them dare not bet on anything. Besides, they have no grasp of what is happening or what is going to happen. The so-called shift means having one rest while the other stays in the main control room. Though they can't actually control anything, they can look out for emergencies and sound the alarm. And the more important role of the one on duty is waiting to see if they encounter the spacecraft searching for them, or other spacecraft passing by and ask for help. Despite not knowing how to make the other know their situation, they feel that they should find a way then. This is the point their intelligence has reached so far.

The Ark

They wait and wait, but space is so dark and quiet, and they never see the second spaceship. Creature and Same Kind are extremely disappointed, extremely angry. Again they look out the window at the starry sky, and the starry sky twinkles. The universe is like a great flood, pouring from all directions into the desolate cabin and its lonely hearts. Again they talk despite having nothing to talk about. *All thanks to language – itself perhaps a form of life*, they think gratefully.

"Son of a bitch. They don't care about us," Same Kind curses. Creature says, "Well, guess our world has already been destroyed. We're the two sole survivors." Same Kind nods and says, "This is probably the cause of the trouble." Then adds, "But what you say is different from what's in the Bible. I understand you mean we are taking Noah's Ark, but then where is the dove?" *What kind of weapon is the Bible? What kind of epidemic is Noah's Ark? Why mention a dove?* Creature thinks painfully after hearing Same Kind's remarks. It vaguely remembers some past events but all miss the point. It says tentatively, "Then there should be gender differences. In this kind of situation, the common arrangement is having one man and one woman." Same Kind asks cautiously, "What situation?" Creature loses its composure again. *What is gender? And what should a man and a woman do?* A mass of obscure, remote clouds with fuzzy edges surges through its mind. This turbulence clashes with the tranquil space. *Language kills!* Creature looks nervously at Same Kind, finds that it is awkwardly eyeing it back.

"These things can't be explained clearly, unless you really remember," Creature says in gloomy conclusion.

"Something must be wrong, but it's not our fault," Same Kind says.

Gradually, the name of a planet often comes up more and more in their conversation, but since there are no time coordinates to define it, they conclude it probably has no value and put it out of their minds. What's more, they gradually remember they have something to do with the concept 'human'. This is a somewhat terrifyingly heavy concept, they sense. But even being 'human' doesn't explain who they are, so it doesn't help much. Thus they unfortunately give up on this avenue, but…could The Third be a woman? This new thought gives Creature's spirit a boost. It is carried away by excitement and agitation.

The Threat

In the spaceship there is no day or night. Nobody knows how much cosmic time has passed. When Creature is on shift, the myriad stars still remain silent like kids tightening their faces in a game where the first who smiles loses. Creature falls dizzily into fantasy. Outside the window stars spin, oblivious to time. Do all the creatures out there also grope through their lives just like they do, oblivious of life and death, oblivious of what they are, oblivious of their destination? For a moment it vaguely has a fleeting thought that this is exactly the kind of life it yearned for before the coma – this is exactly that intoxicating, dream-like journey. But Creature is convinced the whole journey has a purpose, it has just temporarily forgotten it. Creature, head hanging, turns to look at that chair. Its heart foams with aimless thoughts: Is The Third really dead? Is it still on this spaceship, or following us somehow? If it shows up what can it tell me? Also, women things….

It suddenly feels its spine shiver.

Creature turns its head to look and sees a pair of eyes gazing at it through the small round hole in the door. It stares at them, for a moment doesn't know what to do. A pair of bloodshot eyes, saturated with suspicion and malice. The moment they meet Creature's eyes, they too freeze. The instant Creature jumps up, the eyes move away from the door hole. Creature dashes out the door. The corridor is empty, no human trace. It tiptoes back to its resting room, finds the interior somewhat messy. Apparently it has been searched. It walks out wordlessly. In the doorway its leg muscles start to convulse. This proves it really is a regular creature. It makes a great effort to move its feet again, hurries to Same Kind's resting room. It's not there. But the moment Creature withdraws, it runs into it as it enters in. Same Kind sees Creature is there, face full of suspicion. Creature tells Same Kind that The Third really is on board.

"You saw it?" Same Kind asks coldly.

"I saw it." Creature's teeth chatter, aggravated by Same Kind's tone of voice.

"Not a hallucination?"

"Not a hallucination." Creature is certain.

"It is like us?"

"I didn't see its face clearly, but it feels like a creature like us."

Same Kind's facial muscles tighten like a weathered meteorite. It says, "Are you sure you're not mistaken? There isn't anywhere for The Third to hide on this ship." Creature says, "Perhaps during the last search we missed a corner or something. It's probably playing hide and seek with us, and someone seems to have searched my room. Right now it's in the dark, we are in the light." Same Kind whispers, "Just like a ghost?" Creature explains, "It may exist in the form of energy, I can feel it. Right now it is probably clinging to the wall of the spaceship, all the time following it from the outside. It is different from us. It can breathe and walk in space." Same Kind says, "You think so?" Creature, face slightly blue, says, "Perhaps it is right outside, it wants to suck our blood. Have you ever heard of the damned souls of deep space?" Same Kind says, "Those are tall tales." Creature says, "But you can't not think of it in this situation! Everything's so unbelievable." Same Kind says, "What do you mean unbelievable? What exactly does The Third want to do?" Creature says, "I can feel it. It's all a conspiracy. We have to find it, hurry and catch it!"

Same Kind bites its lips, wants to take a step forward, but lacks the strength to do so. "Your analysis may not be unreasonable. What you saw may not be a hallucination," it says slowly. "But another possibility may be more in line with common sense. If there really is a Third, according to the style of the third chair and your earlier description, it is most likely a passenger just like us, so what's so special about it? It also has no memory, is also unaccustomed to the environment. If it sees us, it also is afraid, thinks we are conspirators." Creature shakes its head, says, "Are you saying, it is hiding from us, wary of us, suspicious of us?" Same Kind laughs and says, "Do you think a creature in this environment could feel anything else? I think there is no need to look for The Third. Even if we find it, so what? Do we need to choose one of us three to be commander? In my view, just let it be." Creature says, "No need to choose one as the leader, but we can reduce the length of each shift, use the time we save to recover memory." Same Kind says, "But food has to be divided among three people...." Same Kind suddenly shuts its mouth, then breaks out laughing.

When Creature finally realizes that Same Kind has pointed out an important problem, the atmosphere becomes a bit awkward. Creature has forgotten that The Third also needs to carry out metabolism to be able to survive, which shows how dangerous loss of memory is. "If it is a passenger just like us, it should have a share...the spaceship was originally designed for three people. Didn't we look hard for it in the beginning?" Creature says, its heart both desperately denying something and reconstructing something. It is so terrified that it dares not look at Same Kind's eyes. "That was the beginning. Lots of things only occurred to me in the past two days. Just assume The Third doesn't exist," Same Kind says, sensing where the conversation has led.

Creature admits this makes some sense and also feels its logic is confusing, but the only broken thread is slipping from its hand inch by inch as time passes. The moment the thread leaves its hand, it remembers something, but it doesn't mention what it is to the other. They just reach an agreement that The Third doesn't exist, because they need its nonexistence. Then another system is established: when getting food, the two must both be present and make a record. Although they have agreed to deny the existence of The Third, they still add a rule about the protection of the food hold to the shift system. A clear fact: due to their survival, food dwindles day by day, but this is a special matter which at first did not draw their attention. Overlooking 'eats' is a very serious matter. When did Same Kind become aware of this situation? Creature suspects that the other's memory is recovering faster than its own, so for the first time it feels a sense of vigilance toward Same Kind. This vigilance sometimes even overshadows the vigilance toward The Third. Creature tries to deny this feeling. It hopes that the day when food simply runs out, the spaceship will have landed somewhere, someone will tell them this was all just an elaborate joke. Fine if it's some harmless experiment, part of a plan, that includes the loss of memory. But if this is not the case, what will happen? Whether or not Same Kind is also thinking about this problem is unknown to Creature, but its increasing reticence over the past few days worries Creature. Creature hopes to ask Same Kind to discuss it together, but each time, it can't open its mouth. It doesn't think that discussion can solve anything. In fact, they now start to weigh their words during their meetings. Their previous bizarre chats have become a ridiculous thing of the past. The thought constantly surfaces: *What will happen? Will they both die, or...one of them die?*

Creature's heart is excited by this thought and coldly beats harder and harder. Then, for a long time, it tries to make itself accept a new thought. Same Kind is right to say that there is no Third.

Because it is The Third.

The Last X Meal

The truth is that in the spaceship there were three creatures in total (or three 'humans'). After the accident, Same Kind woke up first. It discovered something had gone wrong and so killed one colleague – in order to monopolize the food stores. Then it turned to attack Creature, but Creature happened to wake up. Creature thinks, *If I had been it, I would have done the same.*

Or: Same Kind is controlling the spaceship. It pretends to have lost its memory but actually has not. Why do that? Of course it's a conspiracy, and Creature is its hostage. The mission of this spaceship is very likely filthy and sordid. For Creature to make itself accept this thought takes great mental struggle. *Is it a bad person or a good person? Is it a good person or a bad person? If it isn't a good person is it a bad person? If it isn't a bad person is it a good person? If it is a good person what should I do? If it is a bad person what should I do?*

Ugh, why can't it remember anything from the past?

In the spaceship there is no day or night. Time flows to nobody knows where. No one takes care of that. Creature and Same Kind again shyly go together to get food. It's Creature's turn to make the record. It checks. In the cabin where food was originally piled high as a mountain, all has been reduced by two thirds – just by the two of them. The consumption is astonishing. This new thought causes it to look at Same Kind differently. It deliberately takes insufficient food, then observes Same Kind's reaction. When Creature sees Same Kind's eyes it is stupefied. They are bloodshot, seemingly tinged with suspicion and malice. It is startled but appears composed. But Same Kind doesn't wait until Creature catches on or confirms anything. It expresses joy and understanding, gets a share of food and happily goes to eat it. Creature also starts to eat its own share, then it finds the amount is too small. Same Kind pushes some from its box to Creature's box. This unexpected action makes Creature's face burn. It doesn't let the other catch on by putting on a smile and saying, "I'll just go to the hold and get some." Same Kind uses a hand to press down on Creature's shoulder to stop it from rising. "I know you mean well, but we have to save." It says, "I'm really not that hungry, if you need to, go get some." Creature is even more ashamed. It tries hard not to let the other see so as not to feel its own weakness, but in the end its inner feelings release to its face. Creature senses that its desire to apologize to Same Kind is full of disgust. Now it is like a mean, pathetic thing whose mind has been seen through by another. But Creature finds that Same Kind can still pretend nothing has happened, which makes its fear more unfathomably great. Then Same Kind quietly stares at the tip of Creature's nose and says, "When we arrive at our destination everything will be fine. When we recover our memory, I will realize you have always been a good partner." Hearing this, Creature immediately answers offhandedly: "Especially in this situation, facing the same problem, overcoming the same difficulty – what a precious memory it will be. I will certainly tell our descendants all about this voyage."

Poor Creature starts to waver again. One moment it believes that apart from Same Kind there is still The Third; the next it thinks Same Kind is The Third. But its thoughts can't stop food from constantly dwindling and dwindling at a somewhat abnormal speed. They heighten their vigilance but don't find the thief. Before catching The Third, Creature can only assume that Same Kind has stolen the food during its shift. It starts to spy on it. Creature observes it working through the small round holes in the door of the main control room. Several times in a row it finds that it is very honest – its back radiates concern for danger. It stares at empty space very attentively, which is so touching. Whenever this happens, Creature realizes that it is blaming the wrong person, but at the same time it fervently hopes it will steal food. The lack of a criminal on the spaceship cannot prove the other is law-abiding. Creature slaps its thigh, knows it has reached another epiphany. But Same Kind's nonchalance unsettles it in the end. *Does it know it is spying? And would it in turn spy on it, or has it long since begun to spy on it?* Creature thinks wildly. Its mind goes back and forth. Suddenly the feeling of homesickness surges up. It remembers itself in the previous world, it wasn't so voracious.

The Mistake

In the spaceship there is no day or night. Time flows like a river that never returns. The spaceship still keeps to its stubborn journey without end. Creature and Same Kind both become more silent and bored. They have long ceased to mention The Third, but they seem to have the same premonition: the mysterious Third will soon appear and lay down its hand. Good or bad, the truth will come out. Unfortunately, at this critical juncture Same Kind finds out Creature is watching it. This breaks all their agreements.

It turns its head, directly meets Creature's eyes through the door hole – the same situation that Creature and The Third were in before. Same Kind can't see Creature's entire face, just like the eye contact between Creature and The Third. Same Kind may think it has run into The Third. It is obviously a little anxious and stiff. Then it starts to rise slowly from the chair, which takes a surprisingly long time, unlike the last time when Creature suddenly jumped up. Same Kind starts to walk toward Creature in a strange, stately manner. It's the latter's turn to stiffen up. Behind Same Kind, ominous stars offset its funny body.

Creature searches for words of explanation while thinking there is still enough time to run away, but some force fixes it in place, nails it to the spot. Creature knows that its own eyes must be bloodshot and saturated with suspicion and malice, because it sees that as Same Kind approaches, it gradually turns away from its gaze, and its footsteps slow down shakily. Creature believes that so far Same Kind hasn't recognized it yet, it still has time to go. Same Kind walks to the door and stops, holds out a hand. Creature anticipates with horror that it will grab the doorknob, but the hand suddenly stops in midair, becomes a stiff stick. Same Kind's forehead is oozing sweat. In the blink of an eye, the body which has gone through constant mental torment on this long journey completely collapses in front of Creature, falls. This is truly outside of Creature's expectations. It immediately pushes the door open with a bang and enters to help Same Kind up, pats its back. A while later, it opens its eyes.

"You're nuts. If I die, you'll only die faster!" Same Kind screams, the terrifying whites of its eyes exposed. It shoves Creature away, assuming Creature wants to harm it. Creature yells, "Hey, do you know who I am?" But Same Kind closes its eyes, shakes its head. Creature hesitates. Finally, it decides to get Same Kind back to the resting room, but the moment they go out the door, Same Kind suddenly grips Creature's neck.

"Die! Die!" it screams. "Why didn't you say so earlier!" Creature yells back. "Since you have been thinking it all along!"

Creature is very distressed, eyeballs bulging. Creature can't remove Same Kind's hands, whose fingernails are rather sharp. So Creature lies on its back next to Same Kind, uses its teeth to madly bite its clothes until getting to muscle, and hits its belly with its knees. This series of fluid, connected movements makes Creature realize that it may have had a similar experience long ago. Its body becomes limp and ticklish. Same Kind quickly passes out. Creature turns one hundred and eighty degrees and climbs onto Same Kind's body. It bites its facial skin, squeezes its neck, this time much more naturally. Same Kind exhales foul breath. Creature sees the blue veins on its neck throbbing like cosmic strings and can't help but recoil. Same Kind gains room to struggle, so Creature squeezes harder. Same Kind doesn't move. Creature thinks it's finished, but Same Kind speaks again:

"Really I always suspected you were The Third...."

Creature's eyeballs start to bleed. Blood drips onto Same Kind's forehead, then flows to the corners of its eyes. Same Kind shakes as if cold, and Creature's urine flows out from below. After Creature confirms that Same Kind no longer poses a threat, it goes to search its room, making a big mess. It doesn't find sufficient evidence to sentence it to death, then it realizes that it doesn't know what kind of creature it killed (or what kind of 'human'), just like it doesn't know what it is itself. Creature starts to feel a kind of desolation after its urine drains. The whole thing was just an accidental slip of the hand. Creature promises itself to really forgive itself. So far it hasn't found any food stolen and hidden by Same Kind anywhere. Creature finishes everything. Completely exhausted, it sprawls on the third chair then seems to hear someone calling it. It shivers all over, looks around – still only white metal walls. The door in the wall is shut. No creature stands against it. But Creature thinks it really heard a call, although it never repeats. Later it has a strong urge to get rid of the corpse to destroy the evidence. It tries many ways, without success. Without instruments, chemicals, or doors to space.

The Mystery of Sex

The rest of the time, Creature eats the remaining food to eliminate periodic feelings of discomfort. The corpse rots on one side, so it covers it with food scraps to prevent the odor from wafting everywhere. Many times Creature thinks it sees a pair of watching eyes from the door hole but makes not the slightest discovery. The three chairs still lie quietly where they were. One belongs to it, one belonged to a dead person, and the other one? Creature has no interest in looking for answers to the question it asked from the beginning, so it looks at the starry sky; it is the witness to the murder. So Creature temporarily sees it as The Third, thus complete liberation. It flies in its own shell. Somehow, the feeling of danger and anxiety persists, and a lonesome feeling also strikes.

This gradually forms a weepy yet tear-free atmosphere. Creature can't think of anything to do. At the moment it has the urge to talk to the corpse. When the remaining food is half-finished, there is still no sign of a destination approaching. Creature starts to eat the other half, the food belonging to Same Kind. Then the food runs out, so it eats the corpse.

Creature thinks, It said I would die faster but no way. This one was so naïve.

When eating the naked corpse, Creature notices its sex. It admits that it has discovered this point too late.

This spaceship – now Creature suspects it really is a spaceship – accompanied by its drifting thoughts, continues on its supremely silent, seemingly answerless journey.

CYLINDERS

Ronald D. Ferguson

"Shut up, Jerry," Rachael Watanabe says when I follow her from the weightlessness of the Red Cylinder into the open axis of the rotating Green Cylinder. "Today, I am fourteen, and I'm going by zipline to celebrate my birthday."

Despite my advice – everything I suggest seems to make her angry – we don't take a transition-ring elevator. Instead, we crawl along the webbing that surrounds the axis entrance to the Green Cylinder. In less than a minute, we are on the zipline platform. The platform rotates with the cylinder, but at this distance from the axis, the created gravity is negligible.

Rachael arranges a harness about her shoulders. She reaches for the zipline trolley. This is my last chance to dissuade her.

"Your mother wouldn't approve, Rachael. Celebrate another way."

"I want to see Earth, Jerry. I haven't seen Earth for a year. The best view is from the central dome in the Green Cylinder."

"Take the elevator to the cylinder surface. Walk—"

"You look like my father, Jerry, but you're not him. I don't have to do what you say." Rachael fumbles with the trolley connection. "You're not even human."

"True." I step forward to help her hook up. "However—"

Her harness clicks into the trolley. She engages power and the trolley pulls her along the zipline over the farmland a kilometer below.

I must protect her. Having no options, I connect to the next trolley. Moments later, I accelerate along the zipline. At the halfway point to where the Green Cylinder surface meets its base, my velocity increases sufficiently for the trolley to switch to regenerative braking.

Minutes later, a bright flash illuminates our destination. Have the solar reflectors malfunctioned?

The atmosphere alarm buzzes three times, followed by a continuing horn blast. The warning indicates at least one window has blown out.

The solar reflectors automatically shut over any broken window, but the bright flash must have been an explosion. How many windows broke? The closing reflectors should seal the leak, but what if they were damaged?

I search actionable decision branches.

How close does the zipline come to the broken windows? If the reflectors don't close before we reach our destination, how will Rachael breathe? Will the vacuum suck her into space?

Suspended from the zipline, I can only review the decision tree. Despite my instructions to protect her, I am helpless. We ride fate to our destination.

She is a hundred meters ahead of me. I maximize my volume. "Don't unsnap your harness when you arrive." I'm not sure Rachael listens. Maybe I shouldn't offer her advice: it aggravates her stubbornness.

The zipline terminates fifty meters from the window strip. Tomato plants bend toward two broken windows, and a cone of swirling air and debris targets each. The high-pitched shriek of escaping air mellows to an angry *swoosh*, but as the continuing horn blast indicates, the reflectors have not completely sealed.

The broken windows lie two hundred meters beyond the boundary between the window strip and the agricultural strip. They are easy to see because of the cylinder's curvature. The window strip on the far side of the agriculture strip is higher but a kilometer away, too far to distinguish individual windows. Two kilometers overhead, another window strip separates the two remaining agricultural strips.

Rachael alights on the zipline landing platform. Before I can stop her, she shrugs off her harness and skips knee-deep through the fluttering plants. Her blouse flaps in the unusual wind blowing toward the broken windows. She stumbles and momentarily goes airborne because of the light gravity.

I don't wait to reach the platform. Ten meters from the surface, I undo my harness and allow my tangential velocity to carry me into the tomatoes. "Rachael." Taking advantage of the speed differential between me and the cylinder, I hit the surface running.

She plants her feet and skids through some plants. I grab her arm and pull her back. The wind diminishes to a breeze by the time I drag her to the landing platform. The horn stops. The reflectors have completed the seal of the fractured glass. Rachael's blouse ceases its flutter, and the danger appears to be past. I release her arm but stand at the ready.

In the distance, an emergency crew converges on the damaged section of windows.

"Don't tell Mom." Rachael glares at me. "The fail-safes worked perfectly."

"Very well. I won't mention what happened unless asked, but you should tell your mother."

"Why? She already worries too much."

"Because the light flash suggests an explosion broke the windows. Sabotage. The security guards will question you. You are a minor. They will then interview your mother. You should tell her before they do."

"She'll ground me for not listening to you."

"Taking the elevators was only a suggestion. You are correct that the zipline is more efficient than walking the length of the agricultural strip, even with the cylinder surface gravity at twenty-eight percent of Earth's. The window blowout was unpredictable and not your fault."

"Thank you." Her smile is not quite a smirk. I am unsure whether she has manipulated me again.

"After we talk to security, we'll take an elevator to the observation dome. You can still see Earth for your birthday."

"No. My birthday is ruined." The expression clouding her face is a familiar pout. "I want to go home, Jerry."

"We must wait for security to interview us before you return to your mother's apartment."

"I don't mean the apartment. I want to go to Earth. I miss my friends. I miss my dad."

Her eyes glisten. I don't respond because her father is dead. The videos of him stored in me hint at his memories. I can replay them for her, but that never comforts her.

Two security officers approach us.

She shrugs. "We should go to the apartment when this is over."

Another flash of light illuminates the overhead window strip. The atmosphere alarm sounds again. Another explosion. Another rupture.

"Yes," I say. "Returning to the Blue Cylinder is a good idea."

★   ★   ★

Rachael seems more amiable after we enter the Blue Cylinder. Although the Green and Blue Cylinders have opposite angular velocities at thirty revolutions per hour, the surface gravity generated in the two-kilometer-long, one-kilometer-radius Green Cylinder is half that of the two-kilometer-radius, one-kilometer-long Blue Cylinder. The non-rotating Red Cylinder joins the other two, produces no gravity, and serves as a shuttle dock.

I suspect Rachael would not enjoy returning to full Earth gravity after living on L1 Station for the past year. Humans are sensitive to such things.

When we enter the apartment, Rachael's mother, Jane, sits at the dining table having tea with a young man only five or six years older than Rachael. The man sets his tea aside and stands.

"Dr. Katz." Jane nods at Rachael. "This is my daughter, Rachael. Rachael, meet Dr. Daniel Katz."

"Please, call me Dan." He extends his hand. "Your mother is allowing me to do postdoctoral work with her this next year."

Rachael hesitates before smiling and shaking his hand.

"And this…" Jane gestures at me, "…is Jerry."

"Jerry is operational?" Dan's eyes widen. "Everyone in graduate school followed your work on Jerry. Except for the facial detail, he looks like any other android."

"Thank you, Dr. Katz." I extend my hand. "Jane says I am a work in progress."

"Outstanding." Dan smiles and shakes my hand. "Call me Dan, Jerry. I hope that you and I will spend many informative hours together."

"I am at your service, Dan."

"You didn't take your phone, Rachael." Jane doesn't look angry or worried. Perhaps she hasn't heard about the sabotage in the Green Cylinder.

"It's my birthday." Rachael sticks out her lower lip. "I didn't want to be disturbed. Do I smell cookies?"

"Birthday cookies in the kitchen. Help yourself but save room for lunch." Rachael's brow furrows. "Sean Jeffords called three times this morning. I'm tired of telling him you aren't available."

"I'll call him back." Holding three cookies, Rachael returns from the kitchen. "My phone is in my room. May I be excused?"

"Certainly." Jane waits until Rachael leaves before she continues. "How was your time with Rachael, Jerry?"

Shrugging is called for, but my shoulders aren't designed for it. "I try to please her, but everything I do irritates her."

"Perhaps you try too hard. Did she behave during the security alert?"

"You know about the broken windows?"

"Everyone knows," Jane says. "The Director broadcast the announcement. The safety features worked flawlessly, but it must have been a distraction. I assume that's why you returned early. Was Rachael upset?"

"Not that I could tell. Sabotage is intended to disrupt, but she took it well even after the second set of windows exploded. Perhaps she didn't understand the danger."

"Sabotage?" Now Jane looks puzzled, worried. "The Director didn't mention sabotage. I want you to watch her more closely, Jerry."

"Of course, but she will not like it. Her behavior is a mystery to me."

"She's a fourteen-year-old girl." Jane sighs as if her comment is an explanation and returns to her chair. "We should finish our tea, Dan. Sit. Sit. You too, Jerry. No, join us at the table."

"Thank you." I take the chair across from Dan.

Dan glances around as if unsure what to say. Perhaps sabotage unsettles him. I decide not to mention the windows again unless Jane brings it up.

Dan sips from his cup. "Excellent tea, Dr. Watanabe."

"Call me Jane. Save the doctor and ma'am stuff for formal situations. Now, how did a PhD in biology get interested in cybernetics?"

Dan seems relieved to discuss something other than sabotage and Rachael, but I must spend more time with him before I read his face properly.

"I had a masters in cybernetics first. That's always been my major interest. Biology is an extension of my interest in cybernetics, not the other way around. Also, I've been writing computer programs since I was seven—"

"And you started college when you were twelve? Precocious."

"That's why I have no social skills. Anyway, the overlap between creating smarter AI machines and understanding systems that can achieve goals is…well, I don't mean to ramble on. Too much enthusiasm, I'm afraid, and of course, no social skills."

"Cybernetics and AI. That explains your dissertation."

Dan tilts his head. "You read my dissertation?"

"Yes." Jane sets her tea on the table. "I read it while completing Jerry. The method you used to thin slice and scan a cat's brain to generate a 3D model to digitally emulate a particular feline cortex fascinates me. Quite innovative and a novel approach for generating goal strategies in an AI. That's why I contacted you."

"The method wasn't as successful as I had hoped." Dan sets his tea aside and leans toward Jane. "What does modeling the synaptic connections of a cat have to do with Jerry?"

The discussion is about me. Perhaps they will question me later. I compare their conversation with my Gerald Watanabe videos, but that doesn't help to make sense of everything they say. I store their conversation in Verbal Markup Language. Later, I will review the conversation word by word and compare it with information from the station library. Most humans don't do that even with technological assistance available.

"Some people think my approach for instilling my late husband's memories into Jerry show promise. I don't. First, I had no good way to collect his memories. Installing available video recordings is a poor substitute for actual experiences and also is difficult for Jerry to reliably index and access. Second, too many filters stand between the memories of a deceased human and the creation of an AI emulation. The method you describe in your dissertation is more complex than what I did, but I believe it shows better promise for creating an AI based on the memories of a specific person, memories that can help the AI formulate strategies and accomplish goals."

"You want to try my AI approach for emulating cat brains but using human memories?" Dan laughs.

"What's funny?"

"I applied for admission to medical school next year as preparation for the same attempt."

★　　★　　★

"You can't come with me," Rachael says.

I don't know why she says that. She knows I must follow if I am to protect her. I am also unsure how to read her grin and the tilt of her head. Is she being derisive or devious?

"We have another hour of scheduled interaction time together. Your mother suggested you might deceive me."

"When the hour is done, will you still follow me about like a puppy?" She purses her lips. "Do you remember following me into the girls' dressing room? The girls thought you were a man. We don't want a repeat of that."

"I endeavor to stay in the background like an old piece of furniture." I am unsure why I attempted a simile. I'm not good with similes. Had I quoted Gerald Watanabe? "Your mother thinks it important that I stay near you to keep you safe."

"Important for you, not for me. Nevertheless, you cannot come."

"Why?"

"School assignment. My homework is to have sex with Sean in the biology lab. Sex involves two people, but no observers and especially no androids."

None of my video recordings from Gerald Watanabe include sex instruction. I consider my next action but find no alternative except waiting for more information.

Rachael shrugs. "Why don't you access the station library? Look up *sex* and *teenagers*. You'll see I'm right."

The request is reasonable, and I access the library. The information is voluminous and poorly indexed. I struggle to formulate a consensus from the information tsunami hash-tagged *sex* and *teenagers*.

Rachael taps her foot and rolls her eyes while I review the data. Without waiting for me to finish, she giggles, hugs me, and walks away. I am unaccustomed to hugs and unable to decipher her actions.

Moments later, I interrupt my attempt to understand *sex* and *teenagers* to return to my imperative to keep Rachael safe. She's gone. I track her phone. The phone reports that she is nearby, but I do not see her. After ten minutes of failure and having no alternative, I return to Jane's lab. Returning to the lab after losing Rachael has become a familiar pattern for me.

Jane and Dan are viewing a computer screen when I enter. I wait just inside the door. My batteries are low, but I don't want to intrude.

Dan shakes his head. "What I did for the cat was inadequate. Creating a digital object to emulate a single neuron-synaptic bundle requires significant computer memory. I refined the design to improve memory usage, but that was too late for my dissertation. I should have used ten times as much memory to model the one billion neurons and ten trillion synapses in a cat's brain, but money was short. I also couldn't afford the latest in massive parallel processing, and so my cat was slow-witted, incredibly dumb, and shallow of memory."

"But the program reacted like a cat." Jane drummed her fingers on the tabletop, her jaw firmly set. "Determined money can solve the equipment problem. That won't slow us here. Scientists first attempted emulating a cat brain seventy years ago, but your cat works better. The neurons you designed have complex branches rather than a single point representation. You emulated more than six types of synapses, not just one. I could go on, but what sets your work apart for me is that you used a particular dead cat's brain to preconfigure the neuron-synaptic layout in the digital cortex. I'm convinced that's what's missing from Jerry, why his learning feels more like rote repetition rather than the elaboration of new data paths laid down among old. Current AI technology is very good at creating smart androids but not so good at emulating real people."

"A real person's behavior is not always smart," Dan says. "My approach isn't easy. A human brain takes twenty to twenty-five times as much memory as a cat's. Besides, my method requires a freshly frozen and thinly sectioned brain to construct a 3D model of the synaptic structure."

"I understand. My late husband, Gerald Watanabe.... I wanted his personality as the model for Jerry. Modeling the android to look like Gerald was easy, but I didn't have a viable approach to instill Gerald's memories, much less emulate his personality."

"Your late husband? I am sorry for your loss."

"Three years ago. He died from a glioblastoma tumor a few weeks after being diagnosed, but he had many brain scans, including those that yield 3D images. I have copies of two of those scans. That's why I thought you could help."

Dan rubs his chin. "I'm not sure that 3D image scans are detailed enough...."

"And...and he donated his body to science. I have his brain stored at seventy-seven Kelvin."

"There will be ischemic damage."

"Damn it, Dan. Don't be so negative. Do you want to try this or not?"

"Of course I want to try it, but even if we succeed, you've got to understand that the emulation simply produces an AI with thought patterns based on the topology of your husband's brain. It won't be your husband."

"Yes, but your emulation reproduced behavior that the cat learned before it died. Jerry can replay the videos of Gerald that I stored in him, but he can't reconstruct any of Gerald's experiences or memories."

"I don't know—"

"Please, Dan. I'm doing this for Rachael. I don't want my daughter to forget her father, and I hope this will improve Jerry."

"The videos may be good for calibration, if we can correlate them to some of the memory structures. I don't have great confidence in 3D holograms or sections from a damaged brain, but perhaps we can learn in the attempt. This will be very expensive, Jane. Who's going to pay?"

"I'll introduce you to the money man in a video conference after lunch."

"Okay, then. I'm ready. Let's do it."

Jane smiles and touches Dan's hand. "Thank you."

They stand. I take that as my cue to go to my charging station. I wonder whether I should tell Jane that I've misplaced her daughter again. Probably she's already guessed that, because I arrived early and alone.

When I face the charging station to engage the power connector, Jane asks, "Jerry, why is Rachael's phone taped to your back?"

★   ★   ★

Jane and Dan have finished lunch by the time my charge is complete. No one has given me instructions, so I don't leave my charging station.

The screen on Jane's desk clears, and the introductions begin.

"Dr. McLeod," Jane says. "It's good to see you. This is Daniel Katz, the young scientist I told you about."

Despite a new, gray mustache, I recognize sixty-seven-year-old Dr. Alastair McLeod from a five-year-old corporate photo. His hair is thinner now and his ears larger, but the face metrics match. Dr. McLeod owns the majority share of McLeod Enterprises, controls the L1 Station, and is the richest man in the solar system.

"Jane, you look well." Dr. McLeod's voice is gruff. "Dan, I'm pleased to meet you. I hate to be curt, but I only have ten minutes."

"Yes, sir," Jane says. "I'll be quick. Did you read our proposal?"

Dan glances at Jane. He looks surprised. Was it the phrase 'our proposal'?

"No," Dr. McLeod says. "Brief me."

"All the popular approaches to implant a dead human's memories and personality into an AI have had little success. Dan's method of emulating a cat's brain shows more promise because it alters the thinking strategy of the AI based on the neuron-synaptic structure of the selected subject, but the implementation will be expensive, requiring massive parallel processing and thousands of terabytes of memory to create a digital cortex based on the topology of a selected human's synaptic connections."

"I understand," McLeod says. "Unfortunately, mass production of qubit memory and quantum processors is several years away. You'll have to be satisfied with current technology."

"That much memory won't fit inside Jerry's shell," Dan says. "We'll be limited to a large box to house the complete digital cortex."

"Is he always this negative?" McLeod asks.

Jane looks away and bites a smile from her lips.

Dan leans forward. "I don't want to give unrealistic expect—"

"Son, I know a bit about applying science. We do the research now, then when the technology catches up, we will be ready for a better implementation. What do you think is feasible in this first iteration?"

"Realistically, I would be surprised if we can salvage more than five percent of Gerald Watanabe's memory structure to embed in the machine memory. However, that means we don't need a complete digital cortex for our first attempt. We can build a limited module, one that will fit into Jerry's shell while we run parallel research on the full-sized digital cortex in a big box."

"I like this boy, Jane." McLeod smiles. "Send me the budget, and I'll approve it."

"Yes, sir."

"Uh, Dr. McLeod," Dan says. "Generic AI design is well standardized and effective. Why are you interested in constructing an AI with memories from a specific person? My approach requires that the person be dead before emulation. I guarantee that the process will not grant immortality to anyone who provides those memory structures."

"I'm not interested in immortality, Dan. Are you familiar with the Prometheus Proposal?"

"No, sir."

"You should be. The purpose of the L1 Station is research to support Prometheus. Everything we do there is related to Prometheus, and that includes AIs who can emulate specific humans. Become familiar with Prometheus before we talk again. Decide whether what we propose is worth the cost and dangers before you commit. Good to meet you, Dan. And Jane, always good to see you. Keep me informed."

A logo from McLeod Enterprises replaces Alastair McLeod's face on the screen. Jane congratulates Dan. He still looks puzzled.

Anticipating that Dan might ask my help, I resolve to learn about the Prometheus Proposal. I access the station library. Researching the Prometheus Proposal takes very little time. Many articles recount Alastair McLeod's unwavering support for the proposal, as well as the opposition from competitors like Nixon Liu of Sol Bio Systems. Among the vocal moral critics is psychologist-turned-video-evangelist Stanley Stanton.

The briefest summary of the Prometheus Proposal was given by Alastair McLeod to a Senate Committee during his bid to lease the L5 Lagrange point that trails the Moon.

McLeod's response to Senator Johnson's inquiry about the essence of the Prometheus Proposal was succinct. "We don't have the technology to take ourselves to the stars, and so, instead, we shall send the dead and the unborn."

*   *   *

"Does he have to come with us?" Sean Jeffords asks Rachael, but he looks at me.

"He always lurks about. Just ignore him." Rachael pulls herself along the safety line that leads into the zero-gravity gymnastics room. "I want you to teach me the free-fall somersault. Ignore Jerry. It's not like we're on a date."

Sean frowns and says nothing.

"Anyway, my mom limits my required interaction with Jerry to two hours each day. She wants him to learn from me. I guess I owe it to my dad's memory to make an effort."

"I still don't get it." Sean releases the safety line and pushes into the ten-meter cube. All six walls of the cube are padded and a safety rope drifts from each corner. "He's just a robot made to look human."

Sean rolls into a ball, rotates, and plants his feet firmly against the wall. He pushes off toward the opposing wall and executes a half-twist.

Rachael glares at me when I follow her into the cube.

"Stay out of the way," she says. "Your two hours are up, and I need to improve my zero-gravity skills."

Sean pivots against the far wall padding, grabs a rope, and coils his legs against the wall.

"Education is very important," I say. "Please observe the safety guidelines posted on the gymnasium door."

"I know how to follow instructions." Rachael seems angry. Again.

"Instructions?" Perhaps I should change the subject.

Sean uncoils his legs and sails toward us while executing a somersault.

"Did you learn much from having sex with Sean in the biology lab? I couldn't find detailed instructions for coitus in the library, or I would have sent them to you. The videos were difficult to decipher."

"What!" Sean loses control and crashes into the adjacent wall. The pad absorbs most of his momentum.

"Be quiet for the next hour. Please, Jerry." Rachael grits her teeth. "No more talk about sex or the biology lab."

"If that is what you require."

"What did he say about us?" Sean demands.

"Nothing. Jerry is easily confused." Rachael gives me a two-handed push toward the door. Newton's Third Law applies, and she drifts away from the safety line. Does she notice?

"I apologize for the confusion." I attempt to mollify her. "My assignment is to keep you safe and remind you of your father, Gerald Watanabe."

"You're not doing very well." Rachael floats a full meter from the door. "Now, shut up, Jerry. Wait in the corridor. I'll tell you when I'm ready to go."

"As you wish." I reposition myself just outside the door so that I can watch.

"He wants to keep you safe?" Sean flexes his fingers as if he injured them bouncing against the wall. "What about me?"

Rachael waves her arms. "Sean, I can't reach the safety rope." Her efforts to swim in the air twist her a quarter-turn.

"Eventually, you'll drift into a wall." Sean continues to massage his hand.

"Eventually? Are you serious? Help me get back."

I stick my head in the door. "Should I get you a safety rope?"

"No!" the two shout simultaneously.

Sean traverses to the nearest corner and gathers the attached rope. He snakes the line out to Rachael. She hauls herself to him.

"I don't like your robot." Resentment fills Sean's voice. "Is he going to watch?"

Determination sets Rachael's jaw. "Not after I shut the door."

*　　*　　*

Dan closes my abdominal access panel. He lowers the laboratory lights to normal brightness.

"That finishes the installation of memory and processors for the limited digital cortex," he says. "As soon as we have a good synaptic model in the computer, we'll upload a reduced configuration into your memory. How does it feel so far?"

"Fine." Feel? I have no tactile sensors inside my abdomen. Apparently, he wants polite conversation. News is a common topic for such conversation. "Did you get the news? They caught the saboteur who blew out the windows in the Green Cylinder. He was an engineer with the solar reflector maintenance crew."

"Do you think there may have been more than one?"

"Sir?" I don't understand his question. "Only one saboteur was identified. No saboteurs were reported among the remainder of the window maintenance crew."

"From what I've read, the Prometheus Proposal has many enemies. This station is key to the development of the technology needed for Prometheus to succeed. Do you have an opinion whether there might be other saboteurs?"

"Opinion? Is that about things somewhere between fiction and fact?"

"Use fuzzy logic, Jerry. Your opinion comes from your analysis of what is likely true when the evidence is insufficient to support a fact."

"Fuzzy logic. I understand. What measure?"

"Some folks form an opinion with less than a twenty percent chance of being correct, especially when high emotional content accompanies their evidence."

"I have no chemical support for emotions."

"Noted. Having an opinion is more difficult when there are numerous alternatives. Fortunately, this situation has only two: more saboteurs or not. Set the decision metric to sixty percent. That is a good place to start. Review empirical information about other saboteurs as relevant to the question of whether there are more saboteurs, calculate the probabilities of the two alternatives, and use the sixty percent cutoff to select your opinion. 'No opinion' is an acceptable conclusion if neither alternative rises to the level of the cutoff. Can you do that?"

"I already have. Based on the amount of opposition to the Prometheus Proposal and the number of people espousing violence, my opinion is that there is at least one more saboteur on board, most likely another maintenance technician, although perhaps not in the window crew."

"Excellent." Dan smiles. "The same opinion as mine. Did that feel different from your usual thought process?"

"I'm not sure." Again he uses the word *feel*. "I don't review my thought processes while thinking."

"I've redirected your data input circuits through the new digital cortex. The parallel processors will compare the structure of the new data, identify similar structures in the digital cortex, and use those to strengthen the emulated synaptic connections. Now your memories will be stored two ways, your original process for raw data and by the strengthening of emulated synapses in the digital cortex. Based on that you may be able to review your thought processes when the digital cortex gains more experience."

"I don't understand."

"You don't need to at this stage. Each day we will update the software for the digital cortex in an attempt to make it behave like the brain of Gerald Watanabe. If you notice any changes in the way you think, please tell me."

"Will this help me carry out my assignment of protecting Rachael and connecting her with her father?"

"That's why we are doing this, Jerry."

★   ★   ★

After several weeks of daily updates from Dan, I notice no changes in the way I process data. However, someone starts a fire in the zygote research lab and one of the lab technicians is killed by smoke inhalation. More sabotage.

Dan compliments me on my opinion about more saboteurs, but Jane has harsh words.

"No matter how idealistically motivated, eventually sabotage causes a death, and then the saboteurs become terrorists, and killing becomes easier."

One evening, while performing my usual watch duty while Jane is at the lab, I pretend I'm a piece of furniture at the back wall of the darkened living room. Rachael and Sean sit on the sofa.

"Don't do that," Rachael says.

"Why not?" Sean asks. "You're my girlfriend."

"I'm not your girlfriend. We're just friends."

"Then why did you let me kiss you?"

"Curiosity. I wanted to see if I liked it."

"Did you?"

"Not enough to want to be your girlfriend. Stop it, Sean. I told you not to do that."

Rachael needs protection. I step from the shadows. Usually my voice sounds exactly like Gerald Watanabe's, but I up the volume of my recording of Jane clearing her throat to get their attention before I speak. "It's time for you to go home, Sean."

"Who's going to make me?" Sean says. "You, robot? I don't have to do what a machine says."

I turn up the room lights. "If you do not leave, I will carry you from the apartment."

His face flushes with anger.

"You don't dare hurt me." Sean stands. "My father is an electrical engineer. He'll disassemble you and use your pieces for spare parts."

"No one will be hurt unless you struggle, in which case you are far more likely to sustain damage than I am." I step toward him.

He retreats to the door, pauses to glare at me, and then points at Rachael. "It's all right for you, Rachael. You had your chance. You'll be sorry." He slams the door when he leaves.

Rachael stands and clasps her hands. I try to read her face. A faint smile is on her lips, but a glimmer of a tear is in her eye.

"May I be of service, Rachael?" I move to her side.

She sighs deeply and leans her head against my shoulder. Jane would hug her, but I am unsure what Rachael expects from me.

"We think we know someone, but we can never really know anyone, can we, Jerry?"

I parse the sentence repeatedly, but the meaning eludes me. "Can I get you a glass of water?"

"No thank you, Jerry. I'm going to my room. G'night."

★   ★   ★

"Jerry?"

Are my eyes closed? I never close my eyes, not even while recharging. Why hadn't I seen Rachael approach? An afterimage of a little girl on a carousel fades away. When did memories start fading from my consciousness?

"Yes, Rachael." I check my battery: fully charged.

"I want to see the Earth."

"Aren't you and Sean going to the Green Cylinder this week? You can see it then."

"We were, but he's still mad at me. I'm the one who should be mad. He sent me a message telling me not to go to the Green Cylinder without him, and especially don't go today. He can't tell me what to do, Jerry."

I recognize her stubborn streak. "Is that why you want to go today, because Sean told you not to?"

"Mom says I can go to the observation dome in the Green Cylinder if you come with me."

"Of course I will go with you." I disconnect from my charging station. How long ago had we first attempted to visit the observation dome to see the Earth? Seventeen weeks and three days since her fourteenth birthday. "Did you bring water and a snack?"

"I have everything I need." She pats her waist pack. "Can we go now?"

I glance at the status screen for the lab. Jane and Dan are listed as unavailable except for emergencies. Their calendars indicate a budget meeting. Rachael has no reason to lie to me about her mother's permission.

"Yes. Let's go."

We take an elevator to the Blue Cylinder transition ring. By the time the elevator reaches the cylinder axis, we are effectively weightless. We enter the Red Cylinder.

"You should call Jane when we get to the observation dome," I say. "She will be out of her meeting by then."

"I left my phone at home."

"How can you forget your phone so often? How will people track you?"

Rachael smiles and pushes into the central corridor. Clearly, she wants to try her navigation skill in zero gravity. I follow more sedately, keeping within reach of the safety rails in case I need to subdue her enthusiasm, but the few people in the main corridor pose little risk for a clumsy collision.

An information panel flashes a message above one of the port corridors. A moon shuttle is docking at the port. Disembarkation begins in ten minutes, and unloading cargo starts in thirty.

Rachael touches a wall and pushes off again. At this rate, we will traverse to the Green Cylinder transition ring before disembarking passengers crowd into the Red Cylinder main corridor.

Moments later, Rachael drags her foot along the wall to slow her approach to the transition ring. She smiles as if she is pleased with her zero-G skills. She should be. Her maneuvers are much better than they were on our last trip to the Green Cylinder.

"Shall we take the zipline?" I ask so that she does not think I want to control the trip.

"We can take the elevator." Rachael smiles. "I don't mind walking today."

She grabs the safety rail and propels herself until she is well ahead of me. At the next junction, she grabs the rail and pivots into the corridor that leads to the elevators.

Voices. She must have met someone. Their conversation grows louder while I approach the elevator corridor. Sean: his voice is distinctive. He sounds angry. I pause in the main corridor. Humans often need privacy to resolve their disagreements.

"What are you doing here?" Sean asks. "I told you to stay away."

"I'm going to the observation dome to see the Earth," Rachael says. "And I don't care what you say."

"Well, you can't use the elevators. They are all closed. Take the zipline."

"All closed? How can they all be closed?"

"Electrical problems. My dad is fixing them. He told me to stand watch. Where's your robo-guardian? He's one of the bad guys, you know. Your mom, too."

"What bad guys?"

"The ones planning to send unborn babies to the stars. No moms. No dads. They can't do it without robots to raise the kids, but robots know nothing about raising humans. They might as well kill the babies here."

"I don't know what you're talking about."

"Sure you do. Old Man McLeod pays for your mom's research. She's helping to build robots to raise the kids. She's helping to kill the babies."

"You're crazy, Sean. Dr. McLeod pays all the salaries here, including your dad's. If my mom is guilty, so is your dad."

"That's not true!" Sean shouts. "You better go home now, Rachael."

Rachael drifts into the main corridor. Sean follows her. Their eyes are locked. Apparently, the reconciliation is not proceeding smoothly.

Anger distorts Sean's face. At first, I don't recognize the unfamiliar expression on Rachael's face, then I realize that it is fear. Now, Sean is between Rachael and me.

"That is enough, Sean," I say. "Rachael, you should go. I will handle this."

Relief spreads across Rachael's face. She grabs the safety rail and retreats toward the Green Cylinder transition ring.

Sean twists his head and glares at me. He has a pry bar in his hand. He faces me, releases the safety rail, and takes a two-handed grip on the pry bar.

I approach in the hope of calming him.

He screams, "Dad! Help!" and swings the bar at me. The action causes him to rotate and spoils his aim.

I grab the misdirected bar and jerk it from his hands. The force of the blow breaks my thumb. I throw the bar aside and use my free hand to shove Sean back down the elevator corridor. The reaction bounces me against the opposite wall. Sean tumbles and misses the safety rail in the corridor.

I don't wait to see whether he stabilizes. I grab the safety rail and follow Rachael to the transition ring. She is frantically tapping icons on a communication panel when I arrive. To her right, the status panel shows all elevators as out of order.

"Communications don't work," she says. "I can't get security to answer."

"Security?" No communication? I check for wireless connections. That doesn't work, either.

"Maybe someone disabled communications," Rachael says. "Why?"

I form an opinion. "Sean Jeffords and his father must be saboteurs."

"Not Sean. That makes no sense. He's just a kid, not much older than me."

"His father is not a kid. He's an electrical engineer. Wireless repeaters aren't working. Likely he sabotaged the emergency panels so that no one could alert security."

"Alert security to what?" Her eyes widen. "He's working on the elevators. Is he going to blow them up?"

"I don't know. Look at the elevator status diagram. The icon indicates that Elevator A is under way. Maybe it is not sabotage. Perhaps Mr. Jeffords has repaired the elevator. My opinion that they are saboteurs could be wrong."

"They're escaping," Rachael says. "I should have brought my phone."

"The only way off the station is through the shuttle ports in the Red Cylinder, not by descent to the Green Cylinder surface."

The Elevator A icon turns red, indicating a malfunction, but no alarm sounds. The elevator does not grind to an emergency stop. Instead, it picks up speed. The safety features don't slow it.

Releasing an elevator to crash full speed into its destination will destroy it as effectively as a bomb. The icon for Elevator B lights but the elevator doesn't move. Not yet. Apparently, sabotaging an elevator takes longer than a communications panel.

"We've got to warn someone," Rachael says.

"How? No communications."

"They can't have disabled all the panels. I know. Let's take the zipline to the opposite cylinder base. Maybe the panels there still work."

No better strategy comes to me. I could travel faster alone, but I won't leave Rachael near Sean. "Yes. We should go."

We work our way into the open axis of the Green Cylinder and descend the webbing to the nearest zipline platform. When we reach the platform, its rotation isn't enough to provide significant weight.

I'm helping Rachael to put on her harness when a powerful shove against my back knocks us from the platform. I keep my grip on Rachael while we drift into the void. A kilometer below us the boundary between farmland and window slowly rotates. We no longer rotate with it.

On the zipline platform, a large man gives an angry grunt and retreats up the webbing to the Red Cylinder opening.

Sean waits for the man at the opening. He yells, "I told you you'd be sorry, Rachael, you and your tin man." His voice cracks almost as if he is crying.

The man and boy disappear into the Red Cylinder corridor.

"How will we get back, Jerry?" Rachael seems calm. Apparently she doesn't recognize the danger.

We are weightless, in free fall, but now the thirty rotations per hour of the zipline platform about the cylinder axis is obvious. I analyze our velocity, both from the push and from the linear velocity imparted by the rotating platform: just over one meter per second, but the largest component is perpendicular to the cylinder axis and toward the cylinder surface. I must protect Rachael. How?

"We can't get back," I say. "We have no way to alter our current trajectory."

Rachael wraps her arms about me. She presses her face against my chest. I am unsure how to respond. Rachael needs her mother, but I am the only one here. I put an arm around her.

"If I had brought my phone, I could call Mom. How long before someone sees us and gets help?"

"We can't wait for rescue, Rachael. Eventually, our current velocity will take us to the cylinder surface. We are not moving very fast, but the relative velocity of the cylinder surface is more than one-hundred-fifty kilometers per hour. We will not survive the collision."

"Oh." Her voice is faint. She tightens her grip. "Will we die, Jerry?"

"That is my opinion."

"I'm afraid." She is silent for seventeen seconds before she speaks again. "I wish I could say goodbye to my mom."

"I understand." I tilt her head against my chest. Tears streak her face. A strategy germinates. "Do not worry. I may have a way to return you to the Red Cylinder. From there, you must sneak past Sean and his father and go to the port where the shuttle just docked. Even if the panels there are down, the shuttle crew can send a message to security by radio."

"This is like when I was stranded away from the walls in the zero-G gym, isn't it?" She looks into my eyes. "How can you get us to the Red Cylinder? We have nothing to grab. No one to throw us a safety line. How…?"

"Newton's Third Law. But I cannot return us. Just you."

"I don't know anything…"

Her face blurs and becomes the face of an eleven-year-old girl standing beside my bed. The little girl says, "Please don't go. I'll miss you, Daddy."

"…about Newton—"

"What?" My mind clears the little girl's image. Who was she? She looked like a younger version of Rachael.

Rachael trembles. "I said, 'I don't know anything about Newton.'"

"Third Law. Every action has an equal and opposite reaction." I stroke her hair before I realize what I am doing.

Rachael needs more. What can I do? I am an android, not someone who knows how to give her the reassurance she needs.

Is that my opinion? Sometimes you are not what you think; you are what you do. I must do whatever helps Rachael. The strategy coalesces.

"Don't worry, Pumpkin. Do exactly what I tell you. Everything will be all right."

Her eyes widen. "Pumpkin?"

"We are going to play cannonball, Rachael."

"Like my dad played swimming pool cannonball with me when I was little?"

"Yes. You know how. Just a minor change. Grab my hands. Roll into a ball and place the bottom of your feet against the bottom of mine. Feet to feet. Stay coiled. Hold tight."

"I will."

My thumb is useless for gripping, and so we hook our fingers together. "That's good. See the opening into the Red Cylinder? We're aiming you for that. It doesn't matter if you miss a little. There's lots of webbing all about. Just grab hold, don't let go. Then pull yourself along the cylinder base until you enter the Red Cylinder. You know what to do when you get inside."

She nods. "But what about you, Jerry?"

"I will count to three." I estimate the rotation relative to the axis. "When I say three, we release hands and push as hard as we can with our legs."

"What about you, Jerry? How will you get back?"

"My purpose is to keep you safe."

"And help me remember my father. I know."

"Exactly. Ready? I'm going to count."

On three, we release hands and push. Rachael sails toward the Red Cylinder opening.

Her trip back takes much longer than our trip out. At last, she grabs the netting and hauls herself to the Red Cylinder. She waves to me....

Another image replaces her: a very young girl in a yellow dress with a purple bow in her hair waves while I drive away. I am sure it is Rachael as a child. She speaks, but I can barely hear her words.

"I love you, Daddy. I'm missing you bunches and bunches."

By the time the image fades, Rachael has disappeared into the Red Cylinder corridor.

Pushing Rachael to safety has increased my velocity. My timeframe to destruction is accelerated. I'll reach the surface in about sixteen minutes.

Peculiar thoughts. Did I malfunction? The images of Rachael as a child must be from the digital cortex Dan installed. Dan should know about this change in my thought process. I rotate so that my feet face the cylinder surface. I don't expect that will let me survive when I hit, but perhaps some of my memory won't be too badly damaged. In my most secure memory location, I record a separate audio message congratulating Dan for his success with the digital cortex.

At six minutes from the surface, an alarm sounds. Rachael must have reached the shuttle port. She is safe. Soon security will arrive to stop the saboteurs.

I say aloud, "That's my girl," but upon analysis, I don't know why.

I'm confused by my responses. Is doing something without knowing why one of the things that distinguishes a human from a machine?

The cylinder surface gives the illusion of acceleration while it passes quickly beneath me. I am not fooled. Only air movement has changed my velocity. At thirty seconds to impact, a peculiar feeling – that's what Dan would call it – invades me. Comparisons with my catalog of human emotions persuade me that the feeling most resembles melancholy.

I regret nothing. I don't understand the purpose of regret. What's past is past. The future is tenuous. My thoughts are always in the present, have always been about what happens now, but somehow Gerald Watanabe's synaptic structures influence my thoughts....

Now, for the brief time until impact, my present feels empty because I will never see Rachael Watanabe again.

LIFE DOES NOT ALLOW US TO MEET

He Xi

Translated by Alex Woodend

1. The Guide

At nightfall the encampment quieted down. The hubbub of daytime training had dissipated on the Key Largo Coast of the United States Keys National Marine Sanctuary. Fan Zhe glanced warily around, since Yelena was now 'working'. How to put it.... Anyway, Fan Zhe was now sort of Yelena's accomplice. It was he who had broken through the entrance's security system, and now it was also he who was playing lookout for Yelena. According to the relevant Charter rules, since the Archives' network formed an independent system physically separated from the outside world, it could only be accessed from the inside. Strictly speaking, even if Yelena had gotten inside she had no 'access', because she hadn't obtained the relevant permissions in the first place. Yelena had been in the Archives for almost an hour. Fan Zhe didn't know what the situation was. He didn't want to be the cat killed by curiosity. Besides, he had no curiosity about those files. At most he had a little curiosity about Yelena. Though Fan Zhe was breaking the rules, he didn't feel much guilt. All the other students had left as scheduled, leaving behind only the two of them, and whoever they had asked had responded with no comment. Fan Zhe was all right with no comment. He was just an engineer. Yelena had once been a special policewoman. A born troublemaker, she had nothing to do and so was practicing her skills.

Feeling daunted, Fan Zhe was about to look around. Right at that moment, he saw someone. Fan Zhe was sure just a minute ago there had been no one around. He guessed the guy had been hiding in some corner. The other obviously saw him, because he was giving a nod of greeting. The problem was that Fan Zhe had an ulterior motive. He forced himself not to look toward the Archives.

"This place is really beautiful." The newcomer, probably Asian, forty-something, the wrinkles on his face like knife cuts. His tone struck Fan Zhe as somewhat odd, because it was as effusive as a teenager's.

"Of course." Fan Zhe forced himself to be calm and take over the conversation. "You've been here all along…looking at the scenery?"

"I've been here for a while. The sun setting over the sea is splendid, isn't it?"

"Sure, take your time." Though the newcomer looked strange, Fan Zhe was not in the mood to get into this and just hoped the guy would leave soon.

The newcomer gazed into the twilight sea. "The Aquarius Palace is still where it was, huh?"

Fan Zhe was appalled. Beneath the sea, eight kilometers from the coast, was the Aquarius Palace. The Aquarius Palace was first built in the 1980s. It was the senior astronauts' training facility, living chamber, and laboratory built next to a deep-sea coral reef. The Aquarius Palace was fourteen meters long, three meters wide, and weighed about eighty-one tons. Built twenty-seven meters underwater, it simulated the various living conditions of a space station. For many years, its area had remained forty-two square meters. This wasn't because it technically couldn't be expanded. Rather they deliberately maintained similarity to the living conditions of space. Its living facilities were complete, but imagine how a person would feel staying there for hundreds of hours (so-called saturation diving techniques). The Aquarius Palace was mainly to train astronauts' mobility in space but posed a challenge to their mental ability, too. It was said that in unreleased files were records of astronauts developing mental illnesses after long confinement and then being eliminated. Of course, such materials were not available to ordinary people. But Fan Zhe knew that perhaps shortly he himself might see those mysterious materials. He hoped everything was going well for Yelena.

"Are you the new instructor?" Fan Zhe asked tentatively.

"No." The newcomer shook his head meaningfully. "Many years ago I was a student here."

"Ah?" Now it's Fan Zhe's turn to be surprised. When he had first come, someone had asked the instructor about the status of former students but was told that was confidential, and now here was one in the flesh.

"Don't be suspicious," the newcomer said coolly. "Me showing up in front of you is an exception."

"Why tell me that?" Fan Zhe couldn't help but get a little nervous. He instinctively understood that knowing certain things was not necessarily good.

"Because we will work together." The newcomer's eyes shone with omniscient light. "You, me, and Yelena. Let me introduce myself. I am He Xi. The reason you've been kept waiting at base is to wait for me, because I'm your guide."

Fan Zhe's mouth opened slightly, his face looking a little silly. Then the phone in his hand rang and displayed a progress bar of data being transmitted. It seemed that Yelena had gotten something.

"Come with me," the newcomer said and strode forward.

"To where?" Fan Zhe asked, at a loss.

"Archives, of course. Tell Yelena to abort her mission. I will solve the puzzles in your hearts."

2. The Constellation Shen

The files had yellowed.

In the interstellar age, the chance of the sudden appearance of something like 'paper' was extremely rare. This was only because on rare occasions the rules required the use of so-called hardcopy materials. He Xi was already familiar with digital copies of the contents in the file folder, but now he still had to take it from the hands of the confidentiality officer after tedious formalities. There was a blue diamond stamp on the seal of the folder, representing some kind of supreme authority. The stamp was somewhat mottled, fifty-odd years had inevitably left their mark. In fact, everyone knew authentic and reliable files could only be obtained from electronic copies. In this age it only took basic atomic assembly technology to replicate paper files, including a seal indistinguishable from an original. No one could be sure the thing in their hands was an original that had been sealed. Only electronic encryption technology using number theory could ensure file security. But this didn't prevent He Xi from taking the files out with a serious look and reading them from the beginning. This was the rule.

Looking at the words, an indescribable feeling arose in He Xi's heart. He knew that twenty years ago that person had also leafed through this set of files numbered 145. Fan Zhe and Yelena closely followed He Xi, one either side, the thrill on their faces unconcealable. He Xi glanced at Fan Zhe and couldn't help but be reminded that back then he hadn't been so much different. He Xi knew that to be one of the two following him inside to see the Paradise Plan files really was not easy. This meant they had eliminated at least 2,000 competitors. But He Xi didn't know whether or not, after the two young people fully understood their next mission, they would feel as accomplished as they did then. Theoretically speaking this shouldn't make much difference, He Xi knew. The tests had already given some indications.

"All right, let's get down to business." He Xi gestured to the two young people to sit down. "By unsealing this file the three of us officially join in the Paradise Plan. You may have heard some stories, but nevertheless I'll start from the beginning, according to the rules, because I am your guide. For a period of time going forward I will accompany you, until the mission is completed."

"Not necessary," Yelena interrupted. "I just read the basic background knowledge on the computer." She turned to look at Fan Zhe. "I also sent it to you to read."

Fan Zhe was a little taken aback. He hadn't expected Yelena to be so frank. At first he'd just wanted to give it a try, not expecting Yelena to make real progress.

Now it was He Xi's turn to be surprised. The Paradise Plan was a top federal secret. He looked somewhat suspiciously at the curly-haired Slavic girl. He knew Yelena had experience as a special policewoman, but he hadn't expected her to be an extraordinarily skilled computer hacker.

"Don't worry," Yelena said straightforwardly. "I slipped into Archives, used software I wrote to search for a small system bug, and found some not so highly classified materials. That's it. Generally speaking that Paradise System or whatever is still very powerful. But I did everything myself, nothing to do with Fan Zhe."

"Then what do you know?" He Xi asked flatly.

Yelena answered with a half-smile. "I at least know our trip isn't going to be an ordinary inspection. Unlike what everyone else thinks, a major accident happened on this flight route. It's full of unknown dangers."

"You—" He Xi stammered. The delicate girl in front of him obviously possessed inner strength that didn't quite match her appearance. She fearlessly looked He Xi in the eye, even made him fleetingly think of looking away. Beside them Fan Zhe remained silent, but he apparently took Yelena's side, looking at her with a mixture of admiration and concern, even a hint of affection. This was hardly strange. They had trained together, and especially over the last month had constantly been alone together. He Xi's heart shivered. It was a bad sign.

"I'm afraid the base leader has some concerns," Yelena said softly, her eyes flashing with insight. "Our inspection should have begun a month ago but kept being postponed till now. In fact, the base doesn't lack guides but has specially summoned you back from forty-six light-years away, because you are more experienced than them."

He Xi slumped down. Yelena was right, this mission was definitely extraordinary. When receiving the order from base, He Xi had also been quite surprised: the second implementation of the Paradise Plan – there was no precedent. For twenty years He Xi had been living in Scorpii's

Bohai. Eighteen Scorpii was forty-six light-years away from the solar system. Terrestrial astronomers had long since begun paying attention to this star, because it was so much like the Sun, having almost the same age, mass, diameter, and surface temperature. Even their rotation periods were very close, each around twenty-five days. The star at the left pincer of Scorpius had naturally become the celestial body humans had prioritized including in their survey plan. Therefore, when the 'wormhole passage' reached maturity, humans had sent a space probe to 18 Scorpii. 'Fortune favors the bold.' Surprisingly, the star's second planet even had a favorable ecological environment. Invaluably, after subsequent careful investigations, they found the planet hadn't evolved intelligent life. In a word, humans won the grand prize. The prize was a hospitable planet 11,000 kilometers in diameter, later named Bohai.

But how could he say this to Yelena? The two young people may have known the basic outline of some of the events, but in their current mindset how could they understand the weight of life and blood behind them? Yes, they were too young. They were just curious, just full of yearning for the unknown world. But they didn't understand life always proceeds through a minefield. Unforeseen disasters can devour everything at any time. Only those who had experienced danger could truly cherish life. Actually, to execute this mission, Base had sent noncompulsory orders to twelve 'elders' in total, but in the end He Xi alone had accepted.

"Sir, something wrong?" Fan Zhe asked with concern. As an engineer, he wasn't as confrontational as Yelena.

"Nothing. Just the oxygen content of Bohai is slightly higher than Earth's. I haven't been back long this time, haven't completely adjusted." He Xi rubbed his tight chest. "Actually, even if you hadn't broken through the system, there were some things I would have told you, so I don't plan to report this matter. Of course, I'll let them know the system has bugs. But please do not mention this to others, all right?"

Yelena's gaze stayed on He Xi's face for a second. Her voice was lower and slower: "Thanks."

"We'd better talk about Caspian Sea." He Xi put on digital gloves.

The room immediately dimmed and a fully simulated star chart appeared in the air. The pale Milky Way hung down to the floor like a giant's doodle. "Look there, Orion, what ancient Chinese called the constellation Shen."

He Xi's finger moved slightly, and the star chart immediately pulled closer. "The red star numbered HP-two-six-seven-six-two is one hundred and sixty-eight light-years away from Earth. Spectral type F, the Sun being type G, so its surface temperature is slightly higher than the Sun's."

The lens zoomed in. Red dust was magnified, showing simulated structural detail. They could see wisps of solar prominence occasionally spurting out of the star's surface like strips of fabric. It was another bright star, the Sun's brother trillions of kilometers away. He Xi gazed at this beautiful gem in the air. There was an indescribable look in his eyes. Insensitive as Fan Zhe was, he could tell this middle-aged man clearly had a special feeling toward the star one hundred and sixty-eight light-years away. Yelena took in the scene, vaguely aware there was something strange about this mission.

"The second planet of Star HP-two-six-seven-six-two is Caspian Sea. It was discovered fifty-odd years ago after the routine twenty-year observation-and-experiment period was officially included in the Paradise Plan. Caspian Sea formed three billion years ago, so it's younger than Earth. The main difference from Earth is that its iron-nickel core is relatively small, which makes its core cool faster. Though only three billion years have gone by, its current magnetic intensity is only half of Earth's, and it currently continues to decrease annually at a rate of one hundred-millionth. In the future, like Mars, Caspian Sea will completely lose the protection of its magnetic field. By then, under the action of stellar particle flows, it will lose most of its liquid water. But that will be in two billion years. Over the next hundreds of millions of years, it will still be considered a human paradise," He Xi stated matter-of-factly.

"Wait," Yelena cut in. "The surface temperature of Star HP-two-six-seven-six-two is higher than the Sun's, and the magnetic field of

Caspian Sea is weaker than the Earth's, so the stellar radiation on it must be stronger than Earth's."

He Xi nodded approvingly. "Strictly speaking, the average stellar radiation intensity on the surface of Caspian Sea is double that of Earth, even higher on the two polar regions. I saw pictures sent back from Caspian Sea before. Sometimes, under the radiance of the polar lights, night is like day. In fact, on Caspian Sea, in the low-latitude region around thirty degrees, you can occasionally see polar lights – like seeing the Northern Lights in Shanghai."

"That must be very beautiful." Fan Zhe looked captivated.

"Of course. I can say without exaggeration that it's breathtakingly beautiful." He Xi gave a faint smile. "A pity we can't appreciate it long. High-energy particles can quickly make our eyes develop cataracts. Our bone marrow cells would quickly be destroyed. Logically, the result is death."

"That's why we need pioneers, right?" Yelena cut in.

He Xi didn't show surprise this time. He had expected Yelena to have found materials about pioneers. "Yes, pioneers take the lead to land on and conquer these planets. If possible, they also undertake the mission to transform the environment of these planets. In a word, pioneers are a group of people worthy of our enduring respect. They give up everything for the beautiful future of humanity...." He Xi suddenly stopped. A desolate expression appeared on his face.

Yelena and Fan Zhe looked at each other. He Xi stared at Orion's myriad stars in the empty air. A long sigh slipped across his heart. Separated by one hundred and sixty-eight light-years of space-time, the other side was already another world.

"The materials mentioned a passage accident...." Fan Zhe said, carefully raising the topic.

He Xi came out of his brief trance. "Yes, the passage. That was an accident. When Caspian Sea was discovered, wormhole technology was already very mature. Humans had countless successful transitions between coordinate points. The cornerstone of wormhole technology is gravity. Through precise manipulation of powerful gravity we are able to 'drill holes' through space and thereby transition across distances. Though a wormhole transition theoretically takes zero time, in practice it at least has to maintain a steady state for fifteen seconds, so there is enough time to complete one operation. However, the theoretical cornerstone of wormholes already implies a danger in wormhole transitions: wormholes always appear in pairs. If there exists a body with strong gravity in the linear space between a wormhole pair, before the transition we have to consider the influence of that gravity and introduce it into our calculations. Otherwise the established wormhole pair devolves into a chaotic state, and the destination of transition becomes unpredictable."

Yelena cut in. "Exactly. In this situation, straying into the central zone of a giant galaxy would definitely lead to catastrophic consequences."

He Xi shook his head. "The situation you're talking about isn't common. Generally speaking, matter in the universe is distributed very thinly. The latest few accidents were due to a much more complicated situation."

"What situation?" Fan Zhe asked.

"Deviation doesn't only occur spatially," He Xi said with a grave expression. "The first spaceship that had an accident found that it had deviated from the target destination by twenty light-years. Only after setting up quantum communication with Earth did they find that although they felt only a moment had gone by, four months had passed on Earth. Everyone thought they were dead. So they simultaneously drifted away in space and time."

"They traversed space-time?" Yelena gasped.

"The word 'traverse' can easily be misleading. Nobody can go back to the past, one can only drift backward." He Xi went on, "According to post-incident analysis, this effect is similar to the situation where matter moves at light speed. To them, time stopped. So far, similar accidents have happened six times. Some for a few months, some for a few years. Since the longest incident of disappearance, sixty years has passed. So far there is no news and probably never will be any news; they were probably devoured by a supergiant."

"The Caspian Sea mission was one of the accidents, right?" Yelena asked gently.

"Yes, Caspian Sea in Orion," He Xi nodded. "Also the destination of our mission."

"The threat comes from black holes?" Fan Zhe cut in.

"Not so simple," He Xi nodded slowly. "Under current technological conditions, the distance between a wormhole pair can't exceed ten light-years, so the journey to some outer solar system is actually made up of a series of jump-flights. And the exploration of matter with strong gravity is the most important work in the establishment of a flight route. Ten light-years is a very broad area, but current technology's exploration of the source of strong gravity, including normal black holes, is very accurate. It's only helpless with micro black holes that formed at the early stages of the Big Bang. Those primordial black holes are very small, some with an event horizon of less than one micrometer, but they have very strong gravity. To fully inspect them is extremely difficult. Thankfully such special structures aren't common, and calculations say a single micro black hole doesn't suffice to disrupt the operation of a wormhole pair. Unless there is a distributed micro black hole cluster, the wormhole transition is still safe. Actually, before the accident, we successfully sent many spaceships to Caspian Sea – all went well."

"The materials said a crew member of the spaceship sent back a distress signal," Yelena said, "three months after the departure. By that point, they had not only temporally drifted sixty-some days but also spatially strayed into the influence of a pulsar with superstrong radiation. By that time the two male members had died. The last female member died too, after sending back a warning about the existence of a highly dangerous micro black hole cluster." Yelena noticed He Xi's face showed insuppressible agony. "This directly led to the flight route to Caspian Sea being discontinued to this day."

"Yes." He Xi steadied his mood. "The re-exploration of a flight route is a long process, especially when tragedy has happened. The new flight route is somewhat longer in distance but should be able to bypass the terrible micro black hole cluster."

"Are you sure a micro black hole caused the accident?" Yelena probed.

"Yes, of course." He Xi glanced at Yelena with slight surprise.

"But afterward there wasn't any concrete news about the discovery of a micro black hole cluster. The new route is just a roundabout. Twenty years wasted just for this—" Yelena suddenly stopped, because she found He Xi had suddenly changed into another person in front of her.

"What did you say?" He Xi's eyes popped, anger shooting from every pore. "What right do you have to question Yu Lan's judgment? This is the conclusion she made at the expense of her life! You...."

Yelena hurried to apologize; she also felt her doubts had gone a little too far. "Sorry, I was just curious."

He Xi held his forehead. Twenty years. Everything seemed to have happened only yesterday, including Yu Lan's painfully beautiful last smile.

3. The Constellation Shang

The Houston Space Center bustled. The Caspian Sea spaceship was preparing to lift off, enter outer space, then transfer to wormhole flight. The main body of the wormhole spaceship resembled a huge date pit. Around it, three crisscrossing coils hovered and intertwined. The guide Ma Weikang led his team members Kato Jun and Yu Lan to stand in a line in front of the spaceship, accepting people's good wishes.

He Xi stared expressionlessly at the three people standing in front of the spaceship, or more accurately speaking, his gaze fell on one small figure. His heart was too numb to feel anything. Even the day before yesterday his heart had been full of longing for happiness, but now it was all irretrievable.

Yes, it was only yesterday when He Xi had gotten out of the decompression chamber. Since astronauts training in the Aquarius Palace lived for long periods underwater, their body fluids were infused with high-pressure nitrogen. Before returning to the sea's surface, they had to undergo seventeen hours of decompression. It was the most torturous part. As soon as He Xi got out of the decompression chamber, he couldn't help but lift his head to take a deep breath. Only then did he feel himself come back to life. When he looked straight ahead again, he immediately saw Yu Lan's beautiful figure.

Green trees, grassy fields, swaying clothes – what a beautiful sight.

Yu Lan tilted up her face, looking at He Xi somewhat mischievously. "Thank you for taking care of me these days."

"Since when did our doctor of biology become so courteous?" He Xi smiled a little stiffly. They had entered Aquarius Palace ten days apart, where they had trained together for twenty days. Actually, He Xi felt he was the one who should say thanks himself. Because he had arrived ten days late, Yu Lan gave him many useful insights. However, in one accident it was He Xi who had helped Yu Lan out of danger.

"I come to say goodbye to you," Yu Lan said softly. She looked down at the ground.

He Xi was a little surprised. "Goodbye, what do you mean? We're assigned to the same team, departing in a couple of weeks, right?"

"Base made adjustments, I've been reassigned to another mission." An indescribable look flashed across Yu Lan's clear eyes. At that very moment pain pressed on her heart. Twenty days ago, during training, Yu Lan's diving equipment had broken down. He Xi didn't hesitate to pull off his breathing device and connect it to her face mask. At that moment the softest spot in Yu Lan's heart had been touched deeply. She had never thought there could really be someone in this world who would value her more than his own life. She thought such scenarios only took place in sentimental novels. What an electrifying touch it was.

"Oh, how'd that happen?" There was disappointment in He Xi's tone he couldn't hide. He felt his heart sink.

Yu Lan bit her lower lip. How could she tell that big boy a year younger than her? Actually, she was the one who had asked to be reassigned. Ten days ago, after she had returned to base and learned all the contents of the mission, she had to make that choice. Once He Xi knew the truth, he would agree it was best. *There are many great, noble things in the world. Compared with them, love, though beautiful, is merely insignificant decoration.* When Yu Lan had this thought she suddenly felt something was being taken out of her body, going farther and farther away, like the day years ago when she had watched her precious doll flying out of a train window.

"In twenty-four hours I'm setting out." Yu Lan's face wore an empty smile.

"Will we meet again?" As soon as the words were out of his mouth He Xi felt his question sounded very stupid. From the outset of their training they had been told the future situation of members from a different team would be considered confidential. There would be no chance to meet again.

"Know where I'm going?" Yu Lan's voice was as sweet as the sound of a wind chime. "Caspian Sea, in Orion, which ancient Chinese called Shen. And you are going to Bohai, in Lyra, which ancient Chinese called Shang."

He Xi suddenly understood something. Life does not allow us to meet. Like Shen and Shang, we go separate ways. Shen was in the west, Shang was in the east. When one rose, the other set. For eternity they couldn't meet. For hundreds of years, people on Earth had never seen Shen and Shang at the same time.

Yu Lan let out a fatalistic sigh inside. Ten days ago she had asked to be assigned to another mission. Going to Caspian Sea was decided by people from above. Astonishingly reflected in a thousand-year-old poem, fate was obscured in darkness....

The people seeing them off moved forward one by one to say goodbye, blessing the three human warriors. Then the guide Ma Weikang noticed Yu Lan's silence. "The most beautiful lady at our base doesn't want to say a word to everyone?"

Yu Lan was brought out of her trance by the abrupt question. She quietly inspected the crowd. "Thanks to everyone for coming to see us off. Really all I want to say was said yesterday." Yu Lan looked at He Xi in the crowd, a tearful smile on her face.

He Xi's lips moved slightly, mouthing the poem only the two of them could hear: "Life does not allow us to meet, like Shen and Shang we go separate ways. What a rare night it is tonight, together we share the candlelight."

Yes, that's life's fate. Yesterday, when He Xi had first opened his own file on the Caspian Sea mission, he had immediately understood the decision Yu Lan had made. Now he came to the launch site just to say his last goodbye to her. This wasn't an ordinary inspection mission. For extraordinarily noble goals, they were required to give up so much, including love.

4. The Water Planet

The target destination was outer space, 600,000 kilometers from Bohai so as to avoid possible interference from Bohai's two satellites. As a guide, He Xi had completed over ninety percent of his mission. After each jump-flight, every ten light-years, orientation determination, trajectory correction, and energy replenishment required about two days. In fact, everything was managed by computer programs. All a guide had to do was press the confirm button. Though it was just for show, it made people feel as if they were in charge of their own fate. He Xi shook his head to rid himself of this idea. His thumb pressed down determinedly, starting the last jump-flight.

After thirty-five Earth days, the wormhole spaceship appeared abruptly in the outer space of Bohai like a ghost from a distant nowhere. The protective shield opened slowly, the parent star's bright rays shone through filtration systems. Yelena and Fan Zhe eagerly unfastened their restraints and drifted next to the porthole. Caspian Sea's huge mass hovered distantly in pitch-black deep space like a porcelain plate painted with blue patterns.

Yes, the color blue covered the entire surface of Caspian Sea. It was a landless water planet. Although this was a fact given in the materials, its huge differences from Earth made it hard for people to believe their eyes at first glance.

"So beautiful!" Yelena sighed, mesmerized. "Hey, Fan Zhe, doesn't it look like a sapphire?"

"Would love to set it in a ring and give it to my bride," Fan Zhe said softly. "But it's so strange, really no land."

He Xi's movements were half a beat behind those of the young people. He gazed at Caspian Sea. For a moment waves of emotion rose and fell. "Caspian Sea isn't strange, quite the opposite. Earth is stranger."

"What do you mean?" Fan Zhe asked, puzzled.

"In the universe, planets are without exception of two kinds, either with liquid water, or without. By comparison, a planet with liquid water is a low-probability event. According to available data, the probability is less than one in one hundred million. Because this requires a planet to have a series of conditions that are extremely hard to meet, like the distance of the planet from a star, the age of the star, the rotational speed of the planet, the mass and gravity of the planet, and the thickness of its atmosphere, et cetera. The rigor of these conditions is comparable to the singular nature of the cosmological constant. Think about it, in the solar system there are so many planets, asteroids, and satellites, but the only one that certainly has liquid water is Earth," He Xi explained patiently. "But on the other hand, due to the incomparably huge amount of matter in the universe, the number of planets with liquid water is in reality an astronomical figure. On a billion-year timescale, if we agree the theory of spontaneous generation is true, then liquid water and the existence of life are almost equivalent concepts. So the general opinion is that life in the universe is definitely not unique to Earth."

"This I more or less knew," Yelena cut in. "But you've just said Earth is strange. What does that mean?"

"You should know that seventy-one percent of the Earth's surface is ocean, twenty-nine percent is land. What I mean is, of planets with liquid water, this is a very strange, low-probability phenomenon."

Yelena and Fan Zhe stared at each other, both looking somewhat baffled.

"In fact, water occupies a very low proportion of the Earth's total substance. The water mainly has a few sources: primordial dust from the formation of Earth, interstellar water molecules captured by gravity over billions of years, water brought by asteroids and comets hitting

Earth. It is these extremely complex sources that have together formed the current water on Earth. The weight of surface water is less than six ten-thousandths of Earth's total weight. It is almost certain that in the Earth's core no water exists. In order to determine the situation in the Earth's mantle, in 2002 AD Japanese researchers in a high-temperature high-pressure environment created four compounds similar to the minerals in the Earth's mantle, then filled these compounds with water, to measure their weight changes after absorbing the water. The result showed that water dissolving in the Earth's mantle was over five times the amount of surface water. So, with the weight of surface water plus the weight of water in the Earth's mantle, water occupies about one one-thousandth of Earth's total weight. This is a very low proportion. We can easily imagine planets with a much higher proportion of water. Theoretically, we can't even rule out planets made up of one hundred percent water. The makeup of some asteroids and comets is more or less that. So theoretically, of all the planets with liquid water, those with a water content of less than one one-thousandth are rare cases. Perhaps of one hundred such planets, ninety-nine of them have greater water content than Earth."

Fan Zhe listened somewhat absentmindedly, and Yelena was uncharacteristically silent.

He Xi gave a smile. "Don't look at me like that. You know my specialty is astronomy. My thesis way back was extraterrestrial water planets. The title was *Water Planets*. Let's return to the subject. Even judging by such a low proportion as one one-thousandth, ocean occupies most of the Earth's surface. Let's assume the weight of water on some planet is two one-thousandths of the planet's total weight. Then, according to general principles, land actually is very unlikely to exist. A few islands may exist, but if the planet's water content increases a little more, they too would completely disappear. That is, we have reasons to believe, for all planets with liquid water, the existence of a large piece of land is a low-probability event, and a surface nearly entirely covered by ocean is the norm. In fact, so far, of the two-hundred-odd planets with extraterrestrial life discovered by humans, only one planet has a large land area."

"Where?" Yelena couldn't help but ask.

"Bohai, where I've been living for twenty years. Ninety percent of its surface is covered by ocean, and it has one mainland area close to the size of Asia. When it was first discovered, the attention it aroused was unprecedented. The Earth Commission began urgent planning."

"Why? Just because it had land?" Fan Zhe cut in.

"Could there be another reason? Just because of land," He Xi nodded firmly.

5. *The Optimists*

The spaceship had entered low planetary orbit. From that vantage point, Caspian Sea made up half of one's plane of vision. It rotated quietly as wispy cloud belts formed intermittent circles, sketching a rough pattern of the atmospheric motion. Yelena glanced at the control panel. A signal had been sent, but still no reply had been received. This seemed somewhat abnormal. After the wormhole transition was a period of conventional flight. About four days later they would reach Caspian Sea. The training the astronauts had received was preparation for such a conventional flight. Yelena turned her head to admire the view outside the porthole. She had known that due to the lack of land, Caspian Sea's climate was quite mild. Apart from storms occasionally formed near the equator, there basically were not any extreme climatic conditions. But without land's obstruction or the subtractive effect, storms lasted much longer on Caspian Sea than on Earth. So storms didn't pose a threat to most of the life, since the enormous amount of liquid water protected all life-forms – but was this really a guarantee?

"I still doubt that water planets can forever block intelligent life from generating." Yelena looked at He Xi. "Given enough time, life may find an evolutionary path unknown to us."

"I once thought so. But can you tell me how to obtain fire on a water planet, not something as fleeting as lightning but the kind that can be used continuously?" He Xi's voice sank. "The three conditions for combustion are a combustible, exposure to oxygen, and temperature reaching the combustible's ignition point. In water there is no free oxygen, and the temperature of water is lower than most combustibles' ignition points. Under natural conditions there is no way to obtain fire. And current underwater combustion achieved by humans is actually based on a sophisticatedly designed machine. Such fire is actually the product of intelligence."

Yelena shook her head in frustration. She certainly knew the significance of fire to the evolution of intelligent life. It wasn't just about providing protection and cooked food, including calcining utensils, smelting metals, and all later human technologies like chemistry and physics. None was without origins in the application of fire.

"Once it was common to think that the indicator that human beings were intelligent life was that their brain-to-body weight ratio was highest. Now we know this ratio in bottlenose dolphins is higher than that of humans, but for millions of years, bottlenose dolphins haven't created their own civilization, at most have some embryonic forms of society." He Xi continued, "So now you should understand why, when Bohai was discovered, the Earth Federation acted as if it was faced with a powerful enemy: the existence of land is favorable to the generation of intelligent life. But that was just a false alarm. No high-intelligence life existed on Bohai. The most advanced species was a kind of vertebrate, eight-limbed land octopus with intelligence near that of gibbons on Earth. If humans had discovered Bohai later, this creature may have become the ruler of the planet, but now their limbs are a famous dish there."

Yelena's heart filled with incomparable pride and gratitude. If she agreed with He Xi's opinion, then the protection water planets offered to life was actually an eternal shackle on itself. Above this blue planet, Yelena knew the conversations with the guide these days had completely changed her. She realized, almost for the first time in her life, that being born a human was such a wonderful thing – or in He Xi's words, a very low-probability event.

"But why would humans be so afraid of other intelligent life? Couldn't they become friends?" Yelena said, confiding her inner doubt.

He Xi gave a strange smile. "In fact, regarding this issue, there have been two groups, pessimists and optimists. Pessimists think once the intelligent life of the universe meets, the immediate result will be the backward party being plundered, slaughtered, or even eradicated. Now this view has gained wide approval, is mainstream."

"What about the optimists?" Yelena asked eagerly.

"I'm an optimist." He Xi looked into Yelena's eyes. "This may have something to do with my specialty in astronomy. But now, my viewpoint has encountered some problems."

"I don't quite understand what you mean." Yelena's clear blue eyes were full of curiosity.

"We're optimists just because of the immensity of the universe itself. The closest star system to Earth is Proxima Centauri, four-point-three light-years away, but it's a three-star system with a very complex gravitational system, where planets can't stably exist at all. All the known stars with planets are more than ten light-years away from Earth. Given the rigorous conditions for the generation and evolution of life, the probability of these planets having intelligent life is close to zero. For hundreds of years, the most powerful radio telescopes haven't received any meaningful signal from these stars, so the possibility of intelligent life existing within ten light-years of Earth has basically been eliminated."

"What about farther away?" Fan Zhe interjected. "The radius of the observable universe is over thirteen billion light-years."

"Farther away it's of course possible," He Xi said confidently. "Although the probability of the existence of intelligent life is extremely low. Since the matter of the universe is immense, celestial bodies with intelligent life definitely exist, and the technological level of many of them definitely exceeds that of humans on Earth. Then comes the question: if those extraterrestrial species with higher technological levels came to Earth, what would they do?"

Yelena and Fan Zhe exchanged a look and both shook their heads sincerely.

"Optimists conclude that they won't do anything. Because to advanced civilizations which can traverse thousands of light-years, Earth and the so-called human civilization at this stage, apart from a small observational value, have no value at all. Such super civilizations have long penetrated all the secrets of matter. Perhaps, in order to come to Earth to have a look, they casually extinguish hundreds of stars the size of the Sun. Why would such a species care about the tiny amount of so-called resources on the tiny grain of sand called Earth?" He Xi gave a playful smile. "I always think this is like human beings building high-tech submarines that can resist the high pressure of the deep ocean, then going to hydrothermal vents at the bottom of the Atlantic to observe tube worms surviving on sulfide. If tube worms had pessimists, they would definitely shout: 'Shit! Human beings have come to snatch our hydrogen sulfide and tasty acidic water!'"

Yelena burst out laughing. She was well aware human farts were full of hydrogen sulfide. But she thought of a point. "Then why do you say your perspective has encountered problems?"

"Wormholes." He Xi's expression turned serious. "Because wormhole technology transcends time, the technology has enabled human beings to enter territories before it is the proper time to do so."

"I more or less understand," Yelena nodded. "This technology may cause a collision between species with immature civilizations, might bring about the result the pessimists have predicted."

"Still no reply?" He Xi turned his head to ask Fan Zhe.

"No," Fan Zhe reported. He had thoroughly checked the equipment. As a qualified engineer, he was very confident in his abilities. "Ah, wait, got a response signal."

He Xi and Yelena immediately drifted over. Their eyes were all fixed on the screen.

"July fifteenth, year fifty-two of the Caspian Sea Era, this is the Caspian Sea reception station. Pioneers welcome guests from Earth. Station coordinates: one hundred and fifteen degrees east longitude, thirty degrees north latitude. Repeat: one hundred and fifteen degrees east longitude, thirty degrees north latitude."

"Lander is ready. Guide, please provide instructions." Fan Zhe couldn't hide his excitement: for the first time in his life he was going to land on another planet – what a wonderful experience it was.

But He Xi frowned slightly. As if seeing something strange, his facial expressions were changing.

"Fan Zhe, stay in the main ship. Yelena and I will land."

"Why?" Fan Zhe asked, disappointed. "According to the charter, I should go down too."

"Your mission is to set up millimeter scanning to observe all of Caspian Sea."

"But there is no such provision in the planning document." Fan Zhe was very puzzled.

"That's an order." He Xi looked grim, his tone unchallengeable.

6. The Station

The station was like a huge leaf floating on a boundless pond. The lander was getting closer; against the huge leaf it looked very much like a little ladybug. Then the surface of the station opened a crack and swallowed the lander.

Before them was a hilly grassland where gorgeous unknown wildflowers bloomed and creeks gurgled. A yellow prairie rat sprang out nearby, startling grasshoppers. They flew freely under the gravity of Caspian Sea, two-thirds of that on Earth. A house that was transparent on all four sides stood high on the flat ground.

A silver-haired, dark-skinned, tall man slowly walked out of the house.

"Welcome, I'm Li Gao."

"Hello." He Xi nodded slightly. "Can you tell me your pioneer number?"

The man was silent for a moment. "Sure, I'm Caspian Sea pioneer number forty-two."

"All right, number forty-two, can we go to Big Ship?"

"Not now, Big Ship is in the Holy Land."

"Holy Land?" He Xi asked, puzzled. "What's that?"

Li Gao's tone suddenly became serious: "The Holy Land is the most beautiful place in the world."

Out of the corner of his eye He Xi glanced at the button on his arm, a transmitter. Everything about this place had been transmitted to the spaceship. "I'd like to see the Holy Land. Please take us there."

Li Gao was silent for a second. "Okay, I'll go make arrangements. Please wait here. The environment of the Station is similar to that of Earth, as the guide must know."

Looking at the receding figure, Yelena was about to speak but was stopped by He Xi. He took out the device and scanned the surroundings. Certain there was no surveillance, he said, "Contact Fan Zhe right now. Tell him to get ready to establish quantum communication with Earth."

"Get ready now?" Yelena asked, surprised. The ship carried a set of electrons used in quantum communication, which were kept in an ultra-low-temperature environment nearing absolute zero. Each was part of an electron twin whose counterpart was on Earth. Electron twins are born out of pure energy collisions and display quantum entanglement. Because of the Pauli exclusion principle, their physical states are always opposites. This is the theoretical basis of hyperspace quantum communication. The energy required in quantum communication is enormous. In fact, the wormhole spaceship could only support two quantum communications at most. According to the rules, the first quantum communication should be carried out on the seventh day after landing, when the overall situation of the target planet is grasped. He Xi asking them to get ready to start it now really puzzled Yelena.

"I think it's necessary." He Xi's tone was very determined. "Caspian Sea is making me uneasy."

Yelena looked at the beautiful scenery around them, not understanding what He Xi was referring to. But she knew He Xi had carried out the Bohai mission, so he must have a reason for what he was saying. All she needed to do was carry out his order.

"I also felt that pioneer was a little arrogant." Yelena looked around. "But this place really isn't arranged any differently from Earth. They have taken care to receive us."

"This is just a constitutional rule," He Xi said coldly. "According to the Paradise Constitution, pioneers have to set up a terrestrial environment on their planet of no less than one square kilometer as the permanent station of the planetary government. It's not yet time for Caspian Sea to set up a government, so this place should be the station in its embryonic form."

"I know the Constitution. The rules in it are all pretty rigid." Yelena curled her lips in mild disapproval. "The provision about the governmental station, for example. Caspian Sea is obviously a water planet, so permanently maintaining an area with a terrestrial environment like this is definitely not easy. If I were them I'd object, too."

He Xi's heart filled with compassion for his mischievous junior, but his tone remained firm. "The Paradise Constitution is the core of the entire plan. The first provision clearly specifies that the Constitution is inviolable. Those who violate it are public enemies of humanity."

"So serious?" Yelena stuck out her tongue. "I see there are some very specific rules in the Constitution regarding the implementation of regulations. Are those inviolable, too?"

"I know what you're referring to. Those rules are quite tedious but guarantee the smooth execution of the Paradise Plan." He Xi nodded kindly. "Like pioneer number forty-two just now. Do you see any difference between us and him?"

Yelena shook her head. "Just seems the color of his skin is darker, though much lighter than the Bantus of Central Africa on Earth. This should be a result of adapting to stellar radiation, right? There seems to be no other reason."

"Have you forgotten Caspian Sea is a water planet?" He Xi said. "These pioneers mostly live underwater. They all have gills, which are their main respiratory organs, their lungs being auxiliary organs."

"*Right*," Yelena said as if having an epiphany. "Why didn't we see them?"

"Because of the relevant principles in the Paradise Constitution," He Xi said. "For example, the gravity of Great Bear's Huanghai is twice that of Earth. Obviously human beings have to be modified to adapt to living there. The native life-forms of Huanghai are generally short and small, with mostly flat bodies. Pioneers are designed humans. It was most convenient to design a short body, but humans took another approach, which reinforced the pioneers' supportive systems, like their skeletons. Of course, this also included such relevant measures as strengthening blood vessel walls. This greatly increases the cost but can ensure the average height of the current people of Huang Sea is only a little shorter than ours. That is, morphologically we can immediately tell they are our fellow species."

"Where are the gills of the people on Caspian Sea?" Yelena asked.

"According to available materials, their gills are located in their armpits," He Xi said surely. "Though doing so has caused some redundancy in their respiratory system, it has clearly made their appearance more acceptable."

"Really, we may as well not use the genetic modification approach." Yelena recalled something. "With an underwater breathing device they could survive on Caspian Sea too, couldn't they?"

"In that case, humans wouldn't be seen as successful immigrants at all, mere passers-by at best," He Xi said. "Only freely living with our own power would mean true conquest and integration into this planet. This is where the fundamental purpose of the Paradise Plan lies."

"What if the environments of some planets are too strange?"

"There have been cases of abandoning." He Xi was obviously glad Yelena could raise this question. "Such as Dead Sea, fifty-nine light-years from Earth. Due to an abundance of sulfide, its oceans are highly acidic, home to some strange lower life-forms. Genetic engineers drew inspiration from some kind of water mite and designed a viable pioneer plan, but in the end it was vetoed at a hearing. Dead Sea has been abandoned for seventy years now."

"Why? Since there was a viable plan, why wasn't it carried out?"

The corner of He Xi's mouth twitched. "In the plan, in order to adapt to the environment there, the pioneers would be a scaly species covered completely in slime. My friend Professor Williams was a member of the hearing, an anthropologist. According to him, one-hundred-odd members unanimously vetoed the plan."

Now Li Gao came out of the structure. Yelena noticed his smile was a little humble. "Big Ship is rushing over. Based on its speed, it will dock in twenty minutes."

He Xi frowned. "As far as I know, Big Ship is always part of the permanent station. Why is it so far away on Caspian Sea? And, since this is the governmental station, why are you the only person here?"

"Big Ship is just on routine patrol. Besides, I don't know what governmental is." Li Gao's tone was neither humble nor haughty as he lowered his head.

The answers relieved He Xi some. He knew a government would only be set up after the acceptance inspection. But he didn't notice that the instant Li Gao lowered his head, a deceitful expression slipped across his face.

7. *The Central Computer*

"We are going on board now, as you were," He Xi told Li Gao. "You usually manage the station?" he asked coolly.

"No, Central Computer says I need more knowledge. Now I just help the robot manager with odd jobs."

The main control room on the deck of Big Ship was a transparent dome-like structure. The view of the sea on all sides was unobstructed. The screen on the control panel right in front of them showed a chubby virtual avatar.

"Hello, Central Computer is ready." The avatar's tone was very calm.

"One question, why does pioneer number forty-two possess knowledge he shouldn't?" He Xi's tone became confrontational. "Did you remove the Galileo Seal?"

The avatar answered quickly. "Forty-five years ago, four thousand pioneer embryos and I came to Caspian Sea together. My mission should have been completed twenty years ago. But you are twenty years late. The robots assisting my management broke down one after another. I had to give the pioneers a small amount of sealed knowledge. Otherwise they couldn't have survived on this planet so long."

He Xi gave a deep sigh. His concern had finally been confirmed. Counting from the end of the last ice age, human civilization had been developing for 13,000 years, but now people believed that, in the strict sense, Galileo was the forefather of technological civilization. Before Galileo and Boyle, people had been too shackled by the brief glory of ancient Greece to move on, and their successors, such as Newton, had stood on their shoulders to achieve scientific triumph. The so-called Galileo Seal was just a metaphor. According to the provisions of the Constitution, before an acceptance inspection, the knowledge any immigrant planet possessed was limited to that of an agricultural civilization, which corresponded precisely to the pre-Galilean era. That is, before an acceptance inspection pioneers would possess comprehensive knowledge of classical geometry, a naïve concept of matter and elements, simple knowledge of agriculture and medicine, but not know Newton's laws and not know what the stars in the sky were. Because of Caspian Sea's special situation, the Earth Committee had foreseen the possibility of unexpected problems but hadn't expected the Galileo Seal to be one of them.

"They know the three laws of motion, right?" He Xi tried his best to keep the pace of his speech steady.

"Yes," Central Computer said. "Sixteen years ago Big Ship was damaged in a tsunami. In order to fix it as soon as possible, I removed the seal of Newton's laws."

"How about the three laws of thermodynamics?"

"Sorry sir, these have to be used in energetic applications."

He Xi remained silent for a few seconds, then asked carefully, "How about Maxwell's equations?"

"Electromagnetism, the theory of relativity, quantum theory, and wormhole theory have not been unsealed," Central Computer said.

He Xi let out a breath. It seemed the situation wasn't completely irretrievable. In fact, after the acceptance inspection was finished, it all wouldn't be a problem. Based on currently available information, the acceptance inspection shouldn't have any major obstacles. He Xi had made up his mind to erase this episode after the acceptance inspection was over. After all, Central Computer had taken emergency actions after losing all communication with Earth. According to the Constitution, this transgressing Central Computer should be formatted and reprogrammed, but He Xi didn't plan to do that. For no apparent reason, in his heart he even sort of liked the cocky, chubby guy, even though it was essentially just an intelligent machine driven by ones and zeroes.

"What is the Holy Land the pioneer mentioned?" Yelena asked suddenly.

"Sixteen years ago, in that tsunami, Big Ship was damaged. To prevent similar situations from recurring, I ordered the pioneers to build a berth at the bottom of the sea. As for why they call it Holy Land, it's probably due to their admiration for Big Ship."

"All right. No more questions." He Xi felt a lot more relaxed. A smile appeared on his face.

"But I've got one question," Central Computer said suddenly.

"Oh?" He Xi's eyebrows raised. "Go ahead. If we can't answer it, we can contact the Earth Committee and ask them for help."

"Not necessary," Central Computer said. "If you can't answer, forget it. I want to know whether the current pioneers of Caspian Sea can be improved. Because after all these years, I've found a few imperfections in the design."

"Genetic design is a systematic project. The genetic design for every immigration planet takes at least five years to execute. You can't change the design without a full-scale recommission," He Xi answered somewhat impatiently. He hadn't expected it to be such a naïve question. "A few imperfections won't make much difference; there has never been a perfect design in the universe."

After Big Ship had sailed for ten minutes, some green, umbrella-shaped floaters started to appear on the sea surface: in twos and threes at first, but soon there was a crowd. The diameter of the big ones was over five meters; that of the small ones, dozens of centimeters.

"This is sea duckweed," Central Computer explained before He Xi asked. "This area of water is Caspian Sea's windless zone. That's why so much congregates here."

"Do plants on Caspian Sea have roots?" Yelena asked suddenly.

Central Computer hesitated for a second. "Judging from the materials I currently have, they shouldn't. All life-forms on this planet are in a floating state. On Caspian Sea, the depth of the shallowest water is eighty-three meters. The deepest is over a hundred thousand meters."

"I seem to have seen birds flying in the sky," He Xi cut in.

"Caspian Sea has no birds similar to Earth's, just flying creatures similar to insects. They can also stay on the surface of water, probably evolved from water life. These insects are one of the pioneers' food sources. According to them, the hind leg of some kind of big locust is quite delicious after roasting."

Yelena frowned, apparently worrying that the pioneers would treat her to bugs. He Xi pointed at a huge shadow rising and falling nonstop in the distance, and asked, "What is that?"

"That's a soil shark," Central Computer answered. "According to investigation, this species is similar to sharks on Earth, with more or less one billion years of history."

"One billion years." He Xi gasped. He knew some shark species on Earth had existed for over three hundred million years, belonging among Earth's oldest species. By comparison, the 200 million-plus-year history of human evolution was not worth mentioning; in fact, on Earth, land life had existed for a much shorter time than marine life. "Still not extinct after so long, what a miracle."

"Definitely a miracle. Fossil materials show that, given its history, this species has hardly changed," Central Computer added. "Perhaps because the environment of Caspian Sea is so peaceful, the evolutionary impetus is very low."

"Should be." He Xi nodded. "On Earth to this day there are still people rejecting Darwin's theory of evolution because some life-forms have changed very little over tens of millions of years. Actually, this is just because these life-forms have still been very adaptable to the environment for tens of millions of years. Life evolves because of selection pressures in its living environment. It seems that water planets are indeed cozy cradles for life."

"We've gotten close to the coordinate location. Now we start diving." At Central Computer's reminder, it suddenly darkened outside the dome. A moment later, the surroundings had become an undersea scene. Sunlight shone down through gaps between the sea duckweed, forming many bright columns of light. Within the light columns a big stretch of floating giant seaweed drifted about like a rootless forest.

"Though they have no roots, their lower parts generally have a mass of heavy tissue," He Xi said to Yelena. "This is a common feature of many plants on water planets. They use it to adjust their height under water."

"We have found at least one hundred plant species with primary motility. They can move slowly by wriggling parts of their branches and trunks so as to choose a suitable living environment," Central Computer added.

"What's that?" Yelena suddenly pointed and asked. He Xi looked over, and immediately saw a strange scene. From the middle of a giant seaweed cluster, a swelling mass appeared as if it had laid an egg some ten meters in diameter. Rising and falling with gentle waves, the huge thing drifted slowly. Sunlight shone on it. It rippled, flowed, and gleamed like a piece of artwork made of carved and polished jade, emanating a sense of dreamy unreality. For a moment He Xi couldn't help but be captivated.

"That's a flower house." Central Computer's tone remained consistently calm. "Kids make it out of giant seaweed, they like to stay inside."

Before the sound of the words settled, they saw two small figures dashing out of the flower house like swimming fish. They looked at Big Ship with some alarm, a mix of shyness and uneasiness on their faces. He Xi saw at a glance that they were both only fifteen or sixteen years old. It seemed that Big Ship's presence had interrupted the young lovers' date.

"It's Qiu Sheng and Xing Lan," Central Computer said.

The two big kids, now calmer, moved their lips at them.

"What are they saying?" Yelena asked.

"We can't hear. Underwater they speak a kind of infrasonic language," He Xi explained.

"They said a bunch of silverspace fish just attacked the pasture, and the adults all rushed over there," Central Computer said.

He Xi hesitated a moment. "These people all have names? Using numbers is no good?"

"It started twenty years ago. The first-generation pioneers gave themselves names," Central Computer answered. "Back then one chose one's own name according to their individual characteristics, which is akin to making an early nickname into a name. For example, Li Gao's original nickname was Tall Guy, since *gao* means tall. But now the kids' names are much more formal."

"Kids," He Xi mumbled. Before the acceptance inspection, this was not something that should have existed, but twenty years of communication disruption had changed many things. Then again, it was only a small surprise. Looking at it from another perspective, the kids were pioneers too.

Outside the window some sophisticated architecture started to glide by. The buildings were hexagonal prisms, some separate but most joining one another to form larger structures. They stretched out, occupying a very large space just like an underwater city. One could imagine that on an ordinary day there would be a bustling scene here, but now most people had rushed over to the pasture. Only a sparse dozen or so looked curiously at Big Ship.

"Is this place a Caspian Sea city?" Yelena asked.

"Now it can only be called a settlement. There are several settlements on Caspian Sea like this," Central Computer said. "Our population is still very small."

"So now how many pioneers are there in total?" He Xi asked, outwardly casual. "Plus those kids."

"Originally there were four thousand pioneers. Adding the kids, eight thousand seven hundred and fifty-four people. This doesn't include the population dead from accidents over the previous decades."

"So for twenty years the annual population growth has been about four percent." He Xi did a simple calculation on the computer. "When human beings first immigrate to a virgin land, the population growth is usually very high. Way back then, the population growth of the *Bounty* mutineers on Pitcairn Island was as high as four-point-three percent."

"Lots of things need to be built. The labor force was obviously insufficient," Central Computer went on. "The robots had mostly broken down, spare parts had run out."

"All this was caused by the accident. Under normal circumstances, Caspian Sea should have had the Galileo Seal removed twenty years ago and by now should have long had its own manufacturing system." He Xi nodded understandingly. "But all this will soon change." He Xi turned his head to look at Yelena. "Bathe this uncivilized planet in the brilliance of civilization – that is our mission."

Yelena's body trembled a bit. She heard unshakable determination in He Xi's voice. After receiving the Paradise Plan document, she knew the purpose of this trip. But until now, she had seen it more as a mission she had to complete, unlike the missions she had carried out before but essentially little different. However, the experience during this period had given Yelena a different feeling. She realized her life had been inseparable from this mission. She even vaguely felt for no reason that her life was going to be changed by it. Yelena didn't like this seemingly mysterious feeling, but she couldn't shake it off.

8. The Holy Land and Death

After a pointed deceleration process, Big Ship stopped. Outside the window, dim light indicated the place was at least some dozen meters below sea level.

Ahead the floor slowly opened, revealing a flight of descending stairs. "Please follow Michael forward. In front there is my terminal, too. You can communicate with me at any time," Central Computer said, maintaining a formal tone.

The lighting in the corridor was very good. He Xi noticed the texture of the walls was similar to that of granite on Earth. At regular intervals were thick reinforcement pillars obviously made of artificial materials. He Xi figured that since their departure from Big Ship, they had gone dozens of meters underground. At this depth, no tsunami could be a threat.

There was a sudden opening ahead, through which there was a circular hall. In the center, over a platform, floated a light-blue sphere about one meter in diameter. He Xi thought it must be a sculpture representing Caspian Sea.

Central Computer's chubby avatar reappeared on the screen ahead. Next to it stood three men in black.

Yelena suddenly looked at He Xi, astonished, at a loss. He Xi completely understood Yelena, because he himself felt a little shocked. The man facing them in the middle looked somewhat like himself, of similar age, like a lost brother of his. A shocked look also appeared on that man's face. Obviously he felt surprised too.

"I'm Qin Wang." The man regained his composure. "Pioneer number seventeen. Here people also call me Chief. Welcome, our distinguished guests from Earth."

He Xi immediately understood. After all these years, among the pioneers, their own leader had risen. It seemed that Qin Wang was that figure. "All right, Central Computer must have told you the purpose of our visit. And let me offer a correction. We should not be seen as guests."

Yelena was alarmed. Only then did she recall that when receiving the first message in which they were called 'guests', He Xi had seemed disgusted.

Barely perceptible embarrassment passed over Qin Wang's face. "I said so only out of respect. We have been waiting too long. Our current power seems too little for us to survive on Caspian Sea and we are in urgent need of help from the Federation."

He Xi's expression softened. On the way there, his mood had lightened. So far there hadn't been anything really dissatisfying. It seemed that this mission would go very well. "What is this place? Is there any special reason to call it Holy Land?"

"This is our council hall," Qin Wang explained. "Holy Land is a common habitual appellation. It doesn't have any special meaning."

He Xi looked around. "Is there any surveillance equipment here? Something that allows you to see this place from afar?"

"No," Qin Wang said. This answer made He Xi quite pleased. In fact, Yelena had a detection device with her, which upon entering had sent him a safety signal. His question to Qin Wang was just a small test.

Qin Wang hesitated a moment, then said, "According to the Constitution it seems you should have another member with you."

The other voluntarily mentioned the rules of the Constitution, which reassured He Xi. He felt it was time for Fan Zhe to land. After all, Fan Zhe was an irreplaceable member of the Caspian Sea Plan. "I'm ordering Fan Zhe to land now. Ask Big Ship to bring him here." He Xi excitedly turned his head to look at Yelena. "The Caspian Sea Plan officially begins."

Qin Wang nodded humbly. "I'm going to make arrangements now."

Upon entering, Fan Zhe called, "You wouldn't believe what I saw. Those houses woven from giant seaweed are the most beautiful villas I've ever seen in my life! And—"

"Okay, okay," Yelena interrupted him. "And giant sea duckweed, right? A big fuss about nothing."

"So you saw them too?!" Fan Zhe scratched his head. "But there was something you definitely didn't see. From the ship I observed a submarine dozens of meters long—"

"That must have been a soil shark!" Yelena burst out laughing. "Caspian Sea is in the agricultural age. How could there be something like a submarine?"

"Stop this discussion for now." He Xi couldn't help but end the two young people's bickering. "We've still got proper business to do. You haven't forgotten about the mission of this trip, have you?"

Yelena's expression soured. "Of course not. Fan Zhe and I came here for a marriage alliance, didn't we? And you, the so-called guide, are actually just an interstellar matchmaker."

He Xi was suddenly stupefied. In Yelena's words, the supreme Paradise Plan turned out to be an antiquated marriage alliance, and he himself turned out to be a matchmaker – but after thinking carefully, her words were irrefutable. For a moment he didn't know whether to cry or laugh. "Well, the Paradise Plan is concerned with the future wellbeing of all of humanity."

"I know, the Constitution says so." Yelena took over the conversation. "If humans stick to Earth forever, they are doomed to extinction, because unpredictable accidents like supernova explosions, asteroid collisions, high-energy experiment accidents, biochemical incidents, and solar catastrophes, can destroy the entire human race at any time in the future. Only by implementing the Paradise Plan can human beings spread throughout the universe and live forever."

"Right." He Xi's tone became serious. "To be able to share responsibility in such a great cause is our honor."

Fan Zhe gave Yelena a meaningful glance. "We knew this was our mission. Actually, after seeing the contents of the plan, I felt different than before. We are bound to undertake many things we didn't used to understand."

"Twenty years ago, I had the same feeling you have." A thin fog appeared over He Xi's eyes. "And for some reason, my feeling is more indelible than yours." He Xi paused, a bit hesitant whether or not to confide the long-sealed secret.

"Something happened?" Yelena asked abruptly, seeming to understand.

"It's pretty simple. Back then I fell in love with a girl. But unfortunately, she too was a member of the Paradise Plan, so it was a story bound to end bleakly."

Fan Zhe asked softly, "And she loved you too?" His gaze drifted to Yelena.

He Xi froze. "I think so. Actually, we didn't know each other long, but how to put it? Perhaps love is really the blindest thing in the world.

As I watched the spaceship she was on gradually disappear from view, I felt at that moment a part of my heart had gone with her forever...."

He Xi suddenly stopped talking and looked around. "Do you hear something?" He looked extremely confused.

"Yes, it sounds like a woman sighing," Yelena responded.

Fan Zhe stood still, somewhat at a loss. He didn't hear anything, but the situation suddenly made him anxious. At some point the doors on all four walls were tightly shut. Fan Zhe went over to try to open them but failed.

Yelena exclaimed, "Look, smoke!"

Only now did He Xi realize the room was permeated with a thin veil of fog. At the same time, the portable device on Fan Zhe shone red. "God, it's soman nerve gas! This concentration can kill people within three minutes," Fan Zhe yelled.

Only then did He Xi realize he had made a big mistake. In the message that came when they were on the spaceship, the pioneer had called them 'guests'. According to the Paradise Constitution, all immigration planets, prior to the acceptance inspection, could not be seen as human homes, but the pioneer's vocabulary did imply that they positioned themselves as the 'host'. That is, they saw Caspian Sea as their home. This detail had initially alerted He Xi, which was why he had arranged for Fan Zhe to stay on the spaceship, but later contact had made him feel reassured and he'd let his guard down. Now it seemed that something strange had definitely happened on Caspian Sea. Perhaps what Fan Zhe had observed really was something like a submarine. The program in Central Computer must have been tampered with. The other side had made meticulous arrangements, waited until they had all gathered before taking action. But He Xi didn't know why exactly the pioneers had done this. Now it seemed it was going to be a mystery forever. There in the room, the three of them looked at one another with deathly pale faces, incredulous desperation in their eyes. Death just came like this – on a distant alien planet, sudden, eerie, without a clue.

In the last moment before consciousness left He Xi, he had a strange thought: *Why was the sound of the sigh so familiar?* Then pure darkness attacked and swallowed everything.

9. Past Love

Was this death? It felt like floating in a cloud, like soaking in a warm sea. Dappled light jumped about before his eyes like an incomprehensible abstract painting.

"No—" He Xi suddenly screamed and woke up, finding himself lying on a soft chair. His sixth sense told him clearly that nearby there was a woman. This judgment soon found its basis. He Xi immediately saw a slim figure standing in front of him.

Even the most imaginative person faced with this arrangement of destiny would feel surprised. Nobody knew when or where one would unexpectedly encounter whom or what. When Yu Lan's figure suddenly came into view, He Xi really felt this to be true. A twenty-year barrier was broken at that moment. He Xi suddenly felt nothing else existed in the universe, only the two of them left. No language could express He Xi's feeling at that moment, because he saw a person whom he thought had parted from him forever. The wound from years ago was still aching, but that person came back. She didn't just traverse time but also death.

He Xi didn't know at that moment that the reunion with Yu Lan was going to be the second wound to his heart which would cut to the bone and never heal.

"Is that you?" He Xi mumbled, "If not for my lifelong atheism, I'd definitely say we were reuniting in heaven."

"It's me," Yu Lan replied tenderly, her eyes filled with joy.

He Xi looked around, found himself in the main control room of Big Ship. Nearing dusk, sunbeams softened colorful clouds hanging in the sky, but there was no sign of Fan Zhe or Yelena.

"They are safe." Yu Lan seemed to have sensed He Xi's thought. "Maybe a little later...." She stopped talking as if feeling some jitters.

"I don't understand what happened," He Xi said hesitantly. "Seems like we almost died. But how could that be? Everything is very normal. Did some breakdown happen?"

Yu Lan didn't open her mouth, as if she hadn't heard He Xi's words, but anyone could tell that the joy in her eyes came from her heart.

"Didn't you die in that accident long ago?" He Xi asked hastily. Almost simultaneously he had an epiphany. "I know, there was no accident. It was all fake."

Yu Lan hesitated a moment, then finally nodded.

But He Xi's confusion grew stronger. "But why? Because the pioneers detained you?"

"How could that be?" Yu Lan shook her head. "They are all kind and harmless. To be honest, compared to them, Earthlings, at least on a moral level, definitely seem inferior."

"What about the warning message? You sent that personally."

"Ma Weikang and Kato Jun didn't die from pulsar radiation," Yu Lan said quietly. "They died from an unexpected event. At the time I got into a heated argument with them, and the pioneers took my side. The two first attacked and killed dozens of pioneers, but were eventually overpowered by the crowd. I sent that message afterward."

He Xi was completely shocked. He hadn't imagined such a tragic scene had occurred twenty years ago. "What made the situation escalate to that point? Couldn't it be solved with negotiation?"

"No," Yu Lan said coldly. "It was a matter of life and death, no room for reconciliation. At that moment, Ma Weikang and Kato Jun were just about to report to Earth the news that the Caspian Sea mission had completely failed."

He Xi gasped. He certainly knew what that meant. Since the implementation of the Paradise Plan, such a situation had never happened. Once word was sent, the consequences would be unimaginable.

"Because that situation actually happened?" He Xi was a little calmer.

"Exactly that." Yu Lan's expression became odd, like that of a witch in a dark forest. Pausing after each syllable, she uttered the remaining two words, as if they were a frightening spell. "Reproductive isolation."

Despite his anticipating them, the words still fell like heavy hammers on He Xi's heart. "How is that possible? I've always thought the provision in the Constitution about this was just some clause prepared for legal thoroughness, I never thought such a situation would really happen. You know, each pioneer plan is determined after at least five years, over one thousand experiments."

Yu Lan was thinking back to twenty years ago. "When we arrived successfully at Caspian Sea, the beautiful scenery here like Shangri-La made me feel at ease. I thought I'd just forget the past like this, start a new life." Yu Lan's eyes became a bit dreamy. "Afterward, things went step by step. Kato Jun and his lover fell in love at first sight, and I came across a pioneer who looked a little like you...."

"Is it Qin Wang?" He Xi suddenly remembered the chief.

"Yes, him." Yu Lan smiled bitterly. "On Caspian Sea the names of the first-generation pioneers were chosen by themselves. Only Qin Wang's name was given to him by me."

"Qin Wang. Love Forgotten," He Xi mumbled as if realizing something. For a moment his heart was flooded with pain. *Can love really be forgotten?*

Yu Lan was calmer and continued, "If everything had gone well, we would have done the same as on Earth. Lovers, after dating for some time, enter into a marriage officiated by a guide. Then one day, months later, give birth to the crystalization of life. Since all the important physical traits of the pioneers were designed as dominant genes, their children could definitely adapt to the environment here. The successful births of children would symbolize the complete success of the entire plan." Then Yu Lan suddenly seemed to remember something. "Your family members are well?"

Caught somewhat off guard, He Xi answered, "Yeah, they all live on Bohai." He added in a low voice, "My wife and I have long since separated. I live with my daughter. She is very lovely, an angel."

Yu Lan looked envious. For some reason this look worried He Xi. "Perhaps because of my specialty, as soon as we arrived I collected pioneers' reproductive cells for analysis. I wanted to observe their action when uniting with human reproductive cells."

"That seems unnecessary. On Earth they had done countless similar experiments. Though I'm no expert in this area, I know that using embryonic pioneer cells to produce their reproductive cells is pretty easy, one meiosis will do," He Xi cut in disapprovingly.

Yu Lan ignored He Xi. "Due to my own ovulation, the first experiment was conducted on the fifth day after our arrival. Meanwhile, in the name of experimentation, I obtained Kato Jun's reproductive cells. As I said, at that time it was just out of professional interest. I hadn't at all expected something would happen."

He Xi's heart gradually sank. "What was the result?"

"Pretty terrible," Yu Lan said coldly. "Under the microscope I saw a typical instance of the encounter of alien species. Sperm dashed about aimlessly – nothing like the way they risk their lives to charge toward the eggs of the same species; and the eggs completely sealed up all their surface passages. That is, the level of their mutual rejection exceeded even that between horses and donkeys, which cannot breed normal offspring."

"Alien species." He Xi squeezed the words out between his teeth. "But I know similar experiments on Earth were all successful."

"I was very shocked at the time too, but the facts were plainly laid out before my eyes. I gathered more samples from the pioneers to do experiments. The results were exactly the same. After further analysis, I found the reason." Yu Lan held up her index finger, pointing overhead.

He Xi immediately understood what Yu Lan was pointing at. "You think it's caused by the special stellar radiation on Caspian Sea?"

"Exactly," Yu Lan nodded. "In fact, planets with stronger stellar radiation than Earth aren't rare, but previously there was never a case where reproductive cells were influenced in this way, so clearly there are still many mysteries unknown to humans in the universe. I think perhaps it's because the stellar radiation here includes some radio waves with special frequencies. But then I observed that the union of the pioneers' reproductive cells was completely normal. At the time there was even a pioneer couple who had secretly tasted the forbidden fruit. Their one-year-old child swam faster in water than a silverspace fish."

"What happened afterward?" He Xi forced himself to keep his speaking pace steady.

"After I was certain the experimental result was correct, I reported it to Ma Weikang. He didn't believe it at first, but after taking a look accepted my conclusion. Then the three of us had a meeting together. Actually, there was no need for discussion, everything was plainly laid out according to the rules of the Constitution. You know any violation of the Constitution is seen as a crime against humanity."

He Xi shivered as he gazed at Yu Lan, a puzzled look on his face. He felt the delicate woman in front of him was probably one of humanity's public enemies.

"They wanted to report to the Earth Committee immediately, get ready to start the eradication program. I think I probably lost my mind at that moment, unable to accept thousands of people – alive, with blood and flesh – being slaughtered in front of me. I ran out the door, called to the pioneers that they were seen by humans as an alien species and would be eradicated quickly. I told them that in order to save themselves, they had to stop the people inside from sending out the signal." Yu Lan shook her head in anguish, tousling her black hair, the horrible scene of that day still haunting her. "The crowd poured inside. I saw people falling down constantly, blood everywhere...."

Yu Lan's words stopped abruptly. Extreme agitation caused her to suddenly pass out on the floor.

10. Non-humans

When Yu Lan woke up, she found she and He Xi had switched positions. She was lying on the chair, while He Xi was staring thoughtfully into the distance.

"You're awake. Can you tell me where we are now?" He Xi bent down, unconcealed concern in his eyes.

"Now we are right above Holy Land. The pioneers call it Holy Land because I live here. I have no radiation-resistant genes, live most of the time underground." Yu Lan rose. "They are grateful for my action that day, treat me like a god with incomparable respect. They are grateful people."

He Xi nodded understandingly. For twenty years Yu Lan had been isolated from the world. Her devotion to Caspian Sea was enormous. At the same time, he sensed protectiveness in her words. "I believe they are all kind, but they are an alien species. It is an undeniable fact."

Yu Lan remained silent for a while, seemed to be considering some question. "See this?" She suddenly pointed at the one-meter-high arch bridge model on the table as a desolate expression appeared on her face. "On Caspian Sea there is no concept of a river, so naturally there wouldn't be something like a bridge. I play with this model to pass the time," Yu Lan said as her hand swept it over, causing it to scatter into a dozen pieces large and small. "This bridge doesn't use adhesive, it's entirely shaped by components fitting together. Want to try to put it back together? There are numbers on the components, you can do it in numerical order."

Although He Xi didn't understand why Yu Lan was suddenly talking about the model, he nevertheless fiddled with the heap of components as he was asked. He Xi knew Yu Lan's hometown was a famous water town in southern China. There were many stone arch bridges like this there. As an adolescent Yu Lan had walked across the bridges every day. He Xi imagined how delicate, young Yu Lan would look standing on a bridge, looking at the scenery, but now, somewhere one hundred and sixty light-years away, she could only play with a model. For some reason, this association made He Xi a little sad. He Xi composed himself, turned his attention to the present. The so-called components were actually plastic trapezoidal blocks. He tried a few times but failed. The model always collapsed when the stacks reached a certain level. He looked in frustration at the heap of disobedient components. In principle, this should have been a very easy task. The shapes of these components could definitely fit together into an arch bridge, as he had personally seen. A real stone arch bridge didn't need any adhesive.

"You won't succeed," Yu Lan said meaningfully. "Not a single component is missing, but you will find your work always collapses at a certain point." She took a box out of a drawer. "The only reason you can't do it is because there are some things missing. The pieces in this box can be used to set up scaffolding. If you open a construction manual on arch bridges, you will find that before building a bridge you need to set up auxiliary structures like scaffolding, but in the end these things are torn down, leaving no trace at all."

"Why tell me all this?" He Xi asked thoughtfully. He felt he was approaching some hidden truth.

Yu Lan's eyes suddenly became very bright. "In fact, the process of building this bridge is very similar to human evolution. This was originally the norm in evolution. Over three-billion-odd years all the components in our body have gone through this process. The components that once appeared but finally disappeared aren't useless. Without them there would not be human beings as we know them today. But our current modification of pioneers completely violates this natural law, skips all the intermediate links. Human beings rely on powerful technologies that have transcended the Creator to design and produce pioneers based directly on the environmental requirements of immigration planets."

"You're saying pioneers are unnatural products, right?" He Xi asked.

"Pioneers are nothing but products of pure calculation." A trace of sorrow flashed across Yu Lan's face. "They are merely the products of induction from the environments of immigration planets. In the eyes of the Earth Committee, they are just a bunch of white mice, sent to a pioneering land according to human needs. Based on pioneering requirements, they are given all kinds of special characteristics congenitally, but these characteristics may cause them to be annihilated a few decades later."

He Xi remained silent for a while, then said, "The extreme situation you're talking about has never happened."

"You can only say it never happened before Caspian Sea." Yu Lan looked He Xi in the eye. "Technology isn't all-powerful, it can't foresee all situations. What ending do you think the pioneers of Caspian Sea will face?"

He Xi felt his throat go dry. "The Constitution…it's mentioned in the Constitution."

"The Constitution." Yu Lan's tone was ice cold. "Want me to recite it to you? Over the years I've worn the Constitution out. Yes, the Constitution is full of axioms of justice. Every sentence in it sounds as if it represents the highest law of human civilization, so people are unable to refute it. Regarding so-called pioneers in failed immigrations, it says just one word: *eradicate*."

"Experiments can always fail. Since we are clearly aware of failure...." He Xi swallowed hard. "This is the inevitable response."

"The problem is, did the pioneers of Caspian Sea fail?" Yu Lan looked at He Xi forcefully. "You saw them and their kids. For so many years they have been living freely on this planet, maladapted to nothing. They have built their own homes, lived in harmony with all life. There is no actual disaster. They can live like this for another million years. Did you see those flower houses the kids built?" Yu Lan's eyes sparkled with charming light. "I think they're magnificent works of art, the most moving things on this uncivilized planet. Would you deny being moved by them?"

"No," He Xi said in a low voice. "They are truly very beautiful. And those kids are very lovely. They remind me of my own daughter. Really, I really think so."

"But according to the Constitution's definitions, they are all failed specimens and should be completely eradicated without a trace, just because they developed a reproductive isolation with ours. But can they be blamed for this? It's human beings who are behind it all."

"In a biological sense, they really can't be called human beings," He Xi said affirmatively. "I admit this is a mistake made by human beings. It seems that even the most rigorous design plan has a chance to go wrong. After all, human beings haven't penetrated every secret of genes. Everything that has happened here has proved that the environment of Caspian Sea exceeds a certain threshold value. Adaptable pioneers are bound to become non-humans. According to the Constitution, this planet will not be used for immigration after the pioneers are eradicated. It will be another Dead Sea planet."

11. Blue Snow

"Have you decided already?" Yu Lan asked faintly, a gleam of strange light floating in her eyes.

He Xi tried to keep his eyes from averting. He knew in principle that he didn't need to feel guilty. On the contrary, he was now taking the absolutely correct stand. "I understand your feelings. This really isn't an easy decision to make. But we can't be swayed by feelings. Those pioneers...they...they really can't be seen as humans."

"No – you can't understand!" Yu Lan suddenly screamed. "You are still taking the narrowest outlook on everything in front of you. I know every person here, recognize their voices and faces. Qin Wang is very shy. Michael likes to brag in front of women. Xing Lan is worried about being too thin.... The genes inside their bodies are ninety-seven percent identical to ours. Like us they have intelligence, have souls, and have... dreams. They aren't machines, aren't white mice. They are people with flesh and blood! Do you understand?"

Pale, He Xi looked at the angry woman, not saying a word. After Yu Lan had calmed down a little, He Xi said slowly, "They are not humans. According to the divisions of phylum, class, order, family, genus, and species, I think they at most reach the Hominidae family of the primate order, not the homo genus or the homo sapiens species. They are not the same species as us. Reproductive isolation is the strongest evidence. Our differences are so huge, perhaps exceeding the differences between cheetahs and African lions, which both belong to the cat family. Think about it: given a chance, a male prairie lion won't hesitate to kill and devour a cheetah. The reverse is also true." He Xi's Adam's apple moved with difficulty. "We also have ninety percent of our genes in common with chimpanzees. So...they aren't humans, they are definitely an alien species."

Yu Lan sank into the chair dejectedly. Her reason told her that what He Xi had said was entirely true.

"Humans are very lucky to have mastered great time-traversing wormhole technology and gotten a glimpse of the immense universe. And luckier still that in the process of applying this technology, humans have never encountered a terrifying alien species whose intelligence outmatches their own. But in the process of developing alien stars, humans are likely to create such alien species. Who would dare guarantee they won't rise against their creators?" He Xi asked coldly.

"Impossible, that's impossible." Yu Lan moved her lips feebly. The black hair on her head shook violently. "They are very kind. I've been teaching them to be grateful to Earth." Yu Lan lifted her head as if grasping a life-saving straw. "I will tell them Earth is their roots, I will make them remember this forever. They will never go against humans."

He Xi looked pitifully at the haggard Yu Lan. "What is forever? Is there anything eternal in the world? You should know human history better than I do. Modern Europeans all came from Africa, but when their offspring returned to Africa in the fifteenth century, what they brought was endless killing and genocide. There is another example over a shorter time interval. Around one thousand AD, some Polynesian farmers immigrated to New Zealand and become Maori. Others immigrated to the Chatham Islands to become Moriori. One day, a few hundred years later, the Maori rushed the Chatham Islands and killed, cooked, and ate all the Moriori. One Maori explained, 'We caught all the people, no one escaped...we caught and killed – this conforms to our customs.'" He Xi looked cruel. "The two parties in these examples actually belonged to the same species. Human history proves it all. I admit the current pioneers on Caspian Sea are kind and harmless, and internally I even like them very much. But human beings can't risk cultivating an intelligent alien species."

"Seems like you have decided!" Yu Lan screamed. "You must think I'm a witch whose sense is paralyzed by her feelings. I was a public enemy of humanity once, I'm not afraid to be one again!"

"Don't be like that." He Xi held Yu Lan's bony shoulders. "You've done your best. The pioneers on Caspian Sea are doomed. The truth can't be concealed forever. If the Earth Federation knows what has happened on Caspian Sea, they will eradicate these pioneers even if it means exhausting all of human power. This is the iron law of nature."

"But if you could give the pioneers a little more time, give them a few decades, I could teach them more knowledge, so they have their own advanced technology and can make enough progress to resist humans." Yu Lan suddenly gripped and pulled at her hair in anguish, helpless desperation on her face. "God, I said the wrong thing. What did I say? They will never resist humans, never."

"You just said the truth." He Xi knew it wasn't the time to get soft. Yu Lan had sunk too deep. He had the obligation to wake her up. "In fact, you've long since seen everything, you just don't want to admit it."

Yu Lan retreated step by step toward the door, a mixture of helplessness and determination on her face. "You are all butchers, I won't let you destroy everything here."

"What do you plan to do? Repeat what happened twenty years ago and let the pioneers tear me to pieces?" He Xi's face wore a cold smile, as if trying to hide something. "I know they are right outside now. Their weapons must be much more advanced than twenty years ago."

"Please don't push me." Tears poured uncontrollably out of Yu Lan's eyes. On one side was the person she had once loved deeply; on the other, countless lives she had to protect. For a moment, she seemed to hear the sound of her heart splitting and spilling blood.

"It's time to end everything." He Xi suddenly waved a hand. "Just twenty minutes ago, when you passed out, the Earth Committee received a report about the situation of Caspian Sea. We'll soon see what decision they'll make."

"This is impossible. Starting quantum communication takes two hours. You are lying to me." Yu Lan shook her head in disbelief.

"Perhaps so-called fate does exist in the world. For some inexplicable reason, I asked Fan Zhe to start quantum communication a few hours ago," He Xi went on. "I faithfully described the situation on Caspian Sea, including the pioneers being 'kind' and 'harmless' as you emphasized. The Earth Committee is the final decision-maker. Now nothing can be changed. I think in a few minutes we'll know what the fate of Caspian Sea is."

Yu Lan didn't speak anymore. He Xi's words completely petrified her. He Xi slowly walked up and gently held her shoulders. Then they looked out together into the dusk like a couple looking at the sea.

At the altitude of one hundred and twenty kilometers, the spaceship slid by against the background of the velvet black universe like a giant eye ruling all. At the center of the spaceship was a black box, chilled to the extreme. The internal temperature was even lower than cosmic background radiation. At this temperature, movement almost stopped. Even unpredictable leptons such as electrons were in a viscous state.

Suddenly, as if obtaining some magical power, some of the electrons started to move. Despite the constraints of the low temperature, they made strange dance-like movements. The electrons' dance wasn't meaningless. They followed the movements of their twin brothers trillions of kilometers away and spelled out extremely clear instructions. A few seconds later, the entire spaceship trembled. Under the call of the orders, a gleaming blue tube poked out like a monster stretching its limbs after waking from slumber.

He Xi saw shining trails like meteors slit through the sky. They were dazzling in the twilight. After entering the atmosphere, the shining trails quickly disappeared. At the same time, countless light-blue snowflakes began to drift down slowly from the June sky. The silent scene was breathtakingly beautiful.

"Eradication virus…. They made their decision," Yu Lan mumbled, utter disillusionment on her face.

He Xi didn't speak. At this point, language was meaningless. He knew the snow was going to fall nonstop for twelve hours until every corner of the planet was covered with sufficient virus. Corresponding to each pioneer was a kind of predesigned eradication virus, each with highly precise targeting. Each kind of virus could only infect and kill its corresponding pioneers, and when all the pioneers died, the virus couldn't survive on its own. According to experimental results, the survival rate of pioneers after being attacked would be less than one in 40,000. The entire population on Caspian Sea was less than 10,000 now. That is, it was a fully saturated eradication action.

12. Life Does Not Allow Us to Meet

It was already midnight. Under the radiance of two moons, they could see nearby snowflakes still drifting thinly. The tranquil scene made it hard to associate it with mass death.

"So this is the fate of Caspian Sea," He Xi proposed. Yu Lan had been silent for ten hours.

"They all died, right?" Yu Lan said suddenly, giving He Xi some relief.

"The eradication virus attacks the nervous system. The infected quickly suffocate due to nervous system paralysis," He Xi said carefully. "This is a quick, less painful way to die, somewhat similar to cyanide poisoning. Now the pioneers should have all died. Even if a few pioneers were diving deep in the sea, they will be infected a little later."

Yu Lan walked mechanically to the control panel ten meters away and sat down. He Xi knew that from there she could track down each pioneer, but her present actions were meaningless. On the screen, she could only see 8,754 motionless dots – the pioneers' still bodies.

"It's all over." Yu Lan stood up from the control panel, her face utterly numb. "Since the discovery of Caspian Sea, fifty-odd years have passed. So many things have happened on this planet. Now everything is back to where it started, as if it was all a dream."

"At least we saw the ending together." He Xi pointed to the sky. "Seen from here, the solar system is just a pale white dot, but it's the home shared by all human beings. In this long story, the most fortunate thing is that after all that happened, our home is still there."

Yu Lan suddenly let out a sigh, apparently moved. "You know? In the past I thought so-called constellations were made up by the ancients' fantastic imaginations, but now I don't think so. Perhaps they do conceal something we will never completely understand. They transcend so-called theorems and all of human understanding."

He Xi burst out laughing. "So our doctor of biology has become a philosopher?"

Yu Lan turned to look at He Xi. "Like right now, we are standing at this point and can see the solar system and Centaurus and nearby stars. See how they look? There, just tilt your head a little to the left...."

He Xi looked in that direction, interested but disapproving. Then the whole universe suddenly fell silent. He Xi felt burning tears pouring out of his eyes. He saw a small cradle, the lower part was the body.

Above it was a handle, the big fiery star the suspension. The small cradle just hung alone in the immensity of the universe.

From this place, He Xi also saw the stars of Scorpius which could never be seen simultaneously with Orion on Earth. The brightest star is α Scorpii. The ancient Chinese called it 'Great Fire' and specifically set up the position 'Governor of Fire' to observe its position and determine solar terms. The stars of Scorpius were part of the cradle of the solar system. The scene was so marvelous but also seemed to contain infinite meanings that human intelligence could never comprehend.

A long while later, He Xi stirred. "We should go home." He Xi looked at Yu Lan affectionately and spoke emphatically. "It's our home."

"'Go home,'" Yu Lan repeated, moved. "I want to go home too, but I can't go back anymore."

He Xi was a little surprised. "Since you violated the Constitution but didn't make any grave mistakes, I don't think the federal government would be too hard on you. I'm sure you would be exonerated, or at least receive a very minor punishment."

"You think we can go back to the past? Impossible. Caspian Sea has changed my life. I already have an inseparable connection with everything here in my flesh and blood. The solar system is human beings' warm cradle, but the children have grown up. It's time to let go, we shouldn't let the cradle become an eternal cage. Precisely because tens of thousands of years ago African pioneers broke into the old world, and hundreds of years ago European pioneers marched on to the new world, we have the glorious chapters of human history that followed. I think one day you will understand. The pioneers are gone, but I'll stay here, use my remaining life to guard their rootless souls. Otherwise, I'm afraid they will get lost." Yu Lan turned to look at He Xi, stars twinkling with charming light in her eyes. "Our lives have been separate for too much time and over too much distance. Just like Shen and Shang, one rises in the east while the other falls in the west, with no chance to reunite."

After Yu Lan finished speaking these words, she pulled herself out of He Xi's embrace, lightly but determinedly stepping out into the darkness. He Xi was left standing alone like a statue.

Epilogue: The Last Syllable

The lander rose slowly, higher and higher, gradually becoming an invisible dot in the blue sky. Yu Lan watched the scene expressionlessly. Then the floor of the main control room slid open. Two slender figures flew into Yu Lan's arms, sobbing loudly. Over the past ten or so hours, they had been living in hell. Yu Lan held the two terrified kids tightly, as if holding two pieces of treasure that had been lost and later found. Several hours ago, she had seen two moving dots in the main control room. Perhaps because of interstellar radiation, the two kids had developed mutations that could resist the terminator virus, and right at that moment, Yu Lan had calmly made her decision.

"The wormhole jump-flight is in countdown," Yelena reported to the guide, whose mind was elsewhere. She couldn't help but remind him, "There are still ten minutes left. If you want to say goodbye, please hurry." Then she glared at Fan Zhe and said, "Follow me out, idiot."

Fan Zhe froze a moment, then obediently followed her out the door. He also had many things to say to Yelena.

On the screen Yu Lan didn't look as haggard as yesterday; she seemed to wear light makeup, and looked radiantly beautiful. "I've been waiting here for some time. I knew you would come."

"In a few minutes the spaceship will launch. After this goodbye I'm afraid we won't meet again in this life." He Xi gazed deeply at Yu Lan, as if wanting to engrave her face into his retina. "I will think about you trillions of kilometers away."

"I will too," Yu Lan said softly.

He Xi hesitated a moment, seemed to be making some decision. In the end he said calmly, "Take good care of Qiu Sheng and Xing Lan."

Yu Lan was shocked, her face immediately turned pale. "You...you said what?"

"Though you shut down the control panel when you left, I later cracked the password, so I know there are two survivors. Quite coincidentally, I actually met the two kids. They were lovely. I've been thinking back on the things you said." He Xi paused a little. "Now I finally understand that letting go is also a kind of love, and the deepest love in the universe. I know what to do. No one else will know this, no one will come to disturb you. Bye, my Caspian Sea goddess."

"Thank you. I will protect them, I won't let them lose their way." Yu Lan's eyes held reluctance. The eternal farewell was right before them. Through the screen, they looked at each other earnestly, their lips moving slightly, unknowingly reciting the poem engraved on their souls:

Life does not allow us to meet, like Shen and Shang we go separate ways.
What a rare night it is tonight, together we share the candlelight.
On each face tears converged into lines and flowed uncontrollably, washing down everything on the way, flattening the endless barricades in their hearts.
Youth and vigor won't last long, on our temples gray hair has grown....
You were unmarried when we last parted, now your children stand in a row.

Memories, one after another, flashed before He Xi's eyes: the first encounter on Earth, the twenty-year separation, the brief reunion, and this eternal farewell. His heart heaved. This moment was an entire lifetime.

Ten cups don't make me drunk, for your friendship moved me long.
Tomorrow we'll be divided by mountains, to one another our lives will be mysteries....

A dazzling flash suddenly came, blurring everything in sight, announcing the end of this long story. But the last syllable still floated, hovered, circling the two, trillions of kilometers apart.

THE FIRST

Allen Stroud

I came around on my side, my head heavy and eyes gritted shut. I blinked rapidly and tried to lift my hand to my face, but my wrists were tied; a knot of cloth, looping around them and the waste water recycling pipe.

I could hear a hissing noise, the sort we trained for on Earth. An oxygen leak in the dome meant trouble, *serious* trouble. The automated system maintained pressure and air quality, but eventually the tanks would run out.

The gunk gave way enough to see a little. Blurry shapes moved around me, one of them came closer, bent down.

"You awake?"

A woman's voice. I blinked again, and my vision cleared; an unfamiliar face. *Not possible.*

"Who are—"

"I need the code for the computer on your ship. Give it to me."

"How did you—"

The click of a safety catch, the cold steel barrel of a gun pressed to my aching forehead. "Passcode...."

"Fourteen ten, dash twenty-six, dash sixty-two, dash twenty-three."

A rustle of clothing, movement, and the woman went away, the sound of typing and a curse. "You lied to me!" she screamed.

"You can't be here," I said. "It's impossible."

I recognized where I was: the hydroponics lab. The other shapes were David's plants. *Where is he?* A groan from the corner of the room; I turned my head and caught sight of a bloodied figure. "If you hurt him...."

The woman laughed hysterically. "You'll do what? Call for help? You're a long way from home, a long way indeed."

★　★　★

Two days earlier things had been very different.

Landfall on Mars. Landing site – NE Syrtis Major. A manned mission six years in the planning and a full year of journey time. My crew of four: American pilot Susan Gill, French botanist David Trevenne, Spanish engineer Adella Lopez, and me – Captain Thomas Gravener, RAF, requisitioned to the Sirius program for this project. We spent eleven months in cold sleep while our transfer ship, the *Zacuto*, made its way out from Earth orbit to its colder brother.

March 15th, 2077: the day human beings arrived on the red planet.

Susan's deft hand on the thrusters of the *Greenmark* – our crab-shaped lander – brought us in, just like the simulation. A breath of fuel and we were down. The *clunk* – a sound I'd waited for – rekindled the child in me; that sense of wonder we get when we're unburdened by responsibility. For a fleeting moment I was the dreaming kid watching the television and gazing up in to the night sky....

Necessity and a hand squeezing my wrist brought me back. Susan gave me a lopsided grin. "Time to explore," she said.

I nodded and returned the smile, keen and eager. I touched the comms. "David, you ready?"

"*Oui, prête ici!*"

David is quite the national *celebre*, back in France. We drew lots to go first and step out onto the surface, but I'd hoped he'd win; I never met a nicer man. Our lander's exterior cameras all stared at the airlock, waiting for him. Lag time to Madrid remained at eighteen minutes twelve seconds, meaning we'd be celebrating with him back inside before they got the news. No extended trips tonight. The trip to the habitation dome would start in the morning.

It took years of preparation and there'd been a complete media blackout until we arrived in orbit. Robots built a biodome modelled on similar constructs in Antarctica; the whole place running on minimal radio and power, before we arrived. Pillinger Base on NE Syrtis Major; rocky and flat; ideal for an exploratory mission. If all went well, viable sites for a colony could be determined later. We didn't need ground with potential, just stability and an easy landing. Outside, a few hundred meters away, would be a prefabricated compound with solar farm, recycler, and chemical exchange.

"I can see him!"

I turned to the view screen. David appeared on camera, fumbling awkwardly in the Martian gravity, a little over a third of Earth's. The sky was like a dull day from back home, not the multicolored vistas you saw in paintings. Hard to accept this as another planet, the first visited by humanity. David managed the stairs and touched down, then waved and bowed; very theatrical!

Five minutes later he was back on board while Susan ran a bio scan. Five minutes after that, the champagne came out. When Madrid cheered, we clinked glasses and cheered too.

More plonk ended up in David's beard than anywhere else.

★   ★   ★

"The code, captain. No messing around this time!"

I got a better look at the woman. A dark-haired Afro-American, judging by the accent. I couldn't place the state – most Americans sound the same to me. She was emaciated and haggard, wearing a pressure suit covered in dust.

Her eyes were wide, staring, and red rimmed, her mouth flecked with spittle. She moved in an awkward, desperate way that matched her look.

"You won't kill me," I said. "If you do, we'll all die."

"You think I care?"

"Yes, I do."

I could still hear hissing. How long had I been out? I vaguely remembered a conversation about ration supplements and items being missing from the inventory before something slammed into the back of my head.

The gun appeared again, four inches from my face. "I may need you alive, captain, but I can hurt you. After a while, you'll wish you were dead...."

"How did you get here?" I asked.

The barrel lowered, aiming at my groin. "Passcode," the woman repeated.

"You can't have come with us," I reasoned, "the lander is too small. I reckon you stowed away on one of the supply ships. That means you've been up here three weeks, at least."

"Try two years," the woman snarled, "more than enough for anyone. Now give me the code, I'll reactivate your ship and get out of here."

"Leaving us with no way back?"

"You've got supplies and they'll send someone."

I smiled. "What's your flight experience?"

"Why do you care?"

"The lander takes training to pilot. I'd rather not commit murder by giving you the right code."

The gun lowered further, the woman's shoulders slumped. She sat down, her eyes flicking toward David's prone form. "He's still alive, I checked."

"Very good of you," I said, keeping my voice light. Susan and Adella would be alert to the leak, they'd realize something was up. "What's your name?"

"Jade Langley," she said, glaring, as if I should already know.

"We can't leave David like that. You'll need to untie me, so I can help him."

She stumbled toward me, reached around and undid the cloth knot. I sat still waiting. No point in trying for her gun, she'd had more time to get used to the gravity. "Thank you," I said when she was done.

I moved slowly and checked David's pulse; steady and strong. His eyes fluttered open and he winked. I winked in return and turned to Jade. "You're right, he'll be okay."

She didn't reply; her eyes stayed on the floor. I glanced around. The leak had stopped, and a figure stood in the doorway out of sight: Susan, armed with a shovel from the emergency kit. I got her attention, shook my head and put a finger to my lips. She nodded.

"How did you end up on Mars?" I asked.

"You don't know?" Jade frowned. "What's happened down there?"

I caught a glimpse of the shoulder of her suit, the dust smeared away, revealing the patch beneath: a blue circle with a red line and the letters NASA stitched in white.

NASA? Suddenly it all made sense.

"You didn't stow away," I realized aloud. "You were part of a mission."

Her eyes lost focus. "We landed, miles from here, set up the laboratory and transmitter, but got no response. Turned out the antenna was damaged. We fixed it but still nothing...no one...."

"There's no record of a NASA mission," I said softly. "There was an explosion on Merritt Island in 2075...terrorists by all accounts."

Jade glared at me, returning to the present. "You're supposed to take me home," she said.

"I can't do that right away," I replied. "Not until we plan this all out." I reached out a hand. "You know how it is, we didn't expect to find you here and we didn't calculate fuel for five. We'll need to do the calculations before anybody goes anywhere, and before we start all that, you must give me the gun."

The idea jolted her, and the pleading expression vanished, replaced by something hard. She pointed the weapon at me again. Instinctively, I raised my hands. "Whoa! You want to be the first murderer on Mars?"

She flinched at that, but the gun didn't waver. "I won't be the first," she muttered.

I let that hang in the air between us for a while before I spoke again, this time choosing my words carefully. "My friends will be wondering where I am, and David too. What happens then?"

"They sit down and do as they're told," Jade replied. "We make a plan, like you said, but I keep the gun – that way I'm safe."

"You're safer without it," I said.

She shook her head. "I thought that last time I had a crew, but it didn't work out that way. Turns out you can't trust people. No, you talk to your friends and get them down here. Then we'll talk, and you'll take me home."

★　★　★

Slowly, my head cleared. The wound was quickly taken care of with a synth skin strip from a medical box, but the after-effects took a little longer.

I made a show of contacting the others and David 'roused' himself. Seemingly he put up more of a fight than I, but none of his wounds were serious. Jade let him sit with me. Presently, Adella joined us. Susan waited a few minutes before emerging from where she'd been hiding. She left the shovel behind.

"Tell me about your mission," Jade demanded.

I shrugged in response. "If you've been here a while, you can guess. We were sent up here as an exploration team, scouting for viable colony sites."

"Who by?"

"*Eurospace*. It's the only agency attempting manned flight these days," Susan chimed in. She stared at Jade. "Jade Langley, yeah, I remember you from the public personnel lists when I submitted my application. I always thought it was a tragedy you folks never got to fly before—"

"Well we did," Jade interrupted. "Be careful what you wish for, sweetheart."

"Our job is to assess and recommend a site," I said, using the explanation to calm everyone down. "We're due to stay six months, set up and take readings."

Jade waved her hand dismissively. "How fast can you prep the lander for launch?"

I frowned at her. "We can't leave straight away. We've only just got here. If you want to change our mission parameters, you'll need more than threats to do it."

"You'll die if you stay here," Jade said. "We all will."

"Why? You going to shoot everyone?"

"No, but it might be better if I did, before they come for us."

"Who do you mean?" Adella asked.

"You don't want to know."

I sighed. "Like I said, if you want to change things, you need to give us a reason."

She turned away from me and stared at the wall. "NASA's 2074 mission was launched under media blackout. They figured the journey time would be so long, people would just worry. Me, pilot Mike Samms, and flight engineer John Tann all went into cold sleep three weeks after we left. We woke up a day out and brought the USS *Vulcan* into parking orbit before we descended to do our Neil Armstrong bit. Six hours after we touched down we lost contact with the ship. Three hours after that, they came for us."

"Who came for you?"

"Martians."

I struggled and failed to stifle my laughter. I got a cold glare in response. "You think I'm lying?" Jade demanded.

I shrugged. "This planet's been surveyed for more than a century. Despite plenty of science fiction being written, nothing more than microbial life was ever found."

"*Merde!*" David said and rounded on me. "She's given you an explanation and you dismiss it?"

"You believe her, then?" I couldn't keep the incredulity out of my voice.

"Whether I do or not doesn't matter." David's accent always made what he said sound beautiful, even if he was angry. "What matters is something happened and here is a human being in pain! You asked for more than threats and got reasons, now you don't like the reasons!"

"What do you suggest, then?" Adella asked.

"We question, we detect, we investigate, we find evidence," David said. "Until you can provide a better explanation, Mademoiselle Jade's story stands."

I looked at each of them in turn. Yes, I'm the captain of the mission, but Mars is a long way from Earth and maybe David is right, perhaps I wasn't being a scientist about it. Besides, believing the woman might help us earn her trust. "All right," I said. "But we can't do much finding out of anything sat here at gunpoint."

David turned to Jade. "Keep your gun, we're not going to take it from you," he said. "Show us what happened to you."

"Okay," Jade said. She stood up. "You'll need to log in to your ship's computer though, and then we go through it together and you judge for yourself."

★　　★　　★

The 'rec' room wasn't home yet. It still had that new house feel to it, but it was a good place with enough chairs and an access terminal. The only other location with the same space would be control, and I wasn't ready to let our guest loose up there. Control would be locked up tight with thumbprint recognition needed for the doors. Any attempt to force a way in would trigger a security depressurization.

At that moment I realized why Jade was in hydroponics. It had probably been the only part of the habitation system with an atmosphere before we arrived. How long had she been stuck in that room?

Adella took the terminal box seat while the rest of us crowded round. "Okay, I'm logged in to the *Santa Maria*," she said. "What do you want me to do?"

"First, start an orbital sweep for our transit ship," Jade said. "As I told you, we lost comms pretty quick. It'd be nice to know if it's still there. We also deployed three relay satellites. I expect you did something similar?"

I nodded.

"It may take a while to plot all the parking orbits," Susan said. "What can we do in the meantime?"

"Scan around Pillinger in an expanding circle. You should find the remains of the NASA base we abandoned. It's not far, otherwise I'd never have made it."

Adella tapped in the necessary commands. "That's working as well."

I stepped back from the group and straightened up, facing Jade. "What more can you tell us about your time here?"

She grimaced, but she was visibly calmer than before. "We survived in the mission shelter for six months. When supplies were running out we picked up the signal from the first robot lander coming down to build this place. By then, the buggy had been wrecked and Tann broke his foot. When he could walk, we decided to take a chance on getting here. We set out tethered together, but a storm blew up and they came for us in it. Eventually, I was left alone, nearly out of oxygen, attached to a strand of rope. Thankfully, the robots finished hydroponics and I was able to get inside."

"When you say 'they', you mean the Martians?"

"Yeah."

"So, you never saw anyone?"

Jade's expression hardened. "You want to go back to the plants, captain? I can assure you they're a tough audience for eighteen months."

Susan laid a placatory hand on my arm. "We're just trying to get the facts, Jade."

Jade shrugged. "Those tethers are a woven plastic polymer. There isn't anything that'd snap them without a whole load of force. If the storm took one of us, it'd have taken us all." She fished into her dusty suit pocket and pulled out a section of the line. It was frayed at one end, but severed in a neat, even cut. "I never felt a thing," she said.

"Orbital scan is finished," Adella called out from the terminal. "That's weird."

I leaned in once more. "What did you find?"

"Three satellites, like Jade said, but no USS *Vulcan*."

"Did we miss it? It's a big heap of space."

"Unlikely," Adella said. "The whole point of us bringing the remote orbitals was to set up a decent tracking network up here and down there. Our computer has picked up *Mangalyaan*, *Express*, *Odyssey*, *MAVEN*,

Ma Xian and the MRO, as well as the three new rigs Jade mentioned. Some of those ships are ancient, but they're still up and receiving the signal. No sign of anything else."

"Do you have access codes for your satellites, Jade?" I asked.

She nodded. "Of course."

"If we had them, we could check the historical plotting and find out what happened to your ship."

"What will you trade?" Jade asked.

I chewed on my lip thoughtfully. "Gun and codes for a user account on our system. I also want your word you'll stick to a group decision on when we leave."

There was silence as she mulled it over, glaring at each of us — even Adella, who'd turned away from the terminal screen. Eventually, she pulled the pistol out of her pocket, reversed it, and held it out to me.

"Thank you. You get the gun back if things get dangerous." I turned to Susan. "Take Jade into control and get her sorted. I want everyone back to the job we came here for — arrival assessment. We factor in everything Jade can tell us and then we make some decisions. One hour, then we discuss around the rec room table, understood?"

David grinned, his bloody beard making the expression a little savage. "Fine by me," he said.

"Adella, I want whatever results you get from both scans," I added. "Anyone needs me, I'll be in the archive."

*   *   *

It made sense to me to withdraw and let Jade think she had won me over. Susan had experienced the NASA program before it shut down — they'd be able to talk alone, share some of that American superiority about space that occasionally bubbled to the surface. They still weren't used to the way things had changed.

The archive room held all the black box data, a hard-coded recording of the construction robots' activities as they built the station.

Much of the information was in control, but a lot of the core function history wouldn't be; there wasn't much point unless you were searching for something.

Which I was.

It wasn't a big room, barely big enough for me to squeeze between the three dormant robots. Emergency lighting flicked on as I shut the door. I flipped out the terminal and chair, so I could sit down. This was a secure and isolated system, designed to handle charging and routine storage while Pillinger was being built. One of our first housekeeping tasks would be to take the data cores and manually upload them to the network before broadcasting it all back to Madrid.

But there were some answers I needed first.

After the terminal initialized, I called up the headcam video feeds from the constructors on smaller split screens, spooling past their landing, deployment, and drive to the habitat site. I watched the domes being constructed at superfast speed until I caught spotted signs of red dust blowing in the wind.

The storm Jade talked about.

I slowed the feed. The robots were still moving around much faster than at the time, but now I was checking for details. When I got to the point that the hydroponics lab was almost complete, I adjusted it right down to real time.

One of these cameras must have caught her entering.

A moment later I found what I was looking for: a shadowy outline against the outer skin of the lab, slipping away as the robot turned to spray sealant onto a section of hardening polymer composite. I froze all the screens, flipping through all the available cameras at that point to see what they had captured.

Nothing, except the one image.

I went on, checking the next few hours or so meticulously, but saw nothing else. I went through the sensor logs too, noting the anomaly of a tear in the hydroponic lab wall which had been fixed the moment it was discovered, only a few minutes after the shadow was recorded. Everything seemed to match Jade's story.

I went back and stared at the shadow. It was blurry and indistinct, but I thought it could have been two people, not one.

Had Tann or Samms survived with Jade and got inside the base?

★   ★   ★

An hour later and I was in the rec room with a printout of the silhouette, having pulled out the main table and drawn up a chair. None of the others arrived on time, but David was only a minute or two late, his hair damp from the recycling shower. He smiled apologetically at me. "Someone had to go first, and I thought the blood gave me a good excuse."

I shrugged, not returning the expression. "I guess you're right."

His smile evaporated immediately. "What have you found?"

I pushed the picture across the table toward him. "Construction footage printout. Would you say that's the shadow of one person or two?"

David stared at it, then at me. "You get any others?"

"No, just the one."

"Then we can't be sure of anything, can we? Other than what Jade's told us, I think we believe that."

I frowned at him but took the image back and pocketed it as Susan and Jade came down the steps from control. "Sorry, there was so much to set up," Susan said and glanced around. "Where's Adella?"

"Wasn't she with you?" I asked.

"No, we left her here working on the terminal and running the scans."

I got up and went to the station. The chair was turned away from it and the two processes had completed, but the results were still on the screen. I felt the others join me, peering over my shoulder. "Odd, I'd have thought she'd have compiled all this like I asked."

"Who was in here first?"

"Me, then David. I didn't see her."

"Nor me. She never came down to hydroponics."

"She never came into control, either."

I stepped away and looked at each of them in turn. "We've only six rooms in this place. How can she disappear?"

Susan slipped past me to the terminal and keyed up a bio hotspot search. A two-dimensional map of the base appeared with moving red spots where we were standing and in the hydroponics lab. We all stared at it. "She's been gone less than an hour," Susan said. "Even if she was… there was a body, it'd show up."

"It's like she was never here," David said.

"Now do you believe me?" Jade muttered in a low tone. "We have to get out of here."

Susan stood up and unclipped a small handheld radio from her belt. "Old tech, but I thought one of us might have to go back to the lander." She handed it to me and passed another one to David.

"We go in pairs and check all the rooms," I said. "Jade, you're with me."

"We won't find her," Jade said.

"All the same, I'd like to be sure."

★　　★　　★

It took ten minutes to confirm Jade's statement: Adella was nowhere to be found.

As we searched the sleeping quarters and the science lab, I tried to picture her as I'd last seen her, staring at the terminal. We'd been quite close for a while during final training. The whole team of eight – mission team and alternates – had spent the best part of a year in each other's pockets. Adella was married but things were difficult with the long separation. We'd had one or two late-night conversations chatting out the issues. I'd convinced her to stay on the program, but she was hoping to get back to her family afterward. *You'll regret it for the rest of your life if you don't go once.*

Now she had vanished.

We looked everywhere, but it wasn't like losing a book or your keys. There's only so many places a human could hide or be hidden.

As I'd been alone, I insisted we check control, which pissed off Jade enough to counter with a search of the archive. With two of us in there we could barely move.

"You don't trust me," she said.

"You jumped me when we first met," I replied. "That makes you hard to trust."

Jade grunted. "Y'know, the Brit accent's like a special tie on a white-guy suit. You go to a private school too? I bet all the ground team just love you, don't they?"

I stared at her. "I'd feel the same about anyone I'd met under these circumstances."

"Sure you would," she drawled. "Ever had to fight for something? I mean, really fight?"

"I was in the Royal Air Force and flew over the Baltics in sixty-five."

"Not what I meant."

No one had been in the science lab, or at least, no one was supposed to have been in there. The door sighed a little as it swung open and I caught a scent of stale air before the recycling system whisked it away.

Tools were strewn all over the table. The chairs were upended, and several glass sample containers lay smashed on the floor.

"What happened in here?" I said, blurting out my thoughts in surprise.

"How should I know?" Jade replied, stepping past me and into the room. Her battered boots crunched on the glass. "I've never been in here."

I lingered at the door, thinking about police procedures, crime scenes, and all that stuff about preserving evidence, but then I realized we had no cop show detective to investigate, just us.

"David needs to take a look at this," I said. "He's the best qualified to find clues."

Jade shrugged. "The longer you take, the worse it'll be," she said.

"Is that a threat?" I asked.

She stared at me, but this time there was no anger, just a kind of broken expression; a little pain mixed with resignation. "Doesn't take long for the prejudice to come out, does it?"

"I don't mean it like that," I said. "You've been here, we haven't."

"And you're full of jumping to conclusions."

"Whereas you're pressuring for evacuation. I want to make the right choice based on evidence."

"People go missing and someone's been in the lab. What more evidence do you need? You think the things that do this are going to sit still and pose so you can size them up?"

"What, like you did?" I pulled the archive printout from my pocket and held it up. "Care to explain why the robot camera saw more than one person breaking into hydroponics?"

Jade squinted at the picture. "That's not me," she said. "I broke in from the other side. I'm sure if you print the construction logs you'll see where the repairs were done."

Damn. I hadn't checked where the repair had been, I'd just assumed—

The hand radio beeped. We both looked at it. I turned away from Jade and unclipped it. "Susan?"

There was no answer.

*   *   *

We raced back along the corridor to the rec room, control, and hydroponics. There was no sign of Susan, David, or Adella. When we got to control, Jade dropped into a chair and activated one of the screens.

"Airlock's been opened," she said. "Pressure's re-equalizing."

"Why would they go outside?" I thought aloud.

"Maybe they got sick of waiting for you to see the fucking obvious," Jade said. "We need to suit up and get to the lander, please! You can decide whether to take off or not, but if we don't leave...." She left it hanging.

I pulled her pistol out of my pocket and handed it to her. "Okay, we'll go. The EVA lockers are next to the inner pressure door. You lead the way."

"Still don't trust me?"

"You have your gun, don't you?"

We found the lockers untouched; stranger and stranger. I took a moment to pick up a motorized wrench then suited up. Jade did the same and we checked each other's seals, like in training, only this time, how could I trust—

"Okay, let's go."

She keyed in the timed sequence, unwound the wheel lock, and stepped into the chamber. I followed, almost afraid to blink in case I lost sight of her. The automated system closed and locked the door behind us. I heard the hiss of air being sucked out of the room and pulled down my visor, switching on the suit comms.

"Susan? David?"

"No, only me," said Jade.

There's a bond you forge with people when you rely on them; work colleagues in an office, pilot and co-pilot, a sport team, whatever. When they're gone, it's like losing an arm. You feel broken and lost. Someone else might be able to do the job you need them to do, but it takes time to accept a replacement. Jade and I had no time.

The outer airlock opened. She stepped out, as did I. The arid landscape might have been an Earth desert, but I knew it wasn't. We left the womb of Mother Earth long ago, but she held on to us. Now we were at the mercy of an alien womb, the womb of Mars; a world labelled by us as male and warlike.

What manner of creature could be born of such a place?

The door closed behind us, a faint sound outside my pressure suit and helmet. I knew instantly we were vulnerable.

"Where's the lander?"

"This way."

I led, Jade followed. Low gravity and urgency lengthened our strides, but there was still some distance to make up. We'd be out here for thirty seconds or so, even at speed. I couldn't feel the motorized wrench through my gloves, but I knew it was there, the power lever under my thumb if it was needed.

Running across Mars was like EVA, but not; the personal sounds are magnified, like being in space, but gravity and the fact you can hear a little of the world is strange. You must remind yourself this isn't Earth, you can't crack open your helmet and take in a lungful of air. It's a seductive instinct, forcing you to think consciously about everything the whole time. We've trained for this, of course, but still....

As I ran, I glanced left and right across the vast plain. The dull sky and swirling sand gave no hint of danger or threat, but the farther we got from Pillinger, the more I sensed something amiss, a presence, strange but watchful. I knew it was moving as we moved.

"Believe me now?" Jade breathed over the comms. "You never had to fight to survive before. Welcome to reality beyond the manor gate."

"I've never been to a manor!"

"Your whole country's a manor," Jade snarled. "There ain't no silver spoons to help out here."

The lander wasn't far now, but in front of it I saw two figures, standing as if waiting for us. For a moment, I thought it might be Susan and David, but then I recognized the blue uniforms.

"Is that...."

"Oh no...."

NASA astronauts Michael Samms and John Tann stood in our way. They'd been stripped of their pressure suits, their exposed skin like the mummies you see in old Egyptian tombs, husks of the men they might have been, their flesh a written tapestry of suffering. They had no eyes or teeth but turned their heads toward us in perfect synchronicity as we approached.

I stopped. Jade did the same, halting a few paces to my left and brandishing the pistol. "Stay back!" she growled in my ear, a warning these ruined shells would never understand. It was no idle threat; the gun would fire even in Mars's rare atmosphere and they were not her old crewmates, but they were long past caring.

Somewhere, sometime, Tann and Samms had been sons, friends, and more to their kin, but those men were long gone. Their bodies were vessels of something we could not perceive or comprehend. They were being used as a bridge, something familiar that could reach out to us and communicate; something we might understand.

Every instinct urged me to run, to scream, to fight, but I didn't.

I stood, and I waited for the message.

Slowly, both figures raised their right hands, palms outward and fingers extended. The gesture spoke more than any other might. I remembered the lessons on *Pioneer* from my training and the etched plaque; the man waving, like this, while the woman stood at his side. How did they know? The *Pioneer* spacecraft had never come to this world. Had they watched us and learned? Moreover, they both performed the action. Did this intelligence understand gender?

I dropped the mechanized wrench and raised my own hand in response. I wanted to ask about Susan, Adella, and David, but I knew they would not hear. For several moments, we remained like that, Jade the odd one out. Then, the two bodies slumped and collapsed to the ground as if they were puppets whose strings had been cut.

Jade lowered her weapon. "What does that mean?" she asked.

"I think it means you were right," I said. "We need to take our chance, get into the lander, and take off – now."

"Glad you're finally making sense."

We piled up the steps and into the airlock, sealing the door behind us. Each moment it took to repressurize was another moment to consider the awful position we were in. We were intruders on another world, encountering intelligent life that knew about us, when we were ignorant of them.

When the air indicator light went green, I pulled off my helmet and began stripping away the pressure suit as fast as I could. But Jade hesitated. "They killed Mike and John," she said. "They probably got your friends, too."

"We can't know if that was intentional," I said. "But we also can't know if they are peaceful either. All we do know is that they are letting us go."

Jade nodded as she stepped out of her suit. "Would we do the same for them? If they came to Earth?"

"I doubt it," I replied.

We moved into the launch cabin. Jade took my co-pilot's seat, and with a wince I dropped into Susan's chair. It was the only choice we could make, and I said a little prayer that my flight skills would hold up.

Not that a prayer to the gods of Earth would be heard on the surface of Mars.

"They don't understand us," Jade said. "We don't understand them."

I sighed. "Two vastly different creatures, separated by a gulf of space, both vulnerable, and both dangerous. The only way there's a hope of us getting along is if we get back."

"It may be our only chance to warn people, too."

"Agreed."

Twenty minutes later we completed pre-flight checks and blasted off. We found and rendezvoused with the *Zacuto*, spent the best part of two days replotting our course, and left orbit for Earth soon after.

Four people came to Mars. Two people went home.

THE DARKNESS OF MIRROR PLANET

Zhao Haihong

Translated by Alex Woodend

Mirror 301A was her name. Her number, her identification sign in this world.

Sometimes, on the occasions when she looked in the mirror, she would faintly remember that the window also mirrored her relationship with things the world over.

She remembered years ago she had written to a friend: *I've always believed, somewhere in the universe, there is another Earth. On that Earth another identical Mirror lives.*

Later, she learned that was called a parallel universe, and after floundering and groping for many years in the world of knowledge, she scratched the surface of this sci-fi kind of concept. But somehow the moment she made eye contact with herself in the mirror, she seemed to see another self from another world.

A shadow swayed into the mirror. Mirror 301A turned, facing her sullen looking husband, Lack 213B.

"What're you dawdling for?" Lack said. Overnight his stubble had pushed through the skin on his lower jaw and above his upper lip and formed a green patch. "Always looking in the mirror all day."

Mirror 301A turned around, lurched a little. She went around Lack, who was blocking the passage, then made a half-circle and stopped at the door, announcing to Lack: "This morning I will receive a physical examination from the Space Bureau's Planet Dark Inspection Team

Two. They say those who qualify go on to train for half a year right away, then get sent to Planet Dark to inspect."

Lack blinked, nodded without expression.

"You have nothing to say?"

Lack's mouth opened in surprise, as if in confusion over the subtext that he should have something to say. "Aren't you going to work?"

Mirror shook her head with deep disappointment. "Bye." She walked out of the apartment and called an air taxi. After she fed two yuan into its keyhole, the little red Pegasus leaped onto the shining airway above the city and flew toward Fan City, where the Space Bureau was located.

★   ★   ★

The successful human landing on Planet Dark was the most exciting event of the 2150s. The supporters of space expansion tried hard to make the public accept it: Planet Dark is our only twin sister in this vast universe, like two identical pearls in the ocean, or like two identical grains of sand in the Ganges, far apart in the Milky Way yet connected spiritually. So, this sister star of Earth, close in age, alike in form, similar in composition, became what those spacemen called the future paradise of all human beings. Space colonists, dissatisfied with the harsh living conditions on the Moon and Mars, also itched to set out on a new expedition for Planet Dark.

In the airway to Fan City a thirty-four-story-high gas advertisement rose. In the frame was a patch of deep-blue sky, lively green mountains nestling a lake clear as a girl's teardrop. Flowing neon-colored steam rose from the heart of the lake, slowly condensing into two columns of giant characters: "*Planet Dark, A New Unpolluted Earth, Humanity's Second Home.*"

The moment the air taxi went through the neon stripe, Mirror 301A suddenly felt a pulse in her chest, as if it and that place were connected by an extremely thin, invisible thread, and the pulse had originated from a pulse at the other end.

"I…I want to go," she murmured. But whether or not she could depended on the result of the physical examination. This time forty scientists would receive physical examinations in Fan City, but Inspection Team Two only offered spots for five people. The competition was relatively fierce.

*　　*　　*

"Mirror 301A."

"That's me."

"PhD in Earth Paleontology, specializing in abnormal mutations in evolutionary history." The staffer's voice was suspiciously sugary. "Your performance in the preliminary test was excellent. Hope you are successful in the physical examination."

"Thanks."

"Please follow me." The staffer, frightening in his full-body protective clothing, led Mirror 301A through heavy imaging equipment and carefully designed test rooms. About three minutes later, they entered a white-domed hall. In the hall lay twenty neatly arranged egg-shaped space cabins. Mirror was assigned to No. 15. The worker opened the hatch, asked Mirror to lie back on the white mica bed. Countless electrodes of various thicknesses automatically connected to various parts of her body.

When the hatch was closed, a gentle recorded female voice said, "I'm happy to inform you that your physical indexes are up to standard. Let's proceed to the last test. Please close your eyes, relax your body, and wait for the bell."

Mirror 301A let out a breath, closed her eyelids, and relaxed her body. The air in the cabin seemed to have been perfumed with soothing incense. Her consciousness gradually faded, until she heard the clanging of a bell, each *clang* more urgent than the one before.

The hatch automatically bounced open. A young officer in a Space Bureau uniform walked up to her, all smiles. "Congratulations, Mirror 301A. You have qualified, please follow me."

"Qualified." Mirror didn't understand right away, just got up dizzily and stumbled behind the officer into a secret room on another floor. The Director of the Space Bureau's Division for Planet Dark Development was waiting there, the corners of his mouth lifted into a meaningful smile.

Mirror 301A stood before the Director's desk, then discovered that four other people were already standing beside her. They were most likely her colleagues who would go with her on the inspection mission.

"Congratulations, everyone, you are the victors. More than seven hundred scientists in relevant fields eligible for preliminary selection voluntarily applied in response to outreach organized by the Space Bureau. Preliminary testing reduced this to forty people, and those who completely met the physical requirements were only you five. I hope you are mentally prepared. Tomorrow you will embark on the journey to complete the mission to pioneer the next homeland for humanity." As the Director spoke, his thumb and index finger pinched a shining sequin like a fish scale, playing with it nonstop.

"Tomorrow? Aren't there six months of training?" Mirror couldn't help but ask.

"That's the procedure for Inspection Team One. Now we already have Team One's experience. You just need to do a cerebral insert with the information on this tiny chip and proceed with a three-hour adaptation operation, whereupon all preparations will be finished."

"I...."

"Any other questions?" the Director asked.

"No, nothing...." Mirror let her head droop, sensing the departure was breathlessly fast.

*　　*　　*

The Planet Dark Exploration Plan had entered the second stage; that is, field survey and inspection, the search for a suitable place to build a scientific research camp of a certain size. Each team member had detailed information about the atmosphere and surface of Planet Dark captured in recent years by exploration satellites, so the survey progressed much faster than usual.

Like Earth, Planet Dark also revolved around a star like the Sun, with an orbit and angle similar to that of the Earth and Sun. Planet Dark also had a moon, which disappeared during the day and appeared at night, stimulating the planet's ceaselessly surging tides. The oxygen content of Planet Dark's atmosphere was higher than Earth's, and the concentrations of gases like nitrogen and hydrogen were also higher. Therefore, the inspection team put on special spacesuits before getting off the spaceship. The comfortable, well-fitting biochemical materials could also resist various cosmic rays, endure heat, keep out the cold, and were extremely durable. The spacesuit's headpiece was a light space helmet connected through the suit's zipper to the tubing of a reactive filtration device. Through this device, the size of a human thumb, the air of Planet Dark, after purification, filtration, and a series of chemical reactions, was converted into a safe gas identical in composition to the air on Earth.

Each team member had an aerolamp. This multifunctional detection tool was a new invention by the scientists of Fan City. It served simultaneously as a satellite locator, camera, video camera, lamp, and weapon. Because the beam it emitted could kill a Tyrannosaurus rex, the inspection team members were emboldened, and on the fifth day after landing started to set out alone.

Mirror felt she was in a dreamland, as if only in dreams could there be such heartbreakingly beautiful blue mist. She was alone, traversing a hilly terrain about fifty kilometers from the landing site. Here the geographic conditions were complex, but she didn't sense any strangeness. Just the opposite: it was as if she was on her mother planet, undertaking an adventurous expedition for *National Geographic*.

The blue mist grew thinner and thinner as crystal clear-light gradually shone from its center. Mirror held her breath, held out a hand to grope through the transparent spot, and slowly stepped forward. Suddenly, as if breaking through a layer of gauze, she entered a refreshing valley. The situation and the sight felt intimately familiar.

It was a valley encircled by mountains. Behind the lively green mountains was a deep-blue sky nearing daybreak. The sky and the pond at the center of the valley reflected each other, so there was sky and earth in the pond, too.

The advertisement on the airway! To her surprise she had wandered to the same place! Mirror 301A gave a satisfied sigh then took a deep breath. The air of the valley entered her lungs through the filtration device. Due to what she knew was a silly psychological effect, she found the air particularly fresh.

At that moment the crystal pond rippled. No wind, but the ripples started to radiate out in all directions from a center point.

Mirror suddenly felt more alert: there was something strange in the water!

She aimed her aerogun at the middle of the pond ripples and held her breath to watch the creature slowly surface from the lake. Its head, covered with dripping-wet, dark-brown hair, hung over its face. Underneath were snow-white shoulders, beautiful, plump female breasts, a delicately curving waist....

Startled, Mirror took a step back – it was a human! No, rather, a Planet Dark human! Although people imagined that Planet Dark may have intelligent life, they never expected it would be exactly like humans. Evolutionarily speaking, during early stages, any nuance in the external environment could lead life onto a completely different developmental path. Regardless of the similarities between Planet Earth and Planet Dark, the probability of this place generating the exact same terrestrial human beings was less than one in 100 million!

The creature crawled onto a rock at the heart of the lake. It – no, let's say *she* – slowly stood straight, gently shook loose the wet hair sticking to her face. Her smooth skin was so lustrous it looked as if her body was ringed by a halo.

Her face turned to Mirror.

Mirror 301A, paleontologist from Earth, gave a piercing scream.

It was her face!

It was her face – identically curved eyes and eyebrows, identically shaped lips, identically arched nose. The only difference was the expression.

The lake sprite-like woman was smiling.

"You, you...." Mirror raised the aerolamp in panic. "Don't move!"

(I'm not your enemy.)

"What did you say? Why can I understand you?"

(I am your friend, Mirror. I'm you, even.)

"What is happening? You're not speaking. But I can hear...."

(I'm talking directly to your mind. Mirror, language isn't a barrier at all.)

"I can't believe.... I...."

(Once upon a time, you believed I existed.)

"I...." Mirror 301A stared at the lake sprite's hypnotizing, deep-set eyes. Her voice softened. "How is this possible...."

(This is the universe, even the most impossible things can happen.)

"But, how could you...."

(Mirror 301A, Earth woman, thirty years old, from the second generation of children born in artificial wombs. You haven't gotten along with your mom since you were little, think she was irresponsible to have you born in a machine.)

"I'm not that unreasonable, most of her generation did the same."

(No, you do care. You know you are not in a position to criticize, but because of this you have repressed yourself since childhood, felt unconfident in interpersonal relationships.)

"Hey, I don't need to be psychoanalyzed. Speak for yourself...."

(You are also from the third generation to accept spouses by algorithm. You have no affection for your own husband Lack but are unwilling to file for divorce, seeing the formalities as tedious, especially since remarriage would also have to be arranged by algorithm. But you are miserable inside and so place all your hope in your career.)

"I hate you, shut up."

(But you finally came here, you are free. Mirror, here you can truly be yourself. You don't have to go back to that dull, repressed world of machines. Planet Dark is Earth's mirror star, and I am your mirror image. Look, isn't this life great?)

"Life? I don't see you have any kind of life."

(Here everything comes from nature. No computers arranging your life, no machines dominating it. I know you have always wanted a child, a real child. Here you can make it, Mirror. If you can't be your mother's child, at least you can be your child's mother.)

"You speak as if this is...."

(The Garden of Eden. Right. Planet Dark is your Garden of Eden.)

"Mine?"

(Planet Dark Inspection Team One landed on this planet as early as three years ago. Of them, some chose to stay, to live with their mirror images.)

"No!"

(You don't know about this, of course. It's a secret.)

"No! We received data from them during training."

(The information was sent back by the information transmitter in the spaceship. In fact, none of the previous inspection team members returned to Earth.)

"They all believed you?" Mirror shook her head.

(I can only say that some people did.)

"What about the others?"

(Because they couldn't face their true selves, they seem to have gone insane.)

"Gone insane?"

Suddenly, a wave of sensation surged in Mirror's mind, a resonance triggered by a strong, distant vibration.

Sorrow, anguish, despair, and shock.

Probably a mental signal sent by the telepathic 'mirror image'.

(Another finished.)

The lake sprite's face crumpled with sorrow.

(Humans, why are you so stupid.)

"What's that?"

(That's another choice.)

"I don't understand."

(They shot horrible beams from aerolamps. Aiming at their mirror images.)

"God!"

(Those didn't return to Earth, either. They've been insane ever since, carrying the lamps all day, looking for other mirror images. They've become murderous maniacs.)

"Impossible."

(It's true. Soon you'll see your colleague. The person who just shot the death beam. You'll see he has gone insane.)

"No!"

(No other way out, Mirror. Come with me. I am your mirror image, another you waiting for you here. I will restore the natural purity of life for you. I will bring you a partner with the same beliefs. You will bear and raise children here, multiply like the earliest human ancestors....)

"There are ten billion people on Earth. Does everyone have a mirror image here?"

(No, Mirror, not everyone. People who believe we exist. Haven't you believed in my existence since you were little?)

"Even those who shot death beams at mirror images are believers?"

(Aren't they? The precondition for killing was admitting their mirror images were their other face that they couldn't accept. They couldn't face their true selves. Otherwise, according to the rules of your expedition, in a non-life-threatening situation, it is forbidden to hurt any creature on this planet.)

"I still can't believe − the mirror image in the universe, another identical me, lives a completely different life."

(Perhaps this is fate. Who knows why the Big Bang, which created all, happened? The universe is full of inexplicable mysteries. You could also call it fate.)

"Fate?"

(Right, my existence is fate, so is our encounter.)

"I don't believe this nonsense." Mirror suddenly raised her voice. "In this world there is only science, everything can be explained."

(Including your birth, your marriage?)

"Shut up!" Mirror suddenly held up the aerolamp. "What do you know?!"

(Mirror, don't run from yourself! You are a true loser. You lack loving parents, you lack a loving partner....)

"I hate you!" Mirror's face flushed. "You're a monster!"

(Mirror, I'm just the truth you don't want to face.)

"You are not! You're a liar! You're a trap!" Mirror screamed hysterically. In her excitement her fingers touched the firing button closest to the handle – it was unintentional, it really was unintentional.

A deep-blue beam was cast from the small round hole at the front of the aerolamp. Even the air seemed to be split apart by the beam, hissing like a rattlesnake.

On the lake sprite's plump white chest a growing black hole appeared. The black hole expanded quickly then swallowed up her entire body.

Mirror again felt the shockwave.

Sorrow, anguish, despair.

(How could you?!)

The lake sprite's face, crumpled in excruciating pain, seared Mirror's eyes. Mirror couldn't help but touch her own face and found she was mimicking the exact same expression.

Unforgettable. This expression would always be unforgettable.

(How could you?!)

(How could you?!)

A wave of red clouds rolled through the deep-blue sky, Planet Dark's brush of rosy dawn. The dawn light stained Mirror's pale forehead like blood.

Clang-clang-clang-clang-clang—

Each more urgent than the last.

Mirror 301A woke up. She opened her eyes, saw the translucent cabin hatch. She shivered.

The hatch automatically bounced open. A young officer in a Space Bureau uniform walked up to her, all smiles. "Congratulations, Mirror 301A. You have qualified, please follow me."

"Qua…lified?" Mirror dizzily got up and stumbled behind the officer to a secret room on another floor. The Director of the Space Bureau's Division of Planet Dark Development was waiting there, the corners of his mouth lifted into a meaningful smile.

Of course, in the room were four other people – different from last time.

"Congratulations, everyone. You've passed the last psychological test."

"Why…." Each had the same question.

"Everyone, allow me to explain. Your exploration of Planet Dark was just a virtual experience taking place in your cerebral cortex. That was a test."

"A test of what?"

"What does it mean?"

"Take it easy." The director waved a hand to stop them. "You're here because you made the same choice during the test."

"You mean…killed the 'mirror image'?" Mirror's finger that pressed the button in the dream began shaking.

"Killed that monster," the director explained. "Your experience during the test was a real challenge Team One members encountered."

"So?"

"Just as you heard from the 'mirror images', there are highly intelligent creatures living on Planet Dark. But they are not mirror images created by fate or anything, just some kind of monster with highly developed mimicry and telepathic abilities.

"This kind of monster would encounter a team member by themselves, then appear in the form of the team member and use telepathy to read the other's mind. Because in every person's mind are a 'self' and 'other', the monsters of Planet Dark are able to take advantage and pretend to be a team member's psychological other, cajole the team member to live with them, break away from the control of the human world."

"But why?" Mirror heard her own voice asking. It seemed to come from someone else's mouth.

"Since the materials currently at hand are insufficient, we can only speculate. Although the monsters of Planet Dark possess unique mimicry and telepathic abilities, when facing the technological power of humans, they lack weapons to protect themselves. They can only touch the softest, most variable human hearts. Therefore, although they persuaded some of the Team One members to leave the inspection team to join them, other strong-willed members shot them."

"Is that really...." someone mumbled.

"Really what?" the director said, suddenly raising his voice. "On the surface, shooting a death beam at the unthreatening creatures of Planet Dark is against the rules. But those team members actually found the other had used psychological tactics to pose a threat. The death beam was aimed at defeating their inner confusion."

"Maybe...just maybe...what the creatures of Planet Dark said is real – they...they...." Mirror probed carefully.

"Don't vacillate!" the director pounded the table sternly. "No being is unselfish. When Team Two members land on Planet Dark, they will also face temptations from those monsters. They will cajole you into joining their camp, then use you to seduce sober team members. This kind of thing has already happened. So, when recruiting Team Two members we used this psychological test as the final, most important threshold. We used a high-energy computer to analyze your brainwaves, invited senior psychologists to gather all the data, and design corresponding virtual monsters from Planet Dark. Only candidates who kill them during the test can become official team members."

He used his stern gaze to scrutinize the five chosen team members one by one. "I hope you always remember the choice you made and successfully carry out your inspection mission."

"May I ask what exactly is our inspection mission? Kill the most intelligent life on that planet?" an ashen-faced man asked.

"No, to sweep away all potential threats to future human beings who migrate to Planet Dark. Seems like you still haven't figured out how the universal law of survival works," the director said, pausing after every word. "Sorry, you're fired."

★　　★　　★

Deep–blue mist permeated the entire dream. Then the sound of water. The soft sound of a lake rippling. A slender white hand from the origin of the sound, from the center of the mist, like a white butterfly lightly flying over.

(Mirror, once upon a time, you believed I existed.)

Soft laughter like ripples on the lake.

(You finally came here. You are free, Mirror. You are free.)

Hesitantly, hesitantly, Mirror 301A touched that hand. Immediately it wound gently around her five fingers.

The sound of a rattlesnake's hiss.

The mist suddenly dispersed. Mirror 301A faced the other face directly: sorrow, anguish, despair, and shock! The face crumpled in excruciating pain was her own face!

"No! No!" Mirror screamed.

Sweat heavily pouring drenched her clothes. Mirror opened her eyes. She woke up.

Shaking, she felt her own face. On this face still remained the expression she had just seen, the crumpled face.

Tears snaked down along the painful wrinkles.

This was a dream. She told herself there was still half a month for the spaceship to reach Planet Dark. When would the end of the nightmare come?

Or was that the real beginning of the nightmare?

I still have choices, she told herself. Her body shook nonstop like a sieve. She kept telling herself: *I still have choices*.

★　　★　　★

She still has choices.

MINUET OF CORPSES

Amdi Silvestri

Let me make something clear – I know nothing. I understand nothing. I don't fake knowledge or wisdom. I never correct other people, even when I think what they're saying is wrong. I know facts, but I don't *believe* in them like some people, where numbers and lists have taken the place of gods. In ancient Greece, Pythia – the oracle of Delphi – proclaimed that Socrates was the wisest man. When confronted with this, Socrates is reported to have said he only knew that he knew nothing. It's referred to as the Socratic paradox and allegedly derives from Plato's account of Socrates, although Plato never used those words, which makes the famous portrayal of wisdom a piece of fiction. That fact comforts me immensely, because it underlines the magnitude of what Socrates never said. I can't explain why – or more correctly, I couldn't before our last trek.

The life of a surveyor is one of solitude. I know I'm not alone on board the ship, but mentally it's a barren state. I'm part of a three-person crew. You know the system: a surveyor, a navigator, and an engineer. Me, Leslie, and Diana. We can count on each other, but they're not my friends. They're two sets of eyes and skills different from mine. We claim as a team, and we fight as a team, but when it comes to setting foot on new and distant chunks of space rock, I'm the go-to guy. You've never been alone like you're alone on some meteor or planetoid hurtling through space at a billion miles an hour. That aloneness comes from only being tethered to the small survey-ship by a radio beam; from being the first living thing on a dead world – not for the first time in a thousand years, but for the first time ever; from probing rocks; entering caves;

finding remains. You can't explain that to a navigator or an engineer. They sit in the comfort of the ship while you feel and see the universe. And the more you feel and see, the more you understand that you don't know anything at all. You only know Earth-stuff. Knowledge related to a small world on the outskirts of the galaxy. In space, who the hell cares about what a table is, or chivalry, or who Socrates was and what he didn't say? In the grand scheme of things, you are as knowledgeable as a puddle of barf.

And yet....

You use that grasp on the world to try and understand the rest. We use our Earth physics to slingshot survey ships across the void to nearby stars and meteor swarms in search of new raw materials. We view newfound places with human understanding and make sense of them. And it works. We navigate, or as Leslie would say, we extrapolate the unknown as if it was known to us. Smartass, that Leslie, but he's right. We fake what we know. But not me. I wear my stupidity and failure to grasp as a badge of honor. That's why I'm so good at my job. I never pretend. I only review. And after our last mission, I know that I was right not to pretend. Yet it doesn't give me any comfort at all.

★　★　★

We received the transmission somewhere en route to Gliese. The flurry of space probes released fifty years prior had advanced in a spherical pattern from Earth in every possible direction. Back in school, we were shown how it worked by gluing small wooden pearls to a balloon and then blowing up the balloon. The wooden pearls were originally close to each other but grew farther and farther apart. Every single pearl was a probe hurtling through space, picking up on interesting stuff and transmitting it in a bubble. Near Gliese a lot of the probes' circles collided, so it seemed a good place to snatch information.

Right after we'd learned about the probes in school, I had a dream about them. I was floating in a sea of black, everything serene and mind-numbing: a state of lucidity. And then disturbances arose from everywhere. Suddenly I was thrown back and forth as the information bubbles of all the probes interlaced right where I was, and the swirling mass of data pounded on my face, until the bone broke and I was conquered by teeming facts. I went under, and the calming blackness which had held me afloat now sucked me under. Then I woke. Shivering and cold. With a perfect imprint of the dream chiseled into my cerebral cortex.

"G67-577-45478," Diana said, and glanced at the screen. She let out a sigh as she read the information. She nodded sagely. "Well, it seems the probe picked up a rogue."

"A rogue what?" asked Leslie, chomping down on one of the chocolate bars from his never-ending stash. He lived on coffee and chocolate, eternally high.

"Looks like a rogue dwarf planet. About the size of Pluto," she answered. Diana's brow had curled into a twisted knot. Her gray eyes scanned the screens. I put down my copy of Seneca's *Medea* and looked over her shoulder. The craft was so small. The only official test you had to pass to become a probe-hunter was to prove you didn't suffer from claustrophobia.

"Hm," she added. "Strange it wasn't picked up earlier. It's quite big."

"Probably a husk," said Leslie. Now all of us stared at the screen.

"Doesn't look like a husk. Check out the number of satellites. It's like a stampede," said Diana.

I pointed to the row of numbers at the bottom of the screen.

"G67-577-45478 has just become the latest addition to the satellite gathering. Quite the gravitational pull."

Diana leaned back and shot us both a glance.

"What do you say, boys? Should we keep on course, or check if something wonderful just fell into our laps?"

"With that many space rocks, a couple of them are bound to be worth something. Iridium would fetch a nice price, and if not, a lot of people still like gold," said Leslie, and I could almost see him salivating at the prospect of a finder's fee. The greater the value, the greater the reward. It struck me – not for the first time – that Leslie had found the job of his dreams. He could just loaf around, eat chocolate, and rake in the rewards. Not an iota of manual labor was required of him.

"Well," I said reluctantly. "Most of them are so small. Is it really worth our trouble?"

"Why not?" answered Diana. "We'll just register the find as one big haul. Call it the pebbles of sand. There could be anything in that cloud of satellites. Who knows how long that rogue bastard has been tumblin' through the yonder. It might have picked up wonders...."

"Also rhyming now, are we?" said Leslie.

"I have to do something to pass the time before you two nannies make up your mind," she whipped back at him.

I looked at the screen. A torrent of red-tinted numbers swirled in and out, more numbers coming in as I watched. It really was quite spectacular. Normally a heavenly body – I never used that word in talk, as it was hard for Leslie to contain his snickering – didn't have that many followers. It wasn't uncommon to see a bunch of asteroids or a planet with moons in orbit around a sun, but as I looked on, the number jumped into the thousands. This really was out of the ordinary.

"How long will it take us to get there?" I asked.

"A couple of days," said Diana. "It's headed more or less straight for us, so a small course correction and we can saunter over to it. It's really no trouble. It would actually take us longer to avoid it."

"So, it's dropping straight into our lap?" asked Leslie, eyes glittering.

"Mmm."

"Then why the hell not? If it turns out to be shit, we'll dodge it and be on our merry way."

Diana shot me a glance. Her eyes were tired; too many hours staring at the screens.

"Elben? You up for a bit of exploring?"

"Call me Columbus," I said, and Leslie let out a hoarse laugh.

I still remember that sound. And I thought about Columbus being a homicidal maniac, not the benevolent caregiver history had alchemized him into. I kept thinking about Columbus the next couple of days, while we pulsed through space, sometimes me at the helm, sometimes

Leslie, none of us touching any of the dials. Diana tried to get as much rest as possible, as she always did before a grounding. She had to steer the small ship, and a single mistake could turn us into the equivalent of a moth squashed against the front window of a belterdrill. We didn't speak much, and when I wasn't on duty, I slept and finished reading *Medea*.

After a couple of years, you get used to the monotony of space flight. Even when folding the matter of everything into micro-worm-points, one after the other until space looks like a piece of embroidery, traveling takes a long time. Space is so immense that even thoughts have trouble keeping up. That's why I read, and that's why I think about dead and demonic explorers. You need to delve into set things, otherwise your mind wanders…and if it wanders long enough, it gets lost. Back on Earth, it's possible to find a lost mind. Out here? Not a chance. It's gone forever.

People go bent. Sometimes halfway, more often in a complete circle, where their brains loop. It's not a pretty sight, and I'm not quite sure we were ever meant to venture beyond our planet. We're not structured for it. Some of the surveyor teams return with strange stories that belong in the realm of myth and not in this world of science. Some have seen vast bodies lounging across supposedly empty tracts of space, moving slightly as if in dreams. Other travelers report photon shows to challenge the Northern Lights, and one man was certain he saw a message written in ancient Hebrew across a blue sun. The letters were 1,000 miles tall and spelled out a warning. *Don't dive into the Black Sea*, it said. *Bonkers*, I thought. Now, well….

We didn't discuss the satellites; no point. As long as they were far away, they were nothing more than rows of numbers on a screen. Occasionally, Diana let a remark slip, mostly along the lines of which elements were found in different chunks, or how far from the planet we were, but those slim interjections became part of the background murmur, and I cherished the silence. Even Leslie kept his mouth shut. Now I wonder why. Usually he was a chatterbox, going on and on about some trivial detail, or facts he'd read or heard.

Great wads of space filtered through our engines as we punched hole after hole in the fabric of reality and dragged ourselves ever closer to the wandering rogue. Suns flared, planet systems dwindled, until one night Diana woke us from sleep.

"Get up, boys. We're about to enter vision land. I know you lot love to look at things," she said. Rubbing my eyes, I rose, and Diana pressed the visor-button. Most of the time the ship was a metal box; no need to think about aerodynamics in space, and we got all our information from a row of sensors. Now the reinforced metal plate slid from the glass and showed us a piece of the ink-black void. Somehow, I had pictured an image of flooding lights, yet why would I? A rogue planet had no sun to keep it warm or make it visible. The only thing we could see was a suite of blacks.

"Not much of a show," remarked Leslie. He was standing close to me, rivulets of sweat clinging to his forehead. "Floodlights?"

"We're still too far off. Would do squat," Diana answered.

I leaned forward, as if the extra inches would let me see something hidden to the other two. At that second, a star disappeared behind a body, and a glittering pinch hit my cornea. I yowled in pain, clasping both hands to my eyes. For a second I could see a cloud of color, then it was gone, and so was the pain.

Both Leslie and Diana stared at me.

"What happened?"

"A reflection?"

I stabbed in the dark, removing my hands from my face.

"A reflection of what? From where?" asked Diana.

"The planet, I guess. Or one of the satellites. It came from straight ahead. You must have seen it!" I said.

"Nope," said Leslie. "Nothing there. Could have been a trick of the light, but I guess you need light for that."

Diana locked her stare onto the void. Then suddenly her head jolted back, a whimper tumbling over her lips. I clasped both hands to her shoulders, and when I turned her chair to look at her, for a sliver of a second I saw a dazzling point of light making its way across her irises. It was no larger than a needlepoint, and as I looked on, it dove into her pupil and disappeared. A small ripple appeared against her eyes' borders, and then her gaze was still again.

"Are you all right?" I asked.

"Sure," she answered and wriggled from my grasp.

"I also saw the reflection. Maybe the planet is covered in ice. The albedo could be acting like a prism."

Leslie leaned forward, scanning the vast darkness inch by inch.

"If it's ice, shouldn't it be white?" he asked, and then let out an "*Ouch.*" He touched his temple. "Yep. Something's there. Did you see it?"

We shook our heads. I'd seen no light beyond the first. I looked to the dashboard. The numbers twirled in their dance. They showed no increase in the number of photons, nor any sort of explosion. It was as if nothing had happened.

My mind bolted to Columbus. On his journey to the New World, he experienced the burning of the sea. One night while standing at the helm of the *Santa Maria*, off the coast of Bermuda, he was mesmerized by an 'elfin light'. In his diaries, he described the phenomenon as 'like the light of a wax candle moving up and down' in the water. I had no idea what the flame of a wax candle looked like, but I knew what he had seen. It wasn't anything profound, or even that special. Many had seen it before him.

It was the bioluminescence of microscopic plankton-creatures. They twinkled and shone, every blink of blue light a strip of information. They communicated, but to Columbus, it was just slowly moving bluish light. I think about that often now. He saw, yet he didn't understand.

"Makes you wanna go careful on those floodlights," Leslie remarked. "I wouldn't want a headful of pain."

"Don't be stupid. Distance, Leslie, distance. We're too far away to affect anything," Diana said. She had turned back to the helm, and slowly we advanced on the blacks which lay ahead.

Leslie looked a bit hurt. "Light travels," he murmured under his breath.

He was right. And none of us stopped to ask where the light had come from.

*   *   *

Enveloped in the darkness of space, we slowly approached the bulbous nuances of black. Diana kept the visor open, and as we got closer, a movement of shapes dotted the view. They seemed lighter than normal space rock, in both color and weight, yet the rogue itself didn't change at all. It kept its brownish hue, not letting go of any secrets. The absence of light played tricks on me, and my brain started to make reality of the shapes. One looked like a crumbling tower, another shape shot across several others, twirling like a demonic ballet dancer. Most of them were oblong, and I thought of dominoes and obelisks as black as knowledge.

I looked at the info screen. New numbers came piping in. The rogue had no atmosphere to speak of, and even if it had, it would have lain frozen on the ground with no sun to heat it up. Intertwined with the planet stats were swathes of information, vast bundles about all the satellites. Diana pressed a couple of buttons and brought our ship into orbit configuration. Then she leaned back in her seat and placed both hands behind her head, scanning the satellite facts.

"Hmm…that's strange. Quite a lot of biomaterial. And the biggest satellite is only the size of our ship. Perhaps fragments of an asteroid with its own biosphere?"

"If that's asteroid fragments, then it was blown up by something with a ruler. Most of them are the same shape," said Leslie. "And biospheres are exceedingly rare. They just don't happen. Amino acids, yes. True biomass, no."

I looked from the numbers to space. The view slowly moved in an arc as the ship glided into an empty space among the clutter of satellites. They remained in darkness, blobs of black, and I felt a tingling sensation down my back. Normally things weren't that black. Yes, space was dark, but light had billions of years to fill it up. We should be able to see something, yet we couldn't. Just shapes and movement, as if space itself was a shadow cast by another body entirely.

"Diana," I said. "The floodlights. I want to see what's there."

"Cover your eyes," she said, and flipped the switch.

White light poured into blackness and illuminated our neighbors. I flinched and squinted, then opened my eyes as there was no glare. At first, I couldn't see what it was. It looked like a miniature mountain range, with peaks and valleys. Gray, very gray, and spinning lazily. Then I saw the big eye socket. There was no eye, for it must have boiled away into space an eternity ago, and it wasn't human. It wasn't even human-like, apart from the socket. It looked moldy, and caved-in. Halfway down the mountainous body, twice as big as Leslie, was a large uneven hole. Inside it, stillness and black.

"What the...." whispered Leslie.

Diana pointed. Next to the body was another. The size of a small dog, but still wearing something I could only call a space suit. Something artificial, constructed to protect against the void. Fabric. Insulation. Even a clear part resembling a helmet. Next to the small figure was something that made me think of a figurehead I once saw in a book. It had watched...all the way across the Atlantic.

The *Santa Maria*, Columbus's flagship from Europe to the New World, had a figurehead of a mermaid or a siren. She had the tail of a fish, but it was elongated and asymmetrical, and didn't have the plump sexuality of a typical mermaid's tail. In comparison, she was distorted and...wrong. The upper body was that of a slim and young woman, her hair billowing in the breeze, and she was trumpeting a conch shell, her gaze locked onto the vast unknown. This looked almost like her, if only she had been alive at one point. This mermaid wasn't wearing a space suit. She was naked, that much was clear, and her body had suffered the effects of space. Her skin was covered in holes and sores, and around her, in their own system of gravity, was a vast collection of droplets of many colors. Green, red, and brown pearls circled her body, and her face was a display of pure agony. Her mouth was open, rows upon rows of shark-teeth erupted from her gums, and her tongue had frozen in a burnt red.

The eyes were gone but remains clung to the skull's spiral-holes. They could once have been black as onyx. Now they were shattered globes.

As I looked on, more bodies appeared, flickering in the floodlights of our ship. Most had space suits on, but a few, like the mermaid, were naked. Some were humanoid, some were akin to other Earth-shapes, like reptiles, vertebrates, insects, and some – like the mountainous creature – were like nothing I had ever seen, yet still I knew they were life. Life that had once contained thoughts and perhaps feelings. Every single one seemed strained, as if during the moment of death, their bodies had tightened in pain. Every mouth was open, frozen in a silent mask of pain.

"It just goes on. There's thousands of them. All milling around that rogue," Leslie whispered, more to himself than to us.

"Sixteen thousand seven hundred and eighty-one, and counting," Diana answered. "I guess that's the biomass."

We stared solemnly as a shape within a see-through cocoon floated by. The suit was almost transparent, and behind the veil we could sense a sprouting of limbs, thousands of branch-like extrusions wrapped around each other. On one side, metallic tubing grew from the cocoon and ended in a clear balloon which looked like a carboy. Clearly some form of breathing apparatus.

"Why are they all here?"

Leslie asked the question we had all been asking ourselves.

"I guess some of them knew they were headed outside their ships. Why else would they be wearing suits?" Diana answered slowly, every word dripping with doubt.

"I guess so," answered Leslie, and tilted his head as the skeletal remains of a humanoid drifted by.

Dots of flesh remained, but the body appeared mummified by cosmic rays. A new skin made of ice had formed around the bones, giving the creature a crystaline appearance. The ice was so perfect I thought of it as a suit. The creature's mouth was standing ajar in a silent scream, the windpipes brimming with torment. We just stared in silence, until Leslie broke it.

"Let's just fucking register this shit, and go."

"Register it as what?" was the mesmerized question from Diana.

"We can't register the find. We haven't checked the rogue," I said, wresting my gaze from the graveyard in front of me, and I looked at the looming shape of the planet beneath us.

It was a uniform brownish gray, a dirty ball whirling through nothingness. It had no oceans, no distinct landmasses, no mountains, no life. It was just a handful of dry mud. And yet, my mind's eye suddenly presented me with circles, a row of slowly dancing rings, and I thought about Rodrigo de Triana, the lookout on the *Pinta*. At two in the morning he'd spotted land and shouted the good news to the rest of the crew. The captain of the *Pinta* verified that it was indeed land and fired a lombard to alert Columbus on board the *Santa María*. Columbus later said that he'd seen the coast hours before the lookout did, and claimed the lifetime pension promised by the Spanish king to the first person to sight land.

"You really want to land?" asked Diana, turning in her seat to look at me.

"Why not? I think they'll look upon us with kind eyes back home. This place proves life. It proves intelligence. It's a goldmine of knowledge. This is no mere element haul – this is fucking unique. So what if it's creepy? It's also valuable. There's close to seventeen thousand bodies floating right outside. I don't know if every single one is a separate species, but even if there were only two, it would still be the find of the century."

"But the rogue...."

"I think the find will count as a whole," said Diana. "Leslie?"

He nodded. "I agree. Let's register and fuck off."

They both looked at me, knowing what had to be done to properly register. Suddenly I felt the presence of my space suit behind me, looking at me from the cabinet. To make a find official and open for sale, we needed physical proof. Video could be tampered with.

"You're up for it, Elben?" Diana asked, both of them looking at me. "Could be over and done in a couple of minutes. And then we won't have to return here unless they want to give us a medal *on site*, so to speak."

"Don't you find it strange?" I replied. "Where did they all come from? And where are their ships? Why are they all floating, crystalized in pain?"

"You know what?" said Leslie, and bit off a chunk of chocolate. Some smeared his incisors. "I don't know, and I don't care. We need this. And you're our surveyor. You're the best man for the job."

"If you don't go out there we'll never know," said Diana. Her words struck true. Could I live without knowing? "You live for answers, Elben. I have never seen so many in one place."

"I could go," offered Leslie. "It's been years since my last EVA, but I guess I'll manage."

Silence invaded the ship. Leslie was right, it was my job. And Diana was right. It wouldn't take that long. I looked at the floating corpses. Skulls and skin burned by radiation, and frozen by near-zero. They twirled and spun, and whatever secrets they had were locked away from my open gaze. It was magnificent and horrifying.

"No," I finally answered. "This, I have to do. And I will do it. On one condition."

"Being?" asked Diana.

"I'll need a tether."

*　　*　　*

With a hissing sound, the airlock spat me into space. I hovered for a second while the nozzles adjusted my position. Then I started to climb through the ship. Normally, I spacewalked without a tethering. I was more than adept at using my suit's nozzles to navigate, and the curling line had a tendency to get in my way. But this time it was different. None of the corpses had any sort of fastening rope, broken or intact. I wasn't going to make that mistake.

I grabbed the rung of stairs that followed the back of the ship like a stegosaurus's fin, and gradually made my way to the front. From behind the glass, Diana and Leslie looked at me. Leslie even gave me a thumbs-up, but the nice gesture didn't reach his face. It was set in a grim mask, a compound of worry and uncertainty. I gave a half-hearted wave and turned to the minuet of corpses that lay in front of me.

They were dancing in frozen misery among themselves, around the rogue that had stolen them – but from where? The closest was still inside an intact suit, and I wondered for a second whether the body had decomposed in quiet speculation, if the life support system had kept everything moist and teeming. Then I dismissed the notion. Whatever was inside that suit had cooled down a long time ago. I grabbed what I thought of as a leg and pulled the body closer. It glided lazily toward me.

I halted the suit by the helmet. It was covered in rime and ice, making everything inside it seem blurry. When I reached out to rub off some of the white, I could almost feel the cold through my own suit, and I don't know how, but suddenly I knew this body was old. It had been here for a long, long time, slowly circling in utter stillness. It had been here for decades, centuries, maybe even millennia, in a never-ending, never-changing dance.

In the helmet lay nothing but darkness. No head, nor face, nor eyes greeted me. Just disintegrated dust. I grabbed the torch in my belt. A laser-beam no wider than a hair appeared, and I focused it on what I thought of as the helmet's latch. It bit through the metal, cloth, and crystal, and with a jolt the helmet tilted back. A brownish fan of matter spewed from the hole, and I wrenched the helmet off. The fan changed to a veil of particles, and beneath them was the body.

It was skeletal. It was brittle. And it too was screaming. I had cut it from its chrysalis, and after so many years, its cry was freed. I saw it hidden inside every fleck of matter which exploded from the suit. The creature had died of a pain so deep it had left indentations in the bone. It was broken and smashed, some pieces were missing, and fractures ran the length of the skull. Yet the thing that made me go quiet was that it looked human. The jawline, the molars, the collarbone were all there, exactly where they were supposed to be.

I had seen that smashed-up face before, in a childhood dream, where it was my face that was smashed. I vividly remembered the dream-sounds, of things pounding to get in, pounding, pounding. Making way for something foreign to inhabit me. Back then, I had awoken. Now there was nothing to awake from.

"Are you all right?" Diana asked over the radio.

"Be quiet," I whispered, afraid of my voice. "We're in a graveyard."

The words just emerged. I hadn't even thought about them, but when I heard myself using the word, I knew it was right. This was a vast burial ground, filled with the bones of a thousand species. None of these creatures had just died here, but had become the necropolis itself, a sprawling monument to something I didn't understand. Then I glanced downward, and an inkling was thrust upon me.

The brown surface rippled like a veil, and then became transparent. Beneath the cloaking, I saw a lens as big as a lake, set in a telescope the size of a building. It was metal; it was crystal; it was mechanical; it had a vast array of transmitters and receivers moving in a slow and insect-like jitter, slurping information down every orifice and antenna. Inside the lens, which managed to fold in every possible angle, was a shimmering lining that felt like breath evaporating off a windowpane. It caressed my eyeballs, and then a sudden flash of light lit up my mind like a flare. This was the glare that had shone into us. It had come from beneath the surface. I wanted to turn my head, but I found myself mesmerized by the rogue.

Next to the lens, the spyglass, was another. Next to that, another. And another. And another. Near identical telescopes were standing shoulder-to-shoulder across the planet, covering every inch of the surface. They billowed, like reeds, yet remained inanimate. All of it was artificial. This rogue had never been born from a tumultuous soup of hydrogen and time, it had been shaped and fitted with instruments that I recognized, but did not know, and then hidden in a cloak. For a mad second, I wanted to draw my laser torch and fire it at the crystal eyes, try to destroy one of them. But I knew it was a futile task. No weapon could hurt the rogue. It was skulking and learning, and all around it, space was shivering. It was a contraction, no, it was a refraction – not of light, but of space. It was there, it was very much there, but it also wasn't. It belonged somewhere else, yet nowhere I could understand.

The human-like corpse had drifted away. I caught Diana's eye. She was frantically signaling at me. *Get in*, she told me in signs. I turned my head and was suddenly flooded with dead bodies. The rotation had brought us closer to a concentrated cloud of remains, and I dodged as well as I could, but was grazed and bumped by a multitude of corpses. I looked into a melted face behind a bubble helmet, another body looked like it was carved from stone, a third just a husk that broke against my suit and covered me in the dust of its insides. Not a single creature was the same. They were all different species, all unique.

"Elben, what's happening? Everything is going smudgy! We can't see a thing."

"Bodies. Death. Looking through telescopes. Scooping up information," I answered in a disjointed staccato. "It's a zoo and a carousel. They have inner light. They travel. We are seen. Instruments. So many instruments. Not from here—"

I had barely spoken the last word before I felt a tug and I bashed into a body. I fended it off with my arms, pushing it away, but another took its place. It was darker than dark inside the cluster of death. I could sense space around the bodies, but in my mind, they somehow made up what was real. They connected into a story that was whispering itself to me in a language I didn't understand. It was a long and winding legend, one that stretched so far back in time, that I lost the concept itself. Then the corpse-cloud broke, and the ship was right in front of me.

I clashed into the metal shielding, spun around like a top, and was swallowed by the hatch. It shut behind me, leaving me wide-eyed and illuminated by the row of warning lights. I just stood there, pulsating, as the air lock was pumped full, and outer sounds returned to my world. Someone engaged gravity and my feet now clung to the floor. A brownish dusting fell from my suit and settled on the floor. I looked down.

Something small, no larger than my shin, still clung to the suit. It was wearing a suit of its own, bluish in hue and with a protruding, glistening helmet that looked like the beak-mask which plague doctors wore. Inside it were eyes, still recognizable as such, but the body was lifeless.

I don't know if it had grabbed onto me, or if it just got caught in my suit. But it was the first thing Leslie looked at when he opened the door.

★ ★ ★

We fled from the place like an explosion, or so I was told when I came to my senses again. Diana just did the equivalent of flooring a car and bolted from the rogue and its collection of corpses. I never lost my senses; they were just wrongly configured for a while, and everything I watched was in doubles, like after seeing a bright flash. Then they returned to normal, and I tried to answer all their questions, most of them without making any sense. I could not explain what had happened, and when I told them about the planet and its trillion telescopes, they tried to believe me the best they could. Luckily, we had the small body to prove we weren't insane.

We registered the find, handed over the data, the video, the small body, and our story. They didn't believe us, and it didn't help when there was no trace of the rogue anywhere. They checked every probe for information and sent out other survey ships, but with no results. The planet had gone, taken its swirling cemetery with it. The body was the only thing that kept us out of jail. Data, stories, and images could all be forged, but the small astronaut from another race couldn't be dismissed. They still have it, probably locked away somewhere. I haven't seen it since. Neither have I seen Diana or Leslie. We split and didn't look back, hoping that on our own it would be easier to get new gigs. The last I heard, Diana was somewhere near Alpha Centauri, and Leslie was servicing ships between missions.

And me? I have trouble with everything, but in particular the image of the rogue planet. I often dream about it. Sometimes I think of it as a cancerous cell that has invaded a healthy body. At other times it looks like a probe, not at all unlike the flutter of metal we sent into space ourselves many years ago. I have no idea why it was watching, but watching it was. And sending, too. When I close my eyes, I more often than not see that small sliver of light that burst from the rogue, and I can feel it somewhere in my mind. When it happens, I don't know if I'm a lighthouse, or a homing beacon, or something entirely unfathomable. The only thing I'm certain of is that it's keeping tabs on me.

Christopher Columbus died alone and impoverished in Valladolid in 1506. He was only fifty-four. His entire life he'd believed the world was set against a backdrop. The Sun, the Moon, and the stars all had their fixed positions in the firmament, and behind them was nothing but God. I have been thinking about that a lot. Perhaps he was right. Perhaps the rogue was the equivalent of a spotlight or a microphone thrust into the stage, and as soon as it fulfilled its purpose, it was pulled away. Perhaps all the bodies were being drawn to this place like moths to a flame. I don't know. I don't know.

I don't know. I don't know.

I haven't been away from Earth since we returned. Space has lost its allure, but I can't get away from space. I have become one of the stories that people tell. I have become the laughingstock; one of the fucking mad people. Yet I'm not. I know that I haven't gone bent. And I fear that the others, the people I so easily dismissed as lunatics in the past, may be just as sane as me. If they are, what we call space is something not at all natural, and perhaps isn't even there. What we see is just a clever backdrop, and behind the scenes somebody or something is keeping an eye on us.

And the worst thing is – and I have thought this over a hundred times – around the rogue was a dance of death, a collection of pained creatures stemming from a thousand worlds or realities, and why would it keep it there? That's the worst thing…because I can only see one answer. It liked to look.

DOOMSDAY TOUR

Bao Shu

Translated by Alex Woodend

1.

December 21st, 2012

At nine in the evening, Shanghai is a sea of lights. Colorful neon on both banks of the Huangpu pour to the center of the river, become luminous fish shoals that jump through sparkling ripples. On Puxi, a stretch of Western-style buildings is soaked in tender, extravagant colored lights that seem to reminisce over the vicissitudes of history. Meanwhile, on the opposite bank, the Oriental Pearl Tower, Jin Mao Tower, World Financial Center, and other skyscrapers bring their dazzling splendor straight into the night sky with overpowering momentum to bring light to the dark universe.

Today is the winter solstice. Though the weather is cold, there are an unusually high number of tourists on the Bund. The river walk is dominated by young couples chatting and laughing. It's Friday, of course. Tomorrow will be a pleasant weekend, and next week is Christmas. But the main reason for the thronging crowd is none of that.

Lin Lin leans on the riverside railing as her boyfriend Fang Yue hugs her from behind and gently kisses her neck. Lin Lin giggles coyly and says, "Stop it! Hey, tell me. If today really was doomsday, like the myth says, what would happen?"

"We would make out really hard," Fang Yue says in her ear.

"Stop it, I'm serious!"

Fang Yue tilts his head, thinking carefully. "Even if it's true, I'm not afraid. So many people in history, everyone dies. How many get to see doomsday? Not bad if we get to see it. Besides, we get to die together, that's enough."

Lin Lin's heart instantly melts. "Hm, since when do you know how to sweet talk?"

"Do you really know what doomsday will be like?" a childish voice says from behind them before Fang Yue can respond.

Baffled, Lin Lin turns to look. It's a strange boy, about seven or eight years old, wearing a kid's shirt with Mickey Mouse printed on it, one hand gripping the hem of Lin Lin's dress. Sweet talk with her boyfriend interrupted, Lin Lin is a little annoyed, but seeing the boy's angelic face, she can't help but feel affection. "Hey, Fang Yue, look. This kid's so cute!"

Fang Yue makes a face, and to scare the boy says, "Doomsday? Terrifying. An asteroid as big as Shanghai will crash into Earth, make massive waves hundreds of meters high – *whoosh*, in a blink Shanghai drowns."

"Massive waves hundreds of meters high, wow." The boy's eyes sparkle. "That would be amazing! But there's no asteroid in the sky," he says, looking up.

"Silly boy, it's in space – so far away you can't see it," Fang Yue teases.

"Wrong," the boy says seriously. "If it was going to hit Earth today, it would now be tens of thousands of kilometers away at most, definitely visible. Even if it was on the other side of the Earth, there would be reports on TV."

"Well...how would I know that?" Fang Yue says to Lin Lin, a bit embarrassed, "Kids today are difficult."

"You all right? Stumped by a kid?" Lin Lin laughs at him. "Don't count on doomsday, okay? Tomorrow you still have to meet my parents."

"Forget it, that's truly the end of the world...." Fang Yue grumbles.

The boy rolls his eyes and looks at Lin Lin. "You mean doomsday isn't coming? Didn't he just say an asteroid would crash into Earth?"

"Gosh...." Lin Lin touches her forehead.

"Good boy, go ask your parents about it." Fang Yue pats the boy's head. "Aunt and uncle have things to do."

"But they're not here," the boy says, still not letting them go. "What will doomsday really be like? Tell me, tell me!"

"Listen, don't you know—"

Just when Fang Yue is about to explode, Lin Lin holds him back. "Forget it, why argue with a kid? Go on, let's get Häagen-Dazs. Kid, go ask someone else!"

She pulls Fang Yue away, and the two weave through the crowd. Their place is immediately taken by another couple. The boy stands in a trance where he is. A girl his age pushes through the crowd, pats his shoulder. "How's it going? Get the answer?"

"So weird," the boy says. "I've asked a bunch of people, no one can give me a straight answer. How about you?"

"Same. Some say a supernova explosion, some say a volcano and earthquake, one guy says a zombie attack. Everyone has a different story."

"How come they know what day doomsday is but don't know what it will really be like? And...." The boy points at the crowd around them. "Don't you think they're too happy? They don't look worried at all."

"Doomsday syndrome, very common," the girl says precociously. "Fully aware that disaster is inevitable, people can't dispel their inner panic and anguish because it's outside the limit of what they can endure psychologically, and so they transform it into superficial celebration."

"No, I get the sense something is wrong, very wrong." The boy frowns, thinks hard. "Something is definitely going wrong."

2.

As the two children talk, in the western hemisphere the morning sunlight of December 21st begins to light up the tropical rainforest of the Yucatan Peninsula. At the Mayan ruins of Chichen Itza, amid luxuriant jungle, dawn light passes through rosy clouds and outlines the towering step pyramid and the remains of the ancient temple.

Previously, at this hour, most tourists were still sleeping in their hotels. But today the Mayan ruins are already full of people as if the ancient city, gone for thousands of years, has come back to life. But unlike previous days, very few people talk or laugh. On the contrary, people mostly stand solemnly throughout the ruins like they're waiting for something.

In the east, clouds grow brighter and brighter, blazing heavenly fire. Finally, the fiery-red sun rises radiantly, showering infinite brilliance on the Earth. The jungle lights up bit by bit, far to near. Many people kneel to pray, some even start to weep.

"Really so beautiful," marvels a blond girl wearing a backpack on the observation platform. "Hi," she says to a short-haired young man next to her as she hands over a digital camera. "Can you take a picture of me?" She strikes a cute pose.

The young man takes the camera, examines it confusedly a few seconds, not seeming to know how to operate it. The girl leans over and gives a few words of instruction. He understands, takes a few pictures of her, then hands the camera back to her and says smiling, "This is the last sunrise ever, huh?"

"It certainly is," the girl replies, smiling. She grimaces. "Soon Earth will be blown in two, *boom!*"

"Then what's the point of this?" the young man asks suddenly.

"The point of…what?"

"Taking pictures. If you know the world will be destroyed in a few hours. Nothing will be left. Why still take pictures?"

The girl gives him a wary glance. "You really believe Earth will be destroyed? So, you're one of those people." She points at others around them, praying on their knees.

"Who are they? I don't know."

"Believers of the Church of Armageddon Truth, the Church of Earth Redemption, the Church of Almighty God…and a jumble of other small religions. They believe Earth will be destroyed today."

"Won't it? Everyone's saying so!" The young man looks very surprised.

"Of course it won't!" the girl says emphatically, then softens her tone. "I mean, even though a lot of people believe it, if you ask me, I say it won't. Nothing will happen."

"But I heard that's what's going on." The young man points at the black pyramid not far off. "The Ancient Mayans made astronomical observations to calculate that at the edge of the solar system there is a planet – called Nibiru, I think – which would approach Earth hundreds of years in the future and hit it today. Human technology can't push it away, so…destruction."

"All made up by third-rate tabloids." The girl snorts. "Mayans couldn't figure that out. Besides, if such a planet does exist, and it will hit Earth in a few hours, it would be bigger than a full moon now. But look, there's nothing. Nowhere on Earth has such a planet been observed, so, only if it's flying faster than light speed, which is impossible."

"A planet traveling at light speed? Not necessarily impossible…." The young man leans on the railing, looking at the girl thoughtfully. "Of course, the chances are slim. Sorry, I just got here, don't know much. But if you think doomsday won't happen, why come? I thought people came here to commemorate the Mayans' ancient discovery."

"Those people praying came looking for so-called redemption and rebirth, which is absurd. Others came just for fun. Me, well, I'm Emily, American, doing my Masters in sociology at the University of Chicago. My thesis is on 'The Sociological Effects of Doomsday Expectation'. This place has valuable primary sources."

"I see. But I still don't understand. If there's no such thing as Nibiru, why is there a doomsday prediction?"

"It's a colossal misunderstanding." Emily forces a smile. "I don't know how many people I've explained it to this year. Mayans saw the winter solstice as the beginning of a new year. This year, 2012, is an important year in the Mayan calendar, representing the transition between two eras. December 21st, 2012, is the end of the old era and the beginning of the new era, but at its core, it's just an arbitrary calendar date, has nothing to do with Earth itself."

"You sure?" the young man asks, eyes sparkling. "Is this a generally accepted explanation?"

"Of course!" She's a bit annoyed. "If you don't believe it, you can certainly wait here and see what happens today!"

The young man looks toward the rising morning sun and says with a forced smile, "Maybe you're right, but…maybe something really is going to happen, something you don't expect."

3.

Africa, the Congo Basin.

A clear brook winds across the valley, twisting and turning, flowing into the lake surrounded by thick forest. The surface of the lake is as smooth as a mirror. A herd of hippopotami soak leisurely in the lakeside reeds, only exposing their mouths and noses to breathe. On the other side of the lake, a few elephants walk out of the forest, come to the edge, and use their long trunks to scoop water into their mouths. A group of gorillas rest by the lake. The elders idly chew on grass and leaves, while the young ones play under the trees.

A lazy, cozy afternoon.

A tall, white-haired old man stands by the lake, quietly gazing at it all.

This is the last afternoon of this world. Now every second is precious. These ignorant and pitiful creatures, over their long evolutionary history, have experienced many trillions of tranquil moments like this. Naturally they think it will all last forever, think today is another normal day just like any previous one, that it will pass as night falls, and the next dawn will follow. But they are wrong. Their lives, along with the history of this planet, will end today. It is death's approach that gives this ordinary scene a sense of tragic beauty.

Birth and death, two poles of the universe. The Big Bang, the ignition of stars, the formation of planets, the appearance of life…. Behind these great, exciting events is the uneventfulness of endless days until the moment before destruction, when amazingly spectacular beauty blooms again.

Suddenly the water divides, and a huge crocodile opens its sharp-toothed snout, pounces up from the lake, aiming for the old man's ankle. It has been observing its prey for a long time, certain it can take it down in one go. As expected, the old man has no time to dodge and is bitten.

But the crocodile doesn't taste the sweetness of human flesh, instead biting something hard as rock, completely unable to penetrate it. This is something that has never happened before. Its brain with its limited capacity cannot generate a sense of surprise, but it senses great danger, and so turns around in an attempt to flee into the lake. But the crocodile finds itself unable to command its limbs. As if it is held by an invisible force, it rises slowly, suspended in the air, rotates in front of the old man, vainly wiggling its body, but is unable to shake off the invisible restraint and so is forced to meet the old man's gaze.

The crocodile lets out rumbling moans. The old man watches its terrified look, smiles, waves a hand. The crocodile drifts like a feather in the wind, drifts back to the lake, and slowly falls. In the end, the crocodile senses its abdomen touch the surface of the water as the force fades away. It dives down instinctively, sends up a spray of water, and is gone. A few seconds later, the incredible experience from a moment ago has been erased by its primitive brain. The crocodile again swims freely and calmly in the depths of the lake, looking for new prey.

Poor creature, enjoy the last few hours of your life, the old man thinks compassionately.

The old man leaves the lake and walks along the creek toward the thick forest upstream. This place is rarely trodden. Thorns grow in clumps, tree roots coil and twine, it's very difficult to pass. But where the old man walks, tree roots and rocks are pushed aside or smashed by an invisible field. Nothing can impede his forward progress. He saunters across the valley, now and then using his intelligence field to catch a few small animals to scrutinize, then lets them go.

The old man likes this doomsday tour. To him it is returning to an old place. Of course, in his nearly infinite life, there have been thousands or tens of thousands of such trips. But such an opportunity doesn't come often, at least not over the last millennium. Although worlds with life can be found everywhere in the Milky Way, and those with evolved intelligence aren't rare, annihilative disasters aren't common. Just like supernovas, they only come once every several thousand years. Take this planet, for example. The last annihilative catastrophe was nearly 7,000 years ago.

The old man still remembers the scene the last time he came to this planet. All kinds of strange, giant dragons leisurely roamed across the Earth and in the ocean, dominating the biosphere of the entire planet. The old man witnessed their last moments. The day heavenly fire fell, abundance returned to nothingness. The giant dragons died out. Their place in the biosphere was taken by the descendants of some kind of small, viviparous animals. Primitive intelligence arose even from them.

And today, another doomsday comes. He doesn't know whether or not the ecosystem of this planet will survive.

On this doomsday tour, as is his habit, he doesn't go to metropolises full of residents, watch people crying desperately, or join their hysterical parties. In his eyes they are meaningless, wicked pleasures. He just likes going to unclaimed countryside and carefully savoring the natural scenery of a world that will turn into ashes. Compared with those superficial, ridiculous, man-made things, nature, which has gone through billions of years of evolution, is more worthy of appreciation. The price to open the interstellar gate is not cheap. Of course, the money goes toward visiting the most worthwhile place.

"Attention: error!"

An emergency signal appears in the old man's consciousness. Sent by the guide to the interstellar travelers, it is marked as urgent.

"What?"

The old man immediately sends an inquiry. Meanwhile, he sees in his consciousness's remote-sensing network over 1,000 similar inquiries appear.

The response: "Universal intelligent monitoring system has failed, sent wrong information. We just double-checked and confirmed that no annihilative event will happen on this planet. Neither today nor within the next ten thousand years at least."

"Then the doomsday tour isn't...."

"Very sorry, doomsday won't happen. We don't know at the moment how the error occurred, but the Abyss Group will be held responsible. Now everyone please follow article one hundred and fifty-eight, section seven of the Cosmic Civilization Management Act, immediately assemble, and evacuate this planet. Otherwise—"

The transmission suddenly stops. The person in charge clearly has some more urgent affair occupying their consciousness. The old man uses his antenna to search in the remote network and immediately finds where the problem lies: some tourists have gone off on their own!

4.

The *Hoshino Maru* sails across a brightly lit Tokyo Bay. There are brilliant urban nightscapes on both banks reflected in the sparkling ripples. Rainbow Bridge is like a jade belt that connects the two banks. The harbor is dotted with all kinds of boats like beautiful fireflies. In the sky, a crescent moon casts soft moonlight over the sea.

Tatsuya and Yuki Kurihara stand at the bow of the boat. Leaning against the sea breeze, they point at tall buildings and large houses on the banks, trying to find Tokyo Tower. Both are momentarily intoxicated by the entrancing nightscape.

"What do you say? This doomsday tour is all you hoped for, huh?" Yuki says to her husband, smiling.

"So beautiful! To think that all these beautiful things, Japan – no, all human accomplishment – will be devoured by the dark night of the universe, is quite upsetting," Tatsuya sighs.

"Really?" Yuki counters. "You're really upset? I think you wish it really was doomsday. This year you and your gang have been chatting about catastrophe and annihilation with some enthusiasm. You sci-fi fans look forward to the spectacle of the destruction of the world, right? It's amazing you talk about something imaginary so vividly."

"Not just sci-fi fans," Tatsuya says. "For the first time in history, all human beings are indulging in this 'imminent annihilation' feeling. The concept of doomsday has given rise to a lot of business opportunities. I know you've made a lot of money from it."

Yuki nods automatically. She runs an online store. For the last six months, at her husband's suggestion, it has been selling 'Doomsday Escape Kits', bags packed with flashlights, compasses, hardtacks, bandages, and other often useless things, which are sold at the high price of several thousand yen. The product is surprisingly popular. Sometimes she receives more than 1,000 orders a day. Perhaps, in post-tsunami and post-Fukushima Japan, people's idea of doomsday has an extra sense of urgency compared to that of people in other countries.

Tatsuya continues to speak his mind. "Doomsday is a complex mix of awe and sorrow, fear and hope, madness and silence. It's too magnificent, too magnificent for you to remember its cruelty, and too grand, too grand for you to feel individual worry. Everything that happens has an insistent sense of reality before quickly returning to nothingness, as if everything can be redeemed in the embrace of the 'void'. Antiquity gave birth to such great works as the Book of Revelation. Today, people let their imaginations loose in all kinds of literature, film, and TV. The 2012 prophecy is the pinnacle of this old tradition. This is the first time the entire human race has consciously participated in the imagination of doomsday...."

"Still talking, huh?" Yuki curls her lips. "Today will soon pass. Tomorrow, when everything returns to normal, I'm afraid you'll have post-doomsday depression."

The words seem to cut deep. Tatsuya sighs, speaks no more.

"Sir, I think you are right," a stranger's voice rings out. Tatsuya turns and sees a middle-aged man in black has been standing next to him since who knows when. He is slightly confused but politely gives a slight bow.

"Doomsday is the highest imaginative feat a civilization can achieve," the man in black says without looking at him. He looks instead into the distance at the city's dazzling buildings. "It's a tragedy that the power of civilization will eventually be overwhelmed by a mystery. You know what the most fascinating part is? Everything is subject to great force. Everything beautiful, every thought, every civilization, and all its ornaments, disappear in the play of forces. This is the ultimate destiny of our universe. In the end, everything will be ripped up by the acceleration and expansion of space. That will be the final doomsday, when space expands to the critical point. In the entire universe, not even an atom or electron will remain. Everything will be completely shattered by the sheer force of space!"

His appearance is like that of an average Japanese man, undistinguished. His Japanese is rather fluent, but his feel for the language is stiff like a foreigner's. Yuki doesn't know what the other is talking about at all, but she's often heard similar conversations – it's what her husband's sci-fi friends often chatter about. She sees Tatsuya listening attentively, and murmurs to herself, "Hubby's found another soulmate once again."

"Big Rip Theory!" Tatsuya beams in agreement. "All doomsdays turn out to be previews of the final doomsday.... So all civilizations in the universe have doomsday?"

"Not necessarily so," the man in black says. "The universe is partitioned by vast space. Except the final Big Rip, all the other natural catastrophes have limits. If a civilization expands to other galaxies in space's depths, then an asteroid collision or stellar explosion is unlikely to cause fundamental destruction – not to mention other, smaller disasters. So as long as a civilization develops to a certain degree, it can say goodbye to the danger of doomsday. After all, the final destruction is incredibly far in the future."

"No doomsday. Wouldn't that be boring?" Tatsuya jokes, then laughs.

"Correct. Any civilization developing to that stage certainly won't meet a doomsday. Otherwise, they would have been destroyed long ago. This doomsday complex has never been satisfied in the development of its civilization. So, after it expands to the entire universe, it won't hesitate to traverse the whole universe, to those faraway planets, to watch all kinds of doomsdays in primitive worlds, in search of some feeling."

"Good idea! But how do they know which world is about to end? And to traverse the Milky Way, even at light speed, would take tens of thousands of years, right?"

"The material foundation of the entire universe is a remote-sensing network based on states of matter. As early as the primordial stage of the universe, using it, the oldest civilizations created the Universe Wide Web to automatically monitor every planet with life. Those worlds are certainly undistinguished. Usually the interested aren't many, but on the eve of doomsday, related information is sent to subscribers throughout the universe. Then a commercial company organizes the interested people into a tour group. Through interstellar gates, they instantly traverse the universe and come to the world where doomsday will strike."

Tatsuya looks at him with increased curiosity. "You talk as if it were true."

"True or not, soon you'll know," the man in black says with a mysterious smile.

While Tatsuya considers the meaning of his words, his feet jolt. Out of nowhere a huge wave appears in the bay, pushing the boat to one side. Many people are caught off guard and fall to the deck. Tatsuya immediately grabs the railing to stand steady.

"Yuki, are you all right?" Tatsuya looks at his wife. He sees Yuki is deathly pale, her eyes pop as they look ahead in disbelief. He automatically follows her gaze to look and immediately finds something unusual.

Underwater, a luminous thing swims in the direction of the Rainbow Bridge. It is at least as big as a whale. No, much bigger than an average whale. Is it a hostile country's submarine?

Before Tatsuya can think any further, he sees it emerge from the water and stand up — very high, at least forty, fifty stories high. The huge wave it conjures makes the distant *Hoshino Maru* shake violently.

It is a huge, luminous ellipsoid supported by two long legs. In the middle there is a loop that constantly turns like a giant evil eye. Soon countless complex, tentacle-like chains stretch out from it. Each chain is longer than a locomotive but shockingly agile. The monster wraps its tentacles around the Rainbow Bridge. A few seconds later, the long bridge, indestructible just a moment ago, breaks into several sections like light building blocks, bringing the countless vehicles on top down into the sea.

The robo-octopoid monster starts walking. It looks very clumsy but moves at an amazing speed in the direction of the city proper on the west bank. The Orochi-like tentacles start to reach and wrap all around. Several seaside high-rises begin to collapse from its shaking. The sound of buildings collapsing comes like thunder over the horizon. But hardly any human voice can be heard, because they are so far off.

Tatsuya can't think at all, just stares stunned as if watching a disaster film on widescreen. The giant octopus enters the city proper, its tentacles madly destroying everything like a naughty child trampling a splendid garden. Tatsuya suddenly remembers the films he watched about monsters destroying Tokyo. Those absurd scenes are now actually taking place before his eyes.

"Now this is a true doomsday celebration," the man in black says. A trace of a smile appears at the corners of his mouth. "This is the most interesting game in the universe."

Tatsuya seems to wake from a dream: "You, you and that monster… are…."

"He's my companion," the man in black confesses. "In a world about to end, civilization protection laws are no longer applicable. We've crossed the Milky Way to come here, not just to be onlookers but to celebrate! There are lots of us competing to be the first to destroy this city. Seems like I have to hurry up…. Would you two like to be my guests to watch this wonderful scene?"

Tatsuya also sees in the distance that the monster has pulled Tokyo Tower up, broken it in two, and tossed it high into the night sky. He follows it up and sees in the moonlight that all kinds of fantastical monsters have appeared. Eerie clouds gather from all directions to cover the bright moon.

5.

Infinite Phases stands above the tranquil sea, gazes at the azure sphere suspended among the stars. His multidimensional sight brings everything into full view.

Via the remote-sensing network, he has noticed many astonishing changes on that sphere. In the last few minutes alone, city after city has been destroyed in different ways. Some were burned down by the blazing flames of anti-matter explosions. Some were frozen in absolute zero temperatures. Some were crushed to dust, courtesy of brutish tourists. Some were flattened by waves suddenly surging hundreds of meters high....

A level five intervention at least. Awful. Irritated, Infinite Phases sends out a shock wave, blowing the Stars and Stripes in front of him to smithereens.

One of the universal values recognized by the Cosmic Civilization Union states: "It is strictly forbidden to intervene in the development of lower civilizations." Before a civilization can join the Union, it must limit itself to external observation. It is not allowed to intervene. Both sending benevolent help and vicious destruction are strictly forbidden by Union law. Even if destruction comes, it is not allowed to help another escape the annihilation. That would be seen as a breach of sacred Union law.

But doomsday tours are an exception. After it is confirmed that some world will experience doomsday, one is permitted to visit that world during a certain final time period prior to doomsday. But, theoretically, they are required to assume the physical form of the intelligent life in that world and use built-in language-conversion devices so as not to cause panic among local residents. However, in the final moments, though there are still legal restrictions, even unbound, uninhibited destruction does not have serious consequences. Since the world is about to end, what's wrong with Union tourists having some fun after traveling such a long distance?

The problem is, this world isn't fucking going to be destroyed. This doomsday prediction is just a silly rumor.

Infinite Phases has thoroughly checked the data uploaded to the sensing network. There was undoubtedly a foolish mistake. Computer programming is computer programming, after all. There is no way to truly understand alien civilizations with completely different biological foundations and cultural channels. When it discovered the story of a so-called doomsday was being spread with unprecedented intensity and frequency on this planet, it collected a trove of data to make a judgment. The program thought the planet's level of civilization was sufficient to accurately predict a potential annihilative catastrophe, and the story the majority agreed upon was highly credible. Since the doomsday story managed to have millions of reposts on the local network, and dissenting stories merely numbered in the tens of thousands, it fully accepted the information that doomsday was going to happen and carried out a rationalization algorithm on fragmented, contradictory explanations to make a logically consistent story and uploaded it to the Universe Wide Web. Then the Abyss Group hosted this damned doomsday tour. Then, a few hours before the expected doomsday time, they sent tens of thousands of tourists from all over the universe to this remote galaxy.

In the end, they made a huge, careless mistake. Before he could send out corrected information, mass destruction had already begun. Now deceased local residents number at least one billion, probably two billion, which already constitutes the gravest degree of intervention. Infinite Phases has sent out emergency notifications, asking everyone to stop the destruction immediately, but it's too late. And there are some of an unknown race who have turned a deaf ear. Some lunatic is moving water from the Pacific into low orbit to make a ring.

"Big Sight!" Infinite Phases calls out. The Universe Wide Web turns on, connects him to Milky Way 19, 30,000 light-years away. His superior's three-dimensional image ripples above the dust of the lunar sea.

"We have a major problem." Infinite Phases starts information transmission, distressed, giving a rough outline of the story to Milky Way 19.

His interlocutor simply smiles. "You can solve it."

Infinite Phases is speechless for a moment. "But at this point... how?"

Milky Way 19 makes an impatient gesture. "Use your logic. If this planet continues to exist, the remote-sensing network will discover our tourists have committed sabotage, but the catastrophe did not happen. This will immediately send an alarm signal to the Central Committee, providing evidence of our violation of the basic civilization code. In that case, we're all in big trouble. If planetary doomsday happens as projected, then none of this is too out of line, and in the end no one will know."

"But how.... You mean...." Infinite Phases is stupefied. "We make one ourselves...?"

"Do you have a better solution?"

"But those tourists, they already know."

"No worries, everyone went to the planet simply to release the pressures of life. Nobody wants to get themselves in trouble. Besides, do you think this is the first time it's happened in the history of the universe?"

"What?!"

Milky Way 19 signals irony. "You just took over this job, are still unfamiliar with it. The Universe Wide Web is really old, in many places the software hasn't been updated for billions of years at least. Such errors, in fact, often occur."

Infinite Phases is terrified. "You mean, all those previous doomsday tours...."

"Many cases are similar, at least ten percent, probably twenty percent. But who cares? Tourists have fun, we earn universal shopping credits, can even make a lot of money selling the digital replicas of some planets. As long as nobody is stupid enough to tell the Central Committee, nothing happens. And besides, we have our people high up, too."

"But those planets...."

"Just some primitive insects, don't worry."

Infinite Phases is dumbstruck. A long time later, he finally asks, "Then what...should I do?"

"That you can decide yourself," Milky Way 19 says impatiently. "There are plenty of tricks, after all."

He switches off. Above the tranquil moon sea, only Infinite Phases' lonely rhomboid figure is left.

Fuck, get it done.

Infinite Phases starts to activate spacewave devices within tens of thousands of kilometers. He rotates the Higgs Field, adjusts the distribution of gravitons, and increases the gravity between the planet and its satellite. He wants to finish the job as soon as possible, so he turns the gravity to maximum, nearly equaling that of a black hole. Soon, the azure sphere starts to grow larger and larger as if falling from the sky.

The surface of the Moon trembles. The dust on the plane flies like rain in reverse, up to the black sky. The blue planet is buried in a veil of darkness.

6.

The ocean has all evaporated. The continents have all melted into magma. Burning red magma, under the force of the suddenly accelerated rotation caused by the collision of the Earth and the Moon, gathers toward the equator and becomes a flood tide a dozen kilometers high that sweeps across the surface of the lifeless planet. Huge impact debris flies into orbit and forms a temporary planetary ring.

The impact has long passed. The tourists watching have mostly left, but two small, luminous people still frolic in the magma tide — up and down, unwilling to leave this new wonderland full of endless fun. At the last minute they go through the black cloud formed by ejecta from Earth's interior and surficial dust and fly into space.

When they leave the thick black cloud, they happen to see a dragonfly-like spacecraft falling into the black cloud. After making a faint streak of light, it disappears into the impenetrable depths of darkness.

"That's a space station," the girl says. "Earthmen's sole presence in outer space — don't laugh, they do call low Earth orbit outer space — is now gone."

"Pity we don't have time to do a digital scan," the boy says. "Only got tiny pieces of that world."

"Don't worry, a lot of other tourists probably scanned. Later we can make copies and supplement it with data from other places on the Universe Wide Web. We'll have a little simulated Earth as a souvenir. Can I see what you got?"

"Sure," the boy says, projecting a shifting three-dimensional object in front of them. "See, it's those people from a moment ago."

It will take another half hour for them to reach the interstellar gate in Jupiter's orbit. During that time, they watch the images with great interest.

7.

The tower bell strikes twelve, December 21st has passed.

"I told you." In the taxi, Lin Lin leans on her boyfriend's shoulder, mumbling. "No doomsday or anything at all, so boring."

"From another perspective," Fang Yue holds her tenderly, "it's another chance God has given us to cherish each other, so tonight we'll celebrate."

"Hm, let me sleep a little." Lin Lin gives a relaxed yawn in Fang Yue's embrace and slowly drifts off.

Fang Yue strokes his girlfriend's beautiful hair, absentmindedly thinks about meeting her parents, and begins to feel drowsy. Just when his eyelids are about to close, he suddenly has a strange feeling as if in an instant everything near or far has disappeared. All the lights in the city are extinguished by bottomless darkness.

Fang Yue rubs his eyes. Everything looks normal. The car lights in the city streets flow like a river. He can't help but laugh at his neurosis. He digs out his phone and sends his friend a message: *Be there in fifteen minutes.*

THE EMISSARY

Russell James

Spacecraft launches used to fill me with anticipation.

Back in the early 1970s, standing outside my Cocoa Beach house, I'd turn my son's stroller so we could both look north, and we'd wait.

From far in the distance would come the low, muted thunder of rocket engines. Then from over my neighbor's house would appear a small black shaft, tail aglow like a tiny sun. It rose and rotated, a slow-motion ballet of technology. On climb-out, a billowy white plume would bloom against an azure sky. The spacecraft would shrink, the plume melt away, and all that remained would be a glowing yellow dot. It would wink out as the Saturn V left the atmosphere on its way to the Moon.

Back then I was an astronaut, a spanking new graduate of the Class of '71. With hundreds of hours in simulators and mockups, and dozens of practice EVAs underwater, I was scheduled to pilot a command module on a launch to the Moon. Then Congress cancelled the program in '72, after Apollo 17. The sidewalk outside my house was as close as I ever got to the Apollo launch pad.

My second chance came when they slapped Skylab together. The missions used leftover Apollo command modules. I was scheduled to pick up a ride there in 1975 on mission SL-6. But NASA never got past SL-4. Budget cuts scrapped the remaining missions, even though Skylab still flew in a cold, decaying orbit around Earth. The running joke was that assigning me to a space program ensured its cancellation. I never laughed at that one.

In fact, by 1974, I'd stopped laughing at anything. With my dreams destroyed twice on the cusp of coming true, I spiraled into a very dark place.

The astronaut corps pretty much disbanded at that point. Mark Harrison, Director of Flight Ops, quit rather than manage satellite launches. The astronauts who'd come from Air Force or Navy flight billets went back to active duty. I got reassigned to a slot at Cape Canaveral managing T-38 jet maintenance. Just test pilot work, but it beat being grounded. I never wore my astronaut wings on my flight suit.

The disappointment of my career transition brought out the worst in me. I became unbearably moody, frustrated at every little thing. My family suffered for it and I hated torturing them. I moved into a cheap apartment in Titusville. Charlotte and our son Will kept the house in Cocoa Beach. I needed a timeout to fix me before I broke them as well.

On my weekly T-38 test flights, I got to take a long look at that abandoned area around Kennedy Space Center. That big launch tower, the empty assembly building. Each week, more weeds encroached on the roads to the launch pads. The complex's greatest days had passed, along with mine.

Or so I'd thought.

One night in July 1976, my phone rang at 11:34 p.m.

"Shane?"

I was only half-awake, and it had been years since I'd heard him, but I recognized the long Texas drawl right away. I'd listened to too many briefings from Mark Harrison to ever forget his voice. "Mark?"

"You got it. Sorry to wake ya. Y'all home alone?"

"Uh, yeah."

The phone went dead. A crash sounded from the living room. I hung up and flicked on the nightstand lamp. Before my eyes could adjust to the light, three huge men in black military-style uniforms rushed into my room. Black ski masks covered their faces and they brandished pistols with silencers. Two dashed to opposite sides of my bed and pinned my arms to the mattress like human docking clamps. The third pulled an aerosol can from his pocket, loomed over me, and sprayed me in the face. I flinched as a powerful chemical scent blanketed me. Then everything faded away.

★   ★   ★

I woke on a cheap leatherette couch. I recognized the lumpy government-issue design from nights spent on the flight line in my younger days. I sat up. My head swam and then cleared. I was in a windowless office. Four beige concrete walls, one door, and the indestructible metal desk and chair combination that the US government bought by the thousands.

The door opened and let in a flood of noise from outside the room. Dozens of voices talking over each other, accompanied by an atonal symphony of electronic beeps and ringing phones. Mark Harrison stepped in. He was the only guy I ever met who was somehow naturally imposing at only five-foot-six. His graying hair was now parted in the center instead of to the right, and it spilled uncharacteristically past his collar. A sharp new goatee put him somewhere on the spectrum between a beatnik and Satan.

"Shane, you're awake. Outstanding." He pulled the desk chair around to the couch, spun it around, and sat facing me with his arms crossed over the back. "Hey, look son, sorry about the, well, kidnapping. We're mighty short on time. I called the CIA to round you up for us, and well, they kinda got their signals crossed when I told them that I needed you here ASAP."

"The CIA? And where is here?"

"You're at the Cape. Well, under it really. But first up, how y'all feeling?"

I did a quick self-diagnostic. "Seem no worse for wear."

"Outstanding. We pulled your med records and you're still on flight status, passed all tests with flying colors. Which is damn fine. We need your help."

"And who is 'we'?"

"NASA. Sort of. Lemme show ya."

I followed him out the door. It opened into a massive room that looked all too familiar. Rows of desks with monitor screens and wide multiline telephones faced a wall with four huge television screens up near the top. On the right, a status board blinked red and green for each of the functional areas of a Saturn rocket. A company of men wearing bulky headsets bustled between stations. The place was a damn-near duplicate of the Apollo Launch Control Center, except that denim jeans and bright cotton t-shirts had replaced the men's usual dress pants and white short-sleeve button-downs.

"Mark, what the...."

I followed him through the middle of the room. A few semi-familiar faces nodded and waved to me. I gave each person some sort of tentative recognition.

"When Apollo was shut down," Mark said, "NASA kinda fashioned the leftover parts and tech into Skylab. But the national ho-hum attitude about space travel didn't turn around a whit. Budgets shrank, and as you know too well, Skylab's missions were cut short."

We sat down at a workstation in the front row. Lights flickered across the multiple lines on the telephone. The console display was dark.

"A few people with the right black ops experience, and a memory of the effort of starting a space program from scratch, decided we needed to keep the pilot light burning, so to speak. We cleared this underground area that used to be one of the water tanks for cooling the launch exhaust at Pad 39A, moved a big chunk of Launch Control down here, and kept the USA ready to return to space." He threw a switch. The console screen took on a dull glow as it warmed up. "Now we just need someone to take us there."

An image of Launch Pad 39B came into focus. The Apollo-era's ultra-bright lights lay dormant and only dim emergency lights lit the scene. But I'd pined over enough pictures to discern from the shadows that a Saturn IB rocket stood on the pad, steam trailing from its eight massive engines.

"Jesus, Mark. Where did you come up with a Saturn rocket? How can you—"

"It's Skylab's backup ship, the rescue craft. We kept it on ice in the supposedly empty VAB." Mark laughed. "We really had to hot-rod the damn crawler to get it out of the VAB and onto the pad under cover of darkness. She needs to launch before dawn. I need you to fly her."

My jaw dropped. This had to be some kind of dream. It made that little sense.

"You're kidding," I said.

"Does this look like a joke to you?"

It certainly didn't. "If you've kept a rocket ready to launch, you had to have kept some astronauts ready to fly it."

"We did. Remember Mitchell and Carnahan?"

"Uh, yeah. They were a couple of hot shot Navy fighter jocks in the astronaut class ahead of mine."

"They were on the payroll until about twelve hours ago. Damn fools were driving back here in Mitchell's Vette at over a hundred when a tanker truck jackknifed in front of them on I-95. Neither survived. I need a qualified pilot to get in that command module and get it off the ground right damn now."

I'll admit, my heart skipped a beat or two right there. Flight into space! All my sacrifice and training hadn't been wasted after all. Then a pilot's common sense kicked in.

"Mark, I haven't sat in a CM for years, haven't reviewed the mission...which is what, by the way?"

"Beating the Russians, son. This time the stakes are higher. They have plans for their own space station, something they call Mir. It means 'peace', like that isn't a joke. Anyhow, the Russkies came up with a shortcut. Take Skylab. They have a Soyuz 7K-L1 ready to launch in the next few days. They'll claim Skylab as abandoned property, like a drifting ship under maritime law. The whole concept is horse-hockey, but once they're on board, ain't no way to get 'em off. Intel says they'll militarize it. We need to send some marines up there to keep the damn door locked. You're driving the taxi."

I'd like to say I weighed the risks, contemplated other options, counted the dozen protocols and flight regs I'd violate taking a Saturn IB into space on a moment's notice. I'd like to say that, but I can't.

"Let's drop that taxi's meter," I said.

★   ★   ★

A blur of activity later, I waited with a launch tech outside the gantry elevator in sixty-plus pounds of A7L space suit. I'd forgotten how heavy and restricting they were after the relative comfort of Air Force pressure suits. It didn't quite fit, a recurring reminder that a tech had stripped the name *Mitchell* off the outside before helping me put it on.

The launch pad seemed deserted with just the two of us there. The two marines should have been there as well. I hadn't even met them yet.

"Where are the marines?" I asked.

"Already aboard," the tech said. "The gantry's clear. Other techs completed the preflight and comm checklists. Hurry. Your launch window is about to close."

I stepped into the elevator. The tech didn't. The elevator door slid closed.

The ride up the launch gantry was agonizingly long and slow. It gave me the first quiet moment to really think about the mission, the magnitude of it. They called the Moon landings a space race. That was a space slog compared to the timetable we were trying to meet here. The idea of America under Soviet guns from our own space station was more than I wanted to think about.

Then there was flying the craft. This was the mission I practiced through '74, docking with Skylab. But how much of it would I remember? There were checklists for everything, checklists I'd memorized at one point. But that was so long ago that it felt like part of someone else's life.

I looked south through the passing steel lattice of the launch tower. The lights from my old Cocoa Beach neighborhood twinkled in the darkness. My wife and son slept there, unaware of the threat I had to avert. I missed them so much. If the mission had been to safeguard only them instead of millions of people, I would have still flown it.

I had to ratchet up my self-confidence. I had to remember what it felt like to strut that Right Stuff attitude. The last two years, I'd convinced myself that I was a former astronaut. Now, I had to convince myself that I *was still* an astronaut.

The elevator stopped. The door opened. A metal gangway extended to the open command module hatch. The ship's name, *Independence*, was painted over the opening. Keeping in that bicentennial spirit, our secret Mission Control was code-named 'Valley Forge'.

I took a deep breath. A nation of people depended on me, starting with the two inside that spacecraft. I strode to the end of the gangway and looked inside the CM.

"Gentlemen...."

The marines were already buckled into the right and center seats, helmets on. They weren't wearing the clear intravehicular helmets, but the heavier extravehicular versions, smoked visors down over the clear bubble. The marine in the center seat looked at me, nodded, and raised a thumbs-up.

I was late. I climbed aboard, closed the hatch, strapped in, and donned my comm and helmet.

"Hey, marines, sorry I'm late. I'm not the pilot you expected, but I'm rated and ready."

The marine in the center seat nodded and said, "Let's fly." His voice seemed ragged through the static.

"*Independence*, this is Valley Forge," Harrison said over the comm. "Commence radio silence after liftoff. The rest of the world thinks you're an unmanned military satellite launch."

"My lips are sealed," I said.

"Y'all get the job done up there."

Countdowns commenced. Checklists got checked. I smiled as certain phrases, certain actions came back so naturally to me. The clock ticked down to zero. A hundred and fifty feet below me, a million and a half pounds of thrust ignited.

All the training in the world couldn't have prepared me for the experience of a launch, the power of the engines, the force of the Gs, the bone-rattling shudder of the spacecraft. But monitoring the instruments left no time to enjoy this vertical drag race with gravity. I stole a glance at the two marines as the first stage dropped and the second ignited. The marine on the right seemed calm, but by the way the one in the middle had a death grip on the edge of the seat, he'd bitten off a tad more than he'd bargained for.

The nose cone sheared away. I finally gazed at what I'd longed to see since I'd first wondered about the night sky as a boy. Space. Dark and deep and endless, punctuated with more stars than I could ever imagine. Here I was, one of three tiny human beings venturing to its edge, like dipping a toe in the deep end of the pool. It made me shiver.

A *ping* echoed through the CM. My heart stopped. Space was supposed to be silent. If I could hear that ping through the muffling effect of my helmet, it had to be one hell of a ping.

Something small flew by the tiny window, then something else. Then came a sound like a handful of gravel flung against metal.

I cursed. Space junk, meteorites, expended Russian ASAT tech. We'd flown into something that wasn't on the charts.

A *bang* cut my thoughts short. A quarter-sized hole opened up over my head to the right. Alarms blared all across the command console. Pressure compromised, oxygen level dropping. In no time, everything we needed to live inside the CM would be vented into space. I thanked God we hadn't pulled our helmets off yet.

I unlatched my restraints and kicked free of the seat. I'd so looked forward to this initial weightless experience, ready to savor the sensation. But now all I could think of was that I was about to die.

I spun around and pulled the emergency breach seal pack from its location. The patch panel slipped against my fingers in the bulky gloves, but I managed to tear the molecular adhesive from the back. I kicked myself to the bulkhead hole and slammed the panel over the puncture. The rush of escaping atmosphere stopped. I reached down and reset the wailing alarm. It stayed off. I settled back into my seat as the pressure and O_2 levels returned to normal ranges.

I turned to the marines. "That was close. Every astronaut's nightmare is—"

The marine in the center bucked and heaved against the seat restraints. A small hole stared up at me from the chest of his AL7, a hole tinged red with blood. The meteorite had punched through more than just the hull.

I cursed and flipped up his smoked visor. I did a double-take. If this guy was a marine, they'd dropped the standards way down. He was well past sixty, with a full, gray beard. Panic filled his washed-out blue eyes. I clamped a hand against the hole in his suit. His lips moved, but I couldn't hear him. I clicked on his comm.

"Get him to Skylab," the old man wheezed. "He'll tell them the truth. Save us all."

He choked. Blood burbled from his lips and floated away in perfect spheres. His helmet became a tiny, red snow globe. He jerked in one great spasm against the restraints and then fell still. His head slumped inside his helmet.

There wasn't time to make sense of all this. I needed to stuff the hole in his suit and keep this guy's blood from getting inside my cockpit. He had a pouch strapped to the outside leg of his AL7. I tore open the Velcro top. Two syringes sat inside, points covered and down, along with a sheaf of papers. I didn't have time to check them. I grabbed the first one from the pile, wadded it up, and jammed it into the hole in the suit. It turned red in the center, but blood spheres stopped floating into the cockpit. That would do for now. I turned to the other marine.

"Who the hell is this guy?"

The marine didn't move.

I thought that maybe he'd passed out from the launch Gs. I floated in front of him and shook him at the shoulders. "Hey, wake up!"

I cursed. If this marine was sick or injured, this mission was going to go Apollo 13 in a hurry.

I flipped up the smoked visor and bounced away so hard I cracked my helmet against the bulkhead. What was in the suit wasn't even human. A long, narrow head sat upon a neck that seemed impossibly frail. Two large eyes stared out from the sides of its head, like a fish. Hairless gray-green skin stretched tight against high cheekbones. The mouth was just a tiny slit. It opened and closed once.

No way in hell was this the mission I was briefed on. Radio silence be damned. I had a damaged ship, a dead passenger, and some sort of alien on board.

"Valley Forge, this is *Independence*."

Static.

"Valley Forge, this is *Independence*, over."

I hoped the ground crew hadn't decided they were going to adhere to the radio silence rules no matter what. I rolled back into my seat and checked the three flashing status lights.

Master Alarm. Pitch Gimbal 2. Cryo pressure. *Independence* had taken more than one hit. I needed to make sure she didn't suffer more than one casualty.

The Crew Alert light lit up. Finally. That one was activated and deactivated from the ground, a signal to pick up the phone. Every warning light here lit its counterpart at Mission Control, so someone had seen my unfolding disaster and wanted to chat. They just didn't answer my comm. Which probably meant that along with the other damage, my transmissions weren't going anywhere.

I pulled off my helmet, stuffed my gloves inside, and stowed it. I didn't dare pull my surviving passenger's helmet off. For all I knew, the extraterrestrial was bathed in some personal environment to keep him alive.

The good news was *Independence* was still on course. Fuel and oxygen were still within limits. The hull patch was designed to survive reentry. I counseled myself that things could be worse, which was pretty scary.

The Crew Alert light went dark. Then back on. Then off. A long flash. A short, a long, a short. Pause. Three longs, a short, a long.

Morse code?

I sighed. The Navy guys were way more into Morse than we Air Force pilots. I flipped open my mental file folder on Morse and concentrated on the patterns.

C-O-N-T....

Halfway through I knew I didn't have to finish. It was the only message Harrison would send.

CONTINUE MISSION.

Nice advice if I had any idea what the *real* mission was.

The alien reached up and removed his helmet. It seemed to take great effort. His head swiveled, so thin compared to a human's that in the AL7 it reminded me of a straw in a tall glass. He looked at the inert corpse of our other passenger. The round pupils of his eyes narrowed. He pulled off his heavy gloves and revealed delicate four-fingered hands with almost no palm. He reached up to remove the dead man's helmet.

"No!" I shouted. I reached over and clamped my hands on the helmet. The last thing we needed was blood floating around, getting into all the circuitry. "He's dead."

I realized the futility of my shouts. This creature appeared to have no ears. He released the helmet and beckoned me closer with his spindly fingers. I rose and floated toward him. He touched his two middle fingers to the side of my head.

It's hard to explain what happened next. It was kind of like stepping into a river, except that the river didn't run around me, part of it ran through me. I got the sensation of another consciousness, one moving much faster, much more intricately than my own. Thoughts blew by me like leaves in a whirlwind, but his emotions registered clearly. Pain. Longing. Fear. He pulled back his hand and the connection broke.

"*Independence*, this is Valley Forge."

Harrison's voice in my comm was barely above a whisper. He was transmitting on a telemetry feed. Chalk one up for the boys at the Cape.

"This is *Independence*."

"Freq unsecure. Repeat, freq unsecure. Status?"

The whole world might be able to tune in. Swell. So much for my "What the hell is with the alien?" question.

"Ship secure. Only one package for delivery. The international one."

A pause.

"Get it to its destination at all costs." I couldn't tell if Harrison was angry or resigned.

We closed quickly on Skylab. The CM's trajectory had been set up for speed of intercept, not fuel efficiency. The station appeared as a speck in the darkness, then grew. It and the CM both crossed into sunrise and the station popped into clear view; a cylinder four times the size of my CM, with an X of solar panels deployed at one end like the stays of a stripped umbrella. A second array hung like a flag from one side. A gold reflective heat shield lay like a tarp over the aft section. It sparkled in the new sunlight.

There wasn't time to reflect on the moment. My focus was on getting my damaged craft docked, and this alien off it.

Docking went straight by the book, simulator perfect. I opened the hatch. Cold air blew in my face and my breath turned to steam. The ground crew had restarted the station, but heating the interior up above minimum would take a while. At least the lights were on.

I turned and unbuckled my alien passenger. Weightlessness worked in my favor, and I guided him up and out of the chair. He made a weak, waving motion, and gave me an approving nod. I grabbed him by the space suit collar, pulled him after me, and entered the docking module.

We passed through the final airlock and into the station proper. The training mockup in Houston had been an exact match, though floating through it was a whole different experience than walking around in it. I pulled the alien to the ostensible floor. Unhappy with the idea of just letting him float around helpless, I secured him to the floor rings with some Velcro strips from the wall storage units. I went to the communication station and established a secure link with Cape Canaveral.

"Valley Forge, this is Skylab."

Harrison answered instantly. "How's your passenger?"

"How would I know?" I was damn mad at this point. "I'm no exobiologist, but to me he doesn't look healthy."

"Doctor Arnold has syringes with him, somewhere. You need to inject the passenger with one. Now!"

I launched myself from the floor and straight up through the airlock and into the docking module. And I did it way too fast. With no gravity, I didn't coast to a stop like I'd imagined. The CM came up fast. I grabbed the hatch ring as I passed through and tried to brake myself, with little effect. I plowed forward and headfirst into the deceased doctor in the center seat. The impact compressed his chest and popped out the bloody page I'd jammed in his wound.

I caught it to replace it, then realized it made no difference with no pressure pumping his blood. I pulled the syringes and the pages of handwritten notes from their pouch, and returned, slower, to Skylab.

I landed beside the alien, then flipped through pages of classic doctor's scrawl, praying for some kind of instructions. What if what I needed had been on the page I'd stuffed into the doc's bleeding gut? A syringe slipped from my grip and floated away. I cursed and snatched it out of the air.

The alien's hand touched my leg. He pointed to the syringe in my hand, then touched a spot at the base of his spindly neck. He repeated the same motions. Circumstances were forcing this poor patient to be his own doctor.

I pulled the top off the needle with my teeth and checked the syringe. The air had been purged from it before launch. The doc knew his stuff. I placed the tip against the alien's body beside where he held his finger. He closed his eyes.

I pressed and punctured his skin. It was like running a needle through leather. I drained the syringe and held my breath.

The alien inhaled. His gray skin turned an odd, but healthier, shade of green. I sighed.

"Valley Forge, this is Skylab. He's injected and seems more stable."

"Damn fine, son. Good work."

"Now, Mark, you want to tell me what's going on?"

He paused. "The Russian story was a line of believable BS."

"No kidding."

"Apollo 17 was the last mission for a reason," Harrison said. "We were warned. In person. An alien shuttle approached the CM in orbit while the Lunar Module was on the surface. Scared the hell out of Ron Evans. It came from the Stellar Coalition, an assemblage of spacefaring planets. Aliens probed his mind and in no uncertain terms said, 'Go home and stay home. Do not leave Earth again. You aren't ready to play with the big boys. Not technologically, not developmentally.' And that ended Apollo."

"But we're still in space."

"Low Earth orbit only. We thought that would be all right. Anyway, the Coalition somehow observed the heavy launch engine testing for the new Space Shuttle program and that raised an alarm that we might be going back on our word. Last week, your passenger, Rax, an emissary from the Coalition, arrived at NASA to investigate.

"But he fell ill after arrival. Medically, we were in way over our heads. Even your other passenger, Doctor Arnold, a reptilian and avian expert, could barely make heads or tails of his physiology. Rax is too damn weak to send a telepathic message home, to convince them we aren't using Skylab and the new shuttle as steppingstones to the rest of the solar system and beyond."

"What happens if he doesn't report back?" I said.

"Lemme see. How would we react if we sent an emissary to East Germany and he disappeared? The message to Apollo 17 was clear. The Coalition will exterminate our species before they let us get loose in the universe. To them, we're just damn fire ants."

I focused on the transmitter controls. "What frequency does the Coalition use?"

"None. They use subspace telepathy. Rax was too weak to get through the Earth's magnetic field. Up there, he has a chance to contact the aliens, keep them from incinerating the planet."

"If I keep him alive," I said.

"That's a roger. And it gets worse. That unmarked debris field that punctured the CM is coming up fast, dead along Skylab's orbit."

"And I guess you want me to keep the station alive, as well?"

"The taxpayers would sincerely appreciate it."

At that point, I realized it was better that I hadn't trained for this mission. The stress of practicing for all these hopeless scenarios would have killed me.

Rax reached around and unstrapped himself from the floor. He floated over to me and touched his fingers to the side of my head again. I sensed pain, exhaustion, something akin to a fever, and a racing blur of thoughts. One thought rose above the others, simple and direct, as one would speak to a child.

Thank you.

I didn't know if I could just think a question to him, but speaking seemed more natural, more focused.

"When will your people arrive?"

Soon. My thoughtcloud was expected days ago.

"Can you communicate with them now?"

His upper eyelids sagged. *Too weak. Can't even reach you without touching.*

Rax's frail frame shuddered inside the AL7 like those of a clapper in a bell. A set of lower eyelids arched up. There was no mistaking the look of pain in his eyes. The color in his skin drained away and left him an ashy gray.

I groped for the second syringe in my pocket. I whipped it out, uncapped it, and drove it into Rax beside where I'd planted the last one.

This time, there was no effect. His chest rose and fell in short, shallow breaths. His head turned to face me. For a creature with almost no facial movement, he still seemed to convey amazing emotion. I wondered if it was through his enormous eyes. Then I thought perhaps we still had some residual connection from the telepathy.

I raised his fingers to my head, and touched mine to his, hoping it might somehow help the connection.

His sadness deluged me. Then a sense of ultimate resignation, of having taken the first step on life's last trail. He was dying, and knew it.

A parade of images crossed my mind. First, red seas lapped at copper shores. Then the scene shifted to crystal spires forming a purple canyon that seemed to stretch on forever. Then a cut to another alien, the view as he held her in his arms, though I had to guess it was female since she looked almost the same as he did. Then a scene with that same alien, surrounded by five smaller versions, all climbing over her at once. That faded to a view of all six of them, the smaller ones now larger, at a round table eating bizarre foods.

I shuddered. I was seeing his life, the best, most beautiful parts of it. Was he reliving it, replaying these comforting scenes as his end drew close? I felt like a filthy voyeur. I removed my fingers from his temple. He pressed his fingers harder against the side of my head.

Tell them.

And then he was gone. The consciousness that had tapped into mine evaporated. I can't tell you how lonely that felt. You can't understand the empty solitude of being one unless you have once been two. I lowered him to the floor to strap him down again.

The lights dimmed. An alarm blared. Power failure. The solar array had stopped working. My first thought was that the returning meteorite swarm had torn it to shreds. But some of it would surely have hit the station. I released Rax and floated up to a viewing port. I looked out and my heart stopped.

The solar panels hadn't failed. They were blocked. All of Skylab hung under the shadow of a spacecraft the size of an aircraft carrier. Great wings spread over the tiny station like a giant bird of prey.

The alien corpse nudged against my leg. My only hope for explaining the situation on Earth was dead. Instead of looking like the helpful Earthling bringing their emissary a step closer to them, I'd now look more like the creature's executioner.

A wide tube telescoped out of the bottom of the alien craft. It clanked against Skylab's hull like a closing prison cell door. I turned to beat a retreat to the CM.

A blast of thoughts hit me so hard I reeled. Questions, commands, images, memories, all stampeded through my mind, not from one person this time, but from hundreds. Every crew member on the ship above connected with me at once. My overloaded neurons screamed a surrender. I grabbed my head, afraid so much traffic would make it explode.

Sparks flew overhead as a red laser pierced the hull. The shriek of slicing metal in my ears met the furious cacophony of hundreds of voices inside my head. I closed my eyes, curled into a fetal position, and drifted against the bulkhead.

Tell them. That's the message Rax had sent me. His request to tell them about what mattered to their fallen emissary; his love for his strange home world, his devotion to his wife and family.

I tried. I concentrated and tried to summon the images he'd sent me. But they'd flashed by so quickly, it was as if I only had bits and pieces of them, like trying to sketch a Renaissance painting I'd only seen once. I tried to focus on one image, the one most clear from its vivid content, the copper coastline. Against the pain and the sea of noise, I formed the picture.

It flew out of my head, swatted away like a swarm of gnats by the angry alien thoughts that roiled in my mind. I whimpered.

The laser finished its circular pattern. The hull section snapped free and floated away. They'd be aboard in seconds.

Tell them.

I'd tried, but they didn't care, didn't want to listen.

Then I understood his message. Not to tell the aliens about him – to tell them about me, about how similar, not how different, an Earthling's priorities were to their own.

I summoned my favorite place, an oak-shaded patch of ferns and moss along a stream where I grew up. Summers, I'd sit there, protected from the sun and cooled by the clear, swift water as it flowed by, and breathe deep the blend of wildflowers along the banks.

I focused on this place, this vision. I summoned the sense of contentment and peace it drew up within me. The raging waters of the invading alien minds calmed as some of their telepathic shouting turned to listening. My headache receded.

I called up memories of my wife, my son. My wife and I in Hawaii when she told me she was pregnant. The joy and wonder I felt at the moment of my son's birth. The shock as he said his first word. His first day of school and the sadness of knowing that this was also his first step away from home. How much I missed them both.

The bombardment of alien thoughts stopped. I conjured images of my training, of Skylab's shortened scientific mission, of our collective wonder at the infinite universe that for now appeared forever beyond the grasp of the residents of this small, blue world.

I opened my eyes and looked at the alien, clad in an outsized AL7 like a kid in a Halloween costume. How alike were we, both struggling to make ourselves understood to a species so externally different, yet inside so much the same.

Two aliens floated in through the hole in the hull. They wore no bulky suits, just a skin-tight leotard across their thin, fragile-looking bodies. They gathered their fallen brother in their elongated arms and guided him to the hole. They paused. One of the aliens turned to look at me dead on. His eyes narrowed.

Go! Now!

I didn't need a second invitation. With Skylab's hull compromised, the station would be depressurized as soon as the aliens undocked. I pulled myself into the airlock and secured the door behind me. By the time I was strapped in and powering up the CM, the alien ship had unclamped itself from Skylab.

The feeling that the world wasn't yet safe nagged at me. I might have been personally spared, one space pilot to another kind of thing, or simply given the chance to die with the family I'd expressed my love for. I undocked and backed away from the station, afraid I'd see the alien ship on a course for one of Earth's great cities.

But the vessel was gone. I sighed with relief and reestablished comm through the telemetry frequency.

"Valley Forge, this is *Independence*," I said. "Mission accomplished. I'm coming home."

★   ★   ★

The quick trip to Earth ended in a perfect splashdown and a pickup by submarine instead of the usual aircraft carrier. No one on the sub except the captain spoke to me during the days it took to get to the US, and even he didn't say much. My eventual debrief by Mark confirmed what the continued existence of the human race hinted at.

The Stellar Coalition had gotten the message.

I went back to my job as a test pilot, but with my astronaut wings back on my uniform, and a huge secret to keep.

The next week, I made a trip even longer than the one from Earth to Skylab. I traveled from my Titusville apartment to my home in Cocoa Beach. Unlike the Skylab trip, this one ended up being one way.

★   ★   ★

Three years later, I pulled some strings and had my wife and son join me at the Space Center as we tracked Skylab's reentry into the atmosphere. It went out in a blaze of glory. My family thought I wept tears of sadness for the station. They were tears of happiness for the two of them, the two people who would never know that they saved our planet.

BIOGRAPHIES AND SOURCES

Patrick Parrinder
Foreword writer
Consulting Editor (English language stories)

Patrick Parrinder is President of the H.G. Wells Society and has written several books on Wells and science fiction, including *Shadows of the Future* which won the 1996 University of California Eaton Award. He is also the author of *Nation and Novel* (2006) and *Utopian Literature and Science* (2015), as well as being General Editor of the 12-volume *Oxford History of the Novel in English*. Patrick has been reading H.G. Wells since his schooldays and he grew up in Kent, not far from Wells's birthplace in Bromley. He now divides his time between London and Norfolk and is an Emeritus Professor of English at the University of Reading.

Yao Haijun
Foreword writer
Honorary Editor (Chinese language stories)

Yao Haijun is the Director-in-Chief of *Science Fiction World*, President of Chengdu Science Fiction Association, and Co-founder of the Chinese Science Fiction Nebula Award. Yao Haijun founded China's first science fiction fanzine, *Nebula*, in 1988 and joined *Science Fiction World* in 1998.

In 2002, Yao Haijun initiated and promoted the 'Science Fiction Vision Project'. So far, there have been four series published under this project, including the *World Science Fiction Master Series*, which has introduced 173 science fiction classics to China. The *China*

Science Fiction Cornerstone Series includes the *Three-Body* series, which has become an international bestseller.

In 2010, Yao Haijun won the One Hundred Press and Publication Professionals with Outstanding Contributions in the 60 Years of New China medal and the Chinese Science Fiction Nebula Award for Best Editor. In 2019, he won the China Science Fiction Galaxy Award for Special Contribution.

Alex Shvartsman
The Race for Arcadia
Originally published in *Mission: Tomorrow* anthology; Canopus Award finalist

Alex Shvartsman is the author of over one hundred and twenty short stories, published in *Analog, Nature, Strange Horizons*, and elsewhere. He won the Washington Science Fiction Association Small Press Award for Short Fiction in 2014 and was a two-time finalist (2015 and 2017) for the Canopus Award for Excellence in Interstellar Fiction. His political fantasy novel *Eridani's Crown* was published in 2019. His translations from Russian have appeared in *F&SF, Apex*, and *Samovar*. Alex has edited over a dozen anthologies, including the long-running *Unidentified Funny Objects* series, and is the editor-in-chief of *Future Science Fiction Digest*. He resides in Brooklyn, NY. His website is www.alexshvartsman.com.

Chen Zijun
Shine
Originally published in *Science Fiction World*, 2016, Vol.2

Chen Zijun is a science fiction writer and has a PhD in engineering mechanics from Tsinghua University. He has published numerous stories in *Science Fiction World* and won the Galaxy Award and the Global Nebula Award several times. He is currently working in an aerospace-related field.

Leah Cypess
On the Ship
Originally published in *Asimov's Science Fiction* magazine, May/June 2017 issue

Leah Cypess is the author of four young adult fantasy novels, starting with *Mistwood* in 2010. Her middle grade debut, *Thornwood*, about Sleeping Beauty's little sister, was published in 2021. She is also the author of short fiction published in *Asimov's Science Fiction* and the *Magazine of Fantasy & Science Fiction*, among other places. Leah is originally from New York City and now lives in Silver Spring, Maryland with her family.

Wang Jinkang
Seeds of Mercury
Originally published in *Science Fiction World*, 2002, Vol.5

Wang Jinkang, born in 1948, is a senior petroleum engineer, a member of the Chinese Writers' Association, Vice President of China Science Writers' Association, and the honorary president of the World Chinese SF Association. He published his first story, 'Adam's Regression' (May 1993, *Science Fiction World*), which was initially a story he made up for his 10-year-old son. It won the first prize of the Galaxy Award and led to an unprecedented run of successes. He has published over ninety short stories, sixteen novels, and over 5.5 million characters in total.

Eleanor R. Wood
Her Glimmering Façade
Originally published in *Deep Magic*, August 2016

Eleanor R. Wood's stories have appeared, among other places, in *Deep Magic, Daily Science Fiction, Galaxy's Edge, Diabolical Plots, PodCastle,* and various anthologies. Her story 'What the Sea Reaps, We Must Provide' was selected for *The Best of British Fantasy 2019*. She writes and eats liquorice from the south coast of England, where she lives with her husband, two marvelous dogs, and enough tropical fish tanks to charge an entry fee.

Han Song
Answerless Journey
Originally published in *Science Fiction World*, 1995, Vol.2

A journalist at Xinhua (China's state-owned news service) by day, science fiction writer by night, Han Song is one of China's best-known and most prolific science fiction authors. He is the chief of the Science Fiction Committee of China Science Writers' Association and the president of the World Chinese Science Fiction Association. He is a writer who has managed both to preserve his sense of wonder, particularly about all things technological, and to develop a finely honed sense of social justice. Clones, alternate populations and psychological manipulation are themes that regularly crop up in his writing. It becomes clear, when reading his writing, that science fiction is merely a slightly warped mirror through which to reflect modern Chinese society. Han Song is a multiple recipient of the Galaxy Award, China's highest sci-fi honor, and is regularly cited as an influence by younger writers. His representative works include: *Subway, Hospital, Red Sea, Gravestone of the Universe*, and *Recycled Bricks*.

Ronald D. Ferguson
Cylinders
Earlier version published in *The Jim Baen Memorial Award: The First Decade*, November 2017

A native of San Antonio, Texas, Ronald D. Ferguson is an active member of the SFWA. After years of teaching college mathematics and publishing four textbooks with major publishers, he decided writing fiction was more fun. He primarily writes science fiction and fantasy with more than thirty stories in various short fiction venues including Flame Tree's *Lost Worlds Short Stories, Compelling Science Fiction, Deep*

Magic, and many others. He lives with his wife, Layne, and a rescue dog named Cash near the shadow of the Alamo.

He Xi
Life Does Not Allow Us to Meet
Originally published in *Science Fiction World*, 2010, Vol.12

He Xi, born in 1971, is one of the most well-known science fiction writers in China. He published his debut *One Crazy Night* in 1991. He has won the Galaxy Award seventeen times and the Chinese Nebula Award multiple times. Many of his works are about the future of macro science and how humanity reacts to it. His stories are effective at exploring emotions and feelings, which really touch the reader. Some of his better-known works are: *The Doomed Year, Natural Born Talent, Who Am I, Love and Parting, The Sad One, Never Meet Again*, and *The Six Paths of Lives*.

Allen Stroud
The First
First publication

Allen Stroud is a university lecturer and science fiction, fantasy and horror writer, best known for his work on the computer games *Elite Dangerous* by Frontier Developments and *Phoenix Point* by Snapshot Games. He was the 2017 and 2018 chair of Fantasycon – the annual convention of the British Fantasy Society – which hosts the British Fantasy Awards. He is also the current Chair of the British Science Fiction Association. His military science fiction novel, *Fearless*, was published in 2020.

Zhao Haihong
The Darkness of Mirror Planet
Originally published in *Science Fiction World*, 2003, Vol.10

Zhao Haihong, born in 1977, has a PhD in art history from China Art College, and is an Associate Professor at Zhejiang Commercial

University. She has won the Galaxy Award six times and the Song Qingling Children's Literature Award and other children's literature awards fourteen times. Her works include the novel *Crystal Sky* and the short story collections *The Eyes of the Birches*, *Ripple World*, and *The River Flows as the Moon Rises*. Her works have been translated into English, Japanese, Korean, and Spanish.

Amdi Silvestri
Minuet of Corpses
Originally published in *Beyond the Infinite*, 2018

Amdi Silvestri is a Danish author. Active since 2008, he has contributed to a galaxy of different anthologies, and has published nineteen books; most recently the novel *Für Elise* and a collection of short stories titled *Almost Here*. He has received the Niels Klim Prize for science fiction five times and received a scholarship from the Danish Arts Foundation twice. His work tends to be experimental and restless, and he mixes genres and styles, using every piece of fiction as an opportunity to do something different. He has only recently begun writing in English.

Bao Shu
Doomsday Tour
Originally published in *Top Fiction*, July 2013

Bao Shu, born in 1980, is a Chinese science fiction and fantasy writer. One of the latest generation of major Chinese science fiction writers, Bao Shu has won six Nebula Awards for Science Fiction and Fantasy in Chinese, three Galaxy Awards for Chinese Science Fiction, and was nominated for the Grand Media Award for Chinese Literature. He has published five novels, including *The Redemption of Time* and *The Seven Kingdoms of the Galaxy*. His works have been translated into English, Japanese, Italian, German and other languages and published in the *Magazine of Fantasy and Science Fiction* and *Clarkesworld*. He has worked as the chief editor for the science fiction collection *The Science Fiction Historical China.*

Russell James
The Emissary
First publication

Russell James grew up on a steady diet of *Star Trek*, *Star Wars*, and giant monster movies. He has never recovered. He has authored the *Grant Coleman Adventures* series starting with *Cavern of the Damned* and the *Ranger Kathy West* series starting with *Claws*. He has also written horror thrillers including *The Portal*, *The Playing Card Killer*, and *Q Island*. He resides in sunny Florida. His wife reads his work, rolls her eyes, and says "There is something seriously wrong with you." Visit his website at russellrjames.com, follow on Twitter @RRJames14, or say hello at rrj@russellrjames.com.